FURIOUS

Furious
Copyright © 2018
Aaron Shaver

Cover art by Christian Young
Cover design by David Warren.

Published by WordCrafts Press
Cody, Wyoming 82414
www.wordcrafts.net

FURIOUS

The Berserker Heritage

AARON SHAVER

WordCrafts

Chapter 1

Reese Little

Waking up in the middle of the night reminds us of a primal truth: that the journey already started somewhere in the darkness—without us. My eyes open wide and stare into the darkness. I see the ceiling fan above me still spinning silently. I hear gentle breathing from the woman next to me. Against my side I can feel Emma turn in the bed and drape her leg over my knee. As comforting as these familiarities can be in the dark early morning hours of our home, I am uneasy. A familiar nervous feeling, warm and anxious, creeps up from my belly. I try counting—a rhyme that my dad taught me when I was a kid. But, I can't remember it anymore. I roll over and reach for the little white bottle on my bedside table. My fingers fumble for it, finding it in the dark, but it doesn't make the familiar rattle when I grab it. Empty.

I try to calm my heartbeat.

WUMP. Clang.

My eyes snap open. Someone is in the house. I fling the covers off of me and drop out of bed on to my hands and knees. I reach under the bed. Tossing a pair of sneakers aside, I find the tool box and drag it out from under the bed. I reach inside for the claw-hammer. Strangely, I've never really felt comfortable about the idea of owning a gun. But now, I wish I had one in my hand.

"Reese…whatareyoudoin'?" Emma whispers with a drowsy slur.

"Someone's in the house," I whisper back.

Emma sits up, blinks, and pulls the blanket to her chest. I turn toward the door. The crack between the door and the cold hardwood floor reveals moonlight that is coming through the living room windows. I try to slow my breathing.

Clang. Clang. Clang. Clang.

A hollow refrain of metal. Someone is in the kitchen. I turn back to Emma with hammer in my hand.

"Call 911."

I whip open our bedroom door and rush toward the noise. I can barely hear my feet hitting the cold hardwood over the *thumpthumpthump* of my own heartbeat. Furious and frightened, I race past the living room into the kitchen, kicking a basket of laundry in the dark. I can't see anyone but I know they're there. Fingers clench like a vice on my weapon. I move in to strike and hear a voice call out:

"Daddy." A swell of fury and confusion rises in my throat and I gag. "Daddy, I'm thirsty." My son. Slumped against the refrigerator. Trying to open it. I fall to my knees almost dropping the hammer. I hear Emma's rushed footsteps behind me.

"Hollis? Baby, are you awake?" she says. Emma quickly grabs Hollis in her arms. "You want some milk, Baby?"

She opens the refrigerator and grabs a sippy-cup already half-full for Hollis. I glance up to see her look at me as she carries Hollis back to bed with her. She hides the panic and worry from our son, but I can see it. I give a weak gesture with my head, telling her, *Go on… I'll be fine.* But, the sweat covering my skin and the knot of sickening anxiety in my chest tell me that I'm not fine. At least they don't see me vomit on the kitchen floor.

~

I finally get back to bed for a few more hours of sleep before my alarm wakes me. I crawl out of bed and start my routine. Shower. Shave. Brush. Comb. Dress for work. Before I leave, I kiss Emma on the cheek while she sleeps. She rolls toward me and moans. Her auburn hair tumbles over rosy cheeks and fair skin. My eyes take in the hour-glass shape of her wrapped in only a sheet and I remember that I'm a lucky man. I leave her to rest in bed awhile longer before Hollis wakes up. I skip breakfast to walk to the drug store about a mile from our house. The sunlight strikes my eyes, sending me into a sneezing fit. One. Two. Three. Four sneezes. The crisp dawn air hits my nostrils with mix of exhaust fumes and hints of sausage and biscuits from the string of fast food joints.

I enter the drug store. The mechanized *ding-dong* at the door welcomes me. There's a line already forming at the pharmacy counter. Good grief.

I check my watch while waiting in line, trying to gage how long this will take. Just twenty minutes until the mainline bus pulls up to the corner. After that, it's a ten-minute ride into downtown. *Cutting it close, Reese.*

My phone buzzes in my hand alerting me to a text message. It's Emma. She's worried.

What happened last night?
Are you okay?

I'm fine. Just another episode. I ran out of my meds.
I'm at the pharmacy now. Getting refill.

It's getting worse. Isn't it?

I'm fine.

Okay.
Be careful out there.

I always am. I love you.

Emma is good to me. I hate to make her worry. I should have refilled my medication weeks ago. I've been popping these pills since I was twelve. Since Mom died. According to Dad and the doctors, I didn't adjust well. Everyone deals with loss in their own way, or so they say. These pills are meant to manage anxiety and hypertension—but lately, I'm not so sure I'm managing it.

"Sir, can I help you?" The mousy pharmacy tech behind the counter politely smiles and presses her glasses up her nose. I step forward and hand her the bottle.

"Just need a refill," I say. She looks at the bottle and punches a few keys on her computer.

"Eh, pardon me, pal." A squat bearded man squeezes through the line right behind me. I step out of his way just before his big box full of smaller pink boxes clips me. The *ding-dong* tone of the sliding door sounds again and I notice the growing line of early risers behind me. The squat middle-aged man walks around the counter and sets the box down at the floor. His shirt has already come untucked around his love-handles. I wonder if his neck-tie is too tight; his round face is a blotchy shade of red. "Carolynn, you see that line?" He says a little too loudly to the mousy pharmacy tech who's got my empty prescription bottle in her hand. "You see how long that line is?"

"Yes, sir, Mr. Beltcher."

"I know you're new here. But, you gotta pick up the pace." He bends over to grab more pink boxes as he loads the shelves behind Carolynn.

"Photo ID?" Carolynn catches me staring at the back of Beltcher's head.

"Oh. Um, yeah. Here you go," I say handing her my driver's license.

"I ain't runnin' a charity. Am I, girls?" says Beltcher clearly making a show of his managerial superiority. None of the women answer Beltcher. Just as he reaches for another box under the counter, Carolynn steps back reaching for a clipboard and, before I can say anything, the two collide. Beltcher blusters and Carolynn cowers. And, for some reason, that's when I decide to chime in.

"I think you can take it easy, Mister. I'm in no hurry."

He's caught off guard and slack jawed until—"Well, good for you. You think the rest of that line behind you has nowhere to go? Or do you think you're the only one that matters. Like, you're some kind of special snowflake." That warm nervous feeling in my stomach is back.

"Not at all," I say taking a deep breath. "I just think… you've got some great employees working for you. Courteous. And, in the 10 minutes I've been waiting in line, I haven't heard any of them complain once about the line or the work they have to do."

"Oh, yeah," he says with a sneer.

"Yeah," I reply. "But, I cannot say the same for you, sir."

I hear a snicker come from one of Carolynn's associates behind the counter. That really turns Beltcher's blushing face red.

"Listen here," he says raising a fat finger to my face. I imagine what it would be like to grab his wrist, stretch him across the counter, and drop my body weight across his forearm snapping the tendons at the elbow. Would he squeal or scream? "You think you can just walk into my store and talk to me like that?" he says spraying spit with each consonant. "You're wrong, pal." I quietly wonder how many pounds of pressure it would take to pull that neck tie so tight that his head would pop like a pimple. "You're one of those Millennials. Can't take any criticism. You don't like the way I talk to my employees? You wanna cry about it, huh?"

He continues ranting at me. Somehow, I press that warm anxiousness down inside me. It wants to climb up and come out. It would take less than two seconds to grab a walking cane from the end-cap on the aisle directly behind me and bring it crashing over his head.

"Well? What do you have to say about it... *pal?*" He says poking that fat finger into my chest. Carolynn gasps. I take a deep breath.

"First, let me just say… that your store has an abundance of breath fresheners; mints, gum, you know? You *really* should use them. Secondly, between the dutiful ladies working behind the counter and the line of customers waiting patiently, you seem to be the only person who can't take any criticism, since shouting like an infant seems to be your go-to response when a *Millennial* like myself tells you to *take it easy.*"

For a moment, he balks. Mouth open and silent, I see the gears turning furiously in his head, trying for a stinging come-back. The little old lady behind me lets out a laugh. I hear the *ding-dong* of the front door. A man and woman who *were* standing in line walk out.

"Uh oh," I say turning back to Beltcher. "Customers are leaving. I wonder if they'll ever come back?"

That sets him off again. As he continues shouting, I notice Carolynn and her friends behind her. Their faces turn from shock and worry—to amusement. One of them even smiles. Beltcher storms off to the back of the pharmacy—still ranting into the air as he leaves.

Carolynn hands me a white bag with a white bottle of pills inside just for me. She says thank you and gives me a smile. Her bubbly associate leans across the counter to me and says, "That… was amazing!" There's a collective agreement from the pharmacy techs: "He had it coming!" and "You know that's right!" Carolynn pushes her glasses against her nose and looks over the prescription, getting back to business. "Mr. Little, you have taken these before, correct?"

"Yes."

"Okay, I think you're all set…" she takes a closer look at the prescription.

"Wow," she says under her breath. "That's quite a heavy daily dose."

"Um, yes. Yes, it is."

"And, this is for… anxiety," she says just as I say…

"Anger… or, um, yes, anxiety is the right word. I guess."

For a moment, her big brown eyes stare at me through those deep lenses. "Maybe *he* should be taking this stuff," she says with a smile and gesturing to where Beltcher left the scene. "It seems to have worked pretty well for you, huh?

"Yeah," I say taking my prescription and smiling. "Yeah, it does, doesn't it?"

Emma Little

I fire up the laptop on the coffee table and dust cereal crumbs from the keys. Just another day in the life of being a stay-at-home mom while running a free-lance marketing business on the side. A ping pong ball smacks me in the temple.

"Hollis," I say.

"Sorry, Momma," comes the reply from my four-year-old holding a plastic two-foot baseball bat behind his back. He lowers his head letting his almost black curls fall in front of his eyes. He especially looks like his daddy right now.

"What have I said about playing ball in the house, baby?"

"Not to."

I open the video chat. The clock on the screen says 8:50 am. I've got 10 minutes until the meeting with my client. Just enough time to get a snack set up for Hollis. I hop up from the couch and walk into the kitchen.

"Where you going, Momma?"

"I am going to make you a snack, baby, and Momma is going to be on a call."

"Do I have ta be quiet?" he asks making the disappointment in his voice abundantly clear.

"Yes, please, Hollis."

Then, I hear another voice from the living room. "Emma? Emma are you there?" I race back to see a conference room of 30-somethings staring back at me through my laptop. I quickly hide the box of Toastie Cereal and check the clock. They're 10 minutes early; what gives?

"Hey… uh, hey there!" I turn the laptop so they can't see the pile of laundry on my couch. I pop my ear buds in, give Hollis a wink, and turn to the faces staring back at me through my laptop. "Are we ready to discuss the latest revisions you requested?"

"Well, first, Emma, the work we've seen so far is wrong." Devon stares over the rim of her glasses. "All wrong." Oh boy.

Being freelance means I have to put up with a little crap from clients. For instance, when, midway through the project, they claim that my "approach has not met expectations" - I have to push back. Negotiate. It's a verbal dance. But, I'm a mother. I can teach a master class in negotiation. And, I'm not afraid of other people's crap.

After 15 minutes on the conference call, Hollis' steel blue eyes peek over from behind the screen of my laptop. His eyes are bright like his daddy's too, piercing, but Reese's eyes are an icy green. There's an urgency in Hollis' face. He silently mouths the word "snack." I never got him a snack. He's been waiting this whole time. Without being too conspicuous for the camera, I reach under the coffee table for the box of Toasties. "So, Devon, you said earlier that the color pallet is too country-chique? Can you elaborate?"

The *short* video conference goes over an hour during which time I negotiate a revised scope of work from Devon and her team. I also get a verbal promise for two more projects for the holiday launch coming up. And, more importantly, I successfully negotiated the plastic baseball bat from my child's hands for a second time with just a snap of my fingers.

I draft an email back to Devon and her crew. Just as I'm about to hit the Send button, Hollis leaps on to the couch demanding I give Beefy a hug. Beefy is a buffalo, Hollis' favorite stuffed toy animal. I click Send, snap the laptop shut, grab Hollis and Beefy, smothering them both in kisses.

We fill up the morning with games. Hide and Seek in the living room is his favorite. It's during our fourth or fifth round of hiding that, out of the blue, he asks, "Is Daddy gonna be okay?" Reese has been dealing with anxiety since he was a kid. But he's always managed it well—until a few years ago. And, at just four years old, Hollis sees very clearly what his dad has been able to hide from so many for so long.

For a moment, I don't know how to answer him. Then I think of how Reese has treated me and how he's cared for us. He's never raised a hand to me or shouted in anger at either of us, which is more than I can say for any of my mother's boyfriends when I was growing up.

He's been working hard at that mailroom job when other men would have quit. It's not much money and Reese certainly wouldn't want to call it a career—but he's provided for us.

"Your daddy is going to be just fine, baby" I say brushing his cheek. For only a moment, he holds my gaze, trying to see the truth of the matter in my eyes. Then, he smiles and the moment passes. He bounces away and grabs his bat again. "Hollis, don't play ball in the house."

"I won't. I'm gonna see the men."

"You're going to see the who?" I ask watching him bounce

over to the front window. He climbs the arm-chair and turns around in it to look out through the sheers.

"The men," he says matter-of-factly. "Two of them… in the car. They have long hair." I get up from the couch and peer through the sheers out the window. I see the row of houses tightly packed on our street. But, no car. And, no men.

"Well, buddy, it looks like they're gone now. Were they out there while I was working?"

"Yeah, I waved but they didn't wave back. The car just went *Varoom*." Hollis races through the living room in his imaginary car.

I look back out the window. Two days ago, I had noticed a car parked across the street outside our house. I'd picked up Reese from the office. It was dark out except for the street lamps. I thought the car across the street was empty. But, just as we pulled in our drive way, the headlights came on and the car drove away. *We live in the city*, I think to myself. *There are thousands of cars on hundreds of streets.*

"Don't worry Momma," Hollis says behind me. He's raised his bat high above his head with both hands. "I'll protect us."

Chapter 3

Reese Little

Derrick waddles into the copy room wearing his typical sleazy grin, pulling the stainless-steel file cart behind him. The cart is overwhelmed with loan files rubber-banded and stacked for us to copy and scan. I glance at the clock that says it's 4 pm. I wish I could say this was a rare occurrence. But, this kind of late-in-the-day project work has become miserably common.

"Is this the project we were supposed to get on Monday?" I ask without hiding my loathing.

"Yup," Derrick answers. Just behind him, another man enters the room. He is a tall black man in a sharp suit with an even sharper smile.

"Mr. Wilkerson, it's good to see you," I say very aware of making my smile look genuine.

"Reese, always good to see you," he says in a jovial voice that is unnecessarily loud for speaking to someone less than three feet away. Mr. Wilkerson isn't a bad boss, he's just merciless at imposing his sunny disposition on everyone. He's the kind of boss that has a big toothy smile for you no matter what bad news he's going to drop into your lap.

"Reese, I have some news for you, son."

"Is that so?"

"Yes, it is. Derrick tells me you've been doing a wonderful job under his leadership, just wonderful!" He leans in with his imposing size and wraps an arm around my shoulder. He guides me to the back of the copy room, giving the impression this is a secretive meeting—just between us, even though Derrick stands no more than five feet away. "Reese, I think it's time we discuss your career. You've been with Iconic Copy & Mail for four years now and I think we..."

"Five years, sir."

"I'm sorry?"

"I've been with the company for five years."

"Oh!" He recovers quickly. "Well let's talk about the future. How would you feel about managing your own Iconic site?" I've been working toward it for the last three years. And, it would mean a bump in pay and I would finally be salaried.

"Yes… yes, sir," I blurt out. "I would like that very much."

"Yes! I thought you would. Management is the right place for a sharp tack like you, Reese." He squeezes my shoulder unnecessarily hard. "And, moving into a management position opens up a wide range of career possibilities for your future. Why, look at Derrick," he says gesturing a big arm toward the lump of a man hunched over manila files on the copy table. "Derrick," Mr. Wilkerson calls out, "the move to management two years ago changed your world, didn't it?"

"Sure did." Derrick gives a weak smile.

"Sure did," Mr. Wilkerson repeats. He takes a deep breath and stares into my eyes a little too eagerly. "Well, I'll let you and Derrick get back to work. And, Reese…"

Uh oh, here it comes.

"… keep that grit in your belly and keep a smile on your face…"

And there it is, the line he always closes with.

"…who knows, Reese, in another year or so, you could be managing your own mail room just like Derrick." He flashes a smile and big wave and he's gone. I can't help but watch him walk out through the hall of the accounting office back toward the lobby. Without fail, he always looks like he owns the place.

"Alright, Mr. Management," Derrick says with a chuckle. "We got work to do." And, he nods to the file cart. It's loaded with the loan files Cheryl promised to have to us four days ago. But, it lands in our lap on a Friday afternoon with a ridiculous deadline. Cheryl is only an associate office manager but Derrick won't make any objections. He likes the way she looks in her pencil skirts.

"Derrick, can't we say something?" I can feel my face getting warmer. "I mean… they hand us a project four days late. Then, we have to make magic happen to copy and file this God-awful mountain of loan approvals before the weekend."

"You wanna tell Cheryl where she can stick these loans? Be my guest, Reese." Then he grins. "We can call it an exercise in customer management." I've seen this reaction from Derrick too often—the tired look in his eyes, the poor attempt at humor that hides his fear of putting his foot down and speaking up. I wonder how long it will take before I become a door mat too.

"I'm just saying, we can't perform magic. Could we at least talk to…"

"Quit yapping." Derrick slaps a messy stack of documents on the copier in front of me. "Start copying."

Three and a half hours later the job is finally finished. Loan files sit in towering stacks on the work island in the middle of the copy room. I take a breath and glance out the office window to see my wife and child sitting in our '88 model sedan in the dark parking lot. Looking at them sitting under a moonless night reflected by the dull black asphalt of the parking lot, I feel a mix of irritation and shame—irritation at the late hour. But, the shame is mine.

"Done!" I announce a little too eagerly. I toss the last file on to the table.

"Well, it's about time," Derrick retorts. He'd found a way to settle in comfortably at his desk checking emails and left me to finish the last 20 minutes of this project by myself. "I see the wife and kiddo waiting out there for ya."

"Yeah," I say moving toward the door. "Mind if I clock out and I'll see you on Monday?" I grab my jacket.

"Hold on, bud," he says without looking up from his computer. I feel my eye twitch. "Go ahead and roll the original files back to Cheryl." I open my mouth to say something. Derrick's dead-eyed gaze reminded me of the eerie evil scientist in a low-budget sci-fi flick I'd seen in college. The scientist looked like a love-child cross between Quasimodo and Steve Buscemi. "Well?" he dares me. I start to say something. To object. To refuse. To tell Derrick to peel his worthless hide out of that chair and deliver the files himself.

"Sure." I toss my jacket and cap on the desk, grip the file cart, and push my dignity down a little deeper.

I race the overwhelmed file cart like a bat out of hell. The vacant halls of the loan office echo the sound of my Brogue dress shoes slapping the granite floor as I run. I'm not wasting another minute in this cubicle dungeon if I don't have to. I jerk the cart to a halt in front of Cheryl's closed office door. I realize I can hear myself panting for breath. I knock on the door and it moves, opening slightly. Light from inside slips through the opening in the door way.

"Cheryl? We finished up last round of copies. I've got the originals here." I hear movement inside but no response.

"My wife's waiting outside… so, I'm gonna drop these off and go." I push the door open and step in. "Oh, wow! I'm sorry!"

"What the hell, Reese!" Cheryl blurts as she fumbles with the buttons of her blouse that is opened to her navel. She turns her back to me. The zipper of her skirt is undone and her hair obviously disheveled.

"Uh, um… Entirely my fault!" I stammer. "I'm so…" Turning to leave, I see Keith Pennington behind the door inside Cheryl's office. Keith, the micro-managing director of accounts, furiously tucks his Oxford shirt back into his trousers. He stares me down. I can't help glancing at his wedding ring.

"Is this what the help does, nowadays?! Just storm in?" says Keith. I feel the sweat beading on my neck.

"I apologize. I'm just going to leave these files here and…" Before I can walk out, Keith slams Cheryl's office door into me. The force knocks me across the file cart, turning it over. A throbbing pain hits my face and shoulder where the door connected. I try to pick myself up. Files are scattered across the hall.

"Shut up and get out!" Keith raises his arm, pointing down the hall, ordering me like a child to go to my room. I roll and get to my feet clumsily. A dull pulse throbs in my head. Blood racing. Too fast. Too loud. But, I can still hear Cheryl cursing Keith.

"Dammit. Did you have to do that?"

"Hell, make him pick it up!" Keith fires back. "He's got nothing better to do."

Something inside me erupts. A rush. I get to my feet and pin Keith to the wall. Without knowing how, I lift a man that outweighs me by 50 lbs. Both of my hands lock around his throat. Keith flails. He chokes as his heels are raised off the floor.

"Nothing better to do... but, go home to *my family*! Where's *your* family, Keith?"

"God's sss-ssake, Cheryl," Keith gasps, "... call security."

I drive my knee into his groin several times. He screams and doubles over. I toss his body toward Cheryl's mahogany desk and hear his head smack the corner—then he's quiet. I turn to Cheryl, every muscle in my body tenses. My heart pounds faster. My eyes—redness surges through my eyes.

"*This* is why I'm working late and my family sits in a dark parking lot waiting for me? *Becauseyou'rescrewingyourboss*?"

Cowering against the wall, she pleads as I grip her face with both of my hands. I hear Derrick burst onto the scene panting for breath.

"What'd you do?"

I'm looking up at him from the hall floor. Dazed, I look around. No one is screaming. No one is lying unconscious on the floor. I stand clumsily still favoring the hip that took the impact with the floor. Keith and Cheryl, the guilty pair, linger in the small office—still fumbling with the buttons on their clothes.

"We're fine here," Keith blurts out. "Just had a little... uh, we were..." and he trails off. Derrick moves toward the pile of scattered copies on the hall floor.

"I'll clean it up," Cheryl says desperately trying to get everyone to leave the scene. "Just go. I've got it. Nothing to worry about."

I don't have to be told twice.

Chapter 4

Emma Little

Hollis and I wait in our little rusty 4-door car, one of only a half dozen left in the parking lot. The typical Friday afternoon exodus came and went hours ago. Any minute that handsome husband of mine is going to walk through those office doors and we can go home. But, I've been repeating that line in my head for the past two hours.

The glass door shimmers in the dark plaza and Reese emerges from the office. He moves quickly, almost a march, with jacket in hand. Even in his drab blue polo shirt with the company logo on the chest, he's an impressive figure. Six feet tall and athletic. He never played team sports in college but he had a love for judo, martial arts. I think his dad even signed him up for a boxing club when he was teenager.

As he gets closer, I see the knot between Reese' eyebrows. He jerks the car door open. A rush of cold air fills the car and he slumps into the passenger seat.

"Hey, babe. Are you okay?" I ask.

"Just drive, *pleasepleaseplease…*" he replies slightly out of breath. "Just go." Of course, I want to know what's with the dark cloud. But, I don't ask. He'll tell me soon enough. Reese turns to see Hollis who is sleeping soundly in his car seat.

"He was asking for you tonight," I say.

"Yeah? Working late… again. Was he upset?"

"I think he worries about you. He knows something is not right."

"Worries?"

Hollis is only four years old but he's an empathetic soul. No one is a stranger to Hollis. Sometimes, he seems to be acutely aware of what others are feeling, no matter how guarded. I like to think it's his mutant superpower.

"Did you two eat already?" Reese asks.

"Oh, Hollis and I already ate, babe," I say with a grin. "We had delightful spread of grapes, Cheezy Pops, and animal crackers."

"That's high-society living, Em."

"You know it! But, I'm pretty sure there's also half a bottle of wine at the house that needs to be finished off tonight."

"Is that an invitation?"

"Uh-huh." I slide my free hand over his thigh. "And, Hollis is already asleep," I whisper. "We can just tuck him in and go straight to wine-and-lingerie time."

"So…" he looks over at me, "is tonight the night when you drink all the wine and I wear the lingerie?" I laugh, letting out a snort. "You always hog the lingerie, babe," he says with a smile. "When is it gonna be my turn?"

"I don't think either of us would enjoy that, Reese."

I pull the car into our neighborhood: a pocket of quaint WWII-era homes that sit almost on top of each other. Most of the houses on our street are rentals—like ours—and it shows. Every other home on the street is in disrepair: peeling paint, missing siding, or the occasional mail box that leans to one side on a rotting beam of wood. The house across the street has a cluster of cars parked on the lawn. They're throwing another one of their weekend parties that literally lasts the whole weekend. Starting on Friday night, the party attracts a swarm of V-neck wearing hipsters who drink gin in red solo cups and smoke clove cigarettes all night. The last car typically doesn't leave their front yard until Sunday morning.

Reese pulls Hollis out of his car seat as gently as he can, trying to let him sleep. My heart swells watching him carry our child into the house. I wonder how something so parental can be so sexy at the same time. Hollis doesn't stir. He's tucked into his bed safe and sound.

On the kitchen table sits the usual spread of bills and clipped coupons. I grab the bottle of wine from the shelf and pour two glasses. Reese looks at me warmly. It's a much different face than the one he had coming from the office.

"One for me and one for you," I say. He smiles. And, then he notices the bills on the kitchen table. He can't help but straighten them into a neat pile – a small measure of control over the ongoing chaos of our lives. "You think the bills will disappear if you keep shuffling them around like that?" I ask with a smirk. He moves to me and wraps both arms around my waist, pulling me close. He presses his face to my neck and breathes deep. My heart swells again and I feel so small in his arms. I trace a hand over the back of his head, playing with his dark hair. "Wine in one hand and my man in the other."

"You like me, huh?" he says through muffled kisses moving from my jaw and continuing down across my neck.

"Nah, I just want you for your body."

His light green eyes stare back into my own. He kisses

me deeply and, for a moment, I think he's going to take me —really take me in the kitchen without even bothering with the bedroom. But, I feel something change. He pulls away and lowers his eyes.

"Emma," he says moving to the kitchen table. "Can we talk for second?" He sits at our table with mis-matched chairs that, like most of our furniture in this little house, was handed down from his dad or my mom.

"Uh-oh," I say. I try to rally his mood, swinging my hips a bit as I walk toward him. I don't sit in the chair next to Reese but straddle him instead and wrap my arms around his neck.

"Emma."

"Mm-hmm." I plant little kisses across his face.

"Babe." He pulls away from me. "At work today, I had another… episode."

"Oh no. They're getting more frequent aren't they?"

"Yeah. Third time this month. I used to only get these freak-out day dreams once or twice a year. But now... I'm stressed, Em. I walked in on our office manager and one of the directors, um, enjoying an after-hours rendezvous in her office."

"Oh my God!" I say unable to hide a shocked grin. "Seriously?"

"Yeah. It turned into a shouting match. I apologized and the file cart got knocked over –it was just – it was just embarrassing."

"Wait, why did *you* apologize?" I stand and feel my brow tense. Reese calls it my court room face. He knows when I don't like something and I'm about to argue it into the ground.

"I... I don't know. But then, I got so angry. That place just treats me and Derrick like trash that they can walk on. I just snapped and…" he looks away from me, "I killed them both with my own bare hands."

"No you didn't, Reese." I move back to him and hold his face, looking him in the eye. "No you didn't. I don't know what these day dreams are but…"

"But, why are they so violent; so real? Do I need help?"

I don't have anything to say this time. I just wrap my arms around his neck and hold his head against my chest. Then I ask the question that needs to be asked, the question he hates.

"Why don't you talk to your dad about this?"

"Emma, come on, you know why." Standing, he shoves the chair aside and paces across the kitchen floor. "My dad would have a heart attack if he heard me say that I get lost fantasizing about brutally killing people when they piss me off. *Self-control is powerful, son… control your emotions or they will control you*," he says mimicking his father's slight Southern accent.

"I know your dad hasn't been the greatest. His advice has always been on the side of doom and gloom."

"Yeah," Reese says with a wry smile. "His motto is 'prepare for the worst and hope for… less than the best.'"

"I don't see why you couldn't just ask him to help." I go back to my glass of wine. "What is there to lose?" I let that question hang in the air, waiting for his reply. The muscles in his jaw tighten. He decides to change the subject.

"We need to talk about money."

"Seriously?" I don't hide the irritation in my voice. "Can't I just show you my boobs and we can drink wine?"

"I'm sorry, Em. And, I love your boobs… but I'm looking at that stack of bills and I know we still need to buy groceries for next week. We're almost out of milk for Hollis."

"Actually, we ran out this morning," I say quietly.

"Oh. So, we need to get groceries… tonight?"

"Yeah, I'm sorry. I can run to the Corner Market and…"

"Not tonight you're not." He turns, grabbing his jacket. "It's after dark. I'll get the groceries"

Our neighborhood is not the kind of place that is safe to walk after dark. Beyond the hipsters' party across the street, there awaits an obstacle course of inner city oddities between our house and the Corner Market including the neighbor's guard dogs, the inebriated homeless man shouting biblical prophecies on the corner, and the occasional tricked-out car parked at the car wash—not using the car wash—just parked there. He throws on his jacket.

"I'll be back before you know I'm gone."

"Okay." I realize I need to give him more bad news. I start massaging the spot between my nose and forehead. "Reese, um, we only have about $100 in the checking account."

"What? No, I should have been paid today. Did my check not get into the account?"

"You did get paid today." I massage the spot, trying to chase away the headache that is growing. "One hundred dollars and fourteen cents is all that's left after we went in the red last week. I won't get paid for my project work until next month." We've lived pay-check to pay-check for a few years now. Neither of our families ever had much money. All of our furniture has been second-hand. Even the engagement ring Reese gave me - his grandpa gave him his grandma's old ring. I don't mind it. In fact, it's kind of sweet to think about that senile Norwegian rough-neck being a sentimental type.

"So… so, just the essentials from the market then?"

"Yeah," I say. "Just the essentials." He starts toward the

door but halts for a moment. He turns and looks at me. He's thinking the same thing I am. The same conversation we've had again and again.

"Emma, this isn't the way it's always going to be…"

"I know."

"But, this is just…"

"I know. But can't we…"

"No, my dad… is just… you know how he is."

"I know but we can't keep this up… paycheck after paycheck."

"I know. I know."

"…so…"

"…so…" He thumbs through his wallet, turning over the same debit card in his hand, again and again. "I'll be back," he says.

"I love you."

"I love you."

Chapter 5

Reese Little

I zip my jacket and make my way down the block. The neighbor's party across the street has added a few more cars to the front lawn since Emma and I got home. I pass the usual cast of characters as I walk to the store at the end of our street. The "kennel" house is guarded by a lone and barking sentry leashed to a stake in the front yard as usual. I pass that house avoiding eye contact with the dog. I turn the corner at the end of the street and see the car wash. Inside one of the self-clean car wash bays sits the same Monte Carlo that I've seen sitting there no less than four nights a week. Though, it's usually parked in the lot outside the wash bays as if the two thugs inside were claiming a small bit of territory on Gallatin Pike.

Finally decided to clean her up, I think.

The car sits empty and parked in the wash bay as if it were hiding from the city.

"Grace and peace to you!" The homeless preacher shouts at me as he leans against the dumpster at the back of the Corner Market. "Do you know the Lord Jeez-us?" he continues in that loud voice unaware that he is shouting at all.

"I do, thank you," I say trying to be friendly while ending any conversation before it starts. I haven't been to church since mom died. I don't particularly claim any religion but I also don't want to give St. Jack Daniels here the opportunity to evangelize.

I pick up the pace and enter the store. The music of some Arabic hip-hop artist greets me from the boom box sitting behind the counter. The smell of incense is heavy in the air. A lone store clerk in his early twenties sweeps the floor in front of the check-out registers and greets me with a silent nod. I grab a plastic basket from the stack and walk to the back of the store. I pick up milk first then peanut butter, sandwich bread, cereal, some fruit, and beef jerky for myself. I trace the aisles in this little store picking up all the groceries that would get us through the next week. The clerk is eager to set aside his broom and ring up my groceries.

"You have a good night, my friend," he says to me in a thick accent. I walk out of the Corner Market with six plastic sacks of groceries in my hands.

The wind picks up and the air even smells different. A thunderstorm is on its way. I pick up the pace hoping to avoid the deluge of rain. As I began to trot toward the street across the parking lot, I see the preacher-hobo standing twenty yards in front of me silhouetted by the street lamps. He faces me standing directly in my path unmoving.

"No man can hide. No, not one."

"Excuse me?" I ask. Immediately, I realize it was a mistake to say anything at all.

"The Lord will call for a reckoning unto everyman. He will curse a man for his sins. And, *ye shall be punished* even unto the seventh generation!"

He gives that last part about being punished some extra gusto. Strangely enough, he shows no signs of the drunken swagger that I saw on him when I entered the store fifteen minutes ago. His stillness appears even more pronounced as the wind buffets his tattered coat around his thin unwavering frame. I walk past him with my eyes to the pavement but I can feel him stare me down as I rounded the corner making my way up the street.

As I climb the rise in the street leading to my house, I can hear the dogs from "kennel house" clamoring like mad. I make my way closer and the barking grows louder. I notice that the owners are conveniently absent. No car in the driveway and all of the lights in the house are off.

Great, I think, *the neighborhood will get to hear the dogs' racket all night.*

I look again. The sentry dog is missing from the in front yard. Where the dog once stood when I passed by earlier, there lies only the frayed end of its leash. My eyes search in the direction the dogs are barking. I find an orange glow in the cloud line over our neighborhood. It's getting brighter by the second. I keep moving towards the house watching the glow flicker and pulse strangely. I grip my grocery bags a little tighter and speed up to a jog. Cresting the hill, I see the source of the orange pulsing glow. A house burns with thick flames climbing through the windows.

My house!

Dear God, my house is on fire!

I sprint toward my burning home. I run without hesitation and a thousand thoughts race through my mind at once. I drop the sacks of groceries and call out for help. My voice shakes and cracks in the night air. My feet beat the pavement racing toward my home. Emma and Hollis, are they still in that house? Did they get out?

"Help! Help," I scream. I see flames bursting from our bedroom window. "My house. It's on fire. Help!" The party at our neighbor's house is watching from the front lawn. "Call for help! Call for help," I yell at the crowd of on-lookers. Just then, the wall along the back side of the house falls. Brick, drywall, and lumber splinter and spill across the back yard. The house is going to come down. I sprint across the front lawn screaming for Emma. No reply from the house. I can see inside through the living room window—shadows and flame—something big is moving inside. I rush in through the gaping hole left by the collapsed wall.

"Emma! Where are you?"

The heat is terrible. I immediately smell burning hair, not sure if it's my own.

"Emma," I scream filling my lungs hot dry smoke. Our photographs on the wall bubble and turn black. The couch is ablaze. My eyes burn. I begin to choke.

"Em..." I can no longer yell for her. No air. My heart beats faster. Everything turns red. And then, everything goes dark.

Chapter 6

Reese Little

"**G**et him otta here, now. You hear me? This place is not secure!"

I can smell the smoke heavy around me and feel drops of water pelt my face. Opening my eyes, I see rain streaking towards me through the black sky. Two firefighters stare down at me. They carry me out of the ruins of my own home. They place me on a waiting stretcher next to an ambulance. A coughing fit hits me and I retch ash from the back of my throat.

"He's conscious," a firefighter shouts. "We need a medic."

"I can move," I say between lurching coughs as I try to sit up. "Emma? Where's my wife?" I look around the scene frantically. Firemen and other EMT personnel walk around the smoking rubble. "Emma?"

"Reese!" She shoves through the watching crowd at the neighbor's across the street. "Reese." She is wrapped in a blanket and holding our son. I grab my wife's face in my hands and kiss her. I pull Hollis to me and hold him. As I pick him up, he pats my face and asks, "Daddy, did you get hurt?" Emma tries to assure Hollis that I am okay.

"Yeah, it looks like Daddy got a little dirty in there, huh?"

Portions of my face and clothing are blackened with ash. Emma offers a towel that the firemen gave her to wipe down herself and Hollis. She wipes the ash from my face and it feels so good to have her next to me that I begin to cry.

"I thought you were…" I choke.

"I'm here," she assures me. "Hollis and I are safe."

"Daddy, what happened?" he asks pointing to our smoking home.

"I don't know, buddy. That was kind of scary, wasn't it?" I respond.

Two EMTs approach us. "Sir, we need to take a quick look at you to be sure you're okay," says one of them. She shines a flashlight in my eyes while examining scrapes and burns with gloved hands. I grow impatient with the repeated knowing looks and mumbled discussion between the two of them. I notice a short woman in a dark suit carrying an umbrella. Unlike the firefighters and the EMTs, she moves slowly, but not without purpose. She's observing everything. The two EMTs finish their work with a few questions: "How do you feel? Any dizziness or nausea? Labored breathing?"

"No."

"How many fingers am I holding up?"

"Three. Wow, you really ask that question? I thought it was just in the movies."

"Sir, can you tell me your name?"

"It's Reese Little." The EMT asks me to sign a 'refusal of care' document basically saying that I'm okay. I do. When I answer all of their questions, they pause and give each other one of their knowing looks I'd already seen a few times. "What?" I say impatiently. The male EMT claps my shoulder with a smile.

"You are one tough beast," he says with nervous laughter. I look back at him wondering what he means.

"Of course he is," Emma says looking at me with pride.

"No, lady," he says. "I mean, he laid in that burning rubble unconscious for at least 20 minutes with part of the roof laying on top of him! We thought he was DOA for sure…" At this, his partner gives him a jab in the side. He gets the hint and both medics excuse themselves. Then, the lady in the suit takes this opportunity to introduce herself.

"How are we doing tonight?" she says with a rehearsed smile.

No one answers right away. I want to say *My house just burned down. I thought my family died but it turns out they're alive. So, considering everything, not a bad night.* But I just nod. Emma hooks her arm through mine and, with her other hand, she holds Hollis to her hip.

"I'm detective Esperanza." She says she wants to check on us and do whatever she can to help. Immediately, I wonder why a detective is present at a residential fire. Detective Esperanza already gathered a few details that Emma gave to the first officers at the scene. Emma told them that, after I'd left to go to the Corner Market, she heard movement coming from our basement.

"Something big was down there. I started to open the basement door but I heard what sounded like the washer and drier tumble and roll across the floor down there." She recounts several details to the detective.

Initially, Emma thought it was an animal. But, the sounds traveled through the house, growing until it was clear that an intruder made their way into the basement from the outside. She ran to Hollis' room and locked the door.

The detective shoves her cell phone a little closer to Emma

as she tells the story, I assume, to record her statement. Emma says she heard a pounding then a splintering crack, like a door breaking. The intruder or intruders were inside. That's when she realized she didn't have her cell phone with her. She heard heavy footsteps, like a man's, but quiet.

"I think he knew I was still in the house," Emma says folding her arms across her chest.

"Him? You saw the intruder?"

"Oh. No, I didn't actually see him… her. Whatever."

"How did the fire start?" Detective Esperanza asks while holding the cell phone even closer to my wife. Emma tells her that Hollis woke and she tried to keep him quiet. She pushed his dresser against the locked door. Then she turned to pick up Hollis when the door knob clicked. They tried to come in the bedroom. She yelled at them to go—told them she'd called the police. She took Hollis to the window and opened it. Just then, the bedroom door splintered open.

"I could hear them ripping the rest of the door open." She looks at me. "The bed and dresser I had put against the door… I could hear it sliding away. The lamp fell from the dresser and I heard glass break. I think that's what started the fire."

"Did anyone follow you out of the house?" The detective asks with a very clinical disposition.

"I climbed out and didn't look back until I got here—across the street. I got to the party and they called for help. By the time I looked back, I could see fire moving through the house."

"It was a monster, Daddy," Hollis chimes in. "A tree mon-ster." I pick up Hollis and hold him close.

"It was a tree monster?" I ask.

"Yeah," Hollis says with absolute certainty. Detective

Esperanza tucks her smart-phone back into her coat pocket and seems to dismiss Hollis' offering to the conversation.

"Detective, there's something else," Emma says. "I ran over here and the folks at this house took me in and called for help. When I came back out on the front yard with my son… we saw something. In the house, while it was coming down, I saw two… shapes." The detective raises an eyebrow.

"Can you describe the shapes?"

"No, just shadows in the fire. But it looked like they were struggling to get out… fighting even."

"So, you're certain there was more than one intruder."

"Yes. Did you find anyone…or a body still in the house?" Emma asks.

"The officers found no one else in the remains of your house," the detective says confidently.

Just then, I realize our car is parked in the driveway without a scratch. What a pity. Insurance might have paid something.

Detective Esperanza hands me her card. She asks if we have a place to stay tonight.

"Any friend or relative you can call?" she asks. "Or a church you attend that might help?" My mind races to think about folks that we could call at this hour. We could rent a hotel… if we had to.

"Yeah, we've got friends," I say quickly. "We'll call around." As the detective leaves, Emma and I look at each other and we are suddenly hit with the absurdity of everything. We're standing outside in the rain with our four-year-old, on the front lawn of a party that just watched our house burn down.

"So, whatcha thinking?" Emma asks, pulling Hollis up on her hip.

"I'm thinking that our house is gone," I reply.

"Yeah."

"I can't think about that. We need a plan."

The rain begins to beat down. We run to our only shelter—my little old four-door parked in the driveway. We weigh our options. Our list of friends or family that can provide a place to stay is a short one. Our closest friends, Mark and Melissa, would do anything to help us. But, they are raising four kids and adding the three of us to that mix is a burden we won't ask them to take on. This leaves the obvious alternative—my dad. Ted Little, my dad, lives alone in the rural area of the county just outside city limits. His house sits on 15 acres of rough farm land that he does not farm. Sometimes we visit him—a few weekends every year. He already as a room set up for Hollis when we visit. I dig my cell phone out of my pocket and make the call.

To understand my dad, you have to understand what happened to my mom. Growing up, my dad was the adventurer, the survivalist, and the kind of guy who'd pack up the family in the car on a whim and take us caving for a week in Kentucky. My mom passed away when I was 12 years old. For a year, I watched her fight cancer. Then, she fought the chemo. Then, she fought cancer again. The worst part was the day after the funeral…when I realized that life went on and the rest of the world didn't seem to notice she was gone. Dad was never the same. After mom died, his larger-than-life personality became protective and quiet.

Tonight, he answers the phone. He's surprised to hear from me at such a late hour. I explain the fire and the house and assured him that we're all okay. I expect him to immediately offer to take us in. But, oddly, he starts asking questions—strange questions: *What time did this happen? What did you see?*

What did Emma see? Any strange activity in the neighborhood the past few days? Did anybody come to the house in the past few days that you didn't know? I try to answer but… this is weird.

"Dad, we need a place to stay. Is it alright if we…"

"Are you still at the house?" he interjects with heightened tone of urgency in his voice.

"Yeah, Dad. We're in my car parked in the driveway."

"You need to leave now," he says. "Right now." This is starting to scare me.

"Dad, we want to leave but we need a place to go. Is it alright if we stay with you for a few nights?"

"Listen to me, Son. You need to meet me at the diner on Highway 231 in half an hour. Pack or buy everything you need for a road trip in that time…" He's not making sense.

"Dad, what's going on?" Willy's Diner was dad's favorite spot. But it would be at least a 10-minute drive past his place. "If you don't want us staying with you…"

"Listen to me," he cuts me off. "You need to run." Now, I'm listening. "You're not going back to that house or that neighborhood. Meet me at the diner in no less than half an hour. I… I need to tell you something. I think a fight has been brought to your doorstep that you and Emma know nothing about. Reese… I'm sorry." He gets quiet. Sitting there, holding the cellphone to my ear, I don't know what else to say.

"Dad?"

"Just promise me I'll see you at the diner in 30 minutes."

"… I promise."

Chapter 7

Ted Little

I see Reese's white car pull into the gravel parking lot just before 10 o'clock, almost an hour after the diner closed for the night. Only three other vehicles are sitting in the parking lot of Willy's Diner at this time of night. One is Pamela's El Camino that sits here every night this place is open. The second is my own pick-up truck. And, the third is a Monte Carlo that belongs to the troll hunter sitting in the booth across from me. He holds a bloodied rag to his arm to suppress the bleeding. Rain pours out of the black sky in sheets. Terrible weather for confessions that are a little too late coming.

Willy's World Famous Diner is a 50's era meat-and-three that has a working jukebox and a sign out front that boasts the "Best Meatloaf in America!" The little plastic sign in the window that says **CLOSED** was turned out over an hour ago. Pamela is the proprietor of Willy's Diner. She inherited it from her daddy when he passed a few years ago. I'd say she's been sweet on me for some time… but, I guess I'm sweet on her too. She's at the diner most nights still taking orders and serving up better coffee then those fancy chain coffee shops.

"Is that your son?" the troll hunter asks as he turns and nods to the car pulling into the parking lot. His black pony tail tumbles across his leather jacket. Before, I can answer he offers to make a quick exit out the back door through the kitchen.

"Don't bother," I say. "No need to worry about keeping your cover at this point. My son is going to learn a few secrets tonight." We both stand and I finish wrapping a proper bandage around his wound. I help him pull his jacket back over his bad shoulder. "You did your job, Christoph." He tucks his custom revolver into the holster at his thigh.

"Pamela?" I shout back to the kitchen.

"Yeah, Ted."

"You got an umbrella out here?"

"In the can at the door." I grab the lone umbrella propped up in the stainless-steel canister just inside the door. A local insurance agent's logo is printed in white and blue.

"Be sure to get some coffee on," I call back to Pamela.

"Coffee's on."

Christoph and I make our way to the door. He's an able troll hunter and half my age but tonight he walks with a cautious shuffle. Christoph and his apprentice had been watching Reese and Emma's house for over six months now. Over the last two weeks, Christoph came to me again and again with a hunch that something was wrong. I regret not listening then.

We step outside and I snap the umbrella open. "You know where to go," I say. "It's just a precaution... I want you to take it easy. Rest, you understand?"

"Don't worry about me, Ted."

"You just lost your apprentice, Christoph." His drops his gaze. "I'm worried and you need some rest. I know how to contact you. Take care of yourself." He moves as quickly as he can despite his injuries and climbs into his Monte Carlo.

I move across the gravel to Reese's car. Reese sees Christoph getting into his car. He looks him over.

"You guys doing okay?" I say smiling. But, I can hear the slight shake in my own voice.

"Yeah, we're okay, Dad. Hollis is sleeping," Reese says. "We picked up a few things on the way." Reese glances back at the Monte Carlo for a moment like he's going to say something. But, the engine roars and the car pulls away.

I hoist the umbrella over all three of them. Reese holds Hollis as we cross the parking lot and get inside the diner. Emma, Reese, and I shake off the rain and I wipe my boot on the mat. I drop the umbrella back in the can pat down my tweed jacket with some paper towels behind the counter.

Pamela comes out from the kitchen dressed in her uniform with a pot of coffee in hand. She's wearing her powder blue waitress uniform with kerchief around the neck.

"Now, I see why you wanted us to meet you here," Reese whispers to me. He's got a grin on his face. He likes to tease me about Pamela. I guess it's his way of showing that he's okay with it—with me dating. I hate calling it that. Hell, that word makes it sound like high school all over again.

"Well, is everybody okay?" she asks with her Southern drawl. "Ted told me what happened. That's just awful."

"As good as can be expected," Reese answers. "It's good to see you, Pamela. I wish it was under different circumstances, though."

"I'm gonna set you all up with some pie and hot coffee. Just sit yourselves down and get comfortable." And, as quickly as she can buzz around greeting everyone and pinches Hollis' cheeks, she disappears into the kitchen again.

Hollis starts to wake up. Emma strokes his hair. He looks around, wondering where we were, and sees me.

"Papa?" he says with a smile.

"Hey buddy!"

"Our house burned down!" he says a little too excited. I reach for him and set him down on my knee. "There was fire trucks and… and…" he looks back at his daddy.

"An ambulance," Reese says.

"A am-BU-lenz," Hollis says struggling to get his mouth around the word. "And there was somebody in our house."

"Oh, did you see somebody?" I ask.

"Yeah, it looked like a tree... tall... and in our house."

My blood pressure picks up. *Like a tree.* I've heard that before.

"Let's talk," I say to Reese. Emma takes Hollis to a booth at the front of the diner and waits for Pamela to come back with pie. Reese takes a seat across from me with an expectant look on his face. I take a deep breath, still not sure how to start. My hands hurt and I realize I'm clinching them together and my knuckles are white.

"Son, let me tell you a story and then you can ask questions… cause… you're gonna have questions."

"A story?" He leans in and tilts his head. This is the part where he would typically tell me he doesn't want to listen to my stories, he doesn't want my advice, he doesn't want my help. I rush into it hoping he won't cut me off.

"This story is a about a young man and a troll in the mountains of…"

"Dad, I know this story." He leans back in the booth folding his arms across his chest. "The one about the man and the troll that are enemies until they join together to defeat the evil king. You and Grandpa both used to tell me that story when I was a kid."

"It's not a story."

"I'm sorry. What?"

"It's not a story, Reese. Not exactly." I take a deep breath. "Trolls are real."

"What are real?"

"Trolls. Norse mythology, tales of Thor and Odin, and berserker warriors with the strength of 10 men… that stuff ain't just stories." Reese isn't saying anything. I keep going. "Just like the Vikings were real men and women, trolls were real too. Nine and ten feet tall, some even bigger, ugly, and living on the edges of society… in caves and coal mines. They are real and they are still around. And not just in Scandinavia. They're here too. Hiding in forests and frigid mountain ranges." Reese leans in, tilting his head again.

"So you're telling me that the legends about trolls are real?"

"I'm telling you trolls are real. But most of the legends are just made up."

"Okay… well, legends or not," he says, "I don't want to talk about trolls and fairy tales. My *house* burned down!" He catches himself shouting and pulls back. He wrings his hands.

"Are you still taking your medicine, son?"

"What? Yeah. Why? What's that got to do with anything?"

"Do you have the pills with you?" I lean in. "Were they in the house? In the fire?"

"I don't know. Yeah, they were in the fire. I mean, I don't have them with me. Why do you care?"

"Reese, do you remember what happened to Billy Dalton when you were in the 6th grade?" Billy was a kid same age as Reese that bullied every other kid at Riverside Elementary. For a moment, he's confused. He looks down at his hands and there's a hint of recognition on his face. But, that's replaced in a flash with frustration.

"Dad, why are we at this diner?"

"Son, calm down. You're gonna scare Hollis."

"Well, you're scaring me. You're talking about fairy tales and trolls and asking me about my meds. And, you clearly don't want us staying at your place." He throws his hands up. "I don't get it."

"You have to run." I pronounce that in a voice that a father only uses with their child to let them know there are no other options; this is the way it's going to be. Looking into Reese's green eyes, I see the 12-year-old boy that he once was. He had just turned 12 when I learned how much like his grandfather he really was. And, I learned how much that scared me.

"Where are we going to go?" With those words he sinks a little into the booth.

"I don't know. Find a hotel. Stay away from family. Stay away from cities you lived in while at university." I reach into my back pocket and pull out a few one hundred dollar bills. "Take some cash."

"Hold on, Dad." He stands and rubs his face. "Who is after us? Why did they come after me?" He freezes for a moment. "Dad," he whispers, "are you involved in something? Do you owe somebody money?"

"I wish it was that easy." I reach into my coat and pull two aged photographs, bent and torn at the edges, and drop them onto the table for Reese. "It's your Grandfather they are after."

He looks over the two black and white photos. One is a portrait of my dad, Grandpa Karl as he was known to Reese, dressed in military uniform when he served under the French Foreign Legion. The other photo is a group shot of several people standing on a hillside, arm in arm, and smiling. My dad is about 40 years old in that picture; though he looks younger. His jet black hair wouldn't begin to turn gray until he was much older. Next to him, there's an old woman in a long skirt, her hair white pulled into a bun. Next to her is a troll with tusks protruding from his jaw, standing at least nine feet tall.

Reese stares at it a moment, mouth open with a question that he just doesn't want to ask. "Uh, is that Grandpa?"

"Yes."

"And, is… uh… is that… What is that?"

"I told ya, son. That's a troll." He stares at the photo again. I'm sure his eyes are looking for some hint that the photo is doctored. He turns it over in his hand, examines the browning photo paper, and turns it over again bringing it closer to his face.

"Where is this?"

"West Virginia. About 10 miles outside of Frost." His head snaps up.

"Frost? Is this Jotnar Valley?" He's eyes are wide with curiosity. How does he know that name? I find my mind returning to people and a life I hadn't thought about since I was a boy.

"Uh, yes. Did Grandpa tell you about Jotnar Valley?"

"It was just stories he used to tell me when I was little… adventures with giants hiding in forests." Reese scratches his temple and looks back down at the photo. "I thought it was make-believe."

"When your grandpa came to America, he was running from his past. He had been a soldier of fortune. As a boy, he was raised in a quite village on the coast of Norway and when he was old enough to leave, he decided to take up arms with the French Foreign Legion. He had certain talents… war suited him…" I realize I've trailed off when I catch Reese staring back at me.

"Dad, what does Grandpa have to do with all this?"

"That group of people in the photo in West Virginia became his refuge."

"The Legion was coming after him?"

"Hell no." I shift in the booth and lean in. "It was trolls."

"Oh, come on, Dad." Reese walks away from me. He paces, shaking his head. "I mean, is this for real?"

"Son, just look at the picture." I stand. Hollis and Emma are watching us from the far corner of the diner. I try to keep my composure for their sake but Reese doesn't make it easy. "I know you don't understand but you need to trust me."

"Trust you? Dad, I'm trying but this…" he says raising his arm toward me, photographs in hand, like he wants me to take them and toss 'em in the trash.

"Just keep the photos," I say. "Take 'em with you."

"That's just it, Dad. I don't know where I'm going. Not to mention my job—I've got to be back to work on Monday."

"No, you can't worry about that. You've gotta git gone." Reese freezes for a moment. He takes another look at the photographs.

"This place. In West Virginia," he says. "We can go here. The village is still there, right?"

"Um. You don't want to go there, Son." I really don't want him to go anywhere near there.

"Why not? You said this was Grandpa's refuge. It was safe enough for him. They've got to have answers. Right?" Just then, I realize something's not right.

"Quiet," I say cutting him off. "Where's Pam? She didn't bring your coffee, did she?"

"No," he says looking over at Hollis and Emma. "And, she didn't bring pie either."

"They're here." I stand cautiously and Reese does the same. "Dad, who's here?"

Just then, the power goes out and the diner is dark. An eerie silence sets in as the electric hum of the diner's appliances all die at once. The orange glow from the street light outside swims across the rain-streaked windows. I look back at Emma. She's clutching Hollis who's calling out for his Daddy.

"It's okay, buddy," Reese says trying to calm him. "Everything is going to be fine."

"But everything won't be fine," a voice says in the dark.

The doorway of the kitchen opens and a bald lean man approaches slowly. The front door behind me opens, two very large men step into the diner without saying a word. The diner floor creaks and dips with their steps. The old training kicks in and I look for exits. I won't be able to punch through this situation without a weapon. Even then, I have to worry about the rest of the family. This is too fast. It shouldn't be like this.

Reese moves towards Emma and Hollis. She's frightened and holding their boy close to her.

"What do you want?" I say.

The lean man standing at the kitchen door… his face… two tattoos on his forehead – one above each eye. And, both eyebrows are shaved. I had heard of these radical neo-Viking wannabe types but hadn't seen one up close. He moves past the counter and begins to walk toward us. His black leather jacket drips rain onto the diner floor. The two others are trolls from the look of their size, just over seven feet with flat faces and wide square-shaped jaws. Now, I wish I'd made Christoph stick around. Could use a troll-hunter right now. They make their way toward Emma and Hollis. Both wear dark oil skin hats and long duster jackets that barely cover them. Inky rags cover their arms and legs where the long coats don't reach—protection in case they need to move about during daylight. Judging from the chalk-white skin at their face and hands, they appear to be albino—likely hiding in caves and tunnels for generations. One of the trolls rests his hands on the chair across from Emma and I see the bright red marks against his pasty flesh, blood on his knuckles. Are these the trolls that came after Christoph? Reese tries to position himself between his family and the two brutes looming over them.

"You already know what we are here for," says the tattoo-faced man. Our employer believes your father stole it and brought it to this country." His voice sounds diseased. Sickly but not frail. Reese is glancing back at me, waiting for an explanation, a sign, something. My mind is racing. Who is the employer?

"Maybe your employer hasn't heard," I say. "But, my father has been dead a few years now."

"No matter. Give us what we want and we'll go away," he says. I hear an accent in that warbled voice. Not quite Norwegian. Danish?

The tattooed man moves away from me and toward Reese and Emma. With a quick gesture of his hand, he signals his two goons and they close in on them. Heavy hands grab Reese, wrapping a giant arm around his neck. Emma screams. I don't know what they want and I can't threaten them with anything. Reese is kicking in the air trying to find the floor. He can't breathe. The other troll forces Emma's face to the table; twisting her hair in his fat pasty fist.

"Stop," I shout. "Stop. Stop! I'll give you what you want."

Tattooed man gives a nod to the troll holding Reese. He lowers him, gasping for air. I consider my options: I can't let them know I don't know what they want because then I am useless to them which means we are all dead. I reach my back pocket and pull out my wallet. I raise it high in the air.

"Here! Inside my wallet is a page from my dad's ledger. It's… a map. He gave it to me before he died… and he told me to keep it safe. It will tell you what you want to know." The trio doesn't say anything. But, I have their attention. "I have what you want. Now, let my boy and his family drive off and it's yours." I have no idea what I'm going to do when they find out there is nothing in this wallet but a driver's license and a receipt for some cheap cigars.

One of the trolls marches toward me cracking his knuckles. Emma screams and I ready myself for what's about to come. A sudden shotgun blast shatters the front window. Tattoo-face ducks and spins to see where the shot came from.

"Let him go now." Pamela stands at the kitchen door with a double barrel shotgun trained on our assailants. A cut over her left eye trickles blood down her cheek to her jaw. She is an impressive sight dressed in her diner uniform and wielding that weapon.

Reese wrenches himself free in the momentary confusion. I glance at the obliterated diner window in front of us. Reese grabs Hollis in his arms and pulls Emma into the opposite corner away from the line of fire.

"You should lower that weapon before you hurt someone," the tattooed man says. "You just wasted a shot. And you only have one. More. Left."

"I got one shot left." She swipes an arm across her eye, smearing blood, painting her cheek. "Well, who the hell wants it? Step forward. I tell you what, walk on outta here and you won't have to find out who's gonna git it!"

The two goons don't move but the leader makes subtle steps towards me and Pam. With a quick movement I get behind the counter and pull the weapon I hoped I wouldn't need tonight: a long-handle bearded axe. I whisper instructions to Pamela and she steadies her aim at the tattooed leader's chest. I step forward with both arms raised—one holding my axe and the other holding my wallet.

"Alright. Alright. I still have what you want," I say drawing their attention. I lower the wallet and place it back in the pocket. "But, you have to come and get it." I turn the wooden handle of the axe over and over in my hands. "You can walk over and try to take that map from me, that is, if you make it past her shotgun and my axe. Or, you can call off your muscle tactics, let my boy and his family drive off, and I'll hand it to you... nicely." The leader thinks for a moment. But, he ain't convinced. He starts to say something but I cut him off. "You don't want to stare down a sulfur-shot loaded 10 gauge. Do you?"

He stops. He gets it. And, the duo behind him are glancing at each other. He waves his hand and signals the two brutes to back off. Emma doesn't hesitate to scoop up Hollis and bolt for the door. Reese hesitates and looks back at me. What the hell have we gotten into?

"Don't look back, son." I want to explain more, to give him answers that I know he wants. But, it's a little too late for that now. "Take care of your family. I'll see you soon."

He runs to the parking lot. I hear the car spit gravel as they pull onto the highway. Through the diner windows, I can see tail-lights fade away as they head north. I hope they make it.

Pamela leans toward me. "What are our chances of making it outta here alive, Honey?" I stare at the scrawny Viking wannabe and the two trolls behind him weighing, combined, roughly 1500 pounds.

"You got more sulfur ammo on you?" I whisper.

"Sure do."

"Then it depends on how fast you can reload."

"Lead the way."

I raise my axe and rush forward. Another shotgun blast rings through the diner.

Chapter 8

Reese Little

The tires spit gravel behind us. I look over at Emma, her arms still wrapped around Hollis. Before it's out of sight, I glance back to the diner we just escaped. Little to see in the dark through the rain. Little to see except for a single muzzle blast from a double barrel shotgun.

I don't stop. I hold the wheel and just drive with desperation fueling me. Too many thoughts cloud my mind to think straight. *Turn around and help dad. No, turn around and take my family home.* But, we have no home. Not anymore.

Emma turns and hoists Hollis into his child seat when we are a few miles up the highway. As soon as she sits back down in her seat. I hear a shuddering breath and she begins to cry. She folds herself into the passenger seat and sobs. I want to reach for her. But, I keep my hands on the wheel, eyes forward, and I keep moving.

"Momma, what happened to Papa?" Emma doesn't answer.

"We don't know, Hollis," I say trying to keep a reassuring tone. "Papa is a smart one. I bet he's just fine."

"Momma, I want some milk." Milk makes everything better when you're four years old.

"I'm sorry, buddy," I say. "We don't have any milk for you right now." Hollis already finished the last of the milk in his sippy-cup at the diner. Emma raises her head. She wipes her eyes with the back of her hand.

"Beefy is in his bag," she says. "How about your buffalo, Hollis? You want your buffalo?" Emma fishes through the diaper bag, finds the stuffed animal, and gives it to him. From the rearview mirror, I see him lower his face into the velvet fur. I can't imagine what my son is thinking about right now. The things he's just seen would frighten any grown man. My own nerves are shot; I feel unhinged. How does a four-year-old process this?

"Are you okay?" I ask Emma, reaching for her. "Are you hurt?" She shakes her head.

"I just. When he was choking you." She trembles trying to speak.

"I'm fine, Emma. He didn't hurt me," I try to reassure her.

"They could have killed us, Reese." She covers her mouth, trying to catch the words that have already escaped. "You know it. I know it. And Hollis saw it. That's the worst part." Tears fall over her cheeks. After driving for 15 minutes in the rain, Emma asks me where we are going. I hesitate to say it.

"I… I don't know. I'm just driving." I struggle to think about where we are going. My mind can't break away from where we just left. Is my dad still there with Pamela? Is he okay? My knuckles turn white on the steering wheel. I glance at dad's photos on the dashboard. "Maybe take a look at the pictures. Dad gave those to me." Emma grabs the photos and looks over both. "It's my grandfather," I tell her, "in a little town in West Virginia. It's not even a town, really. More like a wilderness commune."

"So, what is this all about?"

"Emma, I don't know where to start." I take a deep breath. "My dad told me that trolls are real." I look over at her face. She has the photos in her lap but she's staring out onto the rain slick road ahead. She is motionless.

"I heard that. It sounded crazy until…" We both stare out onto the dark road, silent, except for the beat of windshield wipers marking the seconds.

"So, your grandfather looks like he was pretty friendly with whoever *these* people are." She fingers the corner of the black and white photo of the group on the hillside.

"He was running from something or someone. Dad said trolls were after him. So, he came to the United States. I assume that's when he changed the family name from Lillevik to Little."

"Why were they after him?"

"I have no idea. He was in the French Foreign Legion. Maybe they attacked someone they shouldn't have."

"Babe?" Emma draws the photo closer to her face. "Did you look at the back of these photos?" I glance over. She's flipped it over and I see something hand-written on the back.

"What's it say?"

"Jot-Nar Valley…" She pronounces it with a hard J sound.

"It's *Yaught*-nar Valley, Babe. The J sounds like a Y."

"Oh." She looks back at the picture again. "Jotnar Valley—April, 1922."

"Wait. What?"

"Somebody wrote 'April 1922' on the back of this photograph. And, the one with your grandpa in uniform says, 'Summer 1908.' What does this mean, Reese?"

I keep trying to look at the photos while watching the

road through my headlights. "Wait a minute... Dad always said Grandpa fought for Norway in World War II."

"So what's he doing wearing a French Foreign Legion uniform?"

"What's he doing in photos from 1922? I mean he's almost middle-aged in that photo, right?" I hear my voice crack. That nervous feeling is back. None of this is making sense. Dad and I used to visit Grandpa Karl in the nursing home. But, Grandpa was rarely coherent enough to know who we were. He would tell me the same monster stories and war stories he told me when I was a kid. Mom and dad hated the war stories when I was a kid. But, it was just sad when I was an adult because we thought he was losing his faculties; he just repeated the same tall tales.

"Reese, I don't think... I don't think your dad has told you everything." The sick nervous feeling is growing and I recall how my dad kept asking about my meds. I grip the wheel. I slow my breathing. "What do you need, Reese?" I look at my wife.

"We're not safe. We are running scared. And blind." I take a breath. "I need answers."

"I trust you." She knows I've got a plan. I reach and place my hand on hers. Her ring, that fluorite stone, pokes my skin and reminds me of all the promises I made to this woman.

"We need to go to Jotnar Valley. They knew my grandfather. Maybe they know who's chasing his ghost."

"You father would hate this plan," she replies. I feel my head grow heavier.

"I know, I know. But I think these people..."

"I think it's perfect." She's unflinching but my mouth drops. "You do?"

"I trust you. We're going to Jotnar Valley."

Chapter 9

Reese Little

I grip the steering wheel tighter, take a deep breath, and exhale. Reaching in my pocket, I get my cell phone to make sure the ringer is on in case Dad calls. It is. I dial his number. It rings several times then goes to voice-mail. I hang up and call again. Then, I have another thought. What if these trolls can track our cell phones? The movies always showed cops and FBI-types tracking the bad guy on their cell phone signal unaware. Can trolls track cell phones?

"Emma. Wake up. Emma."

"I'm not asleep," she says raising her head.

"I think we need to ditch our cell phones."

"What?" She looks at me like I'm not making sense. Maybe I'm not. "I don't know if those guys at the diner can track us on our cell phones. I think I need to toss my cell phone," I say trying to *not* sound crazy but failing miserably.

"Baby, I think they need your phone number to do that," she says rubbing her eyes. "And they didn't look like the types who can track cell phones." Emma turns in her seat and closes her eyes just before she says, "You watch too many movies, Baby."

"Too many movies?" I mutter. "We just found out trolls are real. Pretty sure the two big guys who had their oversized hands on us are actually trolls. Sure smelled like it. And, the third guy, the one doing all the talking, he knew how to find my dad, he was talking about my grandpa. They know my family. But, you think I watch too many movies because I'm worried about my cell phone being tracked." Emma turns toward me, fully alert now.

"You're right." She plunges her hand into my pocket and pulls out my cell phone. The passenger-side window hums as it rolls down. She tosses the phone. I hear the smack of plastic against asphalt. We are both silent. Then, when we can't avoid the lingering question any longer, Emma says, "So… how are we going to contact your dad, Reese?"

"I don't know." God, I hate saying that.

We drive in silence. But, Emma entertains no hope of closing her eyes during the rest of our trek to West Virginia. We stop for gas somewhere near Kingsport, Tennessee. I pay with the cash Dad gave me. Every time I look in the rearview mirror I expect to see that man with the tattoos over his eyes just grinning from the back seat. An hour later, I hear a sound emerge from the back seat: snoring. Hollis is fast asleep. At least one of us is resting. The drive into West Virginia takes us through dark wooded hills lit only by the moon and my headlights. The trees are almost bare and I see silhouettes of skeleton branches reaching upward.

We arrive in Frost just after dawn and I pull into the parking lot of a small general store. It's a cinder block building with a sign advertising a sale on horse feed. A metal tank the size of my car sits next to the store and a single gas pump in front of it. Hollis wakes as soon as the car comes to a stop.

"I'm hungry," he says rubbing his eyes. Emma and I decide to see if the store is open and say hello to the locals. I grab the photo of my grandfather at Jotnar Valley and stuff it in my back pocket.

"Um, it may be a good idea to approach with caution," I say to Emma.

"Well, what's our story?"

"Not sure. What do you think?"

"Well, you could say we are taking a vacation; doing a little camping and you remembered this place your grandparents used to talk about called Jotnar Valley. And, wanted to see it for yourself." I think about it for a moment. It's as good a story as any. And, it's at least partly true.

We climb the wood steps leading to the narrow doors of the general store. I notice one of the doors is barely propped open with a small wooden shim. I press against the door and it opens with a creak and a little bell over the door swings and chimes.

"Hello?" No answer.

I step inside and Emma carries in Hollis on her hip. The store is crammed with aisles of hatches, hammers, chicken feed, and motor oil. Hollis tugs at Emma's sleeve.

"Where are we, Momma?"

"Oh, hello." A man emerges from a small open doorway behind the front counter. He's a 20-something with bright blonde hair and thick beard. "Up and about early, I see. We're not open just yet."

"Yeah, sorry, but…" I try to remember the story Emma and I came up with. "Uh, we've been on the road… camping, you see." I realize I'm still wearing my company polo shirt and Emma's in yoga pants—we do not at all look like we've been camping. "My grandfather used to tell me stories about a place around here. Maybe you know about it…"

"Hello. What's this?" Another voice. Behind Emma and Hollis stands a woman with bright blonde hair pulled into a messy ponytail.

"These folks have been on the road," the guy explains. "Camping, right?" he asks looking at me.

"Uh, right."

The guy and girl could be brother and sister, maybe twins. They regard me carefully for a moment. Each is dressed in work trousers and shirts with plenty of wear and tear. I notice a pair of work gloves sticking out of the side pocket of one. Glancing back and forth at them, they have the same slim build, high cheek bones, and both are nearly a head taller than me.

"So, I think we were looking for a camping spot," I say. "It might be close by. My grandfather spent a few summers there… I think."

"You think?"

"Yeah, it was called Jotnar Valley. Ever heard of it?" As soon as I say *Jotnar Valley*, the guy's neck tenses. His glance moves past me, to the girl.

"Yeah." He hesitates for a moment. "I've heard of it." I look back at the girl. She doesn't say anything but pulls a pack of cigarettes out of the pocket of her overalls. I glance at Emma and back at the bearded dude in front of me.

"Well, can you tell me where…"

The front door swings open behind me. The bell rings and a man with long dark hair steps in. He's got a slicked-back ponytail and alert eyes that scan the store front to back in a glance. One arm hangs across his belly in a sling. And, a really big gun sits in a holster on his thigh.

"You open?" he asks the bearded fella. "I'm looking for some parts. My ride's given me trouble."

"Actually… we don't open for another hour." He walks over to front door, moving past the dark-haired stranger, and sizing him up as he does. "But, uh, since we're all here…" he turns the OPEN sign on the window to face out toward the dirt parking lot.

The smell of cigarette smoke hits my nose. The girl has already lit up and takes a deep drag before expelling two streams of gray smoke through her nostrils. Her blue eyes stare back at me through the cloud of smoke, just daring me to say something.

"Astrid, put that out," the bearded twin says to her. "Don't you know we got a sign on the door that says, 'No Smoking.'" She takes another puff walking back to the counter.

"We also got a sign that says we don't open 'till seven. But we aren't paying that any mind, are we?" I notice a hint of an accent from her and the other guy that could be her twin. It sounds Swedish—but I'm not sure. She takes another long drag before stamping the cigarette out on the worn wood counter top. She brushes any ashes away with her hand and dusts her hands on the leg of her overalls. "Hey," she calls out to the dark-haired guy. "These folks were asking about a camp ground near here." She turns to me with that same daring look in her eyes. "What was the name of that place, mister?"

"Uh, Jotnar Valley."

"Jotnar Valley, that's right." She turns back to the guy. "You ever heard of that place?"

"Hmm?" The guy is caught off guard by the question. His black leather jacket is noticeably worn at the elbows and around the collar. Two or three rings on his hand catch the light of the dawn coming in through the windows. They throw faint beams of light across the dusty store. Probably an out-of-towner just like us. "Oh yeah! You wanna stay away from that place. I heard of some weird stuff that goes on out there." That's when I notice the markings on his rings; they have runic symbols on them. He turns and looks at me in a not-so-subtle way of driving home the point. "I'd say your little family would be better off to keep driving to the next little town. Maybe get a hotel or something." Something is wrong. I glance back at Emma and her face is the face of a woman that will not put up with being lied to.

"Oh yeah?" I say to guy with the dark hair. I walk over to the window and stare over the shelf of motor oils. I see another car sitting in the parking lot outside. It's a Monte Carlo; 1980's model. I've seen that car. "Who the hell are you?" The dark-haired ponytail looks at me with a sideways glance.

"Nobody special. But, you should take my advice."

"You were there," I say raising a finger to his face. "Your car… that's the car that sat outside the car wash across from my house every night for months."

"What?" Emma says.

"And, that was you at the diner, just as we got there. I watched your car pull out."

"What?" She says again. "Wait, did you break into our house?" Ponytail throws his hands in the air.

"No. I didn't. Look, I don't have anything to tell you except to stay away from Jotnar Valley."

"I'm going to ask you one more time; who are you?"

"He's a troll hunter by trade," says the blonde bearded one. "At least, that's what he is judging by the ultra violet flashlight clipped to his belt and the .357 magnum strapped to his leg.

"And," the girl says, "he has the stink of sulfur and self-righteousness."

"No one comes around asking about Jotnar Valley," says the bearded one, "unless you already know what it is. And, if you know what it is, you don't come around asking about it."

"Look," the dude with the ponytail says, who is supposedly a troll hunter, "you are getting into some deep stuff and you need to take your family and go somewhere else."

"No one is going anywhere," the bearded guy says moving in front of the door. "That is until me and my sister get some answers." The sister plops down on a stool behind the counter with a defiant look on her face. I suspect there's a rifle hidden somewhere under that counter.

"I think that's a fantastic idea," Emma calls out. She marches with Hollis on her hip over to the window and flips the Open/Closed sign to read CLOSED to anyone who might stop by. "I want some answers. Who are you people and why did my house burn down?"

For a moment, the platinum blonde twins and the troll hunter are frozen. I don't think anyone expected the cute young mom with the child on her hip would start making demands. It's a Mexican stand-off: three parties and each thinks they have the upper hand. The Swedish twins have home field advantage, the troll-hunter seems to actually know what's going on, and then there's me and Emma. And, we just might be desperate enough to do something… desperate.

Chapter 10

Emma Little

It's dawn. My husband and I are standing in a dusty general store in the middle of nowhere West Virginia. I hold my child on my hip while I argue with a troll hunter and a pair of Scandinavian transplants over the location of an Appalachian commune for giants. And, as funny as all that sounds, I am not laughing.

This troll-hunter, who tells us his name is Christoph, has answers. But, he's not giving them. He'll only tell us that Reese's dad hired him. His job was to *monitor* us.

"What for?" Reese asks for the seventh or eighth time. I've lost count. "Why did my dad have you follow us here?"

"I didn't follow you. I left that diner before you did. And, your pop was fine when I drove away."

"So, my dad gave you instructions to come here?" Reese leans in, getting uncomfortably close to Christoph. But, he doesn't reply. "He wanted you to go to Jotnar Valley, didn't he?" He is silent. The brother and sister that, I assume are the proprietors of the store, butt in with their own questions.

"Just who is your dad, mister?" Reese hesitates.

"Ted Little."

"Oh, I wouldn't have told them that," the troll hunter says.

"Why not?" I clinch my teeth trying not to shout at him.

"Less talking and a little more walking," he replies. "That'd be the best course of action for your family."

"I don't know that name." The brother declares. "Is Ted Little supposed to mean something to me?" Hollis sits up on my hip.

"He's my grandpa. He has a axe," he says confidently. "He can fight da bad guys." The room is silent for only a moment.

"Is that so?" the brother asks. "Does he like to fight trolls?" The ice in his voice is unmistakable.

"It's not like that," The troll-hunter, Christoph, says.

"Oh, it's not? But, *you* like to fight trolls, do you not? And, he employed you."

"It's not like that," Christoph says again.

"Then what *is* it like?" Reese's voice shakes the boards and rattles the glass in this little store. I see him recoil—the staggered breathing, the shaking hands. He's barely holding it together. And, I'm not much better. Christoph is silent. He takes a deep breath. There's nothing more he will tell us. I look at Reese. He looks at me. Then, his face changes—an idea.

"Take a look at this." Reese pulls the photo from back pocket and smacks it down on the counter for the brother and sister to see. It's the group shot from Jotnar Valley. "That's my grandfather," he says. "That's Karl Little in 1922." The brother and sister gather around the photo and stare in silence. Christoph sucks air through his teeth.

"See, you don't want to do that either." He paces, clearly losing any ground he thought he had when he came into this store.

"Attans!" The brother whispers with his hand over his mouth. "Look, she's standing right next to him."

"Who?" Reese asks the brother and sister. "Who's the woman he's standing next to?"

Christoph glances out the window looking up and down the country road in front of the store.

"You waiting for someone to show up?" I ask.

"I'm hoping they *won't* show up," he says grimly.

"Who?"

"The two trolls that gave me this," he gestures to his arm wrapped in a sling. "And, they killed my apprentice." Reese and the twins look up at him. The sister rushes over with hellish look in her eyes.

"You mean trolls tracked you down, killed one of your own, and now you've brought them here. Are you a moron?"

"No, but thanks for asking." He stands his ground with her. "We had the neighborhood covered. Trolls shouldn't have gotten into the city. They'd be seen." He hasn't stopped pacing. I can see the wheels turning in his head trying to figure out what went wrong. "They're traveling unseen somehow."

"What did they look like?" I utter the question before I realize it's on my lips.

"The trolls? Small… comparatively. Only seven feet tall. Maybe 700 pounds each. Wearing long coats and wide brimmed hats." He grips his injured arm as he recollects. "Pretty sure they were both albino." I wrap my arms around Hollis a little tighter.

"Oh my God."

"They came to the diner last night," Reese says numbly. "They came to the diner and attacked us. They attacked my father and his girlfriend."

Christoph is frozen, mouth open, and silent. I can see in his eyes the calculations mixed with doubt rattling in his head.

When he speaks again, it's almost a whisper. "Is Ted alive?"

"We don't know," I say preventing Reese from having to answer that question. "We had to run. We drove all night. And, here we are." The room goes silent again. The sun has crept over the hills outside and rays of amber light stream through the dusty covered window panes.

"I remember my grandfather telling me stories of Jotnar Valley when I was a kid." Reese turns to the twins. "Stories of adventures and giants and… It was the only place that I thought would have answers." The brother steps forward and clears his throat.

"I'm convinced. You and your family need to come with me and my sister. We'll show you Jotnar Valley."

"No. Wait," Christoph says. "Reese, you should know that your dad didn't want you to go to Jotnar Valley because… you'd just be walking into the belly of the beast." Christoph stares at the floor. "He wanted to keep you as far away from this life as he possibly could." The way he says *this life* makes me almost pity him. "But," he says adjusting the sling holding his arm, "it appears the beast has already found you."

"So, the question is," says the sister folding her arms across her chest, "do you want to keep running? Or do you want to meet our friends?"

Chapter 11

Reese Little

It's a strange thing to say goodbye to somebody you've only just met; you're never sure what to say. It's even stranger when that somebody is a troll hunter you've only just met today when he's actually been watching your family for months.

"I'm sorry about your apprentice," I say nodding my head. "What was his name?" He looks me in the eyes.

"Lyra. *Her* name… was Lyra."

I don't know what to say. So, I just apologize again.

"Well," he says clearing his throat, "if I can't change your mind about Jotnar Valley, then I'm no help to you here."

Christoph tells me he's driving back to Tennessee to find my dad. He says he'll do everything in his power to find him and make sure he's alright. The way his eyes stare out to the road and into the distance signal the gravity of his promise. He tightens the sling at his shoulder one more time before he climbs into his Monte Carlo. "Reese and Emma," he says. "I hope I don't have a reason to see you again. Take care of each other."

The engine roars and he takes off down the road. I take a deep breath, filling my lungs with cool mountain air. The smell holds just a hint of snow. A little hand finds its way in mine.

"Dad," Hollis says. "I think he was one of the good guys."

"You think so, Hollis?" I look into his blue eyes.

"Yeah. I hope he finds Papa... soon." I do too.

Emma rests her head on my shoulder and snuggles up against me, hiding from the chilled gusts of November wind.

"So," she says. "We're throwing our lot in with them?" The twins are locking up the general store.

"Sorry for being so shady with the introductions, mister," The brother says as he tosses a set of keys to his sister. "We don't get many visitors in this little town. I'm Dag."

"And, I'm Astrid."

"I'm sorry," I say to the brother. "Did you say your name was Dog."

"No," he says miffed. "I said Dag. Get it right."

"Sorry about that. I'm Reese Little." I'm not sure that I really want to introduce my family to these two just yet. Moments later, Astrid drives a beat-up truck from the back side of the store. Astrid rolls down the window and leans out.

"Just follow us," she calls out. "You're in good hands." The fact that she feels the need to reassure me doesn't make me feel better.

The truck is a classic 1940's Ford pickup. A bright blue tarp weighted by cinder blocks covers something bulky in the bed of the truck. Two rifles hang on a rack in the back window – both of which have iron axe heads shaped into the stock. My apprehension is growing. Maybe it's the lack of sleep. But, I don't like the idea of following two strangers who look like lumberjack-Vikings into who-knows-where. Dag jumps into the truck and we get into our car to follow.

"I'd offer to give ya the grand tour," Dag calls back. "But, you probably already saw everything there is to see on your way into town." His accent is there but not heavy.

We take the road away from town. After a few miles, we turn on to a single-lane dirt road that winds through a patch of forest for a mile or more. The longer we drive the more uneasy I feel. Emma and I keep looking for signs of civilization. Thick patches of forest cover either side of the road. Even with the trees nearly void of all their leaves, I can hardly see beyond 50 feet into the woods.

I catch up to the trail of dust coming from the olive-green Ford. We whip through branches and dead vines laying across a path of switchbacks. I realize we've been driving up an incline for the past half mile. And my stomach has been growling for the past half mile too. I wonder what are the chances that Jotnar Valley will have a bed-n-breakfast waiting for us?

"Reese, we're losing them," Emma says. I speed up. They're taking hairpin turns on this dirt road with the kind of speed that suggests this route is very familiar to them. I slow down again at the tight turns. Sunlight streams through the trees in thick beams cutting across the road while the valley below is still covered in darkness and untouched by the dawn. "Look at that. It's beautiful," Emma says. "Reese, look."

"Can't right now, Emma. Don't want to kill us on this mountain."

"Oh… yeah. Don't kill us." I maneuver our car along a thin path cut into the side of the mountain. I raise my foot off the gas pedal realizing the peril lying just beyond the thin tree-line that separates us from a death drop.

"Where do you think they're taking us?" I ask Emma.

"Some place where the authorities will never find our bodies," she replies with a grin.

"You think you're funny, don't you?"

"Seriously, though," she says, "I hope there's food some-where. I'm starving."

The twins keep up their speed around each turn. But, I can't keep up. We round a curve …and they're gone. The truck is nowhere to be seen. I speed up hoping to get around the next curve and find them. But, there's no such luck. I start to sweat.

"Baby, where'd they go?" Emma asks.

"I mean… they have to be in front of us somewhere. Right?"

"I have to go potty." Hollis is clinching his knees together in his car seat.

"Oh. Um, right now, buddy? This is not a good time to stop."

"I have to go now," he says through his teeth.

I drive a little farther hoping to see Dag and Astrid's lead sled of a truck around the bend. Again, nothing. What I do see is a roadblock ahead. Now, I'm starting to panic. We ap-proach a padlocked metal gate blocking the road. The gate is smothered by downed trees and dead vines. You can't climb through the barrier without earning a broken limb and a tetanus shot. There is no way our car could make it through even if the gate could be opened.

"So, where are they?" Emma says. I notice a large rusty sign posted on the gate. It reads:

AREA RESTRICTED

BY ORDER OF FEDERAL COALING COMMISSION AND THE STATE OF WEST VIRGINIA. ENVIRONMENTAL HAZARD. VIOLATORS WILL BE PROSECUTED UNDER U.S.C. V-177.

"Mom!"

"Okay, okay baby." She turns to me. "Let me get Hollis out of here and he can potty in the woods." This is wrong. Where could they be? "Reese?"

"Yeah. Uh, fine. Just be careful." I try to sound reassuring. Calm. In control. "I'll stay with the car. Make sure you can see me and I can see you." Emma pulls our son out of the car and walks him to the tree line. He bounces into the foliage and drops his trousers. I shut the car off and stand looking at the road block. I turn looking back down the way we came, and back to the road block again. I shake my head and decide I need to relieve myself as well. "I have no idea where they've gone. We could double back, keep going, or sit right here. I really don't like the idea of sitting still on this …" Emma is standing perfectly still in the woods. She's clutching Hollis at her legs and both of them are unmoving and looking at something in the distance.

I step closer, scanning the forest in front of us. "Babe, what - " with the smallest gesture of her hand she signals me to be silent. She remains frozen staring into the woods. An enormous creature suddenly breaks from the camouflage of the forest and sprints toward us. I bolt to Emma and Hollis. She spins, grabs Hollis, trying to carry him and run. I can see the shape of a man racing toward us, legs as tall as me, running over brush and fallen trees, only seconds away from my family. Emma sees me running to her then she screams.

"Run!" She points over my head. "Reese!"

I spin in time to see a second monster. The ground shakes and I tumble forward into the cold dirt. Rolling to my back, I see the second figure hulking over me—skin like dark granite. It growls and turns away, moving towards my car. I get to my feet as Emma grabs me. Without a word we run down the hill away from both monsters. I take Hollis from her, throwing him over my shoulder. I dodge dead limbs and vines with each step. My knees are burning. I see our car propelled into a pair of trees in front of us. A concussive crunch is heard as the frame bends, wrapping around its target. We run and run. A third monster flanks us from the left. It's just as big but faster. Oh god, it moves like an ape—arms and legs—it's almost on top of us.

"Whooa," a voice calls out. The monsters halt. I collapse against the burning sensation in my legs. Hollis tumbles with me.

"Whoa," The voice calls again. Yards up the hill at the road stands Astrid and Dag and their old truck. "Calm yourselves, boys. They're with us."

The monsters turn and look at us. I grip Emma's waist and find Hollis' arm, pulling them both behind me. Their heavy breathing is palpable.

"Welcome our guests," Dag says.

Emma mumbles something, trying to process out loud. If these are trolls, they're a helluva lot bigger than the two that roughed us up at the diner. The dark granite-shaped one looks at me, then back at my car in a broken heap, leaking fluids. He steps toward us and takes a deep breath.

"I am so sorry," he says. "And… welcome to Jotnar Valley."

Chapter 12

Emma Little

It turns out that the death squad of giant monsters that attacked us is just Jotnar Valley's version of security patrol. Astrid and Dag lead me, Hollis, and Reese back up the hill to their truck. We have to leave our car—broken in twisted heap—and we climb into their truck to ride into Jotnar Valley.

"You're kidding me," Reese says. None of us are in the mood for kidding.

"I don't kid," Astrid replies. "Your family can pile in the cab with Dag. I don't mind riding in the bed of the truck." She apologized for the car and told us the three trolls that came after us are part of a group that walk the perimeter of the valley during night hours. And, she coordinates the men and women who watch during daylight hours. Evidently, she's quite the kick-ass tracker and hunter and she takes guarding this valley very seriously. I guess it kind of explains the rifles in the back of their truck. "Again, I'm really sorry about your car."

"I want. My car. Back." Reese coldly waits for her reply.

"Uh, well…" She leans in and whispers. "We'll see what we can do about that."

"Where are we going anyway?" My voice is still shaking. "And where did you two go? We lost you on the road."

"Right there." Astrid points to the rusty sign we'd seen earlier hanging on the gate blocking the road. We follow her to the gate. She turns and faces the tree line facing the drop-off to the valley below. A small path is revealed, hidden by the brush, and cut all the way down the mountain. "That's where we are going," she says.

"You're kidding me," I say.

"Again, no." Dag says. "We don't kid." Dag fires up the engine on the Ford.

"You mean to tell me," Reese says with a finger pointed down the near dead-drop of a mud trail, "you want us all to pile into your little farm truck and take a ride screaming down this mountain?" Astrid smiles at me and glances back at Dag.

"No one's ever put it that way before." She climbs into the bed of the truck. "I promise you," she announces, "everything is going to be okay."

"But that's just it," I say. "When someone needs to say that, it's very clearly NOT going to be okay."

"Trust me," she says. "And besides, you're the ones that wanted to find Jotnar Valley."

We climb into the truck. The bench seat only has safety belts for two. Reese is silent and I can see the vein pulsing across his temple. Did he take his medicine yet today? I stretch a seat belt over myself and Hollis. Dag shares his seatbelt with Reese. The truck rumbles to the edge of the road. We can't even see the path under the front of the truck. Dag lines it up with the gap in the tree line. I start to ask how many times he done this—then I change my mind.

"Wait," Astrid calls out. "Let me get situated back here." She's lying across whatever they're hauling under the blue tarp. She twists and shifts her weight.

"What? I can't hear you, sis," Dag shifts the truck in gear and pulls his foot from the break. We roll forward.

"Wait, you mad man…" Astrid doesn't get to finish the rest. From a slow roll, the view before us opens up to the expansive beauty of ashen blue hills, the morning fog burning off, and orange sunlight waving against a cloudless sky. The sight is appreciated for only a moment when the truck tips forward. Our heads sling back and we rocket down the mountain.

I throw my arm across Hollis. Reverberations through the floorboard hammer against us sending shocks through my legs and spine. All the fear explodes out of me and I scream the whole way down. I turn my head to see Dag stiff-arming the steering wheel, fighting to keep us on the trail. Hollis grips me tighter and—I hear him laughing. His laughter is actually infectious. My fear turns to thrill and Hollis and I are laughing together.

We tear through low tree limbs and send mud and debris spitting into the air behind us. I imagine the truck looks like a metal juggernaut, dirt crusted, and tearing open an old scar on this mountain. Through blurred and bouncing vision I can see the bottom of the trail visible where it levels out at the creek bottom.

I see a swift current. If we don't crash, we can still look forward to being carried off in frigid waters. I throw both hands forward bracing against the dashboard. Reese tries to throw an arm over both of us. Hollis shouts, "Look. Water!" The truck jolts. The shocks bottom out and we hit the water, rocking us forward. The truck's momentum carries us through the rushing stream spraying a deluge of water up from each side of the truck.

On the inside, I am ecstatic and more than a little relieved that we made it to the bottom and we're not dead. I reach for Reese' hand. I can see his pulse pounding in his temple, his jaw clinched—he tries to smile back at me.

"Daddy, we did it!"

"I know, buddy, I know." Reese takes deep breaths and shuts his eyes.

"Reese are you…"

"I'm okay. I'm okay." Reese gives a reassuring pat on the head to Hollis.

"Astrid," Dag calls back to his sister. "You doin' a'right?"

We turn and see Astrid flipped over on her back stretched across the bed of the truck soaked and dripping from the run through the creek.

"Yah, I'm fine. Don't worry about me." She says wiping a wet sleeve over her brow. The truck rumbles over the bank and Dag steers us deeper into the forest rising up from the creek bed. I feel the trees closing in around us like a silent crowd of onlookers. "Cigarettes are dry." Astrid announces. I turn to see a lit cigarette hanging from her lips while she carefully examines the rest of the pack.

"Glad to hear it." Dag calls back. Then he lowers his voice, leans towards us and says, "I've been trying to get her to quit the damn things for years. Terrible shit, smoking is." Just as quickly as he says it he realizes, "Um, I mean… sorry about that little guy," he says to Hollis and looks back at me and Reese apologetically. I give a half-hearted smile to Dag then lean close to Hollis.

"We don't say words like that, do we Hollis?" Hollis looks

up at me without a clue as to what I am talking about. He leans into Reese and begins pulling at the hairs on his arm.

"Dad, can we go down the hill again?"

The truck bobs easily over the dirt path that transforms form dirt to gravel, and from gravel to stone. A flicker of civilization is close by – a home, a trailer park, someplace where people live who thought enough to cover the dirt road in a modest rock-scattered welcome. The dawn sun light has not yet made it over the mountains and into the deepest part of the valley. I anticipate double-wide trailers with old bearded men sitting on a torn and stained sofa rotting on the front porch; women in prairie dresses chewing on a leaf of tobacco and raking clothes against a washboard.

The forest opened up and the secret was revealed. A winding valley lay in front of us with cut paths and dirt roads leading to warm log cabins with smoking chimneys. Two or three craftsman style houses from the 1920's back up against the hill as if they actually grew out of the mountain itself. We ride through the community and I feel a sense of awe. It was not what I thought it would be. Harvested half acre fields lay next to each home. Clothes lines stretched from each cabin. Small bicycles with baskets attached lay on their sides waiting patiently for little riders. Rocking chairs sit motionless on front porches next to assortments of barrels, benches, and metal work cut into the shapes of oversized butterflies. I'm suddenly aware that I never made use of my own front porch at home. It all looks so much like a Norman Rockwell painting—home spun and poor by modern standards. Poor but happy.

"Welcome to Jotnar Valley," Dag says with a proud smile. The path we'd been following ends here. Dag slows the truck and I hear Astrid scuttle about in the back then she leaps out and onto the cold ground just as we come to a stop. "Let's go meet some fine folks," Dag says.

"And, get food," Hollis says. "I'm hungry."

As we walk, I take in the smells and sights. Lights flicker from the cabins. I see two little girls carry bowls of food outside—table scraps—for several large white Great Pyrenees dogs.

"Look Momma, doggies." Hollis points to the pack that are alert to our presence. The girls see us and run back into the house. "Can I go see 'em, Daddy?"

"Better not," Dag interjects. "They don't do well with new people. We use those dogs to protect the livestock."

From behind the dogs comes a herd of goats. They run toward an old board and batten barn. "Here nannies," a voice calls repeatedly from inside the barn. "Here nannies." The herd of goats rushes the barn door. Each jostling and butting for position, until every last goat is inside. Mountain air mixes with the smell of a farm… and cooking meat. We catch the thick aroma of smoked meat. I pray that Dag has the decency to introduce us to food before any other introductions are made this morning.

The smell of a fire and breakfast grows stronger. A column of smoke rises from a large pit dug in the ground just next to a small stone building. The cured pig carcass swinging from the post next to the stone house is breakfast. A crowd of trolls, men, women, and little boys and girls are gathered. Men in work pants, suspenders, and little else pass around wooden bowls filled with cuts of meat and pitchers of water to the women and children. The clothing is simple—deer skin vests and deer skin pants mixed with flannel and denim. The ratio of beards and bald heads to dreadlocks is fairly even, giving the whole community a hippy-prepper meets lumberjack vibe.

A man and a large troll, both wearing bloodied aprons, work together cooking large cuts of pork. The troll cuts and pulls the meat from the pig with a hatchet. The man carries a hatchet in one hand and a butcher's knife in the other. The crowd finds tree stumps and large stones for seating. A few picnic tables allow groups to eat together. Two trolls, easily over nine feet tall, sit on the cold ground, greedily picking apart ribs – and I don't mean a half rack on a plate. They are ripping apart a fully cooked rib cage.

"Are we okay… here?" I ask Dag and Astrid. "Like, if one of these big guys steps on us… accidentally, I mean… that's manslaughter, right?" Astrid lets out a cackle and somehow that makes me feel better.

"The big guys are nothing to worry about," Dag says, "unless you get between them and breakfast. You do want to watch out for the little ones."

"Little trolls?"

"Dwarves. The Ivaldi. They're ancient with big noses and big ears."

"Like, a really ugly version of the troll dolls you get at toy stores," Astrid whispers.

"Exactly, and you don't want to mess with them," Dag says. "They're tricksters. They steal shoes, jewelry, metal or stone trinkets." Just then a green troll with a wide flat head brings something to Astrid. It carries three iron skillets in each hand. The forest green moss covering its body shakes with each lumbering step, like the fur coat of a giant bear.

"Here you go! Take some," Astrid says. She shoves an iron skillet toward us that holds hot corn bread. Chunks of corn bread have already been cut from the skillet. We don't hesitate. Each of us takes some and our stomachs are grateful. And, for a moment, we forget all about the strangeness of what surrounds us. Dag brings drinks to us in clay cups and steins. Astrid carries a platter with several racks of ribs. We feast. Our stomachs are full, our hands are messy, and we warm ourselves to the fire.

Shrieks of laughter catch my ear and I turn to see several children in a circle. It takes a second look for me to realize one of the children is not a child at all; it must be one of the dwarves. Its wrinkled impish face hints at the trickery that Dag warned us about. The children clamor and insist he give some performance they've seen before. He rolls his eyes then reaches into his woven satchel and removes a river rock, a smooth blue stone the size of a softball. Between his two hands the rock begins to shimmer and almost vibrate. The children grow quiet, every breath is held, but their eyes are wide in anticipation. In a final concentrated effort, the dwarf closes his eyes and presses the stone between his hands. Impossibly, the rock shrinks, disappearing, until he opens his hand with the flare of a magician, revealing a small orange gem in his palm.

One of the kids in the circle sees Hollis and rushes over to him. Hollis leaps up and joins the group with his new friend.

"Hang on, Buddy." Reese says. "Uh, stay out here where I can see you."

"Let him play," I say before realizing I've said it. "We can watch him from here. Besides, he probably needs something that feels… normal right now." We watch as the dwarf, the Ivaldi, makes the gem disappear from one hand and appear in another. The kids shriek when he makes it reappear under one little boy's hat and then again in another little girl's boot.

Dag takes off saying he'll be right back. I find myself leaning against Reese as we sit. I trace my finger along the muscles at the back of his arm – the ones he knows I like so much. I notice the crowd is dispersing too. They're all moving in different directions. Looks like breakfast is over. I call Hollis away from his new friends and hoist him on my shoulders. The kids give a round of goodbyes and a mix of human folks and trolls are ushering kids away.

Dag jogs back over to us. "Okay," he says. "Let's go talk to Markham." According to Dag, Markham is one of the guys that was cooking the ribs we just devoured. We walk over to the little stone building we'd passed on the way over here. Taking a look around, I notice something. I lean in and whisper to Reese.

"Did you notice…."

"That all the big guys are gone?" He says finishing my sentence.

"Yeah. Where do you think they went so fast?"

"Sun's come up," Dag says. "They avoid direct sunlight. All jotnar have some aversion to it. So, they go home when sunlight creeps into the valley."

"So, trolls sleep during the day." I look at Reese with a smugly raised eyebrow. "Of course. I knew that."

We arrive at the stone smoke-house where the pair of cooks are collecting their knives and hatchets. The pig carcass, now half gone, is held effortlessly by the troll. He raises and secures the carcass to one of the meat hooks from the ceiling of the little house. Two more pigs hang silently inside. I'm remembering a field trip taken in elementary school when my class visited a replica of an old pioneer village. They showed us how life was lived by early settlers: smoke houses, out houses, and one room cabins… oh my. The man and troll work quickly with no need for talking. I admire their efficiency but I also know to stay out of their way. A large empty sack is draped over the troll's shoulder. Together they fill a basin with the knives, tongs and other implements dirtied from the feast. The man removes his apron and tosses it over a wooden table. He wipes his brow with a stout arm and flops a brown wide-brimmed fedora over his head. Without a word, the troll takes the filled basin and empty sack and steps out of the smoke house. As he ducks to miss the top of the old timber door frame, he sees our group and gives a grunt as he passes.

"Markham, you seen Mother Moon?" Dag says to the man still clearing away items in the smoke house.

"Say what?" Markham saunters out of the smoke house wiping his hands on a towel, sleeves rolled to the elbows revealing tattoos on each forearm. His eyes, though slightly hidden under his hat, are obviously fixed on Reese and me.

"We're looking for Mother Moon," Dag says. Yep, I thought I heard that name right. What a moniker.

"Didn't see her at breakfast this morning," Markham answers without ever taking his eyes off of Reese. Now, I am beginning to feel uncomfortable. He's obviously not concerned with offering a warm welcome to the neighborhood. I lower Hollis off of my shoulders just in case this introduction becomes… awkward. Markham shoots a stream of spit from his lips. It hits the ground with a smack. He turns to Dag, nods in our direction and says, "Who the hell is this?"

"Markham, this is Reese Little and his family, Emma and Hollis," Dag says. Reese reaches for a hand-shake but Markham doesn't extend his hand.

"That name sounds familiar." He looks directly at my husband, examining his face.

"Show him the picture," Dag says. Reese pulls the photo from his back pocket and hands it to Markham. It's the group shot of his grandfather in Jotnar Valley. For a moment Markham doesn't say anything, he only stares at the photo. Then he hands it back to Reese. He reaches for his suspenders hanging at his thighs and pulls them back up over his shoulders.

"My grandfather was Karl Little," Reese finally says, breaking the silence.

"Yeah," he says without a smile, "I can see that."

"Mother Moon will want to meet them," Dag says. "Do you know where she might be?"

"Surely don't, Dag. But, I feel like I need to have a talk with her myself."

"What precisely do we need to talk about?" I turn and see a white-haired woman in a shawl and prairie style dress. She's walking toward us with an entourage of women and men. Each one of them is an impressive specimen of a modern-day Viking, like the mountain air has done them good. They look like they walked out of one of those post-apocalyptic TV shows where the clothing looks super utilitarian while at the same time also super trendy. Dag steps forward.

"Mother Moon, this family came into the store just before dawn looking for Jotnar Valley." Dag gestures to us. "They're on the run. Not sure from what. But their house burned down; they've been on the run all night."

Mother Moon looks over each of us with an easy smile. Clearly, this is not the first time she's welcomed strangers looking for refuge. Dag makes the introduction.

"Reese and Emma, I'd like you meet Anika Muninn. Mother Moon."

"Welcome. Whatever is troubling you, you have found safety." The entourage around Mother Moon nods in agreement. "Have you had breakfast?"

"Yes. Thank you."

"A troll hunter followed them into Frost," Dag says. This peaks everyone's interest. The crowd around us shares a few worried glances. "But, we sent him on his way."

"Ah. Well, let's sit down and discuss more at my house. It's just on the hill there." Then she steps towards me. She reaches out with both withered hands and takes me by the shoulders. "I'm sure you'd appreciate a moment's rest." Her pale blue eyes look into mine, reflecting a soul older than her years. I collapse into her for a hug, nearly knocking the woman over. She holds me.

"Yes," I say refusing to let myself cry in front of strangers. "Yes, we really would." Mother Moon gestures to her entourage and says something to them about meeting at lunch. They all go their separate ways. She pulls her shawl snug over her shoulders and begins walking toward the hill.

"Markham, I hope you can join us," she says.

"His grandfather was Karl Little." Markham doesn't move. Mother Moon seems to lose her balance. She turns and the kind warmth has left her face. Her eyes are wide and her mouth opens trying to form a response.

"Is that so?" She looks back at Reese. There's a hint of reluctance in the way she studies his face, like she doesn't want to find what she's looking for. "You have his hair and his eyes." She takes a breath and puts the warm smile back on her face. Her hands tug at her shawl once again. She calls back to Markham. "I hope you'll visit us at my house in one hour."

Markham nods and simply says, "Ma'am." He walks away, his shoulders set forward, and rubbing the back of his neck with a burly hand. As we walk up the hill, Dag looks over to me and gives a quick wink as if to say, *everything is going to be okay, I promise.*

Chapter 13

Reese Little

We make our way up a steep rise to a little hilltop. At the peak sits an enormous Cottonwood tree. Bare branches stretch high in every direction—a few curl back, scratching the sky with enormous skeletal fingers. The sheer size of the tree overwhelms the house sitting under its gray mid-morning shadow. It's a single-story farm house with a wrap-around porch supported with ornate posts. It's much fancier than most houses we've seen in this village already which have been little more than log cabins.

"They're watching us," Emma says.

"Who's watching us?" I look over at Emma. She cautiously points up at the giant tree looming ahead. Crows, by the hundreds, are resting in the tree. I don't know how I hadn't noticed them before. They are totally silent, unmoved by our presence. We climb the front steps, passing a garden of withering bushes next to the stairs. "Mother Moon, what's with the crows? They like it here?" I ask.

"Oh, they're ravens, not crows," she says brushing aside a wisp of white hair. "There's a difference, my dear."

Once inside, Mother Moon asks us to make ourselves

comfortable. She offers to start some tea and coffee. Hollis tugs at Emma's coat.

"Daddy, I need to go potty." In fact, I do too. Mother Moon shows us to the small bathroom at the back of the house. Worn wood floor boards creak and groan under every step. The walls hold row after row of black and white photos in frames; all are from different eras. Some photos show men wearing coats and shirts buttoned to the neck and women wearing dresses and big hats. Clocks decorate the walls as well. Large round face clocks, cuckoo clocks, and grandfather clocks—I count half-a-dozen in the living room alone and four more before we make it to the bathroom. There's a frayed quilt laying over a rocking chair in the corner. Aside from Mother Moon's eccentric decorating tastes, the house is… cozy.

In the bathroom, I help Hollis wash his hands and then send him scampering back to the group in the living room. As I'm washing my own hands, I catch my face in the mirror. The lack of sleep is showing under my eyes. I take a deeper look at my eyes, at the black pupils. For a moment, I wonder if there's someone else there. Mother Moon said I have my grandfather's eyes.

I return to the living room, a small room with a stone fire place set in the wall and a small sofa against the window. A warm bready smell fills the house. Astrid and Dag have set out biscuits from Mother Moon's kitchen.

"Mrs. Little, does your son like sorghum?" Mother Moon asks from behind a cabinet in the kitchen.

"Um, truthfully, I don't think he's ever had it before," Emma says. "But, thank you. Say 'thank you', Hollis."

"Thank you!"

"Not so loud, buddy."

"Thank you!" Hollis replies. Mother Moon chuckles as she rests a bowl of strawberries on the coffee table in front of Hollis.

"Please, have some," she says. "Let me know if the biscuits are too dry. I made them yesterday. I have some jam if anyone would care for it."

I feel like Mother Moon's house smells the way a grandmother's house should smell. Emma talks about holidays growing up around her mom's family. Her grandma always made sure Emma ate two servings of everything—and dessert too. I didn't really get the full experience with grandparents. My dad was estranged from Grandpa Karl until he had to move him to a nursing home. I can remember visiting him when I was six years old and seeing all of the other grandmas and grandpas in that place. Holidays in my mind don't smell like turkey or ham or apple pie. They smell like menthol, cafeteria food, and urine.

Emma and I eat only a little to humor our host. Our breakfast of ribs and cornbread is sticking with us. But, Hollis gobbles strawberries by the fistful. Mother Moon insists on making tea and sets a kettle on the stove.

"I understand that you had an eventful night last night," Mother Moon says taking a seat across from us. "Would you care to tell me about it?" I start to answer but realize that she's not talking to me or Emma. She's talking to Hollis. He pauses mid-bite of strawberry, his fifth or sixth already, and just looks at her for a moment very still.

"There were bad guys," he says.

"Oh, there were bad guys, eh? Tell me about them." I don't like the idea of Hollis recounting last night's events. It is bad enough that he'll likely have nightmares every night for months to come. I pick him up and hold him in my lap.

"The bad guys say, *Arrgh.*" Hollis growls with both hands raised in little claws. "Then Papa says, *Stop*, and the bad guys… the bad guys… they were bad."

"They were bad, huh?" Mother Moon responds. Hollis barely takes a breath between bites of strawberry.

"And we ran away and Daddy drives the car fast!" Hollis flails his arms dramatically telling the story. "So fast! *Var-rooom! Eerrrrgh!*" he says giving the screeching sound of tires on the road. Dag chuckles at Hollis' little show. I guess anything can be cute when a four-year-old says it. Suddenly, the tea kettle whistles. Astrid goes and pulls it off the stove while Mother Moon continues.

"Well, Hollis, thank you for telling me what happened," Mother Moon says in a very grandmotherly tone. "I have another question for you, young man. Do you like to color?" Hollis nods eagerly. Mother Moon taps her chin then finds a few scraps of paper in the top drawer of a buffet. "I'm going to talk to your mom and dad for a bit. Could you draw for me? I'd like it very much if you'd draw a picture of your grandpa. Don't leave out any details."

Hollis sits down at the kitchen table with Astrid. She has a mug of hot tea and a smile on her face. Despite my first impression of her, she appears almost gentle with Hollis. He puts a worn crayon to paper and vigorously begins scribbling.

Mother Moon sits down in the arm chair across from me. She stirs a pewter spoon through her cup of tea. "Mr. Little, you and your wife are looking for answers. You're running." She folds her hands in her lap, leans forward and says, "We are here to help you. And, without any reservation, we will see you through this."

Emma graciously says, "Thank you." But I've got more questions.

"Thank you, Mother Moon… for seeing us through this… and don't get me wrong, you're being gracious… but, what exactly is this? We didn't even know that trolls—is that what they're called?—that they even existed until today and… you're all living in this commune in the mountains. But, I think your pal, Markham, has some serious reservations about us." I can see Dag shifting uncomfortably where he sits but I don't care.

"Yes," she says calmly stirring her tea. "I'm certain he'll come around."

"Yeah, you seem pretty damn calm and confident," I say. Emma places her hand on my arm, warning me to not be a jerk. "I guess what I wanna know is, who are you and what are we doing here?" The pewter spoon slips from Mother Moon's hand. It falls and clatters on the wood floor.

"Oh, my dear." She struggles to bend over and reach for it. I get up and kneel down to collect it for her. Dag leaves the couch to get another spoon from the kitchen. Mother Moon apologizes to me.

"What for?" I say grabbing the spoon.

"Because you're not going to like this," she says just before placing her hand on my forehead.

The room goes dark and I feel the floor fall out from under me. I reach out for balance—the whole room is swimming and black as night. I can see nothing except for Mother Moon. A light radiates from her. Oddly, I don't cry out for help. Objects in the room begin to come into view against dark; they are tossed about and move around us as if blown by a gale force wind that I can't feel. Strawberries fly past, one strikes me in the chest like a dart and is carried away by the same unnatural current. Framed pictures sail past my feet, the same black and white photos I'd see on her wall. For a moment I gather myself and turn, squinting to try and see Emma and Hollis in the dark. I see nothing. No Dag or Astrid, no walls, no floor. No up or down. Only a single point of warm radiance from Mother Moon. She is gripping the arm rests with fingers like talons. The light grows colder; purple... and she disappears. No wait. She's there! A bird, dark and eerie. Then she's gone, and back again—again and again. A crow, with eyes black as ore, stares back at me.

"Not a crow; a raven," I hear a voice say. "There's a difference, my dear." The voice is inside my head, assaulting my ear drums with each word. "Listen well. I am known by several names. The first of these was given to me by a god-king who called me Muninn... *memory*." My stomach turns and I try to steady myself against the nothing that holds me. I reach for the light where Mother Moon once sat hunched forward in her chair. Only a black bird remains—glossy feathers and enormous in size. The voice thunders in my head again. "You demand to know why you are here," she says. "I could well answer this recounting the many millennia journey that started with mankind's creation and enumerate the days that have led to this one. But, I'll not torment you with details. Every life story echoes and ripples into the stories of others. Generation upon generation, your story today turns and flows through the river that has been shaped by those that have come before you. This is the inheritance of all. Your grandfather fled Norway to seek refuge in the Americas. He was running from a bitter and hateful jotunn called Slakter."

I see the image of a grotesque troll. His dark form, the

stuff of children's nightmares, is cracked like knotted bark. He rushes toward me with frightening speed that contradicts his twisted frame. I want to run but can't. Far away in the dark, I hear another voice—Hollis' voice: *It was a tree, Daddy. It was a tree.*

The dark gives way to a consuming orange flame. I find myself in my own home. It burns around me. Curtains dance against the window as fire lifts and consumes them. A figure rushes into the house shouting. It's me. I see the panic on my own face. I watch myself try to wave off the canopy of smoke in the room.

I taste it all over again. I feel it in my chest, choking my lungs. I drop to my knees gasping for air. Just as my body is about to collapse, a monster tears into the room hurling dry wall and lumber over me. It's Slakter. I watch myself stand and react: hands clinched and muscles tense. The house continues to burn but, for a moment, neither of us moves. Then, the giant monster lunges at me. I dodge and strike. It's too fast for me to see detail—only two frenzied blurs attacking each other. Slakter slams my body into the brick chimney with enough force to break multiple bones. Fractured brick sprays in fragments. With a quick maneuver, I clear his grip and drop to the floor under him. Landing with uncanny balance, I look up to see the enemy towering above me.

My eyes—the whites of my eyes are completely red. Not blood-shot—blood-filled. I leap, fists clinched, but the monster is faster. He brings both fists over my head. I collapse. White grit pours from the buckling ceiling.

The monster tumbles and falls into the outer wall decimating a portion of it. Fissures begin to crack in the blackening dry wall. He pivots hard on his twisted frame and races away from the fire. His frantic escape demolishes the kitchen wall. I'm immobile. The ceiling comes down around me. The roof collapses.

Surrounded in darkness again. This time, it is quiet. The smell of smoke and dry wall dust is gone, replaced with a wet earthy smell. My eyes adjust and the inky darkness seems to move, to twitch and flitter. A thousand ravens stand on the hill leading up to Mother Moon's house under a moonless night.

I feel coolness on my skin and frosty air against my throat, filling my lungs. I hear gentle steps behind me. I spin and raise the ax over my head. It's Mother Moon. Her hair is loose and moves with the night air. Her eyes are younger and her face is bolder.

"Where did you get that?" She nods to the long-handle axe raised above me. I don't have an answer. But, here it is… clutched in my hands and raised for attack.

"It doesn't belong to me," I say, shivering as I lower it.

"None the less," she says with a knowing twinkle in her eye "it's in your hands. Isn't it?"

The darkness covers her face. Surrounded in black again. I feel the weight of my own body and the cold wood floor under my back. A voice is calling my name. I blink and see Emma and Dag hovering over me. They pull me up and ask me if I am okay. For a moment, I am dizzy and think I might be sick. Dag brings me water and I drink it quickly. Why, am I so thirsty? I see the frightened look in Emma's face.

"Babe, are you okay?"

I turn to see Mother Moon still in her chair being attended to by Astrid. She's offering her a glass of water as well.

"What was that? What did you show me?" I ask.

"It's what you showed me... your own memories, my dear."

"My memories? What was that thing in my house; that giant monster?"

"That was Slakter. A jotunn from Norway."

"A jotunn?"

"A troll," Dag answers.

"Slakter is the reason your Grandfather fled Norway in the 1920s," Mother Moon says. "He came to America and started a new life in this valley." Dag, looks me over. Once he's confident that I'm fine, he turns to help Astrid aid Mother Moon. She is still catching her breath and struggling to sit up on her own. Emma wraps her arms around me.

"Where did you go, Reese? It was like you blacked out but your eyes were wide open."

"Daddy," Hollis calls out from the kitchen table. He stands on the chair, a crayon in each hand, with worry on his face. "Daddy, are you okay?"

"I'm fine, buddy." I'm not fine. I have to regain control. I kiss Emma's forehead. "I'm okay, Babe." I stand, cautiously finding my balance, and walk over to Mother Moon. Astrid and Dag both turn from her and see me towering over her frail body slumped in that chair. "So you're telling me," I say through my teeth, "that… Slakter chased my grandfather out of Norway years ago and now he is coming after me?"

"That's right," a husky voice answers from the front door. Markham stands in the doorway, casting a shadow on the room. His heavy steps cause the floor to give and groan under his soiled leather boots. "Slakter came after your grandpa. Now, he's coming after you. So you better have a plan for dealing with this monster. Or get the hell outta here." He pulls the burned-down nub of a cigar from his mouth and tosses it out the door behind him. "Cause I don't want your grandpa's mess in my home. You understand?"

Chapter 14

Reese Little

Just like that, it's a shouting match. Dag is nose to nose with Markham telling him he has no right. Markham hands back a verbal lashing to Dag and Astrid for being irresponsible enough to bring strangers into the valley. I'm yelling at Markham while trying to restrain Emma at the same time. She's gone into full momma bear mode and the deluge of verbal threats is starting to get scary. For several moments a cacophony of anger fills this small house. Then, Emma breaks through the noise.

"Wait. Where's Hollis?" He's not sitting at the kitchen table. I call out for him. Emma calls out for him. There's no answer. Emma searches the kitchen, opening the cupboards. "He may have gotten scared," she says. Astrid takes the hallway and I go to the back of the kitchen and turn the corner. There's a back door. And, it's open.

I fling the door open and take the steps down to Mother Moon's patio looking out onto the cold hillside. "*Hollis.*" The enormous cotton wood tree looms silently; weighty branches reach over the house. I keep walking, picking up my pace and scanning the hill. "*Hollis.*" I see him. He's running and about to make it down the hill past line-of-sight. "Hollis!" He keeps running, his steps are frantic. I run after him. "Hollis. Come Back." I can hear Emma behind me.

"Baby, come back!"

I run and run, feeling the biting wind on my face. Hollis stops when I catch up to him. He turns to evade me, eyes panicked, looking for a way to go but not sure where to go. "Hey, buddy. What are you doing?" He's out of breath. I kneel down and scoop up Hollis.

"No, no." He wrestles away from me. "I wanna go home," he says. "I wanna go home."

"Buddy, I do too. But, we can't go home. Not yet." The reality of those words become heavier as I say them. Hollis is still frantic. His eyes dart back and forth, looking for something. Then, I hear Markham's boots approaching behind me.

"I want Papa. Daddy, I want Papa." Hollis repeats it over and over. My breath catches in my throat. A pain rises up in my chest.

"I… I do too, Buddy." Hollis lets me hold him but he's not calming down. His breathing his shallow and rapid. His eyes are restless.

"I want Papa. I want Papa. Can we go home?" I don't know what to do. Markham kneels down with us. I notice that his hat is gone—lost in the sprint. He tries to smile at Hollis.

"Hey little man," he says. "I'm gonna to teach you a little rhyme. You like nursery rhymes?" Hollis doesn't answer but he is listening. "This is something that always helped me clear my mind and calm down. Repeat after me: One is for Grimnir and his missing eye."

Hollis tries. "One is for…"

"You got it. Grimnir and his missing eye."

"Grimmr ah missing eye."

Markham continues, "Two are the ravens watching o'er those gone by." Wait. I recognize this. It's deep in the back of my mind. Something I haven't heard in years.

"Two are ravens… those by," Hollis says. His breathing has slowed. And, his eyes are focused on Markham.

"Three," he says, "Is for jotnar of…"

"Mountain, fire, and frost," I say letting the words fall as they come back to memory. Then, together, we finish it.

Four is the berserker furious in blood, bone, life, and loss.

Markham stares at me as if he sees something familiar—someone he knew. All three of us are quiet for a moment. The wind picks up across the hillside. It howls through the naked trees, trying to mark the significance of something remembered.

By the time we return to the house, Mother Moon has regained her strength. Dag starts a fire to warm the room. Everyone ambles about the house uncomfortably except Emma. She holds Hollis in her lap, humming a lullaby in his ear. The atmosphere is tense, but at least we're not screaming at each other. Markham paces and the house creaks with his every step. He clearly doesn't want to stay but, for all his blustering, he follows Mother Moon's lead.

"Mother Moon, what did you show me?" My body tenses at the thought of this little old woman in my head. Or was I in her head? "I could see my house burning. What was that?"

"That was your own memory, Dear." Mother Moon proceeds to tell me that I ran into the house and fought this monster—Slakter. I haven't been in a fight since… since I put that kid in the hospital years ago.

"I fought him? He's at least 8 feet tall. How could I do that?"

"Another good question. I believe Markham can answer that one for you."

Markham rubs a hand across the back of his neck again. "Kid," he says, "you're a berserker…just like your grandfather." I hear the words but I don't understand what any of it means. Emma looks at me as if I've been given a terminal diagnosis.

"What?" I sit next to Emma and Hollis. "What does that mean?" Markham looks at Mother Moon and shrugs, throwing his arms wide. At well over six feet tall, his presence dominates the room. He huffs, not sure where to start.

"Look, uh, I don't know what your Dad told you. I mean he grew up here but… I don't know what you don't know. Maybe I should back up."

"Tell them about when Norway outlawed berserkers," Dag says. Then Astrid chimes in.

"Explain the changelings."

"Alright Twiddle-dee and Twiddle-dum," Markham says raising a hand to Astrid and Dag. "Thanks, but I've got this." He walks over the fireplace and leans in to toss a log into the flames. The log crackles. "The nine realms are all tied together. Gods, mankind, trolls… everything is linked in the universe. And, jotnar and humans …are not that different from each other. The myths would say otherwise but… you ever wondered how a Grizzly bear and a Koala bear could be so different but the same? A couple thousand years ago, trolls and humans left each other alone. Live and let live. But kings began to unite tribes against the trolls… began to push them further out of their territory. Men made up stories about them and they became the boogey man that steals children outta their beds. Once men began hunting them, trolls hid in the mountains. After a few generations, trolls were only a myth." Markham drops another log in the fire.

"That's why," Mother Moon says, "little communities like this have been hidden all over the world. We offer sanctuary for trolls and humans alike."

"But, what does that have to do with my grandfather? What does that have to do with me?"

"Reese, you're a berserker," Markham says. "Berserkers were a warrior class of trolls. And, damn dangerous, true enough."

"Yeah. Completely, bad-ass," Dag says with a grin. The whole room gives Dag a look letting him know that additional commentary is not needed.

"I don't understand." I measure each word carefully as I say it. "I'm. Not. A troll."

"Your grandfather was a berserker. And you are too." Markham rakes a hand through his graying beard. "Berserkers ain't that far off from trolls, to be honest. It skipped a generation with your daddy but... it's still in your blood." He pulls a wooden stool up and sits in front of me. We are almost knee to knee and I can smell the dirt and sweat on this West Virginia mountain man. "You ever get sneezing fits when you first walk out in the sunlight? You ever get so angry or scared that you lose control?" Just then, I recall my dad at the diner asking me if I remembered Billy Dalton. I'd forgotten until he said his name. When I was 12 years old, I put that kid in the hospital for four weeks. The details are still fuzzy in my head, like part of me doesn't want to remember it. "Your heart quickens. Veins raise all across your body," Markham says tracing his hand over his forearm. "The whites of your eyes turn blood red. And you've got the strength of a bear."

I remember being 12 years old and standing in the parking

lot behind the library at Riverside Elementary. I remember staring down Billy Dalton. He was a bully who'd failed a year of school and, consequently, stood 6 inches taller than any other kid in class. I remember what Billy said about my mom. She'd only passed away 3 months earlier. Then, he shoved me against the brick wall. That was the first time I ever felt the warm nervous feeling. I balled up my fists. He flinched and then—only blurry images and lingering smells remain—like the metallic smell of blood when it hits the air and the sight of my size 9 sneaker raised just over Billy's face as he was losing consciousness. I shake my head trying to clear away the fresh nightmare.

"Don't tell me his skin turns green too," Emma says with a nervous grin. Hollis looks up at her.

"Momma, Daddy smashes da bad guys?" Neither of us are sure how to answer this. Emma turns to Mother Moon.

"So, you know Slakter. Do you know why he attacked us? What do we do now? I mean how long do we stay here?" Emma's questions come faster and grow more panicked.

"Emma." Mother Moon raises a gentle hand. She smiles that warm smile we've seen several times already. "Frankly, we know very little more than you do."

"But, it sounds like you know quite a bit about my grand-father," I say, "and even a few things about me that I didn't know." I turn to Markham. "So, are you asking us to just wait? Because, I don't even know if my dad is still alive." As I say this, I begin to choke on my words. "The last time I saw him…" The words stop. I try. But, the more I try the more my throat clenches, forcing the words back down. Emma lays a hand on mine and squeezes.

"Reese," Mother Moon says, "I assure you your father is

still alive. If it were otherwise, my ravens would have shown me. However, I can't say that your father is happy at the arrangement of you and your family staying here. I'm sure he had his reasons for keeping our little mountain sanctuary a secret from you for so long."

"It's because of Karl." Markham says crossing his arms across his barrel chest. "He don't want you to turn out to be just like your grandfather."

"What is that supposed to mean?" I stand staring at Markham. He raises his chin.

"Let's you and me step outside." Markham sticks a cigar between his teeth. He bites off the end, rolls it to the side of his mouth then gives me a look of disdain mixed with pity. "You look like you need some air anyway."

We step outside onto the front porch. The cool air cuts through my shirt sending my hands deep into my jacket pockets. I move quickly to get into the sunlight and away from the shade of the porch. As soon as my eyes catch the sunlight, I can't help but sneeze. Markham looks at me and gives a knowing grin, as if to say, *See, I told ya so.* I'm knotted up with confusion and frustration.

Markham fumbles with lighting his cigar against the wind. I watch him light one match and another – never keeping a flame long enough to burn the cigar. He curses under his breath and, when he reaches for a third match from the little box in his shirt pocket, I move in with hands raised to cover against the wind. The light stays, burns, and smoke moves in thin gray streams with the wind.

"Thanks," he grunts at me. I think he means it.

"Third time's the charm," I say.

I hear Hollis shout as he bursts out of the house with

Emma and Dag following behind him. Hollis has a red rubber ball in his hand as he runs. I see him turn and attempt to throw it back to Dag. His little arms don't toss it very far.

"So, you say you wanna know about your grandpa." I see Markham pause and take another puff. He's stalling – choosing his words carefully. It's surprising that he'd mince words now after all the insults and sideways comments he's dished out already. "What did you know of him?" he asks.

"He was always Grandpa Karl to me; crazy Grandpa Karl. He told me stories about his time in the war. My dad hated that. Always worried they were too violent or gory or something. When my family would visit him, he would always find a way to pull me aside and show me some trinket or thing from his time abroad. He'd have some story to go with it too. When I was 11 or 12 he showed me a stone dagger—old but still sharp—with all of these carvings in the handle and blade. Said he stole it off a giant who used it for a tooth pick. Crazy stuff like that." As I say this, it occurs to me that grandpa's crazy stories may have been real—but crazy none the less.

"Yeah, sounds like him," Markham says thumbing the cigar held between his gnarly thick fingers. "Karl would leave the valley for months at a time and go on what he called *hunting trips*. He was a mercenary, Reese. Whatever people would pay, he was ready to play."

This seems to explain why I have stories of him serving in the Norwegian military while there are pictures of him in French Foreign Legion uniform. But it doesn't explain the age of the photo.

"His absence was hard on your dad." Markham says. "He was just a boy. One summer, he came back and the kids always wanted to hear his stories. Well he shows 'em a gold necklace with an ornate medallion on it and right in the center is the most beautiful pearl you've ever seen. The kids all *ooh* and *ahh*. Your dad, he was only about 9 years old at the time, he pops up and asks how he got the necklace. So, Karl turns to your dad and his friends and gives this grand story of a dragon and a princess. He says he fought the dragon and rescued the princess. One kid chimes in asking if the princess gave him the necklace as a reward for rescuing her. And he tells the kids 'You know what? She didn't. So, after I killed the dragon, I killed her too and took the necklace anyways.' Karl laughed but the kids didn't. After a while, your dad didn't want to hear the stories anymore."

"Sounds like he… was a shady character," I say. Markham takes a puff on the cigar and lets the story sink in. I still don't understand why he thinks my dad is worried that I'll be just like Grandpa Karl. "So, what's up with Mother Moon? What is she?"

"That's a loaded question." He takes another puff. "You heard of Odin, right?"

"The Norse god? The Allfather?" Markham gives a dismissive grunt at my response.

"Norse god. Yeah, he wasn't the gentle grandpa that the movies make him out to be. Don't get me started. Anyway, he had two ravens named Huginn and Munnin, thought and memory. They flew across the world and brought him the knowledge of all that was, every battle and birth in the nine realms."

"Mother Moon is Munnin? Memory?"

"Yep. Speaking of," he says, "Mother Moon has a notion to acclimate your family to the community."

"Oh?"

"She's gonna call a gathering tonight after the trolls are just waking up. She'll want everybody to see you and make your introduction. We ain't used to outsiders if you hadn't noticed." Markham stares out toward the valley and squints against the sun. "We'll do our best to figure out a place for you to stay," he tells me. "Mother Moon wants you and your family to have your own place as much as we can provide rather than shackin' you up with another family. She also wants you educated on mountain living." I raise an eye brow wondering what that means.

I turn back to the house and see Emma take Hollis back inside. His little body goes limp in her arms, a classic protest tactic. Before she closes the door, she looks back at me. The wind whips her wavy auburn hair. She tucks it behind her ear and looks at me again, making certain that my eyes meet hers. With that look, I know that she is with me. She is ready to weather whatever comes next. I'm reminded of how much I do not deserve her. Markham sees the exchange but he silently works on his cigar.

"I need to know what to expect," I say. "Days? Weeks? When am I going to hear from my dad? When are we going to be safe again?"

"For right now, you're as safe as you can be. You got plenty of questions but I can't answer 'em all. Take a breath. If Slakter is after you for whatever reason, he don't know you've landed here… not yet. Tonight, you're safe. Tonight, you need to sleep. You'll need your rest for tomorrow." He begins to walk away from the house, back down the hill.

"What happens tomorrow?" I ask.

"Training," he says removing the cigar from between his teeth. "Bright and early."

He descends the hill. I turn back to Mother Moon's house and stiffen my shoulders against the cold wind. I trace the crumbs of information I've gathered during the past hour back through my head as I walk. Desperately, I want to have a plan of action… to find my dad… to get Emma and Hollis back to our... And, then I'm reminded that we don't have a home. Not anymore.

I raise my head and examine the quaint and crumbling house in front of me. Inside are my wife, my son, and a few strangers who seem to care. Then, my eyes are drawn from the house to the large ominous tree standing over it like a guardian with countless arms curling and twisting up toward the pale blue sky. The ravens, still and silent, watch me from their branches. I get a nervous feeling that they are waiting to see what I will do next.

Chapter 15

Emma Little

I am so out of my element. I crack jokes. I keep Reese calm. I keep the family running. But, that was at home. The sun disappears behind the unfamiliar hills. A shiver runs through me. The warming bonfire does little to distract my eyes from that crowd that's forming. Mother Moon raises her cane and pokes at a log in the fire. She stands ready to address the assembly of trolls and humans, young and old, in little family clusters gathering to us. I reach for Reese's hand and, when my fingers glance his, he wraps his hand around mine and looks at me. His bright green eyes give that silent reassurance that I've seen before. I am so out of my element.

"Welcome to you all. You, no doubt, notice that we have visitors to our community," Mother Moon says. The crowd gives a collective murmur. Wooden benches hewn from tree trunks are scattered around the bonfire but they are quickly taken leaving many more to stand and listen when Mother Moon speaks again. "Jotnar Valley has always been a sanctuary… to you and your families. And a sanctuary we will always be. These visitors are strangers in a strange land—but they are not totally unfamiliar to our community. Some of you will remember Karl and Lisbeth Little and their son, Theodore." The collective murmur rises again and Reese looks over to me. I squeeze his hand in return. "Let me introduce you," Mother Moon says to the crowd and gestures to us, "to Karl Little's grandson and family. Reese Little and Emma Little and… little Hollis Little." Everyone laughs at the joke and the tension fades. Just like that, Mother Moon beguiles a crowd with matronly charm. She goes on to explain that we are in need of shelter and hospitality but she says nothing of what happened to our home, nothing about fleeing a burning house, and nothing about this troll, Slakter, with a vendetta. She does, however, mention that Markham would oversee our adjustment to this community. "Do not hesitate to show your hospitality to this new family. And, I am sure that Markham will appreciate your cooperation in any capacity that he might request of you while the Little family is within our protection."

The crowd nods affirmatively. But my spine stiffens. *While the Little family is within our protection.* I look down at Hollis and run my fingers through his brown wavy hair and think to myself, *do we need protection—really?* I make eye contact with a mother holding her own little boy who looks to be only a little younger than Hollis. She wraps him in a stitched shawl that she is wearing; even the clothing appears primal, Viking, native to the fabrics and skins found in this valley. She smiles trying to appear friendly. The crowd disperses when Mother Moon gives the word and everyone happily goes about their way. Trolls and humans pass each other with nods and a few words before moving on to their places—trolls to their nightly work and the people to their homes and beds. As if reading my mind, Mother Moon approaches us.

"Well, my dears, I need to show you to your proper quarters. I'm sure you are all in need of some rest," she says with a smile. "Follow me."

Reese carries Hollis on his shoulders and holds my hand as we walk. I'm thankful that Mother Moon's steps are slow over the terrain. Exhaustion is taking its toll and I can hardly keep up.

I raise my eyes off the ground in front of me when I hear the pace of her shuffle-step come to a halt. A small cabin sits quietly against a patch of woods. The windows are missing drapes allowing a view of the inside lit by candlelight.

"It's not much, my dears. But…"

Without realizing it, I blurt out, "It's perfect." Reese looks at me, wondering what I'm thinking. I wonder myself. Why does this cabin that I've never stepped foot in already feel like… home? He smiles and Mother Moon leads us inside.

"This cabin was empty," Mother Moon says around the place. "Has been for about a year. Astrid and Dag were wonderful sports about cleaning it. They were able to move some furniture from folks that… Well, it's like I said at the gathering—this community is a sanctuary. People come together and share with those that have need."

Hollis dashes across the aged hardwood floor. "Awesome! A fire place! Mom, can we make fire?" I smile at him.

"We'll see, baby."

"Oh, I'm afraid you'll certainly need it tonight," Mother Moon says. "It will be a chilly one for sure."

"This is very gracious," Reese says. "But, I'm afraid we haven't brought a change of clothing or food with us. Hollis still needs diapers."

"Only at night-night," Hollis says defending his four-year-old pride.

"We only have a little money," Reese confesses, "and everything else we had was in the fire." Mother Moon leans on her cane and reaches a hand to Reese's arm.

"I have a feeling," she says with a wink, "that it's all taken care of. A little bird told me so."

As she says that, I notice a strange light moving outside the window. Several small lights—warm and drawing closer to the cabin. We step outside onto the porch and witness a crowd of women and children, both troll and human, carrying candles in the dark and bringing bundles of sheets and baskets with clothing. Others bring food in cans. A female troll with red fabric twisted through her hair carries a small infant troll in one arm and giant sack of corn meal under the other arm. The crowd illuminates the night and we are left wanting for nothing.

Reese takes a rick of wood from the stack outside and starts a fire. Even though there is a separate room and small mattress for Hollis, he climbs into our bed. I am wanting Reese, wanting him to hold me and touch me. He traces his fingers through my hair on the pillow; his eyes tell me he's wanting me too. But, after the day we've had, neither of us are letting Hollis out of our sight. All three of us sleep together in one bed on the first night. I call it our "family pile." I feel Reese's arm drape over me and Hollis and my heart swells. When sleep finally comes, it is a deep sleep.

Reese is an early riser. I wake in the dark to find him standing at the window staring into the dark blue sky just before the sun comes over the mountain. He's already dressed in flannel shirt and work pants that fit loose on him.

"I like the lumberjack look," I whisper to him. He turns and looks at me but the humor seems to be lost on him. His eyes, even in the dim pre-dawn light, they look older. Breakfast is a can of beans on the pipe stove and handfuls of granola from a box. Hollis doesn't hide his disappointment. "We can get Toastie Cereal later, baby. But, for today, this is breakfast."

"I wanna go home," Hollis mutters.

"Well, we can't so be quiet," Reese mutters. It stings Hollis. He looks to me.

"Daddy's upset, baby. We're all having a hard time. Just eat for now. We'll get Toastie's later. Okay?"

Reese walks out to the front porch. I leave Hollis to his granola and join Reese. We stare at each other a moment, our breath making little clouds in the cool morning air.

"Take it easy on him," I say.

"I know, I know. I can't… I'm alright."

"You're not alright. You're anything but alright," I say holding his hand. "You're pretty composed for a man who's lost his house and doesn't know what happened to his father. But you are not alright. Give yourself permission to not be alright." He nods and squeezes my hand.

"I also don't have my pills. I'm pretty sure they were in the fire. So…" He won't look at me.

"So can we get more out here?"

"I don't know."

"If you can't, what does that mean for your…"

"I don't know." Reese looks up. Markham is making his way toward our cabin. He's carrying an extra coat in hand. "Looks like training is about to start," Reese says.

"Training?"

"I think they want us ready to help out." he says. "And, to defend ourselves, if needed." My mind goes back to what Mother Moon said last night about protection. "I'm going to ask Markham if this place has a phone." I realize I haven't seen any phones, cell phones, computers, or any 21st century technology in the valley. "I need to let work know I won't be in on Monday."

"You probably won't be back… indefinitely." Reese wrinkles his brow as if I am overstating the issue. "Babe," I say, "we don't know *when* things are going to be safe." He shakes his head, trying to convince me this will be over in a day or two. *You'll see, Emma. Everything's under control.*

Markham approaches and tosses the coat to Reese.

"Wasn't sure if you had a heavy coat," Markham says. "We're gonna be out in the elements all day, you and me." Then he turns to me. "Bring the whole family to Mother Moon's when you're ready and we'll get started."

We make the trek up the hill. The ravens are waiting for us in the colossal tree that over shadows her farm house. She has coffee brewing when we arrive and Markham is at the stove making a breakfast of eggs and bacon. Markham offers and we can't say no to the smell of bacon.

Our assignments are given to us. Markham will introduce Reese to the saw mill and work with Astrid and Dag for the day. Hollis and I will follow Mother Moon and learn more about the community. Before we part ways, I find Reese in the hall looking at the framed pictures on the wall. I join him. The number of pictures on her walls is too numerous to count and stretch on both sides of the hall and into each room of the house, and endless collection of memories.

"This one," Reese says pointing to a black and white photo of a family in front of a two-story home. "This one is my grandpa. He looks so… young."

The man in the photo has dark hair and an easy smile but there is something off about him. He holds a woman close to him, his arm tight around her waist, and they both stare at the camera. A little boy only a year or two older than Hollis is at sitting at their feet with a rifle laying across his lap and a proud look on his face. It is unmistakably Ted's face.

"Ah, yes. Your grandparents," Mother Moons says. For a moment, I think she is going to tell us a story about them but changes her mind. She only smiles.

Reese looks up from the photo and says, "Dad used to tell me everything he knew about wilderness, camping, and survival; that he learned it all from Boy Scouts. That's not true is it? He grew up here. He learned it here." Markham steps forward puts his coat on.

"Reese," he says, "I taught your dad everything he knew." Reese looks like he's been slapped.

"How old did you say you are?" he asks Markham.

"I didn't say." Markham nods to the door and he and my husband leave for the saw mill. I look back at the photograph of young Grandpa Little. I realize what is off about him in that photo. His eyes. He smiles but his eyes… are angry.

Mother Moon leads me and Hollis down the hill, past several pens for livestock, toward a section of dense forest. While we walk, I ask a few questions.

"So, you're Muninn; like, the two ravens—Huginn and Muninn, right?"

"Yes." She answers without pause, not bothered with any need to convince me of her answer.

"And, what about the other raven?"

"What do you mean?"

"Well, where is she? Or he… or it?"

"I don't know. It's been several centuries since I've spoken to… any of them."

"Them?"

"The old gang, I suppose. We served the All Father… Wotan, Odin… the countless names he went by, and then everything changed."

"How? How did everything change?"

"The world just moved on… as it is want to do. Like any kingdom, our time came and went."

We come to a cavernous opening in the side of the hill. Tucked into that opening is a rusted train car, like one of those boxy metal ones that carries coal, rocks, or sand. It sits on the ground—no tracks under its wheels. The giant door on the side is wide open, inviting us in. I start to ask Mother Moon how it got all the way into this valley but then I remember that, yesterday, I saw a troll lift and throw my sedan like it was a card table. A small ramp at the far side allows us to climb up and we enter through the oversized sliding door. My eyes adjust to the dark and look around the vacant expanse inside.

"Would you mind, dear?" Mother Moon raises her cane, pointing to thick twisted rope hanging just inside the door. I reach up and pull it. Just then, the car lurches under me and we slowly descend through the earth. Hollis moves close and clings to my leg as the box car lowers us deeper into the dark. And then, a warm incandescent light greets us. Rows of Edison bulbs illuminate the shaft with yellow light. The car moves down the shaft like an elevator and the dark opens to reveal an enormous cavern hidden from the surface.

"We lovingly call this The Mine." Mother Moon gives a wink. "Very original, I know." From my vantage point in the elevator, it seems to go on forever. Trolls easily lumber about the Mine passing through hollowed-out rooms and halls. The natural formations along the wall and hanging from the cave ceiling create Gothic chandeliers colored by the sepia mix of the Edison bulbs and cast-iron candle sets. There's an effervescent white noise of a waterfall. I see it emptying into a large pool that opens to a river leading deeper into the caverns.

"Mom, is this the troll house?"

"Yes, baby," I say breathless. "This is… a very big… troll house."

As we move closer to the bottom level, I notice bright orange glow from one side of the cavern. They're the dwarves that Astrid described, small with big ears and eyes, and hair that would make Einstein reach for a comb. A group of ten or twelve of them work at chipping a cross section of stone from the cave wall. Some sit in harnesses high up cutting away with pick and hammer. Others are at the base, tugging ropes and pulleys. And, all at once the wall begins to give way. With coordinated precision, they lower a slice of cave rock the size of a small house.

"The Sons of Ivaldi," Moon says. "Or we just call them the Ivaldi around here. Their ancestors forged fantastic ships, weapons… the spear of Odin. They'll smash and fold that stone into axe heads that never need to be sharpened, chains that are unbreakable. But, these days, they mostly keep our farm equipment in working order." I hear a sigh of resignation in Mother Moon's voice. She smiles at me. "Times have changed."

The box car stops our descent with a jolt. The three of us step off. I look back at the Ivaldi. A large form emerges from the corner, one of the Ivaldi rides in a walking mechanical suit - arms and legs made of polished stone and gears—like clockwork. It's elegant. Four more emerge from the shadows riding their own mechanical contraptions. Without a word spoken between them, they lift the stone slab into place, laying it flat. A cacophony of hammering erupts as the company of Ivaldi descend on it.

"There is someone we should meet." Mother Moon leads us down the cave path. I follow, glancing back at the Ivaldi. We pass smaller rooms where a family of trolls are settling in. They have a small child—who is taller than me—with broad hands and feet. He has the same clumsy energy of a child. I recognize the same bed-time routine—the same insistent parents ushering the child to bed—the same little feet dragging reluctantly. The child sees us.

"Mom, mom, mom, mom, mom…" the child troll says repeatedly while pointing at us. Mother swats at his hand and directs the child to bed with no more nonsense. Daddy troll steps forward and greets us kindly. The mother looks back at us before disappearing into her room. She has a tight frown that she's trying to hide. I know that look. Distrust.

"Come on in," the daddy trolls says in his voice that sounds like James Earl Jones swallowed a family of croaking bull frogs.

"You're too kind," Mother Moon says. "I'm just letting Emma see how we live. Forgive me. Arni, I'd like you to meet

Emma Little. Emma, this is Arni. He grew up here in Jotnar Valley. His wife actually came to us from the mountains of Norway years ago and they started a family."

The fatherly pride shows easily on his leathery face. His smile is calming in spite of the overwhelming number of teeth in his head. I hear Hollis gasp as Arni's third arm gestures to the room. He, again, insists we come in. His wife joins us and offers deer jerky and mead to drink. Mother Moon quickly says yes and gives me a look that says, *Don't say no when a troll offers you food.* We sit and Mother Moon lets me ask question after question.

"How does this community, this whole valley, how does it remain a secret?" I ask. "The world doesn't know about this place."

"And, we like to keep it that way," Arni says. "It's all thanks to Mother Moon here."

"I have a knack for holding memories," she says.

"Any intruder happens to come across Jotnar Valley forgets all about us once they get out of line-of-sight," Arni says. Out of sight, out of mind. I can't decide if I'm impressed with Mother Moon's ability or exceedingly frightened. Arni is all too happy to answer my questions. His grin widens at each answer he gives and he responds with the zeal of a master story-teller. "I was part of the original team of four," he says with a proud gleam in his eye, "that fashioned the turbines that pull electricity from that water-fall at the Eastern wall of this cave. Before that turbine, we lived by torch-light down here." He stands as he tells this part. "After four months of sweat and engineering, it all came down to one troll standing at the precipice of the falls, in the dark, giving a mighty push on that turbine to get it all started. It took the sheer strength of all three of my arms to do it. A lesser troll would still be standing in the water, trying to this day." His wife tosses a dirty rag at his face with a cackle. Arni tosses a half-full mug of mead back at her with a laugh that thunders against the stone walls. I wrap an arm around Hollis in anticipation of the next projectile. Hollis laughs right along with him - and then we see a shadow emerge from the back room. The child is awake. I recognize the same cautious footsteps when Hollis would sneak out of his bedroom.

"Hello, boy," the little troll says from behind the bend in the wall.

"Hello," Hollis says back to him.

"Gerda," Arni gestures to his wife and she shoos the boy back to where he came from.

"Mamma," the little troll calls out in protest. "Is that crazy Karl's family?" The mother shouts and smacks the back of his head as he retreats. She turns and gives a look to her husband. The awkwardness is palpable when Arni finally breaks and tosses all three hands in the air.

"Well, it was no secret that Karl wasn't right. He never fit in..."

Arni's wife bursts back into the room shouting something in another language and waving a finger in his face. They both bellow back and forth. Hollis has his hands over his ears. The noise becomes unbearable until Mother Moon quietly stands up. Silence follows.

"You've answered her questions honestly," she says to Arni. "I hope you will continue to do so." Arni tucks his chin and begins to pace slowly. His wife looks directly at me with painful distrust. Then she turns and goes to her child's room. Arni is slow to answer my question this time.

"Arni," I ask. "Why did grandpa... Karl... Why did Karl not fit in around here?" He clicks his teeth together—his crowded rows of teeth, like a zipper.

"Karl was trying to make a new man of himself when he came here back in 1920. Always seemed like he wasn't quite right... but then no berserker really is. You know what I mean?" He laughs at this but quickly becomes quiet again when he realizes that, no, I do not know what he means. "Berserker's aren't the family types. He tried. He fell in love and started a family. But, like I said, some aren't the family types." Arni doesn't offer much more and I don't press him. I get up from the table a little too eager to leave.

"Thank you for inviting us into your home." I say. "Say thank you for the jerky, Hollis."

"Thank you," he says filling his mouth one more time. I signal to Mother Moon that the conversation is over and I'd like to leave.

We get up and Arni waves as we go. Mother Moon shows us more of the cave and Hollis even gets to stand in the mist of the waterfall before we go back to the elevator and return to the surface.

"I'm sorry if you felt uncomfortable back there," she says.

"I did." I watch Hollis run between trees hiding and jumping out to surprise us over and over again. "Like you said; we're strangers in a strange land. And, everyone seems to know more about us than we do." Mother Moon doesn't try to explain or offer kind words. She just reaches for my hand and holds it while we watch Hollis play. I don't have to tell her that I'm thinking about Arni's comment that berserkers aren't the family types.

The daylight fades early inside Jotnar Valley. The hills on

either side block the sky, bringing dusk around four in the afternoon. As if announcing the sunset, a deep rumble sounds from the hill behind us. Several trolls come bounding out of the train car, leaping over trees and rocks. Most carry axes as tall as a man. One holds a giant chain saw, a crudely made device, dripping oil and roaring like a motorcycle.

"Time to go to work," a troll with flat face and bulging arms calls out to the group of at least a dozen and leads them down the hill toward the saw mill.

"They work at night?" I ask Mother Moon.

"Most trolls," she says, "have a weakness to sunlight. Some berserkers simply experience a sneezing fit – like a mild allergy. The very worst would be the fabled mountain trolls —the Fjell Trollet. Supposedly, they turn to solid stone in the sunlight.

"Supposedly? You don't know?"

"The mountain trolls are very much hermits. Not much is known about them because they rarely move and almost never speak."

"What do you mean *rarely move?*"

"Well, they are confused for mountains, my dear. There are Scandinavian legends about mountains moving during the night and resettling at dawn, changing the landscape. But, those legends are almost as old as I am."

I begin to realize that the more answers Mother Moon gives, the more questions I have. I scoop up Hollis and say good bye to Mother Moon. I raise Hollis on my shoulders and we walk back home. I realize I'm already calling our little cabin our home.

"Momma, I'm tall like a troll."

"You sure are, Baby."

"What's wrong with that house, Momma?" Hollis is pointing into an overgrown patch of woods. For a moment I think Hollis is talking about one of the cabins lining the far hill but then I see it. A board-and-batten farm house is hiding in the woods in front of us.

"I don't know. How did you even see that?" I ask genuinely curious.

We move closer and I see the black cavity through the roof. One wall is torn open from the roof to the foundation. A fire destroyed the house and the forest vines have begun to swallow it up.

"Can we look inside, Momma?"

"No, Baby. Stay close to me." But, I can't resist my own curiosity. Some appetite in me wants to explore this haunted anomaly. Then, I see Reese. He's standing inside the house. He doesn't see us. He's holding papers – browning documents and photographs in his hand. Then, I see it all at once. This house, the burned remains of a house, was in the same photo of his grandfather. This was Grandpa Little's house.

Chapter 16

Reese Little

"**D**on't get near that blade unless you wanna lose an arm," Markham shouts as we watch the logs of timber move single file along the belt. The high-pitched buzz of the circular saw cutting through wood is almost deafening despite the ear guards everyone wears. "I ain't gonna send a mangled body back to your wife, so watch where you step."

It's my second day at the mill. Today he has actually allowed me inside the mill, though I use the term *inside* loosely. The structure is nothing more than rough cut log pillars holding rafters and a wood shingle roof over our heads. My back and arms are still sore from yesterday's work. Six hours were spent hoisting cut lumber from this pile to that pile. Every one of the trolls working beside me lifted 10 times as much and they reminded me of that fact, all day long, without fail.

We did take one break in the middle of the day yesterday. Just long enough for Dag to give me a lift into town to use a pay phone. Dag took the Ford and drove us through a deserted mine shaft for 10 minutes before we saw day light on the other side. We burst through a tree line and Dag swerved onto a thin country road. After a few miles, he pulled off at a place I can only describe as a two-story shack painted canary yellow. This was the local garage plus gas station plus diner. *Best skillet cornbread this side of the Mississippi!* The pay phone was actually a lime green touch-tone phone sitting on a desk in the front corner of the garage. Without a word, Dag tossed a quarter to a mechanic with the name Pete stitched on his coveralls. I called the office number and left a message hoping Derek would get it on Monday morning. I told him about the house and then I froze for a moment. I didn't know what else to say. There was so much I didn't know how to explain. So, I just hung up. When we got back to the valley there was plenty more labor to be done.

I'm grateful for the walking tour Markham is giving me this morning, no matter how loud the saw mill may be.

"Astrid is the *Shaver*. She measures every log and finds the right way to cut 'em to get the most out of 'em."

Astrid raises her protective face-shield. "No jokes about being called a *Shaver*."

"No," I say. "Not at all."

From behind the conveyor line, a thin troll with an orange beard, jumps up from his work. "Shaver?" He shouts. "I hardly know her." The other trolls and humans laugh but shut up quickly when Astrid whips around.

Astrid rolls her eyes then turns back to her calculations. Her frame is hidden by a loose fitting overalls and, aside from her hairless arms, you wouldn't know she wasn't one of the men. It dawns on me that she also operates the general store in Frost with her brother—and she coordinates the folks watching the perimeter. I guess there's no time for idleness when you live on the edges of society.

"Watch where yar goin'." Two trolls brush past me. I'm

nearly knocked into the conveyor line. The one with cobalt blue horns curving back from his forehead turns and stares me down as he walks away. "Dunga. Stay outta mah way," he growls back.

"Did he just call me *dunga*?" I ask Markham.

"Don't worry about it. Just keep moving." Markham waves me on and we cross through a large open barn door that separates the line of logs on the belt being cut from what looks like an open-air storage area under an expansive roof. Dag stands at the far end giving instructions to two more men and a troll with an excessive under-bite. New axe handles are hanging from the edges of the roof. Two dozen or more handles made of hickory or ash sway in unison as a chilling breeze cuts through me and I stuff my hands into my pockets.

Markham says something. With the ear guards on, I can't hear him. I quickly pull them off. "So, aside from lumber we also make axe handles," he says without shouting.

"Hand-made axe handles," Dag interjects.

"Excuse me." Markham says. "Yes, hand-made axe handles. Dag is very proud of that fact." Dag motions to me.

"Come on over here."

Dag reaches into the wood pile where several logs have been quartered and pulls out a short piece that has the shape of an axe handle traced on the wood. He hands me the quartered piece of wood, shoving it into my chest.

"We're gonna teach you something about whittling, my friend," he says grinning.

"Whittling?"

Markham, Dag, and the others answer back in chorus, "Whittling."

For the next two hours, the muscles in my arms and hands

are punished as Dag and his crew stand over me and I'm taught how to fashion an axe handle with hand tools alone. At first, Dag gives me simple instructions for scoring and hewing the wood. Every so often I hear one of the guys say something like…

"That's terrible."

"Odin's beard, are ya making an axe handle or a bowling pin?"

A raspy voice comes from an old man sitting in the circle across from me. "One things for sure, you make a pretty piece of firewood." The group laughs. I cut my eyes to the old man. He's a black man which stands out among the valley's nearly homogenous tally of white faces. But, I notice he only has one good eye—the other is blind, colored a milky gray. One side of his brown face is lined with scars; the cut across his brow and ear, reaching into the hairline of his short white coils.

"You want to say something, boy?" His accent is pure West Virginia but there's no friendly mountain charm or home-grown hospitality in it. He sets his wood and knife down, props an elbow the knee of his deer-skin pants and leans toward me. I realize he's not used his right hand at all—his axe handle is propped between his thighs. I see the same scarring that's on the right side of his face also on his arm, just under his sleeve. "You want to challenge me? I won't refuse a challenge that's for sure," he says. I weigh my next move carefully. Any challenge would be suicide at this point. I don't press it. But, I can't cower silently. I decide to simply keep my eyes on him and I give a quick smirk before I go back to whittling. "Oh, you giving us a smile, now?" He takes up his knife again, leans his right shoulder into the handle for leverage, and begins to work again. "Whaddya think, boys.

Think he knows sumthin we don't?" The group murmurs in shared amusement.

I look back and see Markham comfortably rocked back on two legs of a wood chair supervising us. He pulls an apple from his coat pocket and takes a bite. I don't say a word. They want me to complain. My hands ache but I cut away at the wood piece by piece. A bead of sweat falls from my nose. Another rolls into my eyes. But, I keep working. I'm in control.

For lunch, Markham leads me back to Mother Moon's house for a spread of biscuits, hard-boiled eggs, and sweet tea.

"Those damn midgets swiped my hat. I just know they did." He rakes his fingers through his matted hair and mutters. Evidently, he can't find his fedora.

"The Ivaldi? I thought they were dwarves," I say. Markham points a thick finger at me.

"They're thieves is what they are." Markham and I sit down to eat just as Emma and Hollis come through the front door.

"Daddy!" Hollis and Emma join us. Hollis runs through the front door and crashes into me with arms open. "Daddy, I got to play Smell the Blood!"

"What?" I ask looking up at Emma.

"Yeah," she says with resigned amusement, "turns out that Smell the Blood is the troll version of Hide and Seek." Mother Moon hands her a warm mug of coffee.

"HA!" Markham bellows, "Never thought about how terrible that name sounds. I been watching kids play that for years 'round here. *Fee Fi Fo Fum, I Smell the Blood of an English Man*'—or some say '*Christian Man*'—it goes either way." Markham smiles to himself before going back to eating his biscuits. His smile is genuine, but with considerable effort, as if he'd almost forgotten how.

"As I remember it," Mother Moon says as she lays a plate of eggs and biscuits in front of Emma and Hollis. "Your father was quite good at Smell the... I mean, Hide and Seek."

"Two full days and nights he hid," Markham adds with pride.

"What?" Emma blurts out choking down a sip of coffee. "What happened? When did they find him?"

"Oh, he was fine, darlin'. You gotta consider, hiding out in the elements ain't no game for trolls. It's survival. And, we start teaching 'em early 'round here," Markham says with a raised chin. "Remember, I taught Teddy everything he knows."

I decide to take the opportunity for a not-so-subtle segue. "Speaking of..."

Markham's eyes deflect back to his lunch, "Muninn, can I help you clean up here?" Mother Moon gives a hard look from across the table.

"When have you ever volunteered to clean up around my house, Markham?"

"I found my dad's house," I say before the subject can be changed. "Or, I guess it would have been my grandfather's house. The one down the hill that's rotting in the woods. Looks like it caught fire."

"Mmm hmm." Markham finishes a biscuit hurriedly.

"What happened there? What happened to my dad and his parents?" Before Markham can answer, Hollis speaks up.

"That house is sad. It looks sad." Markham stops and looks at Hollis. Hollis tilts his head and without taking his eyes away from Markham asks, "What happened to you?" When Markham doesn't answer, Hollis moves to the living room and starts practicing a game of hide and seek by himself. "Fee, fi, fo, fumm."

Markham abruptly moves from the table and drops his plate into the sink with a clatter. He moves to the door and says, "Reese, get back to the wood mill as soon as you can." He throws on his thick barn coat and turns up the collar. "Dag's got plans for you both after dinner. You two meet me in the clearing when the sun starts to go down. Hollis will stay with Mother Moon for the evening." He pulls the front door open and a chilling wind enters the house as he leaves.

"Is it me," Emma says watching Markham trudge down the hill, "or did our four-year-old just get under his skin?"

"I think so."

I put my arm around her. I look in her honey-hazel eyes. Just behind her I notice a sheet of paper stuck to the ice box. Mother Moon has Hollis' drawing displayed in her kitchen. "Well, look at that." Emma and I move closer and look over the figures drawn in crayon. My dad is the central figure with the stick figures of me, Emma, and Hollis at his side.

"He's even added the facial hair on your dad," Emma says. His drawing makes us smile. But, I notice something else.

"Did he draw my eyes like that?" Big angry eyebrows hover just above the two little dots for my eyes.

"Um, yep." Emma gives me a pat on the arm. "It's okay, Babe."

"I think I have some photos you'd like to see, Reese." Mother Moon gestures to the hallway as she gets up from the table.

Emma looks back at me. "So, more training, huh?" she says with a weary smile. Hollis climbs into her lap and wraps his arms around her neck.

"I don't know if I can take any more today," I say. "I'm sweating through this thermal shirt. Markham's got Dag teaching me to make axe handles."

"Oh?"

"By hand."

"Oh."

"I mean, each handle takes a full day to carve out then several weeks to dry… or cure… or whatever they call it. Then you gotta set the axe head. It's ridiculous."

"Your arms," Emma says with a coy grin. "They do look a bit swollen," she whispers as she traces a finger across my bicep. I lean into her with a kiss. She leans into me in return and I feel an ache for her.

"Hey, don't squash me," Hollis whines trying to balance on Emma's lap between the two of us.

"Let me see what Mother Moon is wanting to show me," I say to Emma. I stride into the hallway and see the small matriarch holding two small photos in frames. The two bare spots on the wall are easily noticeable in the collage of pictures covering both sides of the hallway from top to bottom.

When I approach her she doesn't raise her eyes from the photos but says very quietly, "Reese, I see the love you two have for each other. You and Emma. It's good. It's strong. You will need that. Protect it and nourish it."

"Um, yes ma'am."

"Now," she says with a deep breath. "You can see several of us in this photo shortly after Jotnar Valley was formed." The black and white photo shows several men and women and three trolls standing in front of the saw mill. Two of the men hold a crosscut saw between them. The trolls each carry an over-sized axe. One of the trolls has three arms—all three raised holding one axe over his head in a defiant gesture. "You can see Markham here," she says pointing at a young slender man who looks to be in his early 20's; younger than I am now. "And, your grandfather here." My grandfather is holding one end of the cross-cut saw with one hand and his other arm is over Markham's shoulder. They are both smiling; laughing.

"His eyes look happy in this picture," I say.

"Hmm?"

"The other picture," I say pointing to the second framed photo in her hands. It's the picture I spotted days ago with Grandpa, Grandma and Dad as a boy. "My Grandpa, Karl. He's smiling in this picture. But his eyes look hurt; angry."

I look back at the photo of the group at the saw mill. In the lower corner a date is written—*March 1928*. On the family photo with my dad, I find a date written in the same handwriting in the same corner. It says, *October 1966*.

"My Grandfather, he looks like he hardly aged 10 years between these two photos."

"Berserkers have the longevity of jotnar," Mother Moon says. "Some trolls live natural lives of 200 years. Others, like the Norwegian mountain trolls are still considered children at that age. Berserkers typically live 130 to 150 years today."

"Today?" I ask. "As opposed to what?"

"Berserkers," she says resting a hand on my arm, "are built for battle. Historically, wars and conquests didn't allow berserkers to live long enough to grow old peacefully." I stare back at Mother Moon as this sinks in. "Contrary to what you may see on the news, the world today is actually much more peaceful than it has been for a *long* time." Hers eyes hold mine for a moment and, in those wrinkled ice-blue eyes, I can tell that she speaks from experience.

I return to the mill, push up my sleeves, and punish my hands and arms for several more hours. When I make the trek back to our cabin, I smell food cooking. Emma and Hollis are eating and laughing.

"Look, I made cornbread," she says with a smile. I notice she's pulled her hair into a tight braid one side of her head. It looks very regal and, at the same time, untamed.

We eat. We talk. I hold Hollis and he tells me about his adventures with Emma and Mother Moon. We walk over to Mother Moon's together and he tells me about a little girl he met. Her name is Elise and, according to Hollis, she's the best seeker for playing Smell the Blood. Emma and I give Hollis a hug and tell him we'll be back soon. We tell him to listen to Mother Moon, say *yes ma'am* and *no ma'am*, and that we love him very much.

"I have plans for young Hollis," Mother Moon says smiling down at him. "I'm sure we'll do some coloring together and maybe later we can feed the goats down the hill." Hollis' eyes light up. I hold Emma's hand as we walk down the hill together, against the cold wind.

When Emma and I enter the valley, the sun has already gone behind the hills. Markham is waiting for us along with Dag, five other trolls, and the scarred old man. I recognize the troll with the under bite from Dag's workshop. He repeatedly slides a small flat stone against the blade of his axe that gives a flaming red glow as it reflects the dimming sunlight in the sky. He looks up at us.

"Look thar. They did show up after all," he says with a grin that isn't meant to be friendly. Another troll laughs at his comment. I recognize him too. He's the horned troll that nearly stepped on me at the saw mill this morning.

Dag steps forward and announces several names and points to each of the trolls, "Arni, Rock, Rolf, Bjorn, Eklund, and

Bubba. Remember them. There will be a quiz later." Each of them nod without much ado.

"Let me guess. Bubba?" I say pointing to the old man. He gives a dismissive chirp through his teeth.

"My name's James Eklund." Then he raises an unfinished axe handle and points to the horned troll. "He's Bubba." I do a double take between the old man and the troll. Bubba clearly takes offense to my mistaken assumption.

"Yeah," the troll barks back. "Whassamatter? You never met ah troll named Bubba?"

"No," I say quietly. "I have not."

"Hi, Arni," Emma says waving. The troll with three arms waves back. I recognize him from the group photo in Mother Moon's house.

"Save the small talk," Markham says. "You two have a lot to learn and the sooner we get started the better."

Dag steps forward with an axe in one hand and a revolver in the other. Without speaking, he tosses the axe to me and puts the revolver in Emma's hand. He looks us both over, rakes a hand through his blonde beard and says, "Let's get started."

Chapter 17

Reese Little

"My goal for tonight," Dag announces, "is that no one dies."

"Is that supposed to be funny?" Emma asks.

"Not at all."

"Because it's not funny."

"It's not supposed to be."

Bubba, with the cobalt blue horns, swings his axe overhead stretching his arms. Dozens of torches are staked in the ground outlining our training perimeter. As the sun goes behind the hills, the flicker of torch-light illuminates the faces and frames of these trolls with cruel shadows.

"A rekkr lives an' dies by his weapon, Dunga," he says pointing at me. "But, you ain't rekkr yet."

Rolf buts in, "You ain't no rekkr either, Bubba. Yar a lumberjack. And, not a vary good 'un."

"Shut up. Ah am makin' a point."

"Issa stupid point."

With a yell, Bubba turns on Rolf, swinging his axe overhead, and the two are locked in a fight. Each swing and block with a quickness I had not expected from such large creatures. Emma and I duck and run for safety. I turn back to see both trolls exchanging hits but neither landing a blow. Then I notice Dag, Markham, and the rest haven't moved. They're watching.

It's all a demonstration. And, just as quickly as it started, it's all over. The old man, Eklund, gives a congratulatory whistle.

"Nicely done, boys. You didn't screw it up," he says taking a seat on a cut log. Dag turns to me and Emma.

"Did you see all of that? Because you're going to learn every bit of it," Dag says. "How to use the axe to attack, defend, choke, trip, pull, push, and split your enemy in twain." Emma raises her hand.

"I don't think I'll be splitting anyone in twain," she says with a smile.

"You'll be using a pair of revolvers, Emma," says Dag. "You'll be with me for the afternoon. But pay attention to how these jotnar handle an axe. You may have to use one someday."

Emma exchanges a look with me. *So, this is what training is about.*

"I ain't gonna sugar coat this," Markham says. "You got a nasty troll coming after you. So, you better be prepared to defend yourselves…and that little boy of yours."

"I thought that's why we came here," I say. "For protection."

"You cannot hide in this valley forever." A female troll approaches the group. Her inky black hair is braided against the sides of her head revealing high pointed ears. She carries herself with a dignified presence and an intimidation factor dialed up to 11. "Even a valley that is mystically protected by Munnin is not totally safe from attack. If Slakter wants to find you, he will. You want to protect your family? Then this is where you start – not by hiding, but by taking action."

"Well said," Markham replies. "Reese, this is Tyra. She will oversee your axe training. Markham walks the group to the shooting range. It's a single acre that backs up abruptly to a hill where large troll-sized targets are mixed with smaller human-sized targets cut from scrap metal.

Dag turns and says, "Emma, the gun you have in your hand is called…"

"A Schofield," Emma says cutting off Dag mid-sentence. "It's a six-shot revolver. A little clunky for personal carry these days, but powerful enough."

Silence.

"The hell? She knows her hand guns," Markham bellows and slaps his knee.

"Uh, babe," I say perplexed. I've never seen Emma touch a gun since I've known her; much less has she ever been interested in them. Emma grins.

"Momma's boyfriends were usually military types. They'd go shoot at the range and I went with them. I thought they'd stick with Momma if they liked her kids too."

"Good," Tyra says hoisting her over-sized axe across her shoulder. "You're not totally helpless. You'll train with regular bullets but you should always load with sulfur when carrying your weapon."

"What?" Emma asks. "Load with sulfur?"

"Bullets don't hurt us none," says Rolf. "But sulfur does."

"So, always carry sulfur-lined bullets." Dag extends a hand to Emma with a bullet between his finger and thumb. "You'll see a green hue."

"Now, what about the man," Tyra says nodding to me. Then she turns and Rolf and the other trolls follow her a pace to another part of the clearing.

Tyra stands in the center of the group. The other five trolls, Arni, Bubba, Rolf–the under bite, Rock, and Bjorn create a circle around us. This is the boxing ring, the school yard fight… and possibly the place where I'm going to die with an axe in my hand.

Tyra starts with instruction. Short commands on technique: strike, block, step, strike, step, strike, block—repeat. She is serious in her delivery with no room for humor. She only pauses twice to grab each of my hands and reposition them on the axe. The second time she positions my hands she swats my face with her hand. I rock back but I'm still standing.

"What the hell?"

"Slakter will not care if you fail to remember how to hold your weapon," she says turning her back to me. "And, he will not tap you on the face either."

"Don't hit me again," I say.

"What will you do?" she asks her back still turned to me. She waits for my reply. She ludicrously outmatches me. I remain silent. She starts up the commands again: strike, block, step, strike, step, strike, block—repeat. And, so it goes. Her commands are perforated by the distant report of Emma's revolver and the subsequent echo.

I remove my jacket and I'm sweating through my shirt when Rolf volunteers to step in and spar. He allows me to catch my breath. Then, with a yell he lunges at me bringing his axe down above my head. I block and he holds the axe against mine, pressing down. He is toying with me. Again, I'm outmatched against a creature almost twice my height. He pulls away.

Tyra calls out, "Again."

Rolf swings at me. This time I block and strike without

hesitation. He plays along letting me try out what I've learned so far. We swing back and forth, hickory strikes hickory in a block between both of us. He holds it for a moment, then he shoves me to the ground with force enough to knock the wind out of me. He offers a gnarled hand and pulls me up by the arm almost dislocating my shoulder.

"Whaddya think boys," the old man calls to the group. "Can this city boy be taught?" I hear the one called Bubba mutter something in reply.

"Dunga."

"Hey now, no name calling," the old man says pointing a finger at Bubba. "That's uncivil and churlish."

"Hey, what's that supposed to mean anyway?" I say between staggered breaths.

"It means yar useless, boy." Bubba laughs, proud of his jab.

"Well, aren't you sweet."

"Again," Tyra says.

Training continues this way until the sun goes behind the hills. Each of the trolls takes a turn sparring with me. There are moments when they see that I'm physically beat. They show pity without being too obvious. They pause, let my legs stop shaking, and show me a different technique while I catch my breath: hook the neck, sweep the leg… until Tyra shouts, "Again."

After an hour, Tyra steps into the circle again. "Show me what you've learned, Little man."

She stands ready, axe held in both hands. I wait for the attack. It doesn't come. After a few moments, I make the first move. I duck, roll, and try to use her size against her by getting too close. I swing wild—muscles are spent. She blocks and before I can swing again she punishes me with the butt of her axe handle into my sternum. I collapse on my back breathless.

"Get up," she demands.

I roll to my side desperately trying to inhale. I grip the cold yellow grass at my fingers and try to pull myself up. A kick takes my arm out from under me and I collapse against the cold grass face-first. A blinding pain swells in my arm and chest. The bitter taste of dirt is on my tongue.

"*Never* let go of your weapon, little man."

She presses her foot into my side and rocks me onto my back. I can hear blood throbbing in my head. There's not enough air. A heavy cold stone presses into my neck. Instinctively I reach for it—the axe head pressing into my throat —and feel a hot sting inside my hand against the blade.

"You have failed," she declares as she stands over me. "Do you think Slakter would show you mercy now?" I can still feel the blood throbbing through my head as my vision begins to go black.

"That's enough," I hear Markham call out. Tyra immediately backs off and the weight comes off my throat. I choke and gasp to fill my lungs with air. Markham stares at me; but, it's not with worry or concern. It's disbelief. "Tyra, he took all that punishment and still didn't turn berserker? Damn."

"What's going on?" It's Emma's voice. I can hear her coming closer.

With what strength I have, I raise up on my arms.

"What's going on?" she says demanding an answer this time. She still has the revolver in her hand. Dag is following quickly behind her and I see the other trolls around us shift and turn their attention to her. She doesn't notice the other trolls begin to move in, as if to intervene. But, the old man still sitting on the sidelines raises his good arm, signaling them to hold. And, they do.

Markham chimes in, "It's a part of training, Emma. Reese will be fine."

Emma looks at me. I see her grip the gun in her hand.

"Baby," I say as convincingly as I can, "I'm fine." I look over at Tyra and say, "It's all a part of training." Tyra steps forward and offers me a hand up. Emma makes her way to me and touches my face and grabs my hand.

"Reese, you're bleeding," she whispers. "What was that all about?"

"Your husband," Tyra says returning her axe to a holster behind her back. "I was sure he would turn much quicker during our training."

"Turn?" Emma asks. She helps me up. "You mean berserker?"

"Yes. He has incredible control for being so… untrained."

"Yeah," says Markham wedging a cigar between his teeth. "We're gonna have to do something 'bout that."

"Are you crazy?" Emma whips around and jabs a finger into Markham's chest. "What if Reese turned berserker… or whatever? If it's as bad as you say, he would be out of control."

"But, Markham's in control," I say wiping the blood from the wound on my hand. "Aren't you Markham?" I look up and they're all staring back at me. "Because you're a berserker just like me. And, if I turned, you know you could take me."

Markham grins. "Well, well, well. You're smarter than you look, Reese. I'll give you that."

When we get home, I clean my hand and bandage it with cloth. Hollis is happy to see us. Emma and I try to repeat bedtime stories that we used to read to him at home. After the third request for *Polly Gets a New Puppy*, he finally falls asleep. We curl up together in one bed, our family pile, and we sleep like babies.

I wake to the hint of a pale blue dawn slipping through the curtains. I feel Emma stir. "What are you thinking about?" I ask.

"The training," she whispers.

"I'm sorry about yesterday, babe. I think they want…"

"I don't like the training. But that's not what bothers me," she says moving closer to me under the covers. "It's this feeling; this dread… that we will have to use it. Soon."

Chapter 18

Emma Little

I watch my husband fashion an axe handle. He sits with Dag under a large over-hang canopy connected to the saw mill, several other men, and Rolf. This morning, his face shows the hint of a beard after four days of no shaving. There's something incredibly sexy about watching him work. His sleeves are rolled up, showing the tense muscles in his forearms. The others sit at a distance watching, pointing and, I assume, critiquing his work. He tries to hide his frustration. Even from where I sit next to the bonfire drying clothes from the wash, I can see the strain of his jaw and the twitch in his temple.

From this distance, I only catch the occasional smell of the saw mill on the breeze. Saw dust and sweat mix in the wind for a moment and then it is gone. My morning so far has been spent at the creek that runs through the valley washing laundry in chilly 40-degree weather. A bonfire nearby keeps us warm. The mud and cold earth make me thankful for the thick leather boots given to me. They've even got enough buckles up the calf to be stylish. Several trolls assist with large sacks filled with pants, shirts, and socks. I am ready with the box of soap flakes and a copper cup. From there, the trolls stand in the creek and drag the sack of laundry through the cold water—soap suds foam through the seams of the sack.

"Keep the soap coming," a woman says to me.

"Sorry." I'm distracted. I keep looking over at the saw mill to see what Reese is doing. I toss a scoop of soap into her sack of laundry. She cinches the bag and ties a loop around the opening. A burly troll with wide ears approaches us. His eyes are young and aloof. He's done this chore so many times before, his movements are automatic. He snatches the sack of laundry and swings it over his shoulder and moves on to pick up two more sacks before dunking them into the creek.

"Are you getting used to it?" she asks me. She is pretty with an olive complexion and dark eyes.

"Me? I don't know. There's so much to take in," I say with a laugh.

"Yes, there is. I remember coming here for the first time – it was almost two years ago."

"Oh? What brought you here?"

"Well…" she pauses as if she knows the next thing she says will get a reaction from me.

"That's my son," she says pointing to the wide-eared troll that just took laundry sacks into the creek. I catch my breath.

"Oh," is all I can say.

"Nobody told you about that did they? Trolls and humans are more alike than we look. Turns out you can pass it down while it skips generations – like blue eyes."

"His father wasn't a troll… uh, a jotnar, jotunn…"

She smiles. "No. And nobody cares what you call them around here," she says. "Trolls, jotunn, giants… it's all fine. Really. He was normal for a human child until his tenth birthday. He became very sick with lesions and growths on his skin. Doctors were no help. He missed school and just stayed in bed for about three months. Then, Mother Moon showed up at my door one day, out of the blue, and said she wanted to talk to me about my son. She called it the Changeling syndrome."

I look back at her son, her extremely large son, and I realize I can see the childishness in his face under the wild sandy blonde hair and big ears. I turn back to her.

"And, his dad?" I ask.

"He's not around anymore," she says quickly. "We were never married so…" she stops mid-sentence then finds an empty sack and stuffs a wad of clothes in.

"How do you do it?" I ask. She drops the accommodating smile and her dark eyes become solemn.

"It's hard. It's hard enough to get a boy to eat vegetables and go to sleep on time. Now, I sleep in the middle of the day—when he does—and stay up at night like he does. The other trolls in the community help and, I mean, they help a lot." She pauses and wipes her eyes a moment. "Hey," she says with enthusiasm, "I heard your husband held his own in combat training yesterday!"

"Word's getting around, huh?"

"Yup. But if you ask me," she says leaning in, "I think Tyra takes her job a little too seriously. She needs to pull the stick out of her butt." We both laugh until her son comes back for more sacks of laundry. We realize we have none ready and quickly get back to work.

"I'm sorry, I'm Emma," I say tossing soap into an open bag of laundry.

"I'm Victoria. And this," she says gesturing to her son standing over us, "is Max." Max looks at me and gives the signature awkward wave of a 12-year-old boy, then he's back to work.

I find myself looking back at the saw mill; looking for Reese. I don't know when it happened but something has changed. Reese is standing, stretching his arms. I see Rolf, his large frame is sitting only few feet across from Reese on the dirt floor. He's whittling on his own axe handle. Dag and two other men are doing the same. Reese looks up and sees me. He nods, smiles warmly, and goes back to work. Without a word, Rolf hands him a new quarter piece of wood. I laugh to myself. So, this is it. Reese has been welcomed to the inner circle of wood whittlers.

Later in the evening, Reese and I meet for combat training. I'm being fitted for a gun belt for my Schofield revolvers. Reese, Markham, and the rest of the gang look on while Dag and Tyra cinch the belt, slide the holsters forward, and then slide them back.

"How does it feel?" Dag asks. "It should be low and snug around the hips." I struggle to still against the cool wind – the sun has already set and November is only getting colder.

"I'll tell you one thing, babe," Reese chimes in. "You've never been sexier."

"Enough," I say. "Stop gawking and help tighten this belt - the holsters are still too low."

"How's that?"

"Fine."

"Does it fit? Is it comfortable?"

"I said it's fine."

"Okay, that's enough," Markham adds. "Just let her shoot. Let's see what she's got."

I turn to the shooting range and look down field. Torches

staked in the ground illuminate the iron targets. I slow my breathing. The gang backs away to watch. From behind me, I hear Dag step closer.

"Relax. And, remember what we've taught you," he says.

I steady myself, then, I pull both guns at once. Just like practice, I alternate pulling the hammer, aiming, and fire on the right. Pull, aim, fire on the left. Pull, aim, fire—switching back and forth between my right and left hand. I keep a quick pace and I hear the metallic *ping* every time the bullet hits its target.

Ping

And again. *Ping*

Ping

Ping

I empty both guns and hit every target.

"Nicely done, Emma," Dag congratulates me. I turn and see a big grin on Reese's face.

Markham looks at a stop watch in his hand. "Twelve shots on target in 10 seconds. That's impressive for day two."

"Yar a stone cold killer, Emma," Rolf adds.

"But, can she do it when it counts?" Tyra asks.

"Oh come on, Tyra," objects Arni, "let the girl have a win."

"Well, that's actually the next part of her training," adds Dag.

"What is?" I ask.

"You hit all the targets standing still. Now," he says gesturing down range, "I want you to run down field and hit each target as it comes to you. The targets will be closer as you take aim."

"Uh, I don't think she can run that field in 10 seconds," Reese says.

"Thanks, babe, but I've got this," I say cutting him off.

"I'm just trying to talk sense."

"That's why I'm giving her 20 seconds," Dag says. "Twice the amount of time to run the field and hit all the targets. Simple, right?"

I reload from the stash in Dag's case of ammunition. I drop cartridge by cartridge into the cylinder until the first gun is full then the next. I re-tie the leather strings on my thighs holding the holsters against each leg. When I'm ready, I turn to the range, take a deep breath, and plant my feet.

"Say when," I call out.

There's a moment of quiet and I wait until I hear Dag's voice.

"Now!"

I pull one revolver and run holding it both hands. I move at a quick pace and easily approach first target and fire.

POW—ping

I cross to the next target, a standing profile of a man, and only take three steps before taking aim and I fire.

POW—ping

That sound boosts my confidence and I don't even pause for the next target. I run and shoot the next two without stopping.

POW—ping

POW—

Damn. I miss one of the targets. I stop. Take aim and fire again.

POW—ping

Won't make that mistake again. I move quicker to make up lost seconds. Next target is a larger troll cut-out. An easy hit.

POW—ping. I holster the empty revolver and switch to the other.

POW—ping. Next target.

POW—ping. Next target. I can feel the seconds tick by in my head. I stop here and take aim at the last four targets. All troll cut-outs at least 8 feet tall. I breathe and…

POW—ping.

POW—ping.

POW—ping.

-click-

What? I pull the trigger again.

-click-

I'm staring at the last target, gun raised, and I'm empty. I realize my mistake too late. There are twelve targets. And, I had one bullet for each. No more, no less.

"It's alright, babe," I hear Reese call out. I can also hear Tyra and Markham mutter something to Dag. They don't want me to hear. I holster the gun and walk back to the group. I try to keep my chin up.

"Well, I tried," I say trying to brush it off like no big deal.

"We got one more exercise, darling," Markham says. "And this only requires one bullet."

I try to grin at his little dig. We cross the slight rise separating the shooting range from the rest of the clearing. Markham leads us through the dark to a barn where Albin, the hog farmer, is waiting for us. He's a rotund troll, nearly as wide as he is tall. He simply nods to Markham and asks, "Are we ready?"

"We'll see," says Markham. We walk into the barn and see a huge pig alone in a pin separated from a crowd of smaller pigs in an adjoining pin.

"You aren't going to make me chase a greased pig are you?" I ask with a laugh. Suddenly, both revolvers are snatched from my holsters.

"Hey."

Dag pops one bullet into the cylinder and hands a revolver back to me.

"What's going on?"

"You're gonna put your gun to the back of that pig's head," Markham says matter-of-factly. "And, you will shoot him." The barn is silent except for the shuffle of hooves in the straw. I look back at Albin. His big swollen troll face looks back at me in all seriousness. His eyes do not flinch from mine.

"No, she will not," Reese shouts as he steps in front of Markham.

"What the hell is this?" I ask. I fight back the tremble in my voice. "I'm not shooting a pig."

"Shoot the pig," Markham says to me when Reese takes a breath.

"Is this a joke?"

Everyone is looking at me except Reese. He's shoving a finger in Markham's chest and shouting. I feel like I've stepped into some terrible hazing ceremony and I keep waiting for someone to give me a sign that it's all a terrible gag. *Just messin' with ya, darlin'.* But, it never comes and they are still looking at me. Waiting. I don't know what to do.

"No. Emma," Reese says turning and holding my face with both hands. "You don't have to do this. Let's go home."

"Pullin' that trigger might be the only thing that gets you home safe 'n' sound one day. Might as well practice now. Shoot the pig, Emma."

"You know I can shoot. I don't need to kill a pig," I say unable to hide the shaking in my voice.

"If you ain't gonna shoot a pig," Markham says, "how you gonna be ready to shoot a troll when the time comes? Or a man?"

"Emma, just shoot the animal," Dag says lowering his voice, "and get this over with."

"No."

"Where do you think bacon comes from, darlin'?" Markham says with a chuckle that makes my face hot.

"I know where bacon comes from, and stop calling me *darling*."

Tyra steps forward and puts a large hand on my shoulder. "All of this training is for nothing," she says, "if you hesitate when action is needed. If pulling that trigger might save your son from danger, you would pull the trigger, yes?"

I nod.

"Then," she says stepping away, "pull the trigger."

I look at the pig, minding his own business, laying in the hay. The gun is so heavy in my hand now. Heavier than before. Without a word I get rid of the gun, shoving it into Dag's chest, and I walk out. I can hear Reese yelling at Markham but I don't turn around. I don't want them to see me crying.

Chapter 19

Reese Little

"**I** remember my father teaching me to swing an axe when I was a kid," I say to Dag. He blocks my attack and returns with his own, thrusting the butt of his axe handle to my gut. I barely dodge in time. Today, I am training one-on-one with Dag in the clearing.

"Oh? He teach you to fight too?"

"A bit," I say between staggered breaths.

I swing and Dag moves. I recover and deliver another swing. This time, he blocks it, rocks forward, and sends me tumbling backwards.

I let the momentum take me, somersault back, and hop up in ready position—never letting go of my weapon—as I've been trained.

"Good recovery," he says. "But you're a terrible fighter. You must have forgotten everything your dad taught you," he says with a smile.

I pause then launch into a barrage of swings. He backs up. I duck and roll and get in close range to hook the leg with the beard of my axe and I send him tumbling back into the dirt. I quickly rebound and bring the axe over-head to deliver a killing blow to his chest. I stop the axe only inches above his body.

"Alright," he says breathlessly. "You remembered a *few things* he taught you."

I offer a hand and help him up. He dusts the dead grass and dirt from his pants.

"So, your dad taught you how to handle an axe, how to evade capture, how to build an over-night shelter in the wild, how to find drinkable water in the wild, and how to push all of your anger and frustration into a tiny dark pit in your stomach." He gives a wink with that last one.

"He taught me to be in control of myself," I say.

"Right. Tiny dark pit," Dag says. "Hey, you haven't heard from him yet, have you?"

I shake my head. "Mother Moon has ravens watching him. So she says. If something comes up, she'll tell me."

Dag walks over to a small flat-bed trailer that is attached to his truck parked just off the path that leads to the clearing.

"Let's take a break," he says gesturing to the trailer.

Taking a break means chopping fire wood. The trailer is full of short logs that need to be split and quartered. We each set a log on top of a large stump, take one or two swings at it, and toss the resulting firewood into the bed of his truck. Two days ago, I dreaded this part: the repetition, the aching muscles. Not anymore. Now, I look forward to the concentration, the controlled swing, the focus…

"Sorry about yesterday, man." Dag's words catch me mid-swing.

"Uh, yeah," I say. "It was, uh, not what we expected, you know?"

"Unfortunately, that's the point. Markham thought it might get you to turn as well."

"I know."

"Have you never… you know… turned berserker before?"

"I don't think so," I say taking a swing at a log in front of me. It splits in two in one swing. It occurs to me that I could not have done that a week ago. "My dad told me I put a kid in the hospital once—when I was a boy myself—but I don't remember it much. I think I tried to forget it."

"No kidding?" he asks with a smirk. He stops a moment and props his axe under him like a cane. "I just want you to know that we do what we do to prepare you, both of you. Astrid and I have seen some crazy stuff, over here and in Sweden. What we have here… it's a safe haven like no other. But, we have to be ready to defend it, all of us have to be ready. If the world discovers us…" He trails off, picks up his axe, and goes back to chopping wood.

"So," I say holstering my axe through the leather loop at my hip. "You think you'll stay here, in Jotnar Valley, forever?"

He smiles. "I know what you're thinking. Can't be much to life when you're living in a shack in the woods, working a saw mill every day and making axe handles by hand." He tosses the bits of the last log into the bed of his truck. "Reese, Jotnar Valley isn't much but it's my home. And, if you're real honest, you'd see it could be a home for you and Emma too."

"Oh, I don't think so. I mean, everyone has been very generous and we appreciate the hospitality and all…"

"When's the last time you thought about that job at the office, Reese? You haven't even called them back since we drove into town days ago." He's right. For a moment, I'm caught thinking about all the stuff, the garbage, Emma and I left behind. It feels like ages ago but it's been just over a week. "Did you almost forget you had a job in the *real world*,

Reese?" He puts a hand on my shoulder and dips his head getting eye-to-eye with me. "Face the reality that your life didn't get weird when your house burned down. Your life got weird the moment you were born. You're a berserker. And you belong here."

The evening falls cooler than it has been in several nights. The air mixes an aroma of snow yet-to-fall and oil from the torches illuminating the training field. I stand in the middle of the combat circle—the name Dag calls it—with my axe in hand. He consorts with Markham, Eklund, and Tyra. I wait, breathing in the cold, while they decide what tonight's training holds. Emma decided not to take part in tonight's training for obvious reasons.

All at once, the three of them turn and walk into the ring. They've got another trick up their sleeve. Over the past nine days, I've shown a natural aptitude for combat and wilderness survival. But, they enjoy their little tricks, like their attempts to make me turn berserker or their way of just proving things are not always what they seem. I pull my axe resting in the leather loop attached to my belt. I let the axe fall loose in my grip, running my hand over the slight curve in hickory handle. Markham gives me a grin.

"You will fight one challenger in armed combat," Tyra announces with the refined airs of a drill sergeant. "You will prove your skills with an axe." Markham steps forward swinging his axe over one shoulder, then switches to the other shoulder.

"Since you haven't gone berserker yet, we ain't gonna have you fight none of our trolls one-on-one." Markham looks over to Rolf and Bubba, watching from the sidelines. "Not yet, anyway."

"Dunga ain't ready for us yet." Bubba bellows and jabs Rolf with his elbow. His grating laugh echoes off the hills around us.

So, this is the play. Markham will fight me one-on-one in the hopes of turning me. And, if I don't turn berserker—if I can't turn berserker—will he? Tyra meets me in the middle of the combat circle and announces the dictates of the challenge.

"The combatants will fight until one yields or until I rule the combat to be concluded. The combatant will take measures to preserve life and limb. Quarter may be asked and quarter will be given."

I wait for Markham to join us in the circle. He smiles the smile of a man that doesn't have any reservation about the fight to come, partly because he knows something that I don't, and partly because he doesn't care who the winner is—he just wants to fight. In another time, he would have made one hell of a Viking.

"Let the challenger enter the circle." Tyra pauses and waits. Markham doesn't move. When too many seconds have passed in silence, I glance around the group. That's when I hear a shuffling step behind me. I turn and see Eklund approaching us. He moves with measured deliberation, favoring his right leg and resting his right arm across his belly.

"Told you I wouldn't back down from a challenge." Eklund tilts his good eye to me in a wink, his brown leathery skin folding in tight lines stretching across his temple. I look back at Tyra. I turn and find Markham. No one is laughing.

"What? Um, Eklund? Mr. Eklund, sir? Are you challenging me?"

"The challenger has entered the circle," Tyra announces with more volume than necessary. I realize this must be the trick up Markham's sleeve. But, I don't get it. Eklund is not a berserker, he's at least 30 years older than me, and then there is the matter of his bad eye, his bad arm, and I haven't seen him swing an axe once during all the rounds of my training. "Are the combatants ready?" Tyra asks.

"I ain't getting' younger."

"You don't even have a weapon." I say quietly as if his fly was unzipped.

"I am the weapon," he says. "That's what rekkr means."

"Are the combatants ready?" Tyra repeats the question with insistence. I'm through trying to figure this out.

"Ready," I say.

"Begin," Tyra announces the start of the challenge, turns and walks out of the circle. Eklund immediately lunges at me and I hop-step away. I circle him and try to shake off the swell of confusion in my head. He's slow to circle me but he's quick with lunges. I hold off my attack and look him in the eye trying to determine if he's serious. From what I can gather, this only ends one of two ways: I embarrass a handicapped old man or a handicapped old man embarrasses me. Either way, I don't win. I glance over to Markham, hoping for a signal giving some clue as to what this is about. That's when Eklund throws a lightning left jab to my eye. The sting across my skull is white hot and I stumble back. I feel blood trickle down my cheek. The old man is as hard as an iron coffin nail. And, he just cut my eye.

"Odin's beard, Eklund draws first blood." The peanut gallery cheers. I hear Dag yelling for me too.

"Be smart, Reese. Focus."

I drive forward with a swing of my axe and another. Eklund dodges. I chase him, butting my axe head to his chest, but he dodges that. With the reflexes of a cat, he hooks the axe head with his arm and leans into it. I wrestle the axe back from him, losing my balance in the process. I stumble, turn, and deliver another swing. But, he's gone. I spin and see him running from the circle, hindered by his limp. He makes for the tree line and I chase him. Then, I turn and look back at Tyra.

"Am I supposed to chase him? He's fleeing from the contest."

"Eklund has drawn first blood," she says. "If you do not respond in kind, you lose."

I bite my tongue, turn, and march into the tree line with my axe ready. The night has grown darker and we've moved away from the torch light. But, he's not stealthy. I can hear him gasping for breath. I hear his trudging foot-steps just paces ahead of me. I race to find him. The dense trees open up to reveal another clearing but it's a narrow valley as if a creek once flowed here. A mud path traces the lowest point enclosed on either side by steep bank.

"Hoo-whee! You still lookin' for me?" His silhouetted figure sits high up on the bank across the dry creek bed. Somehow the moonlight catches his good eye and sends a glimmer back at me, mocking me. "Hoo–whee!" I step down into the narrow valley. He stands and shuffles down the bank toward me. The ground begins shaking under my feet in an almost silent tremor. "Hoo–whee!"

A herd of swine race into the narrow chasm in a mad rush. More than two dozen hurry through the mud path and directly into me. His repeated shout called the swine to feed. I'm frozen for a moment. Then, I dash, hard, toward the opposite bank—toward Eklund. But, it's too late. And, the smile on his face tells me I've lost. My leg is clipped by a hog. I try to throw my weight away from the rushing bodies. My hands grip the bank. I pull myself up but the dirt gives way. I slip. Then, a hand grabs me by the shirt and I'm pulled back. Eklund wraps his good arm around me and leans back into the bank. I'm breathless and find myself holding onto him for life.

Markham and Tyra run through the tree line, followed by Bubba, Rolf, and, last of all, Dag. They all take in the scene and the outcome of the challenge is obvious. Dag let's out a snarl and can't hide his dejection. A dark iron blade, the head of my own axe, is lowered over me. Eklund holds the cold iron edge of my weapon firmly against my neck. He looks down on me.

"You ain't rekkr *yet*, boy."

Chapter 20

Ted Little

The smell of ash is strong as I approach the remains of Reese and Emma's house. I'm glad I waited for the cover of night before I approached the house and started digging around. Don't want any nosy neighbors phoning the police about a balding middle-aged man carrying a long handle axe and a black duffel bag down the street. Another good reason to leave the truck parked down the road: nobody is suspicious of a vehicle parked in front of a store—as opposed to a house destroyed and abandoned after a fire.

The neighborhood is timeworn. World War II era houses built on lots that preserve the old trees and foliage hint at the natural landscape that was here long ago. Never understood why Reese chose living in the city, all these people living right on top of one another—no privacy at all. I'd much rather have a few acres where I can pick my nose without my neighbor looking through their kitchen window to see it.

I step over the bright yellow police tape and, as I do, I reach for my conceal-and-carry pistol on my belt just to be sure I remembered it. It's there, like always. Pam would not be happy to know I'm sneaking around here after what happened at the diner. But, while she's staying at her sister's in Kentucky, I'm gonna get to the bottom of this.

I drop the duffel bag and my axe into the middle of the burned wreckage. Most of what is left of the house is a soggy black mess. Unzipping the bag, I pull out work gloves and a fold away spade. I find the living room area and the large book shelf is face down. The fire scorched the bookshelf around the edges but the scattered pile of books underneath appear unharmed except for water damage. I hoist away the book shelf and begin picking through the books one at a time.

Reese is on the run for something my father did long ago, I'm sure of it. But, hell if I know what. Dad, told me stories about the mean S.O.B. he used to run with in Norway. Somehow, I think this is some kinda bad blood between them.

Found it! Dad's old journal. He kept a record of his days recovering precious commodities that had been stolen or displaced during wars. What do you do during peace-time when you're a berserker? You recover stolen artifacts, gems, and artwork for a price. I thumb through the hand-bound pages in the leather clad volume. His scribbled hand-writing switches back and forth between Norwegian and English. Water has swollen the inky letters and a few of Dad's notes are hard to read. Page after page is a record of recovered artifacts, when and where they were found and the date they were returned. He gives brief descriptions of the places he traveled – the bars he drank in and the women he met along the way. I stick my nose deep into the pages and find the tobacco smell still remains after all these years.

I flip the pages quickly and find a sketch. Dad drew one of the artifacts. Did he draw it after he recovered it or before, so he'd know what it looked like? It's an oval shape with lettering written across it. I take a closer look and angle the journal toward the amber street light.

"Wait a minute. That's it. That is it!"

The sound of flittering wings startles me. I look up to see a group of black birds perched in the old trees in the neighbor's back yard. Ravens. I hold the leather-bound journal high for them to see and whisper just loud enough to be heard.

"I found it," I say. "You tell 'em I'm coming. I'm on my way."

I toss the book inside the duffel bag, fold up the spade and toss it in the bag as well. When I reach for the axe, I smell it. Jotunn. Then I see it. Movement at the tree line on the back side of the lot. He steps forward and I see the creature I'd only heard about in dad's stories.

"Are you Karl's son?" a voice hisses and crackles like dead tree limbs. His appearance is masked by the dark but I can see the twisted roots that make up the grotesque body.

"Are you Slakter?" I ask subtly pawing at the pistol on my hip under my windbreaker. "You the one that attacked my son and his family?"

"That I did. Terrible about his house. Forferdelig. It seems your offspring is quite unaware of his heritage." The coldness of his voice is coupled with a terse Norwegian accent. Slakter steps forward from the tree line and the dense cover of limbs. The moonlight exposes his giant and sinewy frame. He takes measured steps toward me. "Have you been keeping family secrets?"

I unzip the windbreaker and reach for the cigar from inside my coat pocket. "Get down to business," I say slowly pulling a small pack of matches from my front pocket. I thumb the pack open, tear a match out, fold the pack over, and strike. "What do you want?

"Oh. *Get down to business.* How very *American* of you."

"What did you expect?" I ask. I bring the burning match toward the cigar between my teeth just as the flame extinguishes. "Damn." I rip another match from the match book and take my time before striking.

"I expected to see your boy, Reese, and his kone, his wife, return here," he says. "Instead I find you. But, I cannot say I am disappointed." He grins at that last part. I strike the match, bring it toward my cigar, and watch the flame waver and die.

"Damn." I pull another match.

"I want the book." he says. Now, we're getting somewhere. "The one you put in your bag. Give it to me and I'll leave your family alone."

"You're pretty bold to come out here in the city …twice in one week. How'd you manage that without being seen by the locals? A troll your size doesn't easily blend into a crowd."

He doesn't answer. The three that attacked the diner got in and got out too easily. Pam wounded one of the trolls—sulfur loaded 12-gauge shot to the eye—and I dealt a killing blow to the tattooed man leading 'em. But, instead of putting up a fight, they fled out the door. By the time I followed them outside, they'd vanished. That diner sits on a stretch of highway and is surrounded by acres of flat farmland. And somehow, they vanished.

"You must really want that book." I strike another match and pull the flame to my cigar. "What's in there that's so important?" Still no answer. "Why do I have the sneaking suspicion that you're not gonna leave my family alone if I give you that book?"

Silent still. But his eyes tell me enough. His almost indistinguishable black orbs, they flinch. The eyes tell the truth. I hold the burning match to the cigar and *puff, puff, puff* draw the flame until the end glows red. The smoke turns from gray to dark blue quicker than I expected. I toss the cigar up with a flick of the wrist and send it towards his face and turn on my heels. I hear the *POP* and see the flash reflected in the rain-slick street in front of me. He screams. Chemical explosives, no matter how small, can leave a mark. The sulfur smell hits my nostrils as I grab the axe and duffel bag. I stand and run. Gotta make it to the end of this street—main road, street lights, traffic, people—he won't follow me there. I switch the axe and duffel bag to one hand and pull my pistol. I fire two shots behind me and keep running. I hit him but do little except force him to raise his arms in defense. I race to the street. My chest heaves. I make it past the next house and the next. I can see cars speeding across Gallatin Pike. My heels smack the ground and I beg my middle-aged legs to move faster, just a little faster. Suddenly, a pain strikes my back between the shoulder blades. I tumble to the pavement. Bricks. He tossed bricks from the rubble—several are spread in front of me on the road. I roll and face him closing in. I've lost the gun. I look up to see the ravens unmoved in the trees watching the scene.

"It's the stone he wants." I shout. "Tell 'em to find the stone."

I grab the axe and ready myself. The old training comes back to me. I stand and run to his flank, tuck and roll toward him and bring the axe down on his knee. He roars. For a moment, I see the chemical burn at his chest and neck, white and still bubbling. My breathing steadies. I duck and move staying on the offensive. I swing low but only graze his ankle. I raise it again. A gnarled hand strikes me in the chest and sends me end over end across the wet grass. My hands are empty—no gun, no axe. My chest aches at every breath. Two massive hands grab my shoulders and pull me into the air. I'm face to face with the monster. I see the abyss staring back at me through both inky eyes before my body is slammed to the ground. Again and again. I hear the caw of ravens. Wet earth fills my nostrils. I taste blood. I can't breathe. Can't think.

Reese.

I'm sorry.

Chapter 21

Reese Little

"**W**here's the party, dad?"

"It's up ahead," I tell Hollis. "Just over the hill. Do you see all the lights in the trees?" Emma and I walk toward the crowd and the bonfire. Hollis can't hide his excitement and races ahead of us, then stops to wait for us to catch up. Then races ahead again. The hollow of cotton wood trees is filled with chatter and raucous laughter. Near each tree is a flaming standard, a collection of torches woven together, burning high over a banner waving gently in the night air—the banner of Jotnar Valley. We keep an eye on Hollis as he runs ahead of us only to turn around and ask another question.

"Why are we having a party?"

"Why do you have to ask so many questions, Hollis?" I reach down and lift Hollis onto my shoulders. "It's a party. There doesn't have to be a reason."

The smell of beer and roasted meat fills the air. The noise of the crowd grows as we get closer. I hear a drum somewhere in the revelry. Several of the dwarves, the Sons of Ivaldi, are gathered at the center of the crowd.

"Reese, there's Arni and Gerda," Emma says.

Arni waves at us with one of his three arms. He holds his wife with another arm. The third holds a pewter stein that is bigger than my head. Both Arni and his wife are wearing bright fabrics and stone jewelry laced around their arms and necks.

"Join us," Arni calls out with a smile. He gestures with his stein, sloshing some kind of drink into the air. I wonder how much it takes for a troll to get inebriated. "Reese, Emma, there's food!"

"Shh…" Gerda waves a finger interrupting him.

"Oh. Oh. Reese. Emma. There's food and drink." He gestures again with the stein, splashing more drink onto the dirt.

Suddenly, a large troll runs past us carrying one of the Sons of Ivaldi on his shoulders. Strangely, the dwarf is wearing a brown fedora that looks very familiar. Two more trolls race past us just as quick, both carrying the little guys on their shoulders, shaking the ground as they run. I barely hold my balance and keep Hollis on my shoulders.

"Daddy, it's blind tag! Blind Tag!"

Sure enough, each of the trolls is blind-folded and the Sons of Ivaldi are directing them by pulling on their ears.

"I wanna play," Hollis yells just inches away from my ears.

"I bet you do, buddy." Not a chance.

"Let's find some food first," Emma says just as one of the "blind" trolls collides with a tree and sends himself and his rider tumbling to the ground.

Following the smell of roasted meat, we find three rough wooden tables each the size of a king-size bed. On each table there lay skewers the length of my arm with roasted vegetables and meats. Copper cups and steins of various sizes made of pewter wait to be filled from several oak barrels, laid on their side, stacked three high with spigots pouring dark amber liquid from each.

We eat standing on our feet. The noise and the energy feels like a festival or a county fair but without the blinking lights and carnival games, without the clanging noises fighting for your attention and your money. Here every laugh is warm, every face is warm, every sound is warm—even in November. Emma leans into me and I feel her fingertips working between the buttons of my shirt. Her touch reminds me that it's been too long since I've been alone with my wife.

Frantic steps race toward us. A young troll with a wide grin of small teeth asks if Hollis can come play. Emma recognizes him and, with a nod, she sends the two off to play.

"Stay in the clearing," she calls out.

"Look who the hell I found," a gruff voice says behind me. I turn and see Markham with a turkey leg in his hand and wearing a nice wide-brimmed fedora—this one is gray and void of sweat stains. Tyra is with him and, though she still keeps a soldier's posture, she's also laced red ribbon through her hair. She smiles revealing fangs, I'd never noticed before. Overall, she actually appears—pleasant. Markham tips his hat to Emma.

"I hope we don't have any hard feelings about the pig."

"I'm fine," Emma says directly. She holds eye contact with Markham and does not withdraw.

"We understand the motive," I interject. "We just don't appreciate the method."

"I understand, I surely do," says Markham. "From here on out, I promise no more tricks. No more pigs, no chickens, no goats. No animals of any kind will be harmed in the duration of your training," he says with a laugh. I can't help looking over to Emma. She gives me a knowing nod.

"That's the thing," I say. "We are done with training. I'm mean, we're fine to work in the saw mill or work doing whatever. But, combat training—we're done." I don't leave any room for confusion or compromise. Markham tries not to let it show but I think he's genuinely disappointed.

"Yeah, I understand." Markham's meaty paw rubs the back of his neck. "But, Reese, we gotta find a way to get you to transform. Your dad got you wound so tight that we can't shake you loose. You gotta let that berserker come out to play." I step towards Markham close enough to catch the lingering smell of cigar.

"You should know better. Isn't this *thing* inside of us dangerous?"

"That it is, boy. And, the sooner you let it out, the sooner you can learn to control it." He takes a bite from the turkey leg and wipes his mouth with his hand. "You're most dangerous to yourself and others right now. Right now!" He shakes the turkey leg at me, emphasizing the point. "Because, you don't know when you might turn and you don't know what you'd do if you did. See, I grew up knowing what I was from the time I was a boy. I was raised in a place just like Jotnar Valley. After the First World War, I found this ragtag bunch before they started callin' it Jotnar Valley. Your granddad was here, Reese. And, he taught me a thing or two about what it is to be a berserker."

"From what you've told me," I say, "he wasn't the best role model. But, you won't tell me why he really left here, will you?"

"My point is, I had help." He tosses the spent turkey bone to the ground and faces me directly. "No man goes it alone. Every step of the way, I had people who took care of me and taught me. And, when you're ready, you have people too."

Standing there listening to Markham, I begin to figure it out. He wants to be my mentor. He would never say it. But, I saw it when he calmed Hollis on the first day we came to the valley. I saw it in his eyes when I figured out that he's a berserker on the first day of training. He wants to teach me what he knows. Tyra steps toward us cautiously, clearly having heard the conversation.

"Markham makes a point. And, it is worth hearing," she says. "But, this is a party, yes? We can always talk more of this tomorrow."

A cheer rises from the larger group near the bonfire. Drums pound faster and faster. We look over to the crowd of bodies – large, small, and dwarfish – and see a circle forming with Astrid being pushed toward the center.

"What's going on?" Emma asks.

"War chant," Tyra says with a grin. "Looks like the crowd has chosen Astrid to lead us."

The crowd jostles with drinks and food in hand, rubbing shoulder to shoulder, invigorated by the drumming. Astrid tries to wave off the mob and escape the circle. But, they'll have none of it. Dag is the primary instigator pushing her back into center of attention with a smile. Cheers go up when she relents, nodding her head and smiling. She shouts something, pops a cigarette into her mouth and a woman runs forward with a light. She toys with the crowd for a moment, taking a drag on her cigarette, tosses her blonde hair back, then exhales one, two, three rings of smoke. The noise from the crowd rises as they grow impatient. Astrid waves someone on and a boy, maybe a teenager, brings her a long-handle axe. The drumming stops.

There's a moment of quiet from the crowd. Astrid raises

the axe above her head and shouts a fierce refrain in a foreign language. Part of it sounds like *Skul guy, Skill I Klofnir.* It's a harsh mix of growls and consonants. The crowd joins with her as she repeats it again and again, becoming louder each time.

Tyra leans toward us and recites the chant in English:

> *an axe-age, a sword-age,*
> *shields will be cloven,*
> *a wind-age, a wolf-age,*
> *before the world's ruin*

Cups and steins are lifted in the air next to axes and the rare sword. The crowd is feverish and recites the war chant with a zeal that reminds me who their ancestors were. Troll and Viking alike. My ancestors.

The war chant shifts to cheers and the cheers to dancing as the drums pick up again. Tyra looks at Markham and makes an awkward gesture to me. For a moment, the two of them exchange awkward glances. Then Markham clears his throat and steps towards me.

"Um, Reese, we wanted to give you this." He opens his coat and produces what looks like a leather pouch with long straps coming off of it.

"It's a holster for your axe," Tyra says with a smile.

"Yeah," Markham says. "It was her idea, really. Just something I had laying around. Thought it might be useful."

It's a set of leather suspenders that crisscross at the back and connect to a pouch. A brass snap holds the axe head in upside down and props the handle between my shoulder blades.

"Baby, it looks good on you," Emma says adjusting the length of the straps at the back.

I look at Emma and then back to Tyra and Markham. Tyra is nodding her head.

"Yeah," Markham says, "You earned it."

"Markham, thank you. Um, what I said earlier…"

"Nope." He waves a hand letting me know it's water under the bridge. "Reese, you spoke your mind. I can't fault you for it. 'Sorrow swallows the heart if the mind cannot speak for itself.'"

Something tackles my leg and I look down to see Hollis out of breath and clinging to me.

"Dad, did you see that? It was awesome! It was so loud. What were they saying?"

"Hollis, you don't need to shout at me. Yes, I saw it."

"What is that?" he asks pointing at my back.

"That's Daddy's new axe holder," Emma says. "Isn't it cool?" Hollis looks at me wide-eyed.

"Cool!" Hollis looks back at me and Emma and asks, "You gonna get the bad guys that hurt Papa?" I don't know how to respond. For a moment we only look at each other. Then Emma kneels down and holds Hollis' face close to hers.

"You don't need to worry about Papa," she says. "We're going to take care of you. For always and no matter what. We are going to take care of you, Baby." He nods. Emma hugs him and keeps him in her arms a moment.

The party carries on later into the night. Emma and I keep up with Hollis as he runs from one group of friends to another—singing songs, playing games, and showing no fear. He seems to have no understanding that he is the smallest child in every group—troll or not. I can't help but wonder how long that audaciousness will last.

We find Arni and Gerda again. This time Arni is propped against a cotton wood tree sleeping. His enormous head is resting in the crook of the tree. His son lies against his belly, fast asleep as well. Gerda and another female troll stand nearby in deep conversation.

"Oh don't mind them," Gerda says as she sees us pass by. "One had too much fun. The other had too much mead."

Just then a low horn sounds. It's three rumbling bellows. Everyone turns toward the bonfire, where the sound came from. Several trolls lumber toward the fire in groups.

"Oh, help me," Gerda says. "I've got to wake him. He won't want to miss this."

Emma and I look at each other.

"Miss what?"

"The song of the mountains," Gerda says. "It's an ancient gentle tune," she says slapping Arni's cheek repeatedly.

"Wha... what? Whattisssssit?" Arni mumbles.

"It's time. The song is about to start."

Arni's eyes pop open, then squint as he grips his head. Gerda hoists her sleeping boy into her arms and rests his head on her shoulder. She makes her way to the gathering. Arni is a sight as he attempts to stand, makes it to one knee, then rocks back on his butt before rolling to all fours, bracing against the tree, and finally standing on two feet.

I hold Hollis as Emma and I walk closer to see what is happening. The congregation of trolls large and small is tightly packed around the bonfire. I see a few of the small ones, the Sons of Ivaldi, on top of the shoulders of the largest trolls. There is a quiet settling over them despite the size and number of the group. I look around and see a scattered host of people observing this ritual, just like I am, from the outside. All at once, they begin.

Every troll begins with a single note held out in a hum that resonates from the chest. The note expands into a harmony and the volume climbs and climbs and then…silence. In unison, the males thump their chest with a closed fist. It's a somber beat that demands attention. The thumping continues when a single troll, thin and pale-skinned, hums a melody that climbs from low to high in wavering timbre. The choir of trolls repeats back the melody, splitting into a dissonance. Then the melody evolves and grows, adding a refrain, and I hear the sadness of these creatures. I hear the ages come and go. I hear the necessity of living in the shadows, living in dark forests where men fear to walk.

The trolls bring the song back together in a single melody. They build a refrain of notes that stair-steps down, down, down… and ends without resolving on the last note. There is only silence leaving the song unfinished. I hold my breath not wanting to break the quiet. Only the crackle of the bon-fire is heard.

I hear a sniffle and look to see Emma dabbing her eye. She's not the only one. Several, people and troll alike, are blinking back tears. A few steins are raised and cheers are given. I pull Emma a little closer to me.

Then faint cry is heard. It grows louder.

"Help… help… help."

I turn looking for the voice. The crowd is parting as a young female troll with large yellow eyes and dressed neck to knee in colorful ribbons slowly walks through the swarm that is now beginning to press in around her.

"What is it?" Emma asks me.

Sounds of panic and alarm come from the crowd. Markham dashes into the cluster of bodies, shoving aside any in his way. He reaches up to the troll with both arms and that's when

I see it. Mother Moon is cradled unconscious in the troll's arms. I move toward the group leaving Emma with Hollis. As I run in, Dag catches my eye and he has the same confused look on his face that I do. Markham has set Mother Moon on the cold ground and I see her trembling.

"She's breathing," Markham calls out.

"I found her like this," the young troll says. "She was lying in the dirt outside her house. She wasn't moving."

Her eyes are rolled back in her head and she doesn't answer Markham when he calls her name over and over. Her arms are clinched together at her chest. She's holding something awkward wrapped under her shawl. Markham pulls her hands back and lifts a splinter of wood the size of my arm and another – it's an axe, broken at the shaft. I see the stone head of the axe, the familiar rune etching, and I feel the world collapse under me.

"Reese," Mother Moon says gasping for air. "I'm sorry."

Chapter 22

Emma Little

I've watched Reese mourn for three days. The silence is heartbreaking.

After Mother Moon was found unconscious, the whole community went into a panic. Even when she came out of it the next day, she couldn't walk yet and barely had the energy to explain what happened to her. The implications of what it all meant were only beginning to be understood. Markham hasn't left her house since. But, there's little he could do to help her anyway. There is no hand-book on caring for a… whatever Mother Moon is.

But, in the middle of all of this confusion, the larger community at Jotnar Valley seems to be unaware that my husband lost his father.

The axe was already broken when the ravens delivered it to Mother Moon. She remembers seeing a cloud of them coming over the hills to the south just before dusk. The ravens were not settled in the great tree but were waiting on the ground for her, anxiously gathered around a white sheet lying on the wet ground.

"I knew," she told me from her bed. "Before I saw the axe

wrapped inside the sheet. I could see his face. Ted, no longer a little boy, a man now. I knew something was wrong."

Reese hadn't heard Mother Moon say this. He didn't have to. He knew what that broken axe meant. It was a message. Since that night at the party, he's been avoiding me. He's been avoiding everyone.

He laid the pieces of the axe across the rough wood table in our cabin and left them there, like some crude memorial. Days have gone by and Reese won't speak a word of it and I don't know what to say to our son. Hollis has asked me why the broken axe is on our table. He is curious, wants to touch it, but looks at me with guarded questions he can't articulate. It's a rough tool that men use to do rough work and that fascinates a little boy. But, it lies splintered in the center of our cabin and that turns Hollis' fascination into apprehension.

"Momma, is that Papa's axe?"

"Yes, it is." His eyes move over the broken archaic weapon. His mouth tightens in a frown but he doesn't ask any more questions.

Later that day, I take Hollis to visit Mother Moon just before a light rain begins to fall. Markham greets us at her door and lets us in before we get soaked. Mother Moon kindly dismisses any questions about how she is feeling.

"Pish-posh, my dear. I'm fine," she says. She offers us tea as she slowly walks into the kitchen.

"Sit down and lemme do that," Markham says. He has stayed by her side for the past several days and nights. I think they've begun to wear on each other's nerves. She pulls her shawl around her shoulders and makes her way to the stove. Though she is small in stature, she casts a very proud profile with cane in one hand and kettle in the other.

"I can take care of myself, thank you very much."

"You can also help yourself to that rockin' chair in the corner while I make tea." Markham knows his way around her house. He gets a collection of tea cups and coffee mugs and preps the kettle of hot water. Mother Moon relents in a huff and walks slowly to the rocking chair.

"Well," I say ushering Hollis to her. "Hollis and I wanted to see how you are doing. You gave us a fright at the party." She sees the look on my face and understands that Hollis needs some reassurance that everything is okay.

"Oh, you don't need to worry about me at all," she says taking Hollis' hand in hers. "This old bird has been around for a long time. And, I'll be around for a long time still to come." Then she looks at me and glances back to Markham, fumbling with a tea kettle at the stove. "However," she says in a whisper, "I do worry about Markham. He's keeping himself occupied with the excuse of taking care of me. He does mean well."

"What do you mean that you worry about him?"

"Well, it was several years ago but… he had a hand in raising Ted Little. Almost as much as Ted's own father did." I hadn't even given Markham a thought. Then, Mother Moon frowns and leans in. "Where's Reese?" I feel a weariness come over me. Mother Moon's face tenses when I don't answer. For a moment her hands fidget with the folds of her skirt. "Well, I need to see him as soon as possible," she says with a nervous smile. "Markham, make yourself useful and find that boy." Before Markham can reply, Astrid enters the house letting the screen door slam behind her.

"No need. He's at the saw mill with Dag," she says. She stomps her feet on the welcome mat, letting rain drip from her jacket for a moment before coming into the kitchen. "He's quiet but he's okay."

"What do you mean?" I stand. "I'm taking Hollis over there. We need to see him."

"Not in this rain, you're not," Markham says. Mother Moon agrees.

"He's fine, really," Astrid assures me. "Fine as can be expected, I guess. Is it true? That axe belonged to his father?"

"I'm afraid so," says Mother Moon. "It belonged to his grandfather, Karl, long ago. It was passed on to Ted." Her face becomes sullen at this. "And now, it has made its way to Reese."

Astrid promises me that Dag will look after Reese. She tells me to go home, to sleep, and to take care of Hollis. She walks us back to the cabin and even offers to stay with us. I ask her to stay just until I make a fire for the night.

She entertains Hollis with stories about the countryside in Sweden where she grew up. Stories about icy lakes and fiery dragons. It's hard to separate what might be fact and what might be fiction. I'm grateful to hear him laugh though.

"What's that?" Hollis asks her. I look over and see Hollis pointing to one of the tattoos on her bare arm. It's a rune that looks like an upside-down V.

"That means will or will power."

"Will power," Hollis says. Then he flexes his arms with a big grin.

"Yeah, let me see those muscles," Astrid says. Just as quickly as the first tattoo caught his attention, he is pointing to another one.

"What's that?"

Astrid looks down at the tattoo, another rune, and says, "That means heritage."

"What's that?"

"That one means danger. Or suffering." Hollis' eyes widen at that.

"What's that?" he says this time pointing to a series of numbers at her wrist.

"That," she pauses, "is a birthday." Hollis' curiosity is peaked.

"Your birthday?"

"No, that was my little girls' birthday. She's not here any- more. I wear that tattoo so I can always be reminded of her." Hollis is confused.

"Where is your little girl?" he asks. I try to interject.

"Hollis, that's enough questions, baby."

"It's okay," Astrid says. "I'm not sure where she is, Hollis. But I know I'll see her again. Someday."

Hollis leans toward Astrid. She bends down toward him and he cups his hands to her ears and whispers something. Her eyes soften a moment. Then, Hollis asks for another story about dragons and she obliges.

I light a fire and listen to the crackle of the wood. Hollis climbs into my lap and yawns just as Astrid is finishing her tale. I tuck him into bed and then meet Astrid at the door to say goodnight. She hesitates at the door. Her hand brushes a wisp of blond hair behind her ear.

"When he whispered to me, he said his Papa would take good care of my little girl." She hugs me there in my door- way for several minutes. "Good night," she says and walks out into the night.

Hollis sleeps next to me holding his stuffed Buffalo doll that he loves so much. I trace my fingers through his hair until he closes his eyes. Sleep doesn't come so easily for me. I wait for Reese to come through that door. I wait and watch. The amber light from the fire fades until only quiet dark remains. Exhaustion finally takes me.

I wake at the sound of the door opening and closing. A blue November dawn is coming through the front window. I sit up, blinking, and search for him. But the house is quiet. I get up gently, letting Hollis sleep. I go to the window and see Reese, already in the clearing, walking away from the house. He's moving quickly. Looking back at the bed, I realize Hollis and I never moved through the night. Reese never came home until just now. The rough wood table catches my eye. Ted's axe—the axe that lay untouched on that table for three days—the iron head is missing. I look back at Reese marching in the direction of the saw mill. What is he doing?

I get Hollis dressed for the cold and we hike to Mother Moon's house. Markham answers the door with a look of confusion.

"You're up early," he says.

"I need your help."

He agrees to go with me to find Reese. I need answers and I'm afraid he'll just try to avoid me. I know he's hurting. But, the silent treatment scares me. I leave Hollis with Mother Moon and tell him to be a good boy.

"Where's Daddy?" he asks.

"Well, I'm going to go see Daddy right now."

"Can I go with you?" he asks with desperation.

"Um, no, baby. I promise you'll get to see him real soon, okay?" He reaches into his coat pocket and pulls out Beefy.

"Can you give it to him?" he asks me. "Make him feel better, Momma."

Markham and I march over to the saw mill walking against a cold mist that blows through the valley hinting at the possibility of snow. Astrid and Dag are inside tinkering on gears under the main line. Both pop up when they see me and realize a confrontation is eminent.

"Where is he?" I ask trying to appear calm.

"He's in the back," Dag answers wiping his hands across his pants. "He was here all night until this morning. He left for a bit. I thought he was going home… to you."

"But, then he came right back," Astrid says.

"He took the axe head," I say. "He just walked in, didn't say a word, took it and left."

"Astrid, did he say anything when he came back?" Markham asks.

"Yeah, uh, not much. But, he asked me for an axe handle that was dried and ready to go. I gave him one from the racks."

"He's replacing the shaft," Dag says with a knowing look to Markham. "He's going to rebuild his father's axe."

"Damn right he is," Markham replies. "Someone killed his father. He's getting ready for a reckoning."

Enough. I need to stop talking about my husband. I need to talk *to* my husband. "Move," I say pushing Dag aside as I walk past him. I find Reese at a work bench under the canopy at the back of the saw mill. He is using hand tools to chip away at the old wood still wedged in the eye of the axe.

"Reese. I need you. I need you to talk to me. I need you to come home."

He doesn't reply. His shoulders move with heavy breathing. He lifts a small hammer and with deliberate calm he goes back to his work.

I can't stand anymore of his silence.

"*Reese.*"

He stops.

"Look at me. Look at your wife."

He quietly sets the hammer on the table, hand quivering. He turns his body, keeping his head lowered. Dark blue veins are raised on his chest under his shirt, across his neck, and onto his jaw. He looks sick.

"Babe, talk to me," I say stepping toward him. Markham grabs my arm, keeping me from him.

"I'll be damned," he says quietly. "He's turned."

"My God," Dag says.

Reese raises his head and I see his eyes - red, full of blood. His breathing is rapid but deep. More veins are visible, throbbing, on his arms.

"Reese," Markham says. "You still there? Talk to me?" Astrid and Dag have taken a step back. Markham, still holding my arm, guides me back and places himself between me and Reese.

Reese opens his mouth and a steady voice speaks—Reese's voice, but unfamiliar and full of fury.

"I'm fine," he says. "And, I'm in control."

Chapter 23

Reese Little

Except for the quarreling, the cavern is unusually quiet. Mother Moon called a meeting with her council and invited me and Emma to sit in. Markham and Tyra have been arguing back and forth for half an hour now and we're no closer to leaving this underground meeting hall with a resolution. Dag and Astrid keep exchanging knowing looks but have yet to say anything. Arni is there and noticeably silent. He sits across the table from one of the Sons of Ivaldi, who also never speaks up. Emma fidgets in her hardback chair. She shares my frustration. Sadly, that may be the only thing we've shared in the past three days since I found out… my father…

I thumb the engraved design on my father's axe. I trace the group of runes on the iron head. I don't understand them but they mean everything to me. This axe is mine now. I replaced the broken long handle with a standard size hickory from the saw mill. I ignore the argument at the table and just concentrate on the weapon, the deep angle of the beard, the sharpness of the cutting edge; dad really kept this relic in good shape.

"Reese," Tyra says catching my attention.

"Yes, what?" I say.

"Reese, what do you think?"

I look at the group. They look back at me. I look over at Emma.

"We need time," she says to the group staring at me.

"Certainly, we understand," Mother Moon says. There is a tremor in her voice. Looking at her, I realize that she clearly has not been sleeping. Her white hair, normally kept in a neat bun, is loose and her eyes appear sullen.

Tyra rises from the table. "As it stands," she says, "we can confirm that Slakter is responsible for both attacks on the Little family. You all know I am of the opinion we must answer this attack."

"And expose ourselves in the process?" Markham asks waving a cigar in his hand. "We are all safer in Jotnar Valley. If this Slakter character wants to get the Little's, he'll have to find them."

"How can you suggest we hide?" Tyra says.

"I suggest we don't give up our advantage, darlin'."

"There is another matter," Mother Moon interjects. "One I have not yet revealed; and it greatly changes this conversation. I believe when I touched the axe several nights ago, I felt power go out from me. I believe it had been cursed. I can no longer shield this valley."

"What? Why didn't you say anything?" Tyra asks. The whole room is murmuring now.

"Are you okay? What do you mean 'cursed'?" Markham asks.

"I wasn't sure until today." Mother Moon answers. "The type of curse necessary to render me powerless would have to be ….well, I believe this was done intentionally to harm Jotnar Valley. I'm sorry but I simply don't have the power I once did.

It may take days or even weeks before I have the strength to influence memory again. For now, we are all exposed to the outside world." Astrid stands.

"First priority; we protect our perimeter. I'll let the boys know we're pulling double shifts from here on out."

"How did Slakter have the power to set a curse like that?" Dag asks.

Mother Moon hesitates then says, "I don't believe *he* does."

"You think someone else is working for him?"

"Truthfully, I don't know. But, our focus for now is the Little family; Reese, Emma, and Hollis. They are in our care and we must come to a decision as to how we will move forward." Markham clears his throat and rubs his brow.

"You mean find the stone?" he says.

"Yes. We must learn what the stone is and find it before Slakter does."

The stone. The ravens allowed Mother Moon to see what happened to my father. He sent a message warning us that Slakter is after the stone and that we need to find it. Guess what? Nobody knows what the stone is or where it is. But, those were his last words and our only clue.

"How do we find it?" Emma asks.

"We don't know," Markham says. "That's all we got. A stone. Slakter wants it and thinks your grandfather had it."

"Well, that's the connection," Dag says.

"What is?"

"Slakter and Reese's grandfather, Karl," he replies. "They ran together in Norway right?"

"Right," I say realizing what Dag is getting at. "Whatever Slakter wants probably originated in Norway."

"So we're going to Norway, then?" Astrid asks. "I'll volunteer to go to Norway. I need some time away from the smelly saw mill."

"Uff da, Astrid. We're not talking about going on vacation," Dag says.

"I'm not either. But, why wouldn't we consider going over there?"

"Why not?" I say standing from the table. Everyone looks at me and the cavern is silent. "Why not travel to Norway?" I ask. "None of the trolls can travel, not easily. And, Mother Moon, you're in no condition to travel right now. But, I can go. I can search records, museums… whatever it takes."

"Reese, you can't even speak the language," Markham says.

"Most of the population speaks English too," I reply.

"And," Tyra says, "with our guard down, it would be no less dangerous than waiting around here for Slakter to find you."

"Look," I say to Mother Moon, "I am going to find my father's killer." I start to choke on the words, hardly believing I said them. "I'm going to protect my family and I'm not going to hide. Not anymore."

The room goes quiet for a moment and everyone looks to Mother Moon. She closes her eyes a moment and lets out a heavy sigh. "You would need a guide," she says. "Someone who knows the area. Someone we can trust with the knowledge of your quest, Reese."

My quest. She called it my quest. Then, I realize that I'm holding my dad's axe in my hand standing over a group that is assembled because of me—because of my family—and I feel the weight descend on to my shoulders. In a matter of moments, plans are being made to fly me out to Oslo. I walk over to Markham and Tyra and we confer on what I need for the journey. Dag confirms that I can take my axe on the plane as checked luggage.

"Seriously?" I ask. "You mean, I can't take a bottle of shampoo in a carry-on bag but an axe in my luggage is no problem?" The energy in the room is busy and anxious at the same time.

"Hey now," Arni shouts from the other end of the table. He stands to his full height and has everyone's attention. "All these plans are well and good. But, I think you're all forgetting something." He looks at me with an ugly stare. "You especially, Reese," he says. "You're forgetting something aren't you?" I'm lost. I stare back not sure what he's talking about. Then he glances at Emma. I look over at her silently waiting to be acknowledged.

"So," she says looking through her auburn locks, staring at the table in front of her, "you're going to Norway." I don't respond. "I noticed there was no discussion with me."

"I'm sorry, babe. We should talk…"

"No, there *was* no talking about it," she says raising her eyes to me. My face grows hot. "You decided. You didn't talk about it. You didn't share it with me. You just decide to put yourself out there. Alone."

Emma stands and leaves the table. I watch her go not sure what to say. But, I know anything I say now is inadequate. She leaves the council room. But, a heavy burden remains. Markham and Mother Moon try to assure me saying that she needs time but we need a plan now.

"Reese, my dear, it would be wise to make a plan of action as soon as possible." Mother Moon crosses the rock cavern floor aided by her cane. There's a frail shuffle to her steps that was not there mere days ago. "Everyone, gather round. Come close. I don't have the inclination nor the voice for shouting." The crowd moves in close, enveloping me and Mother Moon. The smallest of us, the dwarf from the Ivaldi, finds a spot next to me. He gives me a silent wink. Arni and Tyra loom large standing across from me. Tyra voices her approval to send me to Norway. But, Markham is reluctant to have anyone leave the valley.

"Why should we send Reese to go lookin' for a fight when we could have one on our doorstep any day? We need everyone here ready to defend the valley."

"Markham, it is clear that Slakter knows where we are." Tyra says. "Waiting does nothing. We must move against him now."

"What do you say, Egli?" Arni says to the dwarf who has remained silent throughout the meeting. "Are you and the rest of the Ivaldi ready for a fight?" Egli gives a knowing smile. "Oh yeah! The Ivaldi are rekkr, that's a fact!"

Mother Moon clears her throat. "I believe that settles it." She sets both hands on the head of her cane and pulls her shoulders back. "Reese will travel to Norway to discover the significance of this mysterious stone. We have our own resources here in Jotnar Valley to defend ourselves against any force that Slakter might bring against us. I pray that he is not so unwise as to try it." Tyra gives haughty laugh at this.

"Reese will need assistance if we expect him to accomplish anything in Norway," Tyra says earnestly using the least insulting tone she can muster.

"He needs someone with enough muscle to watch his back," Markham says. "But ain't no troll gonna be able to travel. Not out in the open. And, we gotta get him on the first flight over the pond."

"He needs someone who can speak the language, possesses

exceptional knowledge of the locale and culture and knows how to handle opposition of the preternatural variety." Mother Moon's eyes twinkle, giving away that she already has a guide in mind for me.

"Professor Irons?" Arni asks.

"Professor Irons," Tyra answers.

"Professor Irons," Markham agrees.

"Oh," I say waiting for an explanation. "Who?" Markham tells me that Professor Agatha Irons is the Indiana Jones of Norse myth and archeology. Evidently, the professor and Mother Moon have a long history.

"And, if there is anyone I'd want walkin' by my side into enemy territory," Markham says, "it would be her, sure enough. But don't tell her I said that." Markham turns away and starts making plans with Arni and Egli as to how to defend the valley if necessary. They hunker over several onion skin maps of the valley draped over the stone table at the center of the room. Tyra and Mother Moon approach me. Mother Moon leans in with hand to my shoulder. This time she is holding on for balance. I look her in the eye but she doesn't acknowledge it.

"Reese, you will need to fly to Oslo as soon as possible. But, before you leave, I need to impart you with some very necessary information." She glances back to Tyra and says something that sounds like *meen overferg*. Mother Moon asks me to sit in one of the chairs at the stone table. But, Markham and his crew around the table are no longer looking at the maps. They are staring back at Mother Moon. Tyra is frozen as well.

"Minne overføring. Muninn, you cannot be serious," Tyra says with a tilt of her head as if she had not heard correctly.

Markham steps away from the table and approaches Mother Moon.

"You don't have the strength to transfer memories," he says. "At least, not in your condition."

"Do not presume to tell me if I can or cannot do it," she says with a wave of her hand. "This boy is ready to cross the ocean to fight for his family and protect our valley. Do not tell me I cannot do it." She shuffles over to the table before Tyra can catch up with her. Tyra pulls out a chair and Mother Moon sits. "Reese," she says. "Come."

"I'm sorry. What is this?" I ask taking cautious steps toward the group at the table. I take the chair next to Mother Moon and sit facing her.

"Do you remember the day you first came this valley and I read your memories?"

"Oh, no thank you." I stand and start to walk away.

"I'm not going to read your memories. Please, sit down." I don't sit. "I am going to share memories with you. Memories of a past that will, I hope, provide the trail of bread crumbs necessary for your journey."

"A memory transfer," Tyra says, "that could kill you, Muninn." Mother Moon raises a gentle hand silencing Tyra. This sounds rash. I have so many questions.

"How do you… do you have everyone's memories? How can you give me someone else's…"

"Please." She cuts me off. "You don't have the time and I lack the patience." She leans in and reaches for me. "I will need both of your hands." I glance at Markham and Tyra. Their faces are not reassuring. My only consolation is that their worry is not for me but for her. Reluctantly, I sit in the chair opposite Mother Moon. I scoot forward and lay both hands upturned in her lap. She takes a deep breath and exhales. I brace. Then, another question hits me.

"Just whose memories are you giving me?"

"Your grandfather's." She clamps both hands onto mine, wrapping fingers like talons around my wrists. Everything goes black and I hear the throaty caw of a raven.

Chapter 24

Reese Little

The darkness opens to reveal a cold blue daylight. I feel the rise and fall of waves under me. A sail boat carries me into harbor. I arc my neck and squint to gaze at steep mountains capped in white that cradle the harbor. Then, I hear Moon's voice.

"Don't resist the memory. No matter what you are about to see, do not push back." I look left and right but she's nowhere to be seen. "I can guide you… but not for long."

The boat docks. I leap onto the dock with a small weighty bag in one hand and I carry an axe in the other. The same axe that belonged to my dad. Long black hair waves across my face; the wind cuts through my wet tunic and the layers beneath.

A woman greets me at the shore. She is kind, fair skinned with sandy blonde hair. Her eyes crinkle at the sight of me and she embraces me like a mother to a child. I raise my hand to her, holding the small bag, and she smiles. Inside her house, I spill the contents onto her table: silver coins, broaches, and a cup of gold. The warmth of her small house fades and I am transported to a long boat. A crew of three men are with me.

A raven lands on the bow and hops toward me. It speaks in Mother Moon's voice.

"Reese, focus on the details. This is your only road-map to discover Slakter's purpose."

This time, I'm dressed in a patterned wool tunic. A cloak covers my shoulders and I carry the same axe beneath it. A leather-covered box sits in the hull of the boat at my feet. When we land, I see a castle of stone and dirt – a fortress of many walls but few towers. I am expected and five men carrying sabers meet us. They attack me and the crew. I see for myself the speed and fury of a berserker through my grandfather's eyes. My axe dispatches four of the men and leaves the fifth maimed taking his foot at the ankle. Another man approaches me; he's a much older man dressed in fine fabrics. I cannot see his face, as if the memory of him is blurred; scratched in places. He gladly receives the contents of my small cargo, the leather-covered box. He opens it and finds the gold cup inside and pays me handsomely. I look at his face again but, strangely, I cannot see it. He tells me the loss of his men were worth it to prove my skills as a berserker.

The fortress disappears and I'm standing in a green glen. An enormous wooden building looms before me, multiple tiers and spires reach to the sky. A short rock wall circumscribes the perimeter. I walk toward the building counting no less than three Christian crosses, one sitting at the top of each spire. Lush green mountains provide the back drop of this architectural marvel. Mother Moon appears suddenly, standing next to me, looking left and right as if there is something else to see—something missing.

"Karl's memories are clouded. Disjointed. I'm afraid my abilities are not what they should be." Then she is gone. I look back at the church silently presiding over the scenery. The seasons change; summer changes to autumn and then to winter in a breath. The seasons change again and again. I'm standing in front of a headstone in the cemetery. One headstone among dozens. I raise my leg and, with my laced boot, I plant one swift kick against the headstone.

A young woman finds me in the cemetery of the church. A lock of red has escaped the bonnet meant to hide her hair. She clutches her skirts, ready to run. But, I call out to her. Night after night, I return to the cemetery. I check my pocket watch, waiting for her. Night after night, I see her again. She is no longer frightened. I hold her. She runs her hands through my hair, short now. She kisses me. Night after night we embrace in the field of headstones. But the dark and earthy cemetery dissolves and a stale bright light floods my eyes. She is being torn away from me by men and women dressed in white, orderlies in a hospital. She cries. She begs for me as they drag her away. I turn and leave the room. Her screams follow me, echoing through the barren hallway.

Waves. The cold shores of a familiar village come closer as the steam boat carries me into a harbor. The boat docks. I pass the small wooden houses on stilts at the water's edge. The village, has grown and changed but the signature smell of sea air and wet grass remains. I worry no one will recognize me. But, one woman does. It's the same blonde-haired woman but the blonde is fading to gray. Mother. Her eyes still crinkle at the sight of me. She opens her arms and turns to embrace me. That's when I see something that was not there before. A scar over the side of her face, spreading like a web from her temple to her jaw. It's not the kind of scar made by a blade. It's a burn. In the evening, I stand outside her home, watching the sky, waiting for the sun to fall. When twilight arrives, I climb the hill outside the village and enter the dense, wet, forest. I'm looking for something in the dark. Something hidden. It's not long before Slakter finds me.

I return to the stone fortress guarding the coast. This time I am dressed in uniform. I carry a rifle. The man in charge of the fortress meets me outside the walls and invites me to dine. The house staff prepare food and drink. He dismisses everyone and we eat in the great hall. A dark wood table sits in the center of the room encircled by bear-skin rugs. We eat and then he invites me to his study. He produces a small bag of coin. I still cannot see his face.

I am home again. I smell the sea air that is the signature of my village. The axe I have carried aboard many ships and into many battles is tied over my shoulder and hangs at my side. Just outside a house with roof of moss sits an old woman. It is Moon. She sits, hunched over, her shoulders rise with each breath. As I pass, she struggles to speak.

"Not much more. Remember it all."

I walk guardedly in the moonlight; my head on a swivel, scanning the cobble stone streets. I enter the village square and find the woman I am looking for. Between the gaslight of the street and the moonlight overhead I can see well enough that mother's hair has grown white. She is older and she has changed—but the scar is the same. She is stooped over her work. Her hands move quickly in spite of the tremor. I tell her to leave with me. I tell her a boat and a hired crew is waiting to take us away. She is defiant and will not go. Then I see Slakter's cold dark face. Then I see a village burning—homes and barns burning. And, I hear Slakter roaring into the night.

I run. The night turns to day. Wet grass become rocky cliffs.

A busy dock harboring my boat. A hurried and dutiful crew. The harbor gives way to the ocean and, after a thousand miles and a hundred days, I see New York. Then I see the hills of Jotnar Valley. I see cabins tucked into the mountains. Brutish trolls carrying axes taller than a man. They take down an oak tree. And another. And yet another. Several men frame a cabin. And then another.

The Ivaldi ride incredible mechanical devices to clear the coal mine. I see Arni, the troll with three arms, working at something that looks like a giant wheel at the mouth of the water fall inside the cave. Many trolls begin to call the mine their home. My home is a small farmhouse; a pipe stove for heat and water collecting in a rain barrel outside. I bring a wife home. She is a thin woman with doe eyes. She's the woman in the photographs in Mother Moon's house. She brings me ale and moonshine. When I ask for more, she hesitates. I shout at her. I shout at her until she cries. And, when she cries I hit her. I say I'm sorry. I make promises.

Later, I leave to fight in someone else's war. I carry my axe and I carry my rifle and I wear the uniform of my employer. I'm gone for months. I come home. I demand ale and moonshine and she brings it. When I demand more, she hesitates. I shout. I hit. But, this time she does not cry. My son cries. He stands in his torn night shirt, hiding just behind his door, looking back at me with wet eyes. Teddy. My own father, a little boy, stares back at me.

Teddy grows before my eyes. He is tall enough to reach the ale and pour me a drink—which he does when his mother refuses. A large radio in wood casing plays *Light My Fire* by The Doors. Teddy pacifies my demand for more drink but his mother admonishes him for it. I shout at her and she shouts right back. I tear through the cabin to get at her but Teddy pulls at my leg until I shake him off. He grabs at my arm and I toss him away, sending him sprawling into the Hoosier cabinet. The crash of ceramic plates makes me even angrier.

See what you made me do. I charge after her, pulling her hair. She screams for help. Something dense and metallic smacks the back of my head. I fall to the floor and turn to see Teddy with the iron skillet clutched in both hands. Then, I lose myself to the berserker. I feel the blood in my eyes and the rage pulsing. I lunge for Teddy as he throws the skillet, just missing me. The cabin door bursts open. Markham rushes in and moves between me and the boy. His beard is short and he's thinner. Markham raises a hand and tries to talk at me. But, I'll have none of it. He shields Teddy as I attack. We grapple, hands at each other's faces. I see his eyes. The whites turn red with blood. We fight, tearing the cabin apart. Teddy is grabbed by his mother and they flee just a gas oil lamp crashes to the floor. Oil splashes the linen curtains, setting the wall ablaze. I see Teddy—his face has transformed from fear into awe as he looks back at Markham. His mother pulls him out of the inferno and into the night.

I'm consumed in dark and I begin to feel the memory break apart. For a moment, my stomach turns. Then, I feel a heaviness on my shoulders. Hands. Markham is calling to me. I open my eyes and see him inches from my face and shaking my shoulders with both hands. I hear him tell somebody that I'm awake.

"Reese, you okay? Do you know where you are?" I struggle to speak at first; my mouth is dry and I'm overcome with an aching thirst.

"I'm... I'm okay," I say weakly. I try to stand and Markham

helps me, throwing one of my arms over his shoulder for support. It's then that I see Mother Moon is gone. Arni and Tyra are also missing. Markham says that Mother Moon is recovering, that she was nearly comatose from the memory transfer.

"Whatever you saw in your grandfather's memories," he says, "I hope it was worth it."

I look at his face and remember the berserker I saw. I remember the face of my father as a little boy when Markham came between him and Grandpa Karl. I tell him I need to leave. I need to find Emma. Need to plan. Need to go to Norway.

"Just slow down," he tells me. I'm able to get my legs under me to walk on my own. The light outside the cave is setting in the west. I must have been under for hours. "Don't worry none about the details. That's being handled between Mother Moon and the professor. Just get packed and get some rest."

I walk with my head down watching the ground move under my feet, trying to keep balance. I stumble now and again as a sudden rush of memories spill across my mind. Emma and Hollis are outside the cabin. They've started a fire in the fire pit and Emma sits holding Hollis. They are roasting marshmallows. Dag and Astrid are there too. They've already emptied half the bag of marshmallows when I trudge up the path to them. Emma sees me.

"Hollis, go inside the cabin, Baby." She stands ready to say her peace. The glow of the fire dances across her face. Behind her, the mountains meet the clouds in a purple twilight. The picturesque scene beguiles me to believe this conversation will go my way – that she'll understand why I have to do this.

"Daddy!" Hollis races toward me. He wraps both arms

around my thighs in a grip that warms my heart and, at the same time, accuses me of my absence.

"Hollis, go inside like I told you," Emma says. "Daddy and I need to talk." Dag and Astrid glance at each other, stand and begin to leave.

"But, I don't wanna go. Daddy, are you staying with us?"

"Yeah, I'm going to be right here. Now, listen to your momma."

"No. I'm gonna stay with you." He clings to my legs again. I wrap my arms around him and pick him up. A wave of dizziness hits me as I do—memories of ocean mist and the spray of blood—I breath deep and steady myself. I hold Hollis and look him in the eyes.

"Buddy, I'm going to go away for a while. But I promise I'll be back soon."

"We are going with you." Emma's voice is lower, no non-sense, and no discussion. I try to focus on her face. The waves of light and flashes of memories don't make it easy. "Hollis and I, we are going to Norway."

"Babe, you know that isn't safe."

"Nothing about this is safe. You're not safe going alone. And, we're not safe here without you." She holds her ground. I look back at Astrid and then to Dag. They weren't so quick to leave after all. Their faces tell me I'm outnumbered.

"Emma, I don't think..."

"No, Reese. I didn't ask what you think. I didn't ask for your permission." She approaches and takes Hollis from my arms. "We are going with you. I'm telling you this as a courtesy." She holds our boy tight against her chest in a motherly impulse but also, I imagine, in an effort to hold down the incensed fury boiling up inside her. She gestures to the cabin. "Come inside. We should plan our little excursion to Norway together, like a family." She adds an extra dose of resentment in those last few words.

I approach her hoping I can hold her, hoping I can convince her in some last-ditch effort that this is not a good idea. A roar is heard—an engine, like a race car, getting nearer and demolishing the quiet mountain serenity like a sledge hammer to a glass vase. Emma looks past me and squints.

"Is that *our* car?"

I turn and see our 30-year-old white sedan cutting tracks in the hills and spitting mud. It's not only up and running but it's fully restored. One of the Ivaldi is at the wheel and he gasses it as he races toward us and cuts the wheel at the last second for a power slide. The car stops just feet from us.

"Are you kidding me?" I look the car over. There's not a scratch on the white paint. Every dent is gone. It's sitting on a new set of off-road tires and the whole car shudders with the power of whatever boosted engine they've put under the hood.

The dwarf swings open the door and steps out with a silent grin on his face. He's wearing Markham's fedora on his head. The back passenger-side door kicks open too. Two more dwarves tumble out from the back, a man and a woman. Both look like they are about to be sick as they try to collect their bearings. They can't get away from the vehicle fast enough. The driver walks up to me and tosses me the keys.

"This car was destroyed," I say. "How did you do this?" The little guy shrugs, smiles, then walks away. As they go, one of his passengers, the lady dwarf, gives the driver a smack across the back of the head for her trouble. I look over at Dag.

"Did you put them up to this?" I ask. Dag smiles and runs a hand through his beard.

"What is it politicians say? *I can neither confirm nor deny the allegation.*"

Emma and Astrid circle the car. Astrid is impressed but not shocked.

"I knew they could do it," she says kicking one of the tires. "I've seen them press rocks into diamonds and restore warships. But, I never get used to it." Emma and I exchange a look. We both realize what this means. We have a car again. And, we could drive out of here... at any time.

Then, the noise of a crowd approaches. I turn and see men and women, trolls too, most of them carrying torches and a few carry flashlights. They've all come from the mine and move with a hushed anxiousness, like some kind of dread has possessed them.

"There he is." Bubba, the horned troll, leads this pack. He points at me and the crowd hurries. Dag approaches my side and stands with me as the mob converges on us.

"What's going on, folks?" Dag asks.

"Is it true?" Bubba asks. "Mother Moon can't shield the valley no more?" I see the panicked looks in their eyes. I don't answer. But, my silence says enough. Bubba calls out to the crowd like a town crier. "We're out in the open. Mother Moon can't hide us. It's time to take up the old way once again. It's time to *flee*. It's time to *hide*!

The crowd murmurs and fear takes hold. Some converge and continue making plans. *Spread the word, everyone needs to know.* Others split off in little groups but they all move with that same hushed panic. I look around and realize Jotnar Valley is being abandoned.

Chapter 25

Emma Little

Reese and Dag are at the center of a mob that is working itself into panic. As the questions get louder and more insistent, I can hear the growing tension like a tea kettle giving a low whistle just before it lets out a full scream. Astrid grabs my arm.

"You need to get in your cabin." Her eyes look at me and then at Hollis. She follows me inside. I grab a rick of wood, toss a few sticks in the stove, and start a fire. I should say, I try to start a fire despite my shaking hands.

"Momma, what's going on?"

"People are scared, Baby." Hollis squints, confused.

"But, why?" Before I can answer, the door swings open and Reese barges in.

"Dag is trying to keep 'em calm out there. But he's just spinning stories. We need help."

"Where's Mother Moon?" Astrid asks.

"She's recovering, according to Markham." Reese looks unsure. "I'm not sure what it's called but she showed me my grandfather's memories. It took everything out of her."

"What about Markham? Or Tyra?" Just then, we hear the

mob outside clamor all at once and then—silence. We exchange a look.

"I don't like the sound of that," Astrid says. Reese goes to the window and pulls back the curtain.

"Arni is out there. They're listening." I can feel my chest tighten as I realize I'm holding my breath waiting for the next thing Reese is going to say. "They're moving off. They're all headed down hill… toward the gathering spot."

"Why?" Astrid asks. "Someone call a meeting of the valley?"

A rattling knock hits the door. Hollis screams and I jump.

"It's Dag." Reese moves from the window and opens the door. Dag comes in, breathing heavy, and wide eyed.

"Tyra's calling a meeting," he says. "Arni's telling everyone to meet in the clearing now."

When we get to the clearing, the lights in the trees are already aglow illuminating the hundreds of bodies in a yellow haze. I carry Hollis on my hip and, at the sight of the gathering, I instinctively pull him closer to me. The crowd is buzzing and frenetic. I can hear bits and pieces of anxious rumors passed around.

Tyra stands in the center of the crowd. She speaks to Arni in between urgent questions from those in the crowd closest to them. Typically, I would say Tyra is made for this, made for speeches and restoring order to chaos. Her rigid presence and her no-nonsense demeanor make her well suited to command. But, I remember one of my mom's old boyfriends. He was a Marine who loved the military life. But he used to say, "Barking orders will get soldiers only so far." And, I see very few soldiers in this crowd. Tyra raises both hands and the crowd goes quiet.

"Mother Moon is resting and wishes she could be here to address you all. Know that I speak for her." The crowd murmurs, anticipating answers. "She would ask for calm. And, I would ask that you stand ready to do what will be needed of you for the sake of Jotnar Valley. Make no mistake, we are facing an enemy that has breached Muninn's defense."

Voices in the crowd cry out. Others call for quiet and Tyra continues. "The same way our ancestors defended their own villages, every one of us must be ready to defend Jotnar Valley." Dag turns and looks back at me and Reese. Reese turns and looks at me.

"You mean we're out in the open?" A man deep at the back of the crowd shouts. "What if the outside world finds us?" And another voice, this time a woman, calls out to Tyra.

"What happened to Mother Moon? Is she okay?"

"She is resting. But I'm sure she would ask that you would remain vigilant and return to the Mine. Return to your homes. The time may soon come where you will be required to defend this valley." Tyra is losing them. The murmuring becomes louder and one family leaves the group, then another. They don't look like they are calmly returning to their homes. A troll at the back announces to the crowd that he's leading a party out of the valley at midnight.

"Stay and fight if you wanna." It's Bubba. "I'm taking me and mine outta here. We're going east to the Highland Area." This is met with shouts of derision from some. But, Bubba only gets louder. "Meet me at the saw mill at midnight if you wanna go."

"Shut your damn mouth."

I hear Eklund's unmistakable raspy voice full of grit but I can't see him over heads and shoulders towering beside me.

"I survived Vietnam and a Birmingham sit-in. I ain't going nowhere."

"Stay and die, if you want, old man."

"You ain't takin' nobody outta here," Eklund comes back with a shout, "unless you want to be branded a coward." The uproar grows to fever pitch arguing over who's a coward to leave and who's a fool to stay. I hold Hollis close to me and turn to get away from this mob. Reese is gone. I look left and right, avoiding elbows and pointed fingers as rational discussion is abandoned completely. A hand grabs mine. It's Reese pulling us from the fray. Hollis tucks his head under my chin and we scramble to get away from the crowd.

"Where's Dag? Astrid? Reese, where are we going?"

"Keep going." He leads us back up the hill away from the clearing. Reese marches us directly to the car and he pulls the keys from his pocket.

"Reese, where are we going?" I can hear the crowd down the hill growing louder. Reese opens the door.

"Get in!" He starts the engine. It roars.

"What are you doing?"

"Get in." His eyes command something in me. "I've got it under control." Uncertain but trusting, I throw open the passenger door, sit down, and hold Hollis in my lap.

Reese puts the car into drive and rolls down the hill toward the gathering. He stops the car just at the edge of the clearing, throws it in park, flips on the headlights, and lays on the horn. Three hundred faces turn and look at us. Reese pops out of the car and climbs onto the hood. I step out of the car with Hollis and stare up at my husband who may be losing his mind.

"Hey. While you all talk about running or staying, I'm

gonna get on a plane. I'm gonna go to Norway. And, I'm going to figure this out. All of it. And, so help me, I'm taking my family with me." Reese looks at me and Hollis. I see the same thing in his green eyes that made me trust him when he wanted to toss off his father's advice and come to Jotnar Valley in the first place. It's the same thing that made me say yes when he asked me to marry him five years ago. He turns back to the crowd. "Every one of you has family here. And, trouble is at your door. But, this is not the time to run. You're descended from Vikings, right? You jotnar among us are the stuff of legend. Fearsome. You sent armies running back to their commanders? Well get ready to do it again. Because something out there wants to get in here. I don't want that to happen. When I get back, I want a home to return to. And, I want all of you to be here."

Reese steps off the hood. He moves to me and Hollis and wraps his arms around us both. The crowd is quiet. I whisper to Reese.

"You are so hot. But, what are we supposed to do now?" Before he can answer I hear another voice. Eklund calls out from the crowd.

"Now, that's rekkr, boy!" Reese and I turn and see him shoving his way through the crowd. He emerges and does something very peculiar. He places his left arm, his bad arm, over his chest. Then he takes his right fist, swings it across his body and pounds his left shoulder, like a salute. One of the dwarves, the Ivaldi, steps forward and does the same thing. Two other men give the same salute, a slow repeated strike with the right hand across the body to the left shoulder. Eklund calls out again. "That's rekkr."

Chapter 26

Emma Little

A 12-hour flight is brutal on anyone but traveling with a 4-year-old for 12 hours is agony. Charleston to Washington D.C. to Copenhagen to Oslo.

Hollis eats all the snacks and devours the in-flight meal. I place a box of worn crayons in front of him along with a small spiral notebook with plenty of paper. He draws a picture of Mother Moon and a crowd of trolls all around her. Reese reads through all the shopping magazines to Hollis. Of course, he also has to use the tiny closet of a bathroom once every hour while he is awake.

Trying to sleep is futile. I pick up a Shopping Smart catalogue from the back of the seat in front of me. I thumb through looking at the pictures. A clean-cut man with a chiseled jaw models a brown fedora advertised as all-weather —*perfect for travel*, it says. It makes me think of Markham. The hat, not the model. He pulled me aside as we were getting ready to leave Jotnar Valley.

"Look, I know I wasn't very friendly to the idea of taken y'all in when you first showed up in the valley. And, I did my share of griping," he said, "But, I've come around since then and I've decided that—you're good people." He tipped his hat, concluding his vague apology.

"Why, Markham, I think you mean to say that you like us," I said chuckling. "Is that about right?" He took a step toward me and lowered his voice.

"What I mean to say is, I want you to take care of yourself. You, and Reese, and Hollis… take care of each other. No matter what happens over there or what you find. This ain't about trolls or Vikings. It ain't about protecting this valley. Don't worry about us. It's about family. You and Reese and Hollis. You protect your family. You hear me?" I heard him.

I turn to Reese sitting in the seat next to me. His eyes are closed.

"Are you asleep?" I ask.

"Absolutely not," he says without opening his eyes. His brow tightens. "I keep seeing my grandfather's memories. They're so… vivid… persistent, like flies or birds… diving toward my brain." He rubs both eyes with his fists. "I'm awake now." I'm afraid to ask but I need to know.

"What did you see? In his memories."

"Huh? Oh, it's just flashes. Mountains bigger than anything I've ever seen. I can even remember the smell of the snow on the air. And, the jewels and artifacts. He stole… or reclaimed treasures lost in wars." Reese's face goes sour as if he's going to be sick. "And wars. I can see wars. He… relished it." He takes a staggered breath. "I need you to talk to me. About anything. Just need to get my mind off of it."

"What did Markham tell you before we left?"

"Markham? He told me not to lose myself in revenge," he says raising his head and looking at me. "And, I promised I wouldn't." I reach for his hand, lacing my fingers through his.

"What about you?" he asks. "What did Markham say to you?"

"He wanted me to bring back some Norwegian liquor," I say with a smirk.

"Yeah?"

"Yeah. Oh, and he said we should take care of ourselves."

"It's good advice," Reese says and lays his head back against the seat closing his eyes.

I can't stop thinking about where we are going and wonder what Norway will be like. The professor that is supposed to meet us, Mother Moon said she is a dear friend that she met when the professor was only a child in Norway.

"Every so often," she told us just before we boarded the plane, "I learn of a little boy or girl who is, shall I say, linked to the mysteries of the Norse world. And, they need guidance to navigate daily life when they are surrounded by people who do not believe in such things as jotnar or the supernatural."

When she said that, I immediately thought of Victoria, the young mother I met washing laundry at the river, and her son, Max, the troll.

"Agatha Irons is a woman of special skills, not the least of which is her knowledge of artifacts and antiquities that relate to Scandinavian culture." When Reese and I pressed Mother Moon for more information on this professor, she only told us, "Professor Irons has developed a reputation for not only being an archaeologist, but also a trouble maker, an escape artist, and a miracle worker. Trust her implicitly."

Somewhere over the Atlantic Ocean, around hour number 10, my body finally reached the point of exhaustion. I close my eyes and drift to sleep a mere half hour before the plane lands in Oslo. We land in clear skies and a thin blanket of snow on the ground. Reese grabs our go-bag from the conveyor inside our terminal. Then, we make our way to the customs gate. This is the moment of truth as we present the passports Dag acquired for us only 48 hours ago. "Trust me," he had said. "Astrid and I know a little something about crossing borders."

The customs agent glances at us from behind the glass. "Passports?" she asks.

I pull all three from my backpack and hand them over. My hands desperately want to take them back and flip through the pages again just to be sure everything looks legit. The agent quietly looks through mine then Reese's. She asks for the CBP form that will allow me to bring the Schofield revolvers into Norway. That's something I never thought I'd be doing. The agent looks at my forms then looks at us without saying a word. She smiles and reaches for the radio attached at her shoulder and mumbles something in Norwegian. A tall man in a nice suit and bright tie arrives. He wears a lanyard around his neck with his name and credentials hanging in front of his belly. The man and the customs agent exchange words quietly then they both turn and look at the three of us and smile.

"Reese, what's going on?" I ask.

"I don't know. But, they are smiling so we should be smiling too." I smile but I'm afraid it looks more like a grimace. The man in the nice suit approaches us.

"Please, step over here." He gestures as he smiles even bigger than before. He leads us away from the agent and the line of passengers waiting behind us.

"What is the nature of your visit to Norway?" he asks with an enunciated Norwegian accent. Reese speaks up.

"We've always wanted see the fjords and visit the museums

in Oslo. We might even show our little boy where his great grandfather grew up," he says and gives Hollis' hair a tussle.

"Ah," says the man in the suit. "So, you have family here?"

"Well, we had family here," Reese answers. The man waits for a further explanation but Reese simply smiles silently matching the man to nearly comedic effect. The man breaks first and pulls out his cell phone.

"And, where will you be staying?" he asks while dialing a number.

"Uh, we'll be traveling between destinations. Several hotels."

"And, when will you be returning to the United States?" he says raising the phone to his ear.

"Probably, sooner than we want to," Reese answers. The man says something sharp and unfriendly to whoever he's called on the phone. Then he looks back at us.

"And, the guns? The hand guns?" I take a deep breath and give the performance of my life.

"Yes, Professor Agatha Irons has instructed me to deliver them to her by end of day tomorrow. Both revolvers are antiques, exquisite remnants of a by-gone era, and the professor requires them for her featured exhibit next week."

"Yes ma'am."

"And, they simply cannot be delayed. Her exhibit centers on these exquisite antique artifacts of American lore."

"Artifacts?" he asks. But, I don't even pause.

"And I'm sure you'll see that all the paper work is in order for a temporary import of these firearms. Is that correct or should I give Professor Irons a call?"

The man turns says something to the person on the other end of the cell phone. He raises a hand toward the customs agent who has since let two more passengers cross without incident. She nods and waves at us. She hands our passports to me and smiles.

"Enjoy your visit," she says. We don't wait and we don't ask questions. I scoop Hollis up and fight the urge to run. We walk quickly toward the escalator. Without slowing down, Reese looks at me slack-jawed.

"Babe, that was *awesome!*"

We make our way to the lower level of the atrium. The smells of food get stronger as we approach restaurants leading to the main floor where arriving passengers mix with departing passengers. We were told that Professor Irons would find us and to wait in the lower floor of the atrium.

"God, it feels good to just walk around again," I say.

"Yeah," Reese says. I know that tone of voice. He's not really listening. He's watching everyone. His eyes scan the floor looking for danger and exits.

"See anything interesting?"

"Hmm?"

"Reese, I'm talking to you."

"I'm listening."

"Any sign of her?" I ask.

"Not yet."

We find the find the exits leading to the railway. People come and go on the main floor, jostling carry-on bags while pulling suitcases and boxy pieces of luggage. Reese moves into the crowd when I see a flickering light reflected in the floor and the windows that stretch two stories of the atrium. I turn and see a bright white ball of light floating like a balloon. It's not flickering – it's pulsing. What is…

My head rocks back and my eyes water. The sudden smell of ammonia overwhelms my nostrils.

"Oh God. What is that smell?" I say. In front of me stands a black woman in a wide dark Edwardian hat and dark coat. She is close enough that I can see my reflection in her rose-colored spectacles.

"Keep your head down, love. Don't look at the light," she says pulling the capsule of smelling salts away from my face and tucking them back in her coat pocket.

"What?"

"Keep your eyes down, Babe," I hear Reese say. I look at the floor though I still see the flicker of light against the walls of the atrium. Reese grabs my hand. I glance to the left and right without raising my head.

"My name is Professor Agatha Irons. I've just tranced the entire crowd with that mineral flare. They're immobile now but we only have minutes. Keep your eyes on my heels and follow me."

She moves quickly and carries our travel bag. Reese is carrying Hollis. I feel my backpack on my shoulders that wasn't there when we approached the carousel. Was I unconscious? How long was I out? Then, I see in my peripheral vision that no one else is moving. Legs frozen mid-step. I pass by a woman crouched down to pick up a cell phone she'd dropped. She is unmoving, her hand mere inches from the phone. I begin to panic.

"What is going on?"

"One of my many tricks," she says without slowing down. "Paralysis de Lumine. It will only last another two or three minutes. Which means, I need you both to move faster."

I grip Reese's hand tighter. Professor Irons leads us weaving in and out of the crowd of passengers that are still as statues. I push to keep up her pace. The folds of her long dark coat spread and move like a cape. She carries a cane, black with an ornate polished metal grip, but she does not use it. There is something very early 1910s about her style that is the opposite of inconspicuous.

"How do we know you're really Professor Irons," Reese says. Until this moment, I had not even questioned it. What if this is a trap?

"You don't," she says without looking back at us. No calming tone. No reassuring glance. "But, I don't think you want to take your chances with those blokes."

I glance to the right as we near the exit onto the train platform. Just inside the atrium is a pale man with nice leather coat and gloves. I notice a small tattoo just above his eye. He is holding a sign that says "Reese/Emma." Two more men are frozen in mid-stride. Nothing remarkable about their appearance except they each carry a sign with our names on them as well. They know our names.

We cross the platform, dodging several bundled riders exiting the train, and step inside. I hear frightened shouts from several of the riders as they enter the atrium and see the crowd of human statuary. The train hums and the doors close. Hollis comes to and looks around, confused.

"Where are we?" he asks.

"We are in Norway, Baby," I say.

"Are we safe?"

Chapter 27

Reese Little

Professor Irons gazes at us over her ruby spectacles. I place Hollis between me and Emma in the back seat of the luxury car and buckle him in. The car was waiting for us at the train station and the professor didn't even have to tell the driver where to go when we rode away. It dawns on me that this car is not a rental service. It's her car. And her driver.

"Now that we are safely away," she says, removing her hat and spectacles, "proper introductions are in order. I'm Agatha Irons and you three must be the Littles. I hope." Taking a second look at her, I notice her strong jaw and thick lips. She's attractive even now in her mid-age. Her eyes are deep set and flanked by lines of crow's feet. I wonder what they've seen.

"Yes, Reese, Emma, and Hollis," I say pointing to each of us. "Do you mind me asking where we are going?"

"Very direct, Mr. Little. I do appreciate that."

"You can call me, Reese. We need answers as soon as we can get them. I'm sure Mother Moon explained some of what we've been through over the past three weeks and, well, I just don't have the patience I used to."

"I understand. I will be brief. Mother Moon put you in my

care because Jotnar Valley is no longer safe against an enemy whose motives we do not understand and whose next move is hidden from us. This enemy wants something your family once possessed, Reese. A stone? We find the stone, we find answers."

"That pretty much sums it up," Emma says.

"But, you didn't answer my question," I say leaning forward. "Where are we going now?"

"Oh, you're right. Apologies. We are in route to the mental hospital 50 kilometers outside of Oslo."

"The mental hospital?"

"Yes. More precisely we are going to break in to the psychiatric wing that was condemned over 20 years ago.

"Ah," I say. Emma looks at me and we both sit in silence.

As we got closer to the hospital, the road becomes uneven and cracked. Weeds have grown up through the cracks in the pavement. There's a sense that we are approaching forgotten places. The afternoon sun in Norway gives a silvery glow to the grounds of the hospital. The four-story facility sits alone on several acres surrounded by dark woods that hide it from view of the road. It's an intimidating stonework structure with narrow windows across the face giving the bearing of a barracks rather than a psychiatric hospital. Instead of taking us up the drive to the front door, the driver leads us past the hospital and Professor Irons calls to him to stop.

"Here, Gerald. And, do make that phone call now." Gerald, the driver, replies in a thick North-English accent.

"Yes, mum. Sure you won't have a need for me inside?"

"No. We need you with the car, ready to go."

Gerald, pulls over against the tree-line where we are hidden from view. He pulls out a cell phone and dials a number. Professor Irons opens the door and steps out inviting us to do the same. She opens the trunk of the car and removes a large suit bag, handing it to me. She also reaches in the trunk and, with considerable effort, pulls out a metal cylinder as wide around as a car tire and measuring as high my knees. Dials and wires inlay the face of the strange piece of equipment.

"What's that?" Hollis asks with cautious curiosity.

"This contraption," she says, "is just for you, dear Hollis." He can't hide a look of surprise. I can't hide a look of worry. "But first," she says turning to me and Emma, "you two need the proper attire." She gestures to the suit bag in my hand. "Get dressed. Quickly."

Minutes later, we enter and approach the security desk. The three of us, Emma, the professor, and I are dressed in bright yellow hazmat suits with serial numbers across the chest and a biohazard symbol on the back. Emma carries a coiled hose over her shoulder and a device in her hand that looks like a graphing calculator that beeps rapidly every few seconds. Professor Irons leads and quickly introduces herself to the orderly at the desk. I can't understand a word she's saying but I assume it's Norwegian. The orderly is a balding overweight man wearing a uniform, a white button-down shirt and matching white slacks. He hangs up the phone seemingly flustered from whatever conversation just transpired. Then, I remember that Professor Irons' driver made a phone call just as we got here. Gerald's call must have been the opening act of our little con job.

The orderly stands and leans over the computer monitors in front of him, his gut hanging over his belt. At this point, the professor is probably telling about the "rush order" to investigate and clean old state-run facilities that may be in disrepair. Her cover story makes the condemned psychiatric wing sound like biohazardous nightmare and lawsuit waiting to happen.

The orderly looks past the professor and sees me carrying the heavy metal cylinder. He arches an eyebrow, clearly suspicious of the device. I adjust my grip on the single handle at the dome of the cylinder. It begins to feel heavier as I wait, anxiously hoping Professor Irons' plan is going to work. I turn to Emma and begin barking a few Norwegian phrases that Professor Irons told me to say should anyone in charge begin asking too many questions. Emma barks right back at me with a few phrases of her own. Professor turns and tries to calm us but we only get louder and more obnoxious by the second. Then, right on cue, the orderly steps out from behind the security station waving a dozen small keys on a carabiner and offers to take us where we want to go. We all smile.

He leads us past a bank of monitors flickering a feed of camera angles. Cameras cover the common room, the front door we just came in, and a loading dock presumably somewhere at the back of the hospital.

"You okay to carry that?" Emma whispers, referring to the cylinder in my hand.

"I got it."

The orderly lumbers down the hall. We pass large windows that gaze into the common room. Something is strangely familiar about these halls. But, I can't place it. There are a few patients, all men, playing cards or reading books in there.

One of the men, still wearing a brown bathrobe over his white hospital-issued t-shirt and pants, slowly shuffles across the dark hardwood floor. One hand is extended slightly above the waist as if he is holding something or something is pulling at his arm. He gently talks to himself, changes direction, and continues shuffling, arm still extended. Then, I realize what he is doing – he thinks he's walking his dog. The winter sun filters through the tall windows and gives a surreal glow to the dawdling activity of the room, like watching a milky gray lava lamp.

We climb a set of stairs to the second level. With each step up, the cylinder seems to get just a little heavier. The orderly finally leads us to an expansive landing that is dimly lit by a single sky-light high overhead. A large arch in the wall has been boarded over and a small door was built into the original structure. The orderly fishes through his dozen keys, unlocks the deadbolt, and opens the door. He doesn't go inside. He doesn't even look through the door to the other side. He simply exchanges a few words with the professor and looks back and me and Emma gravely as we cross over to the abandoned wing.

There is little to see in the dark but plenty more to imagine. Small metal carts lie turned over, wires protruding from instruments that were silenced decades ago. Metal rusts and wood warps but sounds—the sounds in a place like this grow sharper, stronger, over time. Like the sound of wooden floor boards creaking and snapping against each other with each step. Like the sound of an incessant drip from a pipe somewhere over head and the faint splash of that drop into a shallow puddle unseen somewhere in the dark.

"Let's get to work." Professor Irons unzips the hazmat suit

and draws her cane from her cloak and raises it. The silver head begins to glow with an iridescent purple light. The cavernous hall before us is illuminated.

I open the dome of the cylinder with a quick turn. Hollis lies coiled up in a ball, holding Beefy the Buffalo. I reach in and pull him out.

"How you doing, Buddy."

"Good," he says rubbing his eyes. "But, Beefy got scared. I told him it's all okay." He clutches Beefy a little tighter.

"The plan," the professor says, "is to find six patient dossiers in the records room of the abandoned wing. According to my sources, these six souls were committed here for various reasons but all six claimed to have seen or otherwise inter-acted with jotnar. I have their names."

"So, we grab the six files and go?" I ask.

"Precisely. Let's be quick about it." We all strap mold res-pirators over our faces. Emma pulls a smaller disposable one over Hollis' face.

"Reese, leave the cylinder behind."

"But..."

"We won't need it again. In fact, get rid of the suits here as well."

Once we strip off the bright yellow suits, the professor moves quickly and we push to keep up with her. The hall is more like a giant room with tall thin windows on one side and endless doors on the other. The doors hang open as if all the patients fled at once. Our hurried steps sound almost thunderous in this empty space. I look back, sure that someone will burst through the door and we'll be caught. The professor leads us to a wide door at the end of the hall. Paint peels off in little coils from the wood face. She assess the door for a moment and raises her cane, and I notice the head of it is a decorative wolf's head.

"Step back, my dears. And, you may want to look away." I cover Hollis' eyes and turn away just as a shot of bright light fires from the head of her cane. It illuminates the hall in a purple hue. She fires two shots total—one at each of the hinges.

"That cane of your is… impressive," I say.

"Did you get that on Amazon?" Emma says. Professor Irons gives the faintest smirk.

"Not exactly. Reese, will you do the honors."

I set Hollis down. Even through our respirators, the smell of burnt dust is potent. There are black burn marks where the hinges once sat undisturbed for decades. I lift the door out of the frame. On the other side is a small room with a low ceiling and metal file cabinets as tall as a man lining every wall. The faint smell of sour wood rot hits us. Emma tells Hollis not to go inside.

"Just stay in the doorway, Baby, where we can see you."

The three of us work quickly. Professor gives us the six names and we begin searching. The cabinets are stuffed with browning file folders containing pages of patient records, family names, death dates and, strangely enough, some birth dates as well. On top of the cabinets are shoeboxes stuffed with more patient's records, letters from loved ones and the occasional photograph. Emma finds a hat box filled with more of the same. Professor Iron's tells us to start in the cabinets first.

"If we can't find the names we're looking for in the cabinets, we move on to shoeboxes."

"Hollis, how you doing?" I lean toward the door and see

him tracing a finger through the dust. He recoils and wipes his hand over his pants. He looks at me and shakes his head in disgust.

The first four names are found easily enough—two men and two women. All four born just before or just after the dawn of the 20th century. The Professor finds name number five, Johann Lillegard, born 1871, much older than our other prospects, and was admitted by his own family during his declining years. I don't find the last name in the cabinet it should be in so Emma and I begin looking through shoeboxes.

Then, I notice three or four files scatted on the floor collecting dust. I pick one up. I open it and have to shut it quickly. I feel my pulse rise. I open the file again and read the name inside.

Irons, Agatha

The patient's profile is in Norwegian. But, I scan the text and, having glanced at several dozen just like it already, I determine these are the discharge papers for an 11-year-old girl named Agatha Irons. I find a photograph. It's her. It's Professor Irons' deep-set eyes and resilient jaw but as an 11-year-old. The year is written on the back in faded pen: *1978.*

"What'd you find?" Emma looks over at me.

"Nothing." I say closing the file. "Still looking." When Emma looks away I turn and find the professor opening the lid on another shoe box. I look down at the file in my hand and back at her. *Who the hell am I looking at?* I move to pick up another file from the floor. At the same time, I calmly slip Professor Irons' file under my jacket and tuck it in my waistband.

"Found it!" Emma shouts. I nearly come out of my skin.

"Jeeze, keep it down."

When we have all six files we make our exit. Professor Iron's directs us back down the abandoned residential hall. But, instead of crossing back over to the hospital she takes us further down a set of decrepit stairs leading to a basement level.

"We aren't going out the front door, Professor?"

"No, Reese. We are not. The plan is to sneak out the back, cross the lawn, and meet Gerald waiting for us at the car."

We descend further into the cold dark of the basement. The dark has an oppressive power that causes us to move even more cautiously and quietly. The iridescent glow from the professor's cane is our only source of light. It shines a pale light on a pair of enormous boilers with icy black mouths gaping open like iron dragons frozen mid-roar. We also pass four steel cages each the size and height of a kitchen table—just big enough for an animal—or a person. Emma moves in closer to me and I put an arm around her. No one says a word.

Professor stops at a small set of stairs and, just above us, I see a thin line of white daylight. She climbs the stairs and reaches up to the storm shelter doors that lead to the outside. The doors budge but do not open.

"Locked from the outside." She steps down and raises her cane again. "Cover your eyes, dearies."

She hits it with a fiery blast of purple light and we are awash in bright daylight and crisp Norwegian air. My eyes blink against the light and I can't help letting out a series of sneezes as we climb the stairs. We cross the lawn of the hospital following the path traced against a security fence. We turn a corner around the fence and see the car waiting at the tree line. We also discover a group of patients taking recreation time, bundled in coats and knit hats, just on the other side of the fence. Maybe six or seven orderlies are supervising. We can't avoid being seen.

"Keep walking," Professor Irons says to us without slowing down. For a moment, I think we are going to make it without incident. But, an orderly does take notice of us. He walks toward us briskly, looking back at where we came from. He pulls a radio from his belt and says something to whoever is listening.

"Professor, he's coming at us," Emma says. "He just radioed somebody."

"Just keep walking." Professor Irons even gives the orderly a wave and a smile. The car is mere yards away but two more orderlies join in and now three of the seven are moving toward us with a little too much interest. Then a shout is heard from the group of patients.

A small wiry man in a parka rushes to the fence. He points at us screaming. He reaches through the fence as if he's going to grab us and pull us through the wrought iron bars. The other men in the yard are agitated and begin to act out; one of the patients spits and flails at an orderly. We seize the opportunity, while the orderlies are occupied, to pick up the pace and jump in the car. But, as I open the car door and set Hollis inside, I hear the patient that charged the fence. I look back and see him being restrained. He's raving about Odin and I hear the word berserker. He says it over and over, pointing at me. I don't understand anything else he's saying and I don't wait around. We pull away and, even when we're out of sight of the hospital, I'm certain I can still hear him screaming.

Chapter 28

Emma Little

Breakfast at a 5-star hotel in Oslo tastes even better when someone else is paying for it. Eggs and open-face fish sandwiches sit on fine china at our table. The maroon walls of the dining hall are minimally decorated with black & white photos of the Norwegian coast. Hollis takes up each of the forks at his plate and begins drumming them on the table.

"Don't play, Baby."

"Momma, the eggs are weird."

"The eggs are wonderful, Hollis. Eat up."

"The fish is weird."

"The fish is fine," Reese says. "Eat." Interestingly, Reese is beginning to learn the Norwegian language. When we were deciding what to eat, he stared intently at the menu for five straight minutes. Then he raised his head slowly and whispered, "I think I can read this."

"Possibly a residual side effect from the memories Mother Moon imparted to you," the professor says with a clinical curiosity. Professor Irons calls for a server who brings more coffee. I thank her for the third time for the breakfast and the wonderful room at this resort-hotel. "My dear, it's nothing.

I'm glad to provide a little comfort while you are all so far away from home." She pulls her napkin tucked in the collar reaching almost to her chin. Again, she wears a long skirt, high collared blouse with a buttoned vest, coat, and hat—all reminiscent of text book photos I'd seen of wealthy women aboard the Titanic. "Reese, how are you doing?"

Reese wipes his mouth and chin—I think this is the first time I've noticed his full beard. I like it. He folds his napkin very deliberately and then asks the professor how she's come by so much money. I'm taken aback by the question.

"Take it easy, Larry King," I say hoping Reese will get the hint.

"Very direct, Reese," the professor replies. "I appreciate that. My skills and education have brought me into a line of work that can be very... lucrative. One can make quite a lot of money rescuing the world from imminent danger of the supernatural variety. That is, one can make a lot of money, if one survives." She finishes her coffee and smiles. "Historically, my line of work has terrible benefits and no hope for retirement." I can't help but laugh. But, it's clear that she's not joking.

The professor reaches into her satchel and pulls out one of the six files we'd recovered yesterday. I say recovered but, really, we stole them. This particular file is of the red-haired woman, Ellinor.

Last night, when we'd made it to the hotel here in Oslo, all of us sat down and rummaged through each of the patient files. Hollis tried to entertain himself playing Hide and Seek with Beefy, his toy buffalo. But, that didn't last long as Beefy was neither very good at hiding or seeking. We essentially combed through the patient files, trying to find a lead in this investigation. And, we got one as soon as Reese laid eyes on Ellinor's black and white photograph. He recoiled as if he'd been slapped. Then he pointed at her photo and kept saying, *she had red hair, she had red hair,* over and over. Evidently, Grandpa Karl left her in the mental asylum years ago. Professor Irons studied the file, reading carefully every line, and determined she was the daughter of the Lutheran minister at the Heddal parish. She pulled out her smart-phone and searched directions and photographs to the stave church in Heddal. It's a marvelous piece of architecture and, when it was built in the 1400s, it may have been the largest structure in all of Norway. Reese took one look at the wooden sanctuary and confirmed he remembered that church and Ellinor…they were linked in Karl's memories. We'd found our lead! No one said it but we could feel the electricity in the air. Which made it all the more strange that Reese was so unmoved by it all. His head was a million miles away. Come to think of it, this morning, he avoided all conversation except to ask probing questions of Professor Irons about where she got her money, where she was from—originally, and how long she'd known Mother Moon.

"It's time to get on, my dears," Professor Irons says folding her napkin and rising from the table. "We don't want to be late for church."

Gerald speeds us across beautiful country roads. Snow blankets the fields and caps rustic farm houses. While I'm watching the scenery, Hollis is trying to reach the professor's cane.

"Oh, you don't want to play with that," Professor Irons says picking up the slender black cane. With the flare of a stage magician she reaches into her jacket and holds out a small object between two fingers. "Hold out your hand," she says to Hollis. She places a small blue bird made of folded paper, like origami. Hollis looks at me, giving a wide grin. "Blow on it," the professor says, "like a birthday candle."

Hollis looks at the paper bird in his hand, takes a breath, and blows. As soon as air hits it, the bird comes alive. Paper flutters and the bird takes flight through the cab of the car. Reese ducks as it swoops toward him. Hollis squeals, eyes glued to the bird's every movement. Then, it is consumed in a brief flame and leaves behind only a wisp of smoke. The professor opens a window letting the smoke dissipate.

"How did you do that?" Reese asks. "The bird, your cane, and when we met at the airport… how did you create that light that stopped everyone cold?

"You're wondering if it's *magic*. It's really not. I'm sorry to disappoint." The professor admires her cane, tracing her gloved hands across the ornamental wolf's head. "My tools are ancient science that has been forgotten. Burning certain minerals give off a bright pulse of light at just the right frequency that captivate any animal with eyes to see. This cane is the product of Nikola Tesla's work, drawing power from the static electricity all around us. It was a gift from my husband years ago."

"So, there's no such thing as magic?" I ask. She pauses before answering.

"Let me be clear. Magic is real. But so much of what we call magic just… isn't.

"What about ghosts, gods, or trolls? What about the supernatural?"

"It's all very real. But, we call it supernatural only because we don't understand how very natural it really is."

"You mentioned your husband," I say. "Do you mind me asking..."

"That's a story for another time, my dear." Just then, Gerald pulls the car onto a side road that leads into a parking lot across the street from an enormous old wooden church building.

We make it to the stave church around noon but, with jet lag, my body tries to tell me it's still early morning. The church appears even larger in person than it looked in the pictures online. We park across the street along with two dozen other tourists—couples with pets, moms and dads with children—who are enjoying the sunshine and snow on a windless day. The site is a strange mix of holy reverence and commercial attraction. There's even a café serving sandwiches and coffee only a few feet from the church.

"Do we need our weapons here?" Reese asks the professor. We'd kept our day bag in the trunk along with Reese's axe and my Schofield revolvers and just hoped no police officers decided to stop us and search the car.

"It's the middle of the day and there are plenty of people around," the professor says. "I don't anticipate any... excitement here. No need." By excitement, she meant Slakter's minions. "And besides, we have Gerald." She looks over at Gerald dressed in his pea coat, sharp sunglasses, and well-polished combat boots. "He's always good to sniff out trouble before it happens."

"Yes, mum," he says dutifully then takes a long sniff of the air. So, he does have a sense of humor. The professor leaves us to inquire about the next tour. I let Hollis run across the grounds and play in the snow while we wait. That's when Reese asks Gerald how long he's known Professor Irons. "Longer than most."

"That's not really answering the question," Reese replies coldly.

"Isn't it?" Gerald doesn't say anymore and I see Reese clinching his jaw. What is going on with him?

"Hey Babe," I say putting my arm through his. "Can I talk to you?" I pull him to where Hollis is playing, scooping up snow and packing it into little balls. "What's going on?"

"Don't you think we're putting a lot of trust in her? We barely know who she is?"

"What? Of course we barely know who she is. But, you were okay with that coming over here." His eyes shift to Gerald and then back to me. "What gives, Reese? What changed?" When he looks over at Gerald again, I place both my hands on his face and turn him to me. His eyes soften for a moment. "Babe. What's going on?"

"I'll tell you later." The professor is crossing the lawn, coming back to us. "Just keep your eyes open." Reese dusts the snow from Hollis' pants and scoops him up. He looks back at me as the professor hands each of us a ticket for the next tour. I turn and look back at Gerald who's been watching us. He reveals nothing behind those sunglasses but only nods.

Inside the church, I find myself… conflicted. The church is a sheer wonder of medieval craftsmanship. I'm awestruck at the beauty, the clarity of purpose, mission and design. But, here we are bumbling through Norway just waiting for a clue to emerge from the mess of memories that Mother Moon gave my husband. And Reese, he's been acting shady. He knows something but won't tell me.

We follow the tour with the rest of the crowd. Thankfully, this tour is for English speakers and the guide rattles off the history of the place concisely. Then, she shares that legend tells that it was a troll that actually built the entire church by hand. Five farmers challenged the troll and he built it all in three days. The crowd kindly laughs at this, scoffing at such a quaint bit of lore. Reese and I do not laugh. Gerald and the professor do not laugh. This is when Hollis announces that he's seen trolls and they like to play Smell the Blood. The laughter of the crowd dissipates into awkward smiles and shifting glances. The tour guide moves on.

I admire the floral patterns painted in the walls hundreds of years ago on top of the reds, yellows, and tans of each beam and panel of wood. And every corner, knot, and arch of this church is layered with Gothic proportions like it was designed to be the cathedral of an old-world fairy tale.

Each of us separate and begin wandering through the church on our own. While Professor Irons is speaking with the head of staff, I find Reese sitting quietly in a church pew.

"Where's Hollis?" I ask. Reese puts a finger to his lips and gazes down under the pew. Hollis is hiding under there, watching the tourists and coloring on a crumpled sheet of paper with a stub of a purple crayon he's hidden in his coat. "What are you coloring, baby?" Hollis looks up at me.

"A troll."

"Of course you are." I take a seat next to my husband. Then I scoot in closer and closer until he puts his arm around me. "What's next?" I ask. He exhales and reaches for that pressure point between the eyes.

"Don't know. There's so much history. It's overwhelming." He leans forward and stands, needing to pace. "But, I've got nothing. I don't see anything else from Grandpa Karl's memories."

"But, you saw this place in his memories. Right?"

"I saw a lot of places. I saw boats, small coastal villages. I even saw Markham."

"You saw Markham in your grandpa's memories?"

"I saw a lot of things." His voice rises, showing his exasperation. "But, they're all just points on a map. They're no good if I can't connect them. I don't know where the map ends or where it begins." Just then Professor Irons and Gerald approach.

"I think I may be of some help, Reese. Let's step outside." The professor leads us outside to the snow-covered lawn. As soon as the bright winter sunlight hits his face, Reese sneezes. Professor Irons gestures to the cemetery that covers nearly two acres of land attached to the church. "The curator here was very obliging and filled me in on some additional history that is not well known. These graves and their headstones were frequently used for stashing illicit coin or treasures." She turns, a smile on her face, clearly impressed with the cleverness of these robbers. "Their loot was hid in plain sight where no decent person would snoop around… in a cemetery. And, in fact, the curator mentioned a particular Christian artifact that was stolen from this church in the late 1800s; St. Olav's cross. It's a sacred ornamental cross made of iron with gold-leaf and jewels set in it—a thing of beauty—but, I digress."

"Where is it now?" I ask.

"Well, no one knows, except for me and a few of my counterparts in academia." The professor goes on to say that a particular Norwegian fortress built in the 1200s has mysteriously accumulated Viking and Christian treasures over the last few centuries. It was all very technical, but from what she and her colleagues could determine, these artifacts essentially didn't belong at the fortress. There is no history of acquisition of these artifacts either by purchase or bequest, so they are assumed to have been stolen. But, no one could prove that with spotty historical records spanning over 700 years. "And, what the curator just described to me as the missing cross of St. Olav… is sitting in Stenholmen Fortress."

"Stenholmen Fortress," Reese says. "What's that?"

"That's our next lead."

We begin walking to the car. Gerald and the professor are discussing travel plans and accommodations for the night and tomorrow morning. Then, Reese takes a turn into the cemetery.

"Babe, where are you going?" His steps are deliberate but sluggish. He leans on a tall headstone of a cross before he continues stumbling through the cemetery.

"Reese?" He turns to look back; his eyes squinting and in pain. He waves us toward him and keeps moving. I take Hollis' hand and we all pick up the pace to reach him.

"I'm seeing something," he says when we catch up to him kneeling at a headstone. "I'm seeing a headstone… and Karl kicks it… knocks it over." He raises a hand to the headstone in front of him, a modest stone only as high as my knee. On the front face is carved the soul's name and directly under that is the birth date and death date.

"Who are they?" I ask. "They died in 1790. They didn't have any connection to your grandfather, did they?"

"It's not the person. It's the headstone," Reese says. "We need to move it." Gerald positions himself behind the stone and pulls it towards him while Reese pushes. I glance across the cemetery at all the tourists walking about and hope no one looks over at us. It rocks back and reveals a hole set into the half of the stone in the earth, only a foot deep and a foot wide. Reese reaches inside and finds a folded piece of paper, a note. A few sentences scratched in black ink, it's a sparse message. The professor carefully unfolds it and reads.

"I am done working for you. I want to love you and you to love me. I am ready to follow where you go. Take me. Show me the world. Ellinor."

The words settle on us like a black cloud. Reese stands and pulls the stone back in place. The professor clears her throat and tucks the note into her vest.

"It appears," she says, "that Ellinor was complicit in moving artifacts and other valuables through this cemetery."

"Ellinor and my grandfather were lovers," Reese says looking back at the headstone. "He convinced her to help him. And, she fell in love with him with hopes of seeing the world. She was a liability. So, he had her locked away in that hospital." He takes in a breath and lets out a heavy sigh. "Grandpa sounds like a stand-up kinda guy." Reese stuffs his hands in his pockets and walks further into the cemetery alone. Hollis tries to go to him but I hold him close.

"Daddy?"

"Not right now, Baby," I say. "He needs… time." Professor Irons approaches me.

"Your husband has taken on a terrible burden. Family can be so… complicated. We don't get to choose who we came from. And, we are forever marked by those that came before us and the stories they leave behind for us to finish." She reaches for me and Hollis in a gesture that is very motherly. And, I'm thankful for it. Then, she almost faints. She stumbles and I reach for her. Gerald moves with alert speed and catches her before she falls. She is shaking. He calls to her but she doesn't respond.

"What's happening?" I ask.

"I don't know. She needs a hospital," Gerald says gently laying her to the ground. "You stay with her. I'll get the car." He runs to the parking lot.

"Momma. What's wrong with her?"

"Reese," I shout. He turns and races back to me and Hollis.

"What happened? What's going on?"

"I don't know. I think it's a seizure. Oh god." I try to hold her upright in my arms. She continues to shake. Reese stands and begins shouting for help. Men and women turn and stare, shocked and confused.

Chapter 29

Emma Little

"**Y**ou will *not* lower this helicopter, Gerald. I will say it one last time. I have no need for a hospital." Professor Irons has repeatedly insisted since the moment that she woke up from the seizure that she is fine. By the time that Reese and Gerald got the professor in the car at the church, she had already come to. She insisted that it was not a seizure. She said she could hear and see everything but couldn't move. Again and again she apologized for giving us a fright—in very typical British manner.

"Mum, I have to insist." Gerald wasn't giving up easily. Though the professor pressed us to continue the course to Stenholmen – and had even acquired a helicopter for Gerald to fly us to the coastal fortress—Gerald wasn't about to let her ignore the need for medical attention without a fight. "There's a hospital only 10 kilometers east of us. I can have us there in five minutes."

"You have your instructions," was the last she said about it. Gerald huffed and flew us straight on to Stenholmen.

We circle the fortress and land just outside the walls. It's undeniably an impressive sight. Hollis can't stop pointing at it. It's not a castle like you might imagine. It's a bulwark of stone walls forming a perimeter that marries the cliff's edge against the ocean.

Function is favored over form. The focal point of the fortress is a single large tower overlooking the walls. As towers go, it's as wide as it is tall. Somehow the rustic functionality of the whole thing dismisses the romantic ideal of a medieval castle while, at the same time, making this fortress seem even more… romantic. It helps that the setting sun throws a warm amber light over everything.

A woman in a white pant suit greets us as we exit the helicopter. She shakes each of our hands with vigor and speaks Norwegian with an endless smile. We grab our day bags and are whisked through the gates of the stone walls and into the manor house adjacent to the tower. Professor Irons explains that Stenholmen was converted several years ago into a destination location, kind of a venue space plus museum with accommodations for an overnight stay. She catches my eye and easily reads the dreamy hopefulness on my face.

"This is unreal," Reese says. "I've seen this place. In Grandpa Karl's memories." He reaches for my hand, for balance, and his eyes blink rapidly—like he's trying to clear something from his vision.

The professor speaks to the lady that greeted us and they exchange a few words back and forth. She called ahead as soon as we knew that the place was our next lead. I don't know what she told them but they are rolling out the red carpet, so to speak. Professor Irons turns to me and Reese.

"She says that we'll be able to see our rooms and freshen up before dinner."

"Rooms?" I ask.

"Yes. I thought it best not to rush. We'll meet the steward of Stenholmen for dinner and stay the night here."

We're staying in a castle! I look to Reese wide-eyed but his brow is furrowed. He's agitated. The kind lady in the white suit leads us into the manor, it opens to a large hallway with an arched ceiling. The interior is made of that same stone and mortar and is decorated with flags hanging from walls; swords and pikes are mounted over the archways at each end of the hall.

Reese and I take Hollis to our room on the second floor of the manor. We pass two men in black turtlenecks carrying cello cases. Evidently, there are musicians staying here as well. Hollis runs to the window looking onto the courtyard below us and the stone wall surrounding the manor. It offers a serene but strange view. The sun has already dipped behind the wall, leaving an orange, pink, and pale blue palette in the sky. We can hear the waves against the rocks outside but the wall blocks us from seeing the water or the cliffs. A manor that was built in the 1200s doesn't have plumbing in every room so we use the hall showers. One for men and one for women. Fortunately, we seem to be the only visitors using the showers this evening.

I put on a simple prairie dress that I packed, champagne color and fitted at the waist. It's the only dressy item of clothing I have from our cabin in Jotnar Valley. I just know it's too frumpy and old-fashioned until I see the look on Reese's face. He's wearing a simple white button down and has Hollis dressed in suspenders, a white t-shirt and jeans. Reese stares, open-mouthed.

"Oh, I like that dress." He walks toward me, puts his hands on my waist and kisses me. He kisses me deeply.

"Yeah?" I ask a little breathless. Reese takes my arm and we all walk down to the dining hall together. Passing through the historic halls and rooms of this place, I look at my husband and my little boy and, for a moment, it feels like happiness. Like a dream vacation. Because that's what normal families do in Norway when they're not chasing mythical monsters, right?

"Babe, I need to tell you something." Reese uses that tone of voice that tells me something bad is coming. No. Not now. Not yet. "I found a file. At the hospital."

"What?"

"The professor didn't tell us… that she was in that mental asylum too." My legs feel heavier. I need to sit. I concentrate on just getting to the dining hall. "It was her name and her photo inside the file," Reese says in a hushed voice. "She was a kid."

"Are you sure it was her?"

"I'm sure. It was Agatha Irons. Discharged in 1978."

We make our way into the dining hall; antlers are mounted on the wall, there's a dark wood table that could easily seat 20 people, and herald flags hanging from every corner. The lady in the white pant-suite is waiting for us, clipboard in hand. She flashes that endless smile and gestures for us to have a seat. Men and women in white suits cross back and forth across the hall, some wear white aprons and hats, and move with speed and focus. Professor Irons and Gerald are already at the table with two bottles of wine. Gerald isn't drinking but the professor is already enjoying a glass of red.

"My! Don't you all look lovely?" She smiles at us. I don't know what to say. I smile an awkward smile right back at her. But, all I can think about is the mental hospital. And, a little girl named Agatha Irons. Reese and I take seats opposite of Gerald and Professor Irons with the entire table separating us.

"No need to get too close, love," Gerald says with a grin. I try to smile back.

"You know, I've traveled all over Europe, the Americas, and the UK." Professor Irons removes her ruby glasses and wipes them with a cloth. "And, I've sampled some fantastic food everywhere I've been." She puts them away, tucking them into a pocket inside her vest. Her eyes begin to wander as she speaks. "But my favorite food—my comfort food—will always be Mother Moon's drop biscuits." A wide smile forms across her lips. "I'd smell them baking early in the morning in her house. They were golden brown at the tops, had just the right amount of butter baked in."

A thin man in a white suite approaches the table. He introduces himself speaking English in a heavy Norwegian accent. His name is Christian.

"I regret to tell you, our host, Steward Lars Bakken, will be late. He ask that you enjoy our food and he will come soon. Yes? Yes." With that, he leaves the dining hall by a small door that, I assume, leads to the kitchen. For a moment, the five of us sit silently in a medieval dining hall. A large fire warms the hall and the pop and hiss of the fire seem to become louder with our silence.

"So, what do you think?" the professor asks. Reese and I mumble a reply.

"It's wonderful."

"Yes, very nice." I sit staring at Professor Irons wanting to ask her about the mental hospital and, at the same time, not wanting to ask her. I can see Reese in the corner of my eye, shifting uncomfortably. I wish Hollis would just say something silly or ask to go to the bathroom like a four-year-old does. Just as I'm about to break the ice, a team of men in white suits enter the dining hall and set a plate of food in front of each of us. Christian follows them with the nervous energy of a Pomeranian.

"Ladies and gentleman, your appetizer is served. Fried Brunost with Cloudberries and Parsley." And, just as quickly as they entered, they return to the kitchen. We eat in silence. Several minutes pass and I swear I can hear every bite Reese takes of his food. Every clanking sound of his fork against the china sounds frustrated and accosting.

"When are we going to meet the steward?" Reese finally speaks up having finished his food well before anyone else. He makes a production of letting his fork fall to the plate with a clatter.

"I understand he will be along sometime this evening," the professor says. "Our arrival was unexpected for the staff. They typically take reservations months in advance."

"Is he going to be able to tell us where Slakter is?" There's a brazenness in Reese's question. Luckily, no one from the staff is in the room with us…at the moment.

"I don't know that he can tell us who Slakter is, much less tell us where he is."

"Then why are we here?" Reese asks. "Aren't we just wasting time?"

Just then, the two members of the staff enter with a rolling cart. Christian follows behind them with a smile.

"Dinner is served! Ja!"

Our appetizers are taken and a large plate of grilled tørrfisk is set before each of us. When the staff has left, the professor takes a measured tone with Reese.

"Why do you think we are wasting time, Reese?"

"Well, where's the steward?" He wipes his hands with the cloth napkin and tosses it on the table. "And why are we waiting on him if he's not going to have answers? And, why are we in this, this castle? How much is this costing you? Does Mother Moon know where we are?"

"Whoa," I say. "Reese, take a breath." Then, Gerald decides to speak up.

"We're here because you're trying to find a bloody rock."

"Hey, if you don't mind, I'm talking to your boss, not you."

"Reese!"

Just then the woman in the white pant suit enters the dining hall again. She walks the length of the table to Professor Irons. Past her smile I can see her eyes darting back and forth between us. Everyone is very quiet. She whispers something in the professor's ear and leaves us. Just before she exits, she gives another big smile.

"Mr. Bakken is here and will join us momentarily," the professor says.

"Mom, what is this?" Hollis pokes at his food.

"It's fish, Baby. Don't play with it."

"Reese you have been very direct with me," the professor says, "until now. Why do you seem to circle the point you are clearly anxious to get at?"

"I just want to know what the plan is?" Reese stands. Gerald stands in response but Professor Irons places a hand on his arm, letting him know to sit back down. "I'm here to find my father's killer. And, yeah, I'm here to find a bloody rock. So why are we wasting time with dinner and bottles of wine?"

"Reese, you are the reason we are here. More specifically, your grandfather's memories are the only link we have to

Slakter and discovering his agenda. You're the lead in this dance."

"I'm the lead? Then why didn't you tell me that you were in the mental hospital?" Her face settles into a disappointed clarity. Gerald crosses his arms and huffs. He knew. "I found your file in that records room," Reese says. "Why didn't you tell us?"

"Were you… committed in that hospital… as a child, Professor?" I ask. But, I'm afraid to speak too loud as if the secret might echo outside of these stone walls.

"That right there," she says gazing directly at Reese. "That look on your face is the reason I didn't tell you. That's the same look given to poor souls who say they've seen a ghost, or a demon. Or a troll. I'm sure it's the same look pretty El-linor received from the orderlies every day at that psychiatric hospital. Where do you think they would put you if you were to tell the world you'd seen trolls? Go on. Tell them you're a berserker too. They will take away your son. Emma and Hollis will be allowed to visit you once a month under state supervision. It's just the way of things in this world." Hollis is at my elbow having left his chair. He hugs my waist.

"I don't want them to take me away, Momma." I pick him up and hold him.

"Oh, Baby. No one is going to take you from us." I look over at Reese. He is still. He looks at Hollis then back at the professor.

"There's much more at play in this story than you under-stand," she says. "And, much more than I understand. Where Mother Moon found me almost 40 years ago is the least of your worries, Reese."

"Am I interrupting?" A tall bearded man dressed in a

three-piece suit stands in the large doorway leading to the dinning hall. "I'm Lars Bakken, the steward here at Stenholmen."

Chapter 30

Reese Little

We stumble over introductions with our host. He's gracious and doesn't mention the argument between me and the professor that he obviously overheard. He's refined and older, close to 70, with thinning hair and beard that was once red but has turned a pale blonde with age. He apologizes for being late; something about a band or an orchestra rehearsing in the great hall for a concert tomorrow night. He seems like the kind of man who is made of manners—like the kind of man who would rise from his chair whenever a woman entered the room. At the same time, he speaks to Professor Irons like a respected colleague, an equal, rather than the "fairer sex."

He takes a seat and we have dinner while he entertains us with stories of the history of Stenholmen. It was initially built to withstand the Danes from the south who tried several times to over-take the fortress from the sea. He doesn't hesitate to share some of the bloody and bawdy details.

I glance at Hollis hoping that it all just goes over his head. It does not.

He looks at me wide-eyed when Mr. Bakken shares a

particular story of a previous nobleman and his seven mistresses. *One for each day of the week.*

"I must ask you Professor Irons, have we met before?" He looks at the professor over his glass of wine, eyes twinkling. For a moment, I wonder if he's attempting to flirt. I look over at Emma. She raises and eyebrow right back at me.

"I don't believe we have, Mr. Bakken. Why do you ask?"

"Please, call me Lars. You know, I'm not sure why I ask. As steward, the state has allowed me the opportunity to meet and work with a diverse range of historians. Maybe in our work we've crossed paths, as they say."

"Speaking of crossed paths," the professor leaves her chair taking her glass of wine and approaches the fire place. "This is a beautiful piece," she says pointing to a shimmering cross just over two feet in height sitting on the mantle. "I don't recognize it. And, in my line of work, that's saying something."

Out of the corner of my eye, I see Emma. She's making a hard face at me, raising her hand to her temple to hide it from the steward. I glance at Gerald and he's giving me a knowing look. What's going on? I look back at Emma and, without turning, she tips her head back toward the professor. Then, I figure it out. The cross! It's the one Professor Irons described that had been stolen from that stave church over a century ago.

"Ah. Christian artifacts are not my specialty," says Bakken. "But, you certainly have an eye for beauty. Notice the rough-set jewels on that cross." His eyes wander over the table as he traces his finger over the rim of an empty wine glass. "I so enjoy seeing the 'fingerprints' of the craft—when you can see where the artisan attempted to set the ruby into the metal work—but it didn't set the first time. Not properly. He'd made a mistake. So, he had to set it again."

"You have quite an appreciation for this piece," the professor says.

"Oh, I'm attached to the history of this place and everything in it." He rises from his chair and tugs at his vest as if straightening his appearance just before a speech. "Stenholmen is a bastion of the old ways; the old history of Norway, of all Scandinavia."

"Would you know the history behind this piece?"

"How do you mean?"

"Crossed paths—how did it get here?" Professor Irons plucks the cross from the mantle, carefully weighing it in her hands. "It's Christian. And, looking at the metal work, it was made before Christianity was introduced to Norway. So, Stenholmen could not have been its first owner. Tell me, am I spot on?"

Bakken is quiet for a moment. He's reading between the lines of the professor's question but he doesn't lose the twinkle in his eye. Waiting for his reply, I realize that Emma, Gerald, and I must look like spectators watching a verbal tennis match between these two.

"I believe it was a gift," Bakken says with a wide smile. "A previous steward received it—actually, four stewards before me—and I can't recall who gave it to him. It may have been a priest wanting to bring the Christian god's favor upon Stenholmen."

"Ah." A silence follows that lasts only five seconds but feels like five minutes. Then, Mr. Bakken gives the professor another relaxed grin.

"Are you sure we haven't met before?" he asks. She answers

only with a smile right back at him. Then, he smacks his hands together in a jolting clap and raises a finger in the air. "I've got an idea! Why don't we all take a walk to the great hall—just on the other side of the manor—the concert is rehearsing tonight!"

We all stand, ready to stretch our legs. Hollis leaps out of his chair clearly bored from all the talking. As we make our way down the hall, passing a glass case with a mannequin dressed in full Norwegian military garb from the 1700s, Steward Bakken excuses himself to use the restroom. Before we all split up and do the same, Professor Irons leans in with a whispered voice.

"Dearies, he's not going to give me anything. He clearly knows where that cross came from but didn't want to discuss it. He's not going to give us information on your grandfather, even if he knows something."

"So, what do we do then?" I ask. "I'm not going to let this be a bust."

"Depends on how bold you want to be? Do you feel like snooping around a castle tonight?" Emma and I look at each other and back at the professor.

"What?" we both ask in a hoarse whisper. I hear the water turn on over the sink in the restroom – he's washing his hands.

"You two need to break away from us. Act like Hollis is sick or you need to get him to bed. Then, sneak through this place and find documents, books, ledgers; anything that might show a record of your grandfather's activity here."

"How am I supposed to know where to find that stuff?" I throw my hands in the air just because I can't shout. Professor Irons leans in and taps her temple.

"You're the one with your grandfather's memories, my dear."

"And, if you get caught snooping around—it's easy-peasey, brov," Gerald says. "You're Americans. Just act like dumb tourists and got lost on the way back to your room."

"And, by the way," the professor says as Bakken opens the door of the restroom. "If you want to continue a certain conversation about a certain hospital later, just ask." I open my mouth to apologize but the professor turns and smiles at the steward and… I'm awkward. I stiffen my shoulders and feel every bit of Emma's eyes staring into the side of my head.

We walk through corridors lit by chandeliers as the steward leads us to the great hall which I can only assume will be even bigger than the dining hall we were just in. As we get closer, we hear music—strings and drums. It's not a classical orchestra. It sounds more like… Viking music. There's a somber strength in it. The drums hold a constant beat that make me think of a long ship moving inland on shallow waterways, oars rowing in time. Then, I see them—oars rowing —and I feel the ship moving under me and the wind against my back. I wince and reach for my head.

"You okay, babe?" Emma whispers.

"Memories… are coming back." And, they come back with force. I can see the shore and Stenholmen fortress looming like a hill carved out of rock. Then there's the man whose face I can't see. He leads Grandpa Karl into the manor. The chandeliers are gone; everything is lit by torchlight. I shake my head trying toss off the rush to my senses. Professor Irons notices I'm not keeping up with the group.

"Reese, are you not feeling well?" She nods to Emma.

"You know what," Emma says, "he hasn't felt well all day. Let's get you back to the room."

I don't need to do very much acting to convince Bakken.

He seems genuinely concerned and disappointed that Emma and Hollis and I won't see the rehearsal. Professor Irons and Gerald stay with him and continue on toward the Viking drums.

"How are you feeling—for real?" Emma hoists Hollis on to her hip and we walk back toward the room.

"Not good. For real. Like I'm staring into a strobe light of images. And, I can feel it too... the waves."

"Yeah? Are you feeling bad enough that you might need to apologize?" Here it goes.

"Yes. I need to apologize to her. I'll do that as soon as Mr. Bakken's away…"

"No. To me, Reese."

"Yes, I need to apologize to you too.

"Do you understand why?"

"Uh… let's turn this way." I point down a thin hallway that has no windows. Emma stops, stares down the small arched corridor and looks back at me.

"Why?" She raises an eyebrow at me. I tap my temple.

"It looks familiar."

"Are you trying to avoid this conversation, Reese?" I turn and walk briskly down the hallway.

"Not at all." The corridor narrows the further we go —and gets darker—no torches or chandeliers to light the way.

"Daddy, where we going?" We come to the end of the hall-way and find a spiral staircase circling upward. I glance up the stairway but I can't see anything but a faint warm light against the stones.

"Reese, do you understand why I'm mad?"

"Yes, yes. We need to go up here." I climb the stairs and Emma follows after me with Hollis. The landing opens up to a bare room with two small square windows deep set into the stone. Opposite the windows, a tapestry hangs across the wall. It depicts Viking long boats entering a bay. A naked bulb hangs crudely wired along the bare beams of the ceiling. No chairs or tables furnish this room. "Well, I think we're off the beaten path up here."

"Daddy, where are we?"

"I don't know, Hollis." I don't mask my frustration. "I'm just… I'm following what I see." I walk toward the tapestry. Something is familiar about it and I can't help but reach out and touch the fabric. My hands trace the weave.

"Why didn't you tell me, Reese?"

"Emma, please." I can feel my brain flickering trying to make the connection. A certain memory, just a hint of something, is hidden from my mind.

"No. Talk to me." I whip around feeling my blood pounding.

"Dammit. Do you want us to get caught?"

"I don't care." Her eyes are wide, angry and pleading at the same time. "Talk to me. You let your wife and child walk around for two days with a woman who was raised in a mental facility." She pulls it back to a whisper but steps closer to me, refusing to back down. "And, then you let the cat outta the bag while we're all sitting at dinner. What the hell was that?"

"I'm just trying to make the best decisions possible. For us. Maybe I'm not very good at it but it's the best I can do." I throw my hands in the air turning away from her. "I didn't tell you because, I didn't know what it meant. I barely know what any of this means," I say staring into the ceiling. I close my eyes, feeling my blood continue to pound, and I take a deep breath. "I don't want to scare you with information I don't have." She sets Hollis down and moves toward me.

"You didn't tell me because you want to do it all yourself. You *want* to be in control."

"*Yes.* Yes, I *want* to be in control. I want to take care of you. I want to take care of Hollis. But, now we're all in the middle of Norway snooping around a castle with no clue what I'm looking for. Why couldn't you just let me take care of this?"

"You *are* taking care of this." She lays her hands on my shirt, grabbing and pulling herself to my chest. "But, that doesn't mean I sit at home just waiting. Whatever this is, it's my burden too. We're married, babe. That means we share everything—good and bad." I drop my gaze and lean into her. She hugs my neck and I hold her to me. I feel the rise and fall of her breathing.

"I'm sorry." I raise my eyes to hers, those golden-hazel pools staring back at me.

"Are you going to start kissing?" Hollis does not hide his disgust.

"We just might, baby," Emma answers with a grin. I turn back to the Viking scene on the wall and rub a hand over the back of my neck.

"I'm stuck," I say. "I don't know what to do from here." Emma leans against me and raises hand to the tapestry, gliding her fingertips across it.

"What would your grandfather do?" What would he do? Whatever brought me up here is fading from my mind like waking from a dream at 4 am. I look over the tapestry, left to right and top to bottom. The raiders in the ships all face the same direction. The boats are all moving east to west. Is it a clue?

"What would a troll do?" Hollis speaks up from behind us. I turn and he's sitting on the floor, elbows propped on his knees, hands holding his face. "Play *Smell the Blood.*"

"Do what?" I ask. He points to the tapestry.

"Play *Smell the Blood*. A troll would hide, right there." I look at the tapestry again taking a step back.

"What do you mean, baby?" Emma says. "Hide where."

"Right here," I say grabbing the tapestry in both fists and jerking it to the ground. Behind it is a thin passage way leading to a dark interior room. I peer in and feel the air around me being pulled into the dark hall. Hollis shoves past my knee and climbs into the passage way.

"Told ya. Let's go."

The room on the other end is furnished with a small writing desk and a simple wooden chair and a floor lamp. When Emma turns on the lamp we see the book shelves on either side of the desk filled with leather bound ledgers covered in dust. Our shadows loom large across the stacks of ledgers. I pull one off the shelf. At the touch of leather to skin, a face flashes across my mind—the man whose face I can't see. But this time, beyond the blur of pink flesh tones that I can see, there's a hint of a smile.

"Yeah. We're in the right place," I whisper. I fan through the browning pages. It's mostly Norwegian—and I can read it! Each page is a list of hand written dates, names, and payments.

"What are we looking at, Reese?" Emma picks up a ledger, blows the dust away, and fans through a few pages. I take another look at the pages in my ledger and see dates for the year 1759, 1760, and 1761. I close the ledger and look for another. At the very bottom a shelf, I find it. A ledger with the years 1860–1890 written on the spine.

"He's gotta be in here." I look up at Emma. "Grandpa Karl's in here somewhere." I flip open the ledger and fan through the pages. I get closer to the 1890s when we hear a noise.

Voices. Coming closer. Emma grabs Hollis and gives him the signal to stay quiet. I turn off the lamp, crouch down and peer through the passageway. A faint amber light moves against the curved wall leading down the stairway. It gets brighter and the voices are closer. A man and woman emerge, both wearing the white uniform of the Stenholmen staff. They whisper to each other. He puts his hands on her hips and pulls the woman to him. She does not seem to mind. They kiss. Then, they tug at each other's clothes—unbuckling belts and unzipping zippers. The man almost drops the gas lantern before he quickly sets it to the floor. That's when she turns and sees the tapestry. She gives a shocked gasp and, for a moment, they both look at the room wondering what happened. But, worried that his chances are diminishing, the man quickly turns her attention back to the matter at hand. And, without much effort, they both forget about the tapestry lying in a heap in the floor and they make love on the stone stairway by the light of an oil lamp. I look at Emma and Emma looks at me. She puts both hands firmly over Hollis' ears. I slump down against the cold stone wall and… just wait.

The man and woman finally leave, stumbling back down the stairs by the light of a lantern. I wait and listen. When I think they are truly gone, I stand and turn on the lamp. I pick up the ledger again and flip to the last few pages.

"Momma," Hollis whispers, "what was happening out there?"

"No questions right now, Hollis."

"Here," I say pointing to a line in the ledger. My grandfather's name appears on a line that says April, 1891 with a payment in sliver pieces. "I found him!" Emma leans in over my shoulder.

"Can I see?" Hollis reaches for the ledger. I sit down next to him and we all gather in close for story time about dear old Grandpa Karl and his thieving adventures across Europe. The record keeping is loose but consistent. Right next to the description King's Stone is the name Karl Lillevik. It has my grandfather's surname as it was before he came to the United States and changed to Little.

"This is it! This is it! The King's Stone. This is what he took and brought to the steward over a hundred years ago." For a moment the atmosphere is climactic. Emma gasps and hugs my neck.

"So, where is it?" She asks.

"Um, I don't know. I mean, it has to be here. Right? This looks like a record of the old steward's, um, acquisitions, for lack of a better term."

"Wait. Reese, look." Emma points at a line toward the bottom of the page. "His name is right there too." And, so it is – right next to an entry for the Green Amulet of Margaret I. Below that his name is next to an entry for the Egg of Eric II. I turn the page and my heart sinks. The next three pages are entries filled with the name Karl Lillevik. Sometimes his name is listed alone and sometimes there are other names next to it. I trace my finger down the page to the last entry with his name—the Stone of Remembrance. Every one of them are payments for emeralds, diamonds, and ornate jewels —all stones.

"They're all jewels," I say. "Stones that he obtained for the steward here during the 1890s." I lower the ledger and look at Emma. "Slakter could be after any one of these." She stares back at me, waiting for me to say more. But, there's nothing more to say—we still don't know what he's after.

"No. Wait, Reese," she takes the ledger from me, "this is small—it's a bread crumb. But, it's progress. Now, we know your grandfather was working for the steward here over a century ago." She holds the book to her chest and reaches for my hand. "The professor needs to see this. Let's get outta here."

We decide to head back to our room and meet with Professor Irons whenever she returned to hers. We walk the narrow passage out of the room and then Emma helps me re-hang the tapestry. I listen at the stairway for a full minute deciding that I can't hear anyone on the lower level coming nearby. When it's safe we make our way down the stairs; I carry the ledger with me. Emma whispers something to Hollis about us using our ninja skills to sneak quietly.

We turn the corner and find ourselves in a long hall, passing the row of herald flags and decorative shields. Then we come to the end of the hall only to find that it splits between two stone arches we hadn't seen before, leading to a stair case on one side and the other opening to the great hall. The musicians are just wrapping up and a two-person sound crew is making final adjustments on a small sound board.

"Uh. We didn't come this way," I say.

"Are we lost?" Emma asks.

We turn around and retrace our steps to the corridor that led to the spiral stairway and keep going. We pass the chandeliers then cross over the front foyer of the manor. And, that's when I feel it. Behind us—someone is following. I look back and see the profile of a man walking toward us. We turn and pass the dining hall and find the stairway leading back to the upper floor with our rooms. I hear the faint footsteps on stone coming up behind us. I keep the ledger tucked in front of me. I look back and see the man is gaining ground on us.

"Move quickly," I say with a whisper. Emma glances at me. "Someone is coming." We pick up the pace and Emma grabs Hollis, carrying him. We climb the stairs and, as we reach the rose-carpeted second floor, I hear the creak of the wood staircase behind us announcing that we are indeed being followed. We round the corner to our hall and nearly collide face-to-face with Gerald and Professor Irons.

"Oh!"

"Bloody hell!"

"So sorry. But you gave us a fright," says the professor. With my adrenaline still pumping and the stranger approaching, I quickly whisper to her.

"We stole a ledger that shows my grandfather was involved with the previous steward—lots of stones—someone is following us. Quick, take the ledger." She looks at the book, then back over my shoulder.

"There's no one following you two." She's matter of fact. I turn and look, holding the ledger just behind me in case she's wrong. Emma peaks around the corner too. There's nothing to see but the airy second floor landing. Over the banister is a view of the first-floor hallway below. The dark wood staircase is silent—no creaking boards, no footsteps following us.

"We played Hide and Seek." Hollis says. He points to the ledger behind my back. "Show her, Daddy."

I'm not entirely convinced the coast is clear. But, if I'm to believe my eyes… I decide to hand the ledger to her. Emma explains what we found; tapestry, a secret passage, and hundreds of ledgers just like this one, all collecting dust. We walk back to the professor's room across the hall from our own.

"This is clearly a record of 'services rendered' at Stenholmen, most likely for the steward." She turns the pages, one at a time, with care. "And, you said there were hundreds of these?"

"I mean, we didn't count them,' I say, "but that's because there were too many to count. And, they're all shoved into that tiny room that they don't want people to find."

"Judging by the dust," Emma says, "I don't think anyone has been in there in a few years."

Professor Irons opens her room to us and we pass the ledger around as we make our selves comfortable. Gerald takes pictures of it using his cell phone. I look through it again, finding my grandpa's name. I go through each entry, searching for another clue that might give us the answer to this riddle. Hollis, curls up on the professor's bed and, as if signaling the futility of the search, falls asleep.

"They're all stones," the professor says with a quiet disappointment.

"Yeah. Do you recognize any of them?" I ask.

"Some. Most of those jewels are in museums now. So, I doubt Slakter is after those."

"This name," I say pointing to a column next to my father's name. "*Alsunndr*. What is that? It's repeated in each of his entries in the ledger?"

"Ah. You're getting better at this detective work.

"Alsunndr. Is it a place? A town?"

"It's a small village on the western coast, in fjord country. Alsunndr was and still is a community whose lively hood is based on fishing. The modern world has hardly touched them even in the 21st century." My mind suddenly recalled the shores of the village I saw in the memory transfer; I could smell the mix of snow and ocean brine on the air.

"But, why is it in the ledger every time Karl did a job?" Emma asks. Gerald scratches his chin and speaks up.

"See, you don't always show up face-to-face to get paid for a job like that. This is hush-hush stuff. The steward has these bad-ass blokes, like your grandfather, gallivanting around the world, jumping in an out of battles, wars, skirmishes and stealing loot, relics, booty." Gerald sounds like he knows about this stuff from personal experience. "Well, he can't have berserkers and the like hanging around the fortress waiting to get their coin. It's not a good look—even in the 1890s."

"So, my grandfather had his payments sent to Alsunndr? And, you're telling me it's some fishing village?"

"Well, that means we found our next lead," Emma says, "doesn't it?" Gerald looks to the professor.

"Follow the money, know what I mean." He leans back in his chair. "I'll sort out the helicopter at dawn." Professor Irons nods and smiles.

"Do you see what we've been able to ascertain in under three days, Reese? There is hope. You will not be without answers." My face grows warm. She's right. For the first time since we stepped off the plane, I feel like my wild goose chase of an idea that started around the council table in The Mine is actually leading somewhere. That warm feeling is also seasoned with humility.

"Uh, professor, I need to apologize… for calling you out like I did during dinner. I'm sorry." She smiles at me and there's a softness in her eyes I hadn't expected.

"Apology accepted." She stands and arches her back. "Now, if everyone would please get out of my room. I need some rest." I scoop up Hollis, resting him against my shoulder, and move to the door. Emma takes my hand and gives it a squeeze. The professor walks to the door and opens it revealing Steward Bakken standing there, hand raised, about to knock.

"Oh! Good evening," he smiles awkwardly, eyes bouncing between all of us. "I'm sorry to come by so late. But, I'm headed to Oslo in the morning. Before I go, I wanted to give you this." He hands Professor Irons a hardcover book, a slick gray dust jacket with his name printed on the spine in bold white letters.

"Call it ego, but I thought you might enjoy it. It's simply a collection of Norse legends I've translated and edited." The professor takes the book and I catch Bakken stroking his beard and staring just a bit too long at her face, awaiting her response.

"Of course! I think I read your version of the Dwarves and the creation of Odin's spear printed in Scandinavian Scholarly." She takes the book with a smile and thanks him. He turns to me.

"Reese, I do hope you're feeling better."

"Oh, yes. It passed. Thank you." I give a nod and he smiles and says good bye. The professor smiles again as he leaves. When, we are sure he is significantly out of ear shot, we cannot refrain from goading the professor.

"That's enough," she says but her eyes disappear behind a smile that betrays her feelings. For all her academic knowledge and cunning she is, after all, human. She opens the book and finds that the inside cover page is signed by the steward. We give another chorus of *oohs* that sends her eyes rolling. She reads the message aloud.

To Professor Agatha Irons—Do not heed knowledge found in towers or in dusty tomes. Answers lie within yourself. You need look no further. Yours, Lars.

We go silent. I look at Emma and we share the same squinty-eyed expression.

"What's that all about?" Gerald asks. Emma asks the same question that's running through my mind.

"Do you think that he overheard us talking?"

"Overheard?" I mumble. "Emma. *Dusty tomes in towers*. He knows we snuck around and found the ledgers." Professor Irons closes the book.

"It means nothing." Her gaze is steely-eyed. "It's either a poorly phrased remark or it is a cryptic acknowledgment of our true purpose here. Either way, he's content to let us be. But more importantly, I need sleep. We all need sleep." We each say good night, and make our way to our own rooms. With Hollis between us, Emma and I lay our heads down. We stare at each other through the night silently asking the questions we can't answer, like, do the wrong people know that we are in Norway? Why was Professor Irons left in a mental hospital as a child? Can we trust the steward here? And, how much does he know about what his predecessors were involved in?

When sleep does come, I dream of the face I can't see. I dream of the fishing village. And, I dream of hollow black orbs, Slakter's eyes, staring into mine.

Chapter 31

Emma Little

I wake to the sound of laughter. I hear Hollis giggling and my eyes open to bare wood beams in the ceiling above me, dark stone walls around me, and my husband next to me. I sit up just in time to see Hollis come bounding into our room from the hallway. He's still wearing the clothes he fell asleep in last night. The professor follows him in.

"No, Dearie. Shh." She takes him by the hand, trying to lead him back outside before she realizes I'm awake. "Oh. So sorry to wake you." She's different this morning. Her eyes are brighter, her collar isn't yet buttoned all the way up to her neck like usual. She seems… relaxed. Hollis races out the door back to the hallway where Gerald finds him. Hollis quickly raises finger guns and shoots him.

"Pow, pow, pow!" Hollis shouts and Gerald roars, collapsing in the hall.

"Gerald," the professor says over her shoulder, "do you mind keeping it down."

"Yes, mum. Sorry." He grins and gives a wave to me before ushering Hollis down the hall, telling him not to giggle so loud. "You're disturbing the peace, mate."

"Sorry," I say wiping the sleep from my eyes. "I didn't realize Hollis was up." Reese rolls over and sits up, realizing that we are not alone.

"Oh, it's nothing," the professor says. "Hollis is fun." She glances out the door at Hollis. "It's hard to remember when mine were that little."

"You have children?"

"I have three. They've all grown and… gone off their own ways now." The corners of her mouth turn down and she changes the subject. She tells us that the helicopter is ready for a trip north—but, no rush. She assures me that she is keeping an eye on Hollis. And Gerald. And, breakfast is on its way to our room.

"It should be another 20-30 minutes before it arrives, though." She grins. "You'll just have to find something to do while you wait." She leaves us with a glint in her eye and quietly closes our door. Reese looks at me, head cocked with confusion. I toss the covers back and walk to the door feeling the cold stone on my bare feet. I lean against the door and slide the latch, locking it with a dull click.

The room is quiet—a quiet neither of us have heard in weeks. My eyes trace the shape of his shoulders through his t-shirt. Reese catches me staring at him and he stares right back. I take a step toward him, my skin cool in the castle air. With a rush, he takes me in his arms and his mouth is on mine. Sweet, deep kisses. I feel his hands holding me against him. He holds the back of my head, reaching into my hair and tugging to bring my head back, exposing my neck. He finds the flesh just under my jaw and I can feel his mouth against my skin, his beard feels new and different. A flurry of kisses and rough hands follow.

"Wait." My breath is staggered. "I want you to hold me." Reese looks confused—like a puppy.

"Hold you?"

"Just… I need…" I'm not sure how to explain it. "Too much. I just need you to hold me."

I see the recognition in his eyes. He takes my hand and gently pulls me to him. We wrap our arms around each other and just breathe. The smell of his body is earthy and sweet. Minutes pass—quiet minutes—and the knot in my back loosens. And, then we are kissing. He is smiling, I can feel it in his kisses. Firm hands grab my hips and pull me closer to him. I kiss him a little deeper and pull my shirt up and off. A flurry of clothes fall to the cold floor and we dive under the bed covers, wrapping arms and legs around each other.

I feel his skin warm against mine—the man who I have been aching for. We've been running and hiding for weeks and I've forgotten how much I've needed my husband. I can tell he's been needing me too. He is so familiar; the way he touches me, the way he moves. His hands are so strong. My heart beats faster when he holds my face in his hands.

"What are you thinking?" I ask, my breathing staggered.

"Well," he says, "didn't you tell me you've always wanted to do it in a castle?" I laugh like it's been too long since the last time I laughed.

"I don't think I've said that, exactly." My fingers comb through his hair. "I love you, Reese. I need you. I need you with me."

"I love you. I'm with you, Babe. Always." He kisses me deeply and takes me.

The helicopter rises, just skimming over the mountain

and pulling snow into the air. Below us, a range of white mountains are displayed. The valleys are filled with deep blue ocean water that is deceptively calm. Professor Irons calls over the head set, getting our attention, and points to a speck in the distance.

"There. Alsunndr is just there." She points to a peninsula protruding into the fjord from a steep mountain. As, the helicopter gets closer, we begin to see the small colorful houses, the pattern of thin dirt streets, and boats of all shapes and sizes docked at the water's edge. Gerald finds a wide patch of green just outside the village center to set us down. When we land, Professor Irons reminds us that there is no cell service here, no one is waiting to greet us, and we are outsiders. "There is no amount of trickery that I can offer to assuage their natural suspicion of us. So, remember to follow my lead at all times… and smile. And, bring your weapons."

"Uh, Professor did you say…"

"Yes, I did."

After, Reese helps me set my holsters, he throws on his axe carrier. With one motion he raises his dad's axe over his head, turns it head down and drops it in place between his shoulder blades. The iron head rests in the leather pouch against the base of his spine.

"Daddy, is that Papa's axe?" Reese turns and takes a breath before answering our boy.

"Yes, it is, Hollis. And, it was his dad's before that."

"Is it yours now?"

"Yes. Yes, it is."

We throw our coats on as quickly as we can. The wind off the ocean is bouncing between the mountains, following the fjords inland, and creating an icy chill that is unforgiving.

Hollis is wrapped in multiple layers and a name-brand parka provided by the professor. I pull his knit cap down over his ears. Reese and I both throw on a set of gloves and pull the hoods up on our jackets.

We walk into the village following Professor Irons as she takes point. Her fur-lined cloak moves like a living thing, breathing the coastal wind and folding itself around her. Gerald brings up the rear. I look back and notice him constantly glancing left and right. I hold Hollis on my hip as we walk up the rise toward the village. Except for the occasional gust of wind, it's quiet.

"We don't have much time," the professor says. "The sun sets around 3 pm up here. In a remote area like this, trolls are sure to be present. After dark, we are strangers in their home."

"Can't we just tell them that Mother Moon sent us?" Reese asks.

"We can. But, I'm not sure that they know or care who Mother Moon is." She continues toward the row of short log cabins with grass-covered roofs. Over the rise, I see a mix of architectures. Log cabins sit next to wood panel houses painted a bright red or yellow. These houses are much newer. By *newer* I mean they were possibly built 50 years ago.

"I remember this place," Reese whispers to me. "I can see her."

"Who?"

"I think she's Grandpa Karl's mom." He blinks rapidly trying to clear his head. "I can see her scar. On her face."

We make our way into the village walking past the first street and crossing the wood fence meant to contain some kind of livestock. But, there's no livestock. There's nobody here.

"Awfully quiet," Reese says.

"I don't mean to sound like a cliché," I say, "but, it's a little too quiet." Just then a dog begins barking at us. It's a Shepherd of some kind, hiding between two log cabins. He barks while pacing nervously, neither approaching nor backing away from us. Professor Irons readies her cane. When no one emerges from the houses to see what the barking is about, we continue into the village. Just as we pass the stone water well, I see it. Faint smoke is fanned by gusts of wind. It's coming from a burned cabin that is still smoldering. We move deeper into the village and see two more cabins charred, burned to the ground, the smoke and fire are long gone.

"How the hell did that get up here?" Gerald points to small fishing yacht, overturned, crushed and laying in the mud in the middle of the village 200 yards from the shore. Under the overturned hull, I see a pair of legs, unmoving, and lifeless. I cover Hollis' eyes and turn back.

"We need to leave here. We need to leave now." Then I see another body slumped face-down over the post of a wooden fence. A man. He still holds a rifle in his hand. The fence post protrudes through the back of his wool coat.

"Professor?" Reese says. "What's going on here?" He peals his coat off and pulls his axe free. Gerald unzips his jacket and pulls a pistol. I move quickly toward the fence, leaving the village, but holding Hollis and swinging three pounds of steel on each hip slows me down.

"Hang on, love," Gerald calls out. "We gotta walk out together. Stay with the group." Footsteps race behind me.

"Emma, slow down." It's the professor. She's not even winded when she catches up to me. "We need to determine what happened here."

"No. We don't." I do not slow down and I do not look back.

"You know this is Slakter's work. And, this is why we are here." She reaches for my arm, trying to slow me down. When she does, I feel her weight fall against me a moment. I turn back in time to see her collapse in the mud and snow.

"Agatha?" I stop and reach for her, setting Hollis down. "Professor, are you okay?" She looks at me but doesn't respond. Gerald races to us and begins tugging at her collar.

"Professor, breathe deep, now. Can you hear me? Can you hear me?"

Just then a thunderous concussion shakes the ground. A troll with long claws and fur trailing over its back pounces, nearly landing on top of Reese. He springs back, swinging his axe defensively. I see the veins swell in Reese's arms and across his face. He leaps at the troll and they collide like furious wild animals. Gerald spins and levels his pistol. I hold the professor in one arm and grab Hollis with the other. Reese and the troll are so fast, unbelievably fast, and vicious. Gerald can't make a clear shot and that's when the men tackle him to the ground. Three men, one carrying a whaling harpoon, knock him to the ground. They climb on him. One pins his legs, while another wrestles his gun away. They slug him in the face. I leave the professor and shield Hollis behind me. I throw my coat open and pull my Schofield, aiming it at the troll. Reese lunges and swings at the monster over and over. Then one of the men turns away from Gerald and moves toward me, raising the harpoon. I turn the gun on him. He stops. My hand shakes. I turn to the troll again and pull the hammer back on my revolver. I swing the gun back to the man. The other two have joined him. I steady my hand. I exhale. I squeeze.

A blast of purple fire hits the wet grass at the troll's feet. The troll stops. Reese stops. The men stare. I turn and Professor Irons has rolled to her side, cane in the air.

"*Stoppe.* Vær så snill. Stoppe."

Hollis peaks from behind my leg. The men see him. One gasps and says something, pointing at Hollis. All three share a look of confusion, glancing back at Reese, Gerald, and me. The big one lowers the harpoon and says something in Norwegian. I don't understand it but the look on his face and the tone of his voice is universal. *Who are you?*

Chapter 32

Reese Little

They take all of our weapons, except Emma's guns. The professor makes a request, something about the mother being allowed to protect her child. Three more trolls emerge from the cliffs buttressing the mountain wall. They surround us. The men exchange a few words with them. These trolls are clad in leather and furs from ankle to wrist and pull wool hoods over their heads against the light of the sun and snow. The largest of the trolls nods, then gives an ear-piercing whistle. At that sound, several older men and women emerge from their homes.

We don't get to watch long before the trolls give us the order that it's time to follow them. As we march toward the cliffs, I look back and see the people looking on the devastation in their village. One man helps another pull a lifeless body out from under an overturned yacht. Another woman pulls her shawl tight around her shoulders and stares silently at a cabin that has burned and collapsed.

We follow the cliffs and the trolls force themselves between us as the path narrows along the fjord. The particular troll that attacked us marches behind me. He lumbers like a bear and always stays close enough so I can hear his heavy breathing and smell his wet fur.

Without a word, we march along the wall of the cliffs until we reach a waterfall mid-freeze. The water seems to simply emerge from an unseen icy fissure in the middle of the cliff wall, pouring 50 feet down over us. Behind that waterfall, hidden from the world, a dark cavern waits for us.

We step inside and my eyes adjust to the dark. I find my footing. We are descending with each step. I try to glance ahead, looking for Hollis and Emma, but I can't see past the bulk of the stone-gray troll in front of me. But, that's when I notice the shafts of light from directly overhead. The cave walls climb straight up on each side to thin openings at the ceiling. I can't tell if the openings are 30 feet overhead or 100 feet.

The cold white beams of light hit rising stalagmites that are as large as columns you might find upholding Roman ruins. When I get a better look, I realize they *are* columns—not stalagmites at all. The floor is carved with lines and symbols under our feet. I see runes and I see knots. One symbol that shows up again and again is a swirling horseshoe shape. The symbols spread across the floor as the narrow cavern widens, step by step, to reveal the cliff within the cave that we are all marching across. I'm thankful that I'm not close enough to the edge to look down and see how far the chasm really goes.

Then, the trolls stop and fan out, leaving us standing in the center of a stone plateau. Emma catches my eye; she's holding Hollis. I see Gerald holding his jaw. Even under the faint light in this cavern, I can see the trail of blood from his mouth and the mark over his eye that will leave a dark bruise for weeks to come. Several more trolls emerge quietly from the dark—tall and scrawny, pale and carrying war hammers larger than any man.

Then, a guttural voice fills up the cavern, like toads croaking through a lead pipe. I don't see him at first but he's sitting right in front of us, completely still, like a natural fixture in the cavern wall. He has a wide body covered only by a cloak that was a red color ages ago but time has faded it to a dull brown and worn the edges down to bits of string. He reclines on a stone throne, naked except for his cloak tied at the shoulders, looking like some crazed emperor. The troll speaks again, addressing us, and the professor quickly interprets.

"Who sent you here?" The professor quickly responds. The troll shifts in his throne, taking a laborious breath and leans into a shaft of light that illuminates his face. His skin appears calcified, scaly, and his eyes… are gone. Deep pits, pink against chalk white flesh, remain where his eyes should be. He utters another question.

"Who attacked us?" The professor says, translating. She looks back at me and Emma. She replies giving a long explanation. The king troll listens and comes back with more questions. For several minutes they go back and forth. I can only pick up bits and pieces of Norwegian. The rest of it is—something else. Professor Irons mentions Munnin. And, she mentions Slakter. At his name, the king troll lowers his head, taking another laborious breath.

He raises a scaly hand to one of his spear-bearers and grunts. This sends the trolls into action and several more grunts are sounded. The expansive cavern becomes crowded with a dozen or more trolls, male and female, scaly and furry. One of them looks like a miniature version of the bear-like troll that attacked me in Alsunndr; its eyes are wide with immense fear.

"Professor?"

"What's going on?" Emma clutches Hollis to her as more and more trolls fill the space, shuffling and carrying ruff hewn clubs and iron axes.

The troll king gives an abrupt grunt and the room comes to attention. His great sagging girth rises with another breath and he launches into more croaking speech. The trolls listen. Professor Irons snakes her way between the trolls to us.

"He's telling them that we are not the same marauders that burned the village and attacked them." She leans in whispering, trying not to draw attention to us.

"Attack them?" I ask. "You mean these trolls? Why would Slakter attack the trolls too?"

"I don't know. But, the one that attacked us …Slakter took the mother of his child." The professor nods behind me. I turn and see the large hairy troll, silent and somber. With him stands the smaller version of himself, his child. "Ranka is without a mother and Willum is without a mate. They took her as collateral… to keep King Dovregubben from pursuing them."

"Who's *they*?" Gerald asks. Professor Irons hesitates to answer.

"Slakter's army. He's recruiting."

The trolls listen to their king. They sway and grunt in collective response. A low growl is given from somewhere behind me. Then, the king turns the attention back on us. He tells us the story of Slakter while the professor interprets.

For a time now, jotnar and mankind shared this land, peacefully. I had to fight for that peace and those loyal to me have been rewarded with quiet lives in these mountains. But, in years long past, this was a land of strife, fear, and blood. Slakter was a child during that time. He saw how the men hunted jotnar. He saw how they feared us. And, he understood them more than any other troll in this land. You see, before he was Slakter, his name was Oscar. He was born to a human man and woman.

Emma and I both turn to the professor in confusion. She whispers the word *changeling*. Emma covers her mouth and pity fills her eyes.

As a boy, Oscar began to change…slowly. Surely, his people believed it was an illness—that it would pass. But, when the transformation began to overtake his body, he saw that their fear and their hate turned to him. His mother tried to protect him but his father put him out. A mob pursued him like prey. He fled into the water and was thought to have drowned in the fjord. He returned to these shores years later fully a jotunn. He hid in caves and among the forests with me and mine as we plied for peace. But, though his family was human, he was not agreeable to peace with man. He neither belonged to the village of men, nor to the den of jotnar. Strife was his way. After a time, I dismissed Oscar from our number. And, I regret that to this day.

Over the years his mother grew frail. Her husband died and no man would marry her. Oscar could not care for her. The men of the village scorned her and the women abused her. He saw the scars upon her face and the hump in her back. He saw how the children taunted the "Witch of Alsunndr," the one who bore the changeling. His wrath came upon the village. But, one man was able to withstand him. That man had the strength of 10 men, he could withstand a jotunn in combat.

I realize this man with the strength of 10 men was a berserker; he was my grandfather. The vision of Slakter's face staring down on him fills my head.

This man fought Oscar in the streets, sending all the people running from the village. Then his mother appeared to him. She implored them both to temper their wrath. But, she was struck and she fell into the stone well. Oscar wailed and called to her but she was already gone and he could not reach her. The man fled and never came back. Oscar's wrath was fully laid upon Alsunndr that day. My warriors arrived and drove him out. And, he was called Slakter, the butcher, from that day on.

The king concludes his story and the cavern echoes with silence. Professor Irons steps forward and asks what happened in the village today.

Last night, he returned to Alsunndr. He brought his wrath to us again. His army moves without being seen—without warning. His army carries the weapons of man. His jotnar fight for the promise of bloodshed—and nothing more. And, they disappeared in a cloud of flies born from the mouth of Hel, herself.

"Slakter's army arrived without being detected and fled without being followed?" The professor pauses, mouth open, stumped and staring at the troll-king, not sure what to say next. "Hilmir Dovregubben, I hope you will allow us to pursue Slakter. Our presence here is an effort..."

The troll king lets out a bark so sharp and deep. Hollis clings to my leg. The troll king rejects the professor's request to continue our search. She straightens her shoulders and prepares to plead our case when I speak up with the stilted Norwegian gleaned from my grandfather's memories.

My wife and child have been threatened and my father has been killed by Slakter. King, why do you refuse a father the right to face his adversary?

Man. Your language is pitiful. Yet, I hear you well. Odin thought it worthy to sacrifice an eye for knowledge. I sacrificed both of mine years ago to bring peace. To challenge Slakter is to bring war to my shores. I did not sacrifice my eyes in vain.

But, King, your peace was *destroyed yesterday. Peace is gone and Slakter has already brought war to your shores. Together, we can challenge him. Together we can...*

He cuts me off with a snarling growl. He lunges forward and takes a lumbering step forward from his throne. Trolls move aside clearing a path for the blind king. Step by heavy step, he moves to the center of the chamber until he is standing over me, eclipsing the faint light from the crevices at the cavern's ceiling.

You say you want peace but do you intend to sit down with Slakter? Will you offer him mead and discuss the merits of mercy? I know the one who travels with you. Do you? Sorrow follows her wherever she goes. Where are her children? What has she told you of her family? I glance at Professor Irons but her face is like stone, giving nothing away. When I cannot answer, he gives a wheezing chuckle.

I bargained for peace years ago. And, it was mine. It's time to bargain, again. We have no use for money or gold. But, secrets are precious. Silence is survival. You may leave here, oh man, and you can pursue Slakter's army if you are willing to go alone. Your family and fellows must remain here... as my prisoners. You may return for them when Slakter is dead.

I hear the blood pounding in my veins. My eyes glance back and forth, looking over the faces of the trolls surrounding us, eyes hidden in black shadows. I feel Hollis' small fingers grip my leg.

"Reese." Emma's voice is slight and cautious. "What's going on? What's he saying?" The troll-king takes in a heaving breath and offers another option.

Or, call off your quest—now. Leave our land. Leave Norse land and do not pursue Slakter. Do not disturb my people again. Do we have a bargain? He glares at me, reveling the in non-choice he's left me. My voice catches in my throat. But, I calm the pounding in my skull and say what needs to be said.

Let us go… and we will leave this land. We have a bargain.

Chapter 33

Emma Little

We are silent in the helicopter as we fly east to Oslo. I reach for Reese's hand but his gaze is fixed out the window, watching the sun set over the mountains. Hollis clings to me through the night and has his buffalo zipped inside his jacket, tucked against his chest.

The next morning we leave our hotel room and schedule a flight back to the United States. Professor Irons tells Gerald to get back to Manchester and take a vacation.

"You sure, Professor?" He keeps up a ready-for-anything attitude that ignores the bruises on his face and the fact that he reaches for his ribs every time he coughs.

"Absolutely. You've earned some rest. Take care of yourself, my dear. And, be sure those photos of the Stenholmen ledger are emailed to me."

"Already done, mum." Gerald checks his gear and his gun one more time. Reese shakes his hand, claps him on the shoulder, and says goodbye. He climbs into the helicopter and we wave as he lifts off the helipad.

We walk into the city center. The buzz of people and buses feels strange – good strange, almost familiar. But, the normal buzz of the city is deceptive, like it's trying to make me forget the last four weeks of surreal insanity. A double decker bus stops in front of us as we begin to cross the street. I see a little girl and her mother inside; the mother stares at her phone but the little girl spots Hollis and waves. He waves back.

There's a Nordic history museum and the professor pays for our tickets. We quietly walk through the exhibits with statues wearing Viking era breeches and tunics. We stare numbly at glass cases displaying pewter and silver jewelry. Even Hollis has nothing to say. As, I look over a miniature village scene made of wood-carved Vikings and felt livestock, I begin to laugh. The professor, Reese, and Hollis all turn and stare.

"Is this the way it always feels?" I ask the professor. "When you've seen the things you've seen—and you look at things like this behind glass cases—is this how it feels?" A smirk crosses her face and she looks back at the village scene.

"Yes. This is how it feels." From the corner of my eye, I see the professor's shoulders rise as she breathes a deep sigh. "You both have been very gracious by not questioning me about my family." Reese and I turn, hoping she's going to tell us more. "Hilmir Dovregubben questioned the whereabouts of my children. Clearly, my reputation proceeds me—and then some." She turns back to the village scene, keeping her eyes steady on a little family of farmers behind the glass. "My children have pursued similar interests as mine—the mythic and the supernatural, even the unnatural. But, they have followed their father's path and not mine." She takes another deep breath and pulls her gloves back on and fixes her hat. "We are a house divided. But, we are still a family. I hope that is all I will need to say on the matter." She gives a perfunctory nod and suggests that we get a spot of lunch.

There's a grouping of fast-food and local restaurants in the city center near the train station. We eat outside; the sunshine makes the chill in the air bearable.

"The food's good," Reese says indicating a fish sandwich and fries, "but not quite like Mother Moon's biscuits, eh Professor?" She smiles and sighs. Her eyes wander a moment.

"Looking back," she says, "I think I love the memory of those biscuits so much….because, in the mental hospital, no one asked a little girl what she wanted to eat. I had to take what I was given. But, Mother Moon would make those drop biscuits anytime I asked her."

"Did she raise you?" I lean toward her.

"She raised me in Jotnar Valley until I was old enough to attend boarding school."

Reese and Professor Irons decide to cross the square to the train station and check the schedule for trains going to the airport. Reese carries both of our overnight bags, one over each shoulder.

"You look like a pack-mule," I tell him. He smiles at me.

"You like it when I lift heavy stuff. Just working out my muscles, Babe." It's good to see him smile. The last 18 hours have been a crushing disappointment. We've come so far, and I don't know what we'd do if we'd actually figured it all out—Slakter, the stone, Grandpa Karl's wild weird life. But, it feels like we were close, so close. And, now…

Hollis and I wait at the courtyard while Reese and the professor visit the train station. Hollis plays, running from table to table saying hello to commuters and families. They all smile politely at the boy speaking English.

Over the noise of the crowd and the hissing brakes of a commuter bus, I hear a scream. I turn as do several other men and women waiting in line to board. There's a commotion in the alley between the eatery building and the railway station. I see people running out of the alley towards us. I reach down and pick up Hollis.

A dull buzzing sound comes from the alley and grows louder. More panicked faces are rushing toward us. I turn with Hollis in my arms and move away from whatever is going on. The sound of buzzing disappears but now the shouts of panicked families and tourists are matched with a low rumble. The whole square trembles and the thundering sound echoes off of the ornate facades of the buildings surrounding us.

"Reese," I shout not sure where to find him. "Reese!"

The crowd is rushing past me as I carry Hollis to the eatery nearest to us. The ground is shaking; I can't hold my footing and tumble over the steps.

"Mom. Look!"

I look over my shoulder and see two massive trolls racing toward us. The sound wasn't thunder. They found us. Black rags cloak their bodies against the day-light. My blood goes cold and I fight against my own panic. I drop my hand to my hip searching for my Schofields.

Damn. They're packed in my bag.

I snatch Hollis and we bolt for the doors to the eatery only to see them slammed shut. The crowd is desperate, seeking refuge from monsters that only seconds ago were nothing more than myth. I turn back to see the brutish trolls lean in to seize us. I press my face to Hollis's. My voice catches but I manage a forced whisper. "Hollis, it's going to be…"

A figure leaps in front of the monsters and swings wildly. It slashes and cuts at the two with furious zeal and ribbons of red spout from their legs and hands. When the figure stops moving for a moment I see my husband, axe in hand and eyes red.

A purple light sails through the air striking the face of the building several stories above my head. An agonized roar is heard and a cloaked stocky troll plummets to the square. The stone walkway cracks from the impact. Ribbons of dark oily cloth cover the troll's face and arms against the sunlight.

"Get inside the building," I hear Professor Irons shout as she raises her cane and delivers another shot of violet fire. I pull Hollis to me and race to the door again. Still locked. *No. No. No!* I slam a fist against the window. I turn to see Reese and the professor back to back as three hooded monsters surround them. The troll's body that cratered the walkway in front of us begins to move. He sputters and growls as he comes to, rolls, and raises his massive girth. The monster rips a street lamp from the pavement and moves toward the fight.

"Daddy, watch out," Hollis cries.

I want to look away. It's two against four. My husband and the professor are outnumbered and I'm frozen—helpless to watch. The professor fires violet bursts of light, peppering the monsters, keeping them from closing in. Reese is a blaze of fury—hacking, leaping, rolling, and slashing as if he was born to it. I cover Hollis's eyes. A monster roars in pain and a bloodied tusk is cut from its face. The oversized fang the size of my leg drops to the ground. Reese picks it up and returns to the fight, swinging two weapons—both dripping blood.

Professor Irons rises into the air, clearing herself from the fray. She grips her hat with one hand and cane in the other. She levitates to the metal frame tower just over the train station, beyond the reach of the squad of trolls below. She clings to the metal frame. Her cane flickers and trembles in her hand for a moment. Then it wraps around her arm from wrist to shoulder. The sky darkens overhead and thick clouds build with a swift unnatural wind. Umbrellas and patio chairs tumble across the square. The ragged cloaks of the trolls flail in the wind around them like leathery wings.

"Momma?"

"Hold on, Baby," I reassure Hollis gripping him tighter.

We feel heat against our skin just before the lightning strikes. The tower blinks with a white unbearable light for a split second. Then the sound hits—a deafening *Crack* that rocks us back. I cover Hollis with my body, shielding him. I look back and see, like crooked fingers, trails of lightning coming from the tower and landing directly on one troll. Then another. Then another—each flash of light discharging from the Professor's outstretched hand. The trolls stop and fall in their tracks, smoldering and writhing in pain. For a moment, I hold my breath.

The square is quiet. My heart pounds in my ears. Then I hear the sirens. Emergency vehicles are on the way. Reese drops to one knee, panting, and the Professor quickly descends from the tower.

"We're leaving. On foot. Now." The Professor waves her arm and the cane releases its grip on her and becomes rigid once again. Hollis pulls from my grasp.

"Daddy!" He runs to Reese while I can barely stop from shaking.

"No, no, buddy," Reese raises a hand. "Stay there with Momma."

From behind me, an explosion of glass knocks me forward. I think the building is coming down but then I feel the grip of what feels like petrified lumber wrap around me. I hear

Hollis scream. Reese scoops him up, pulling him away. A cold enormous hand wraps around my neck and face and I hear his voice.

"We're done here. Vi drar nå." It's Slakter. I'm gasping for air through his grip.

At once, the four trolls reach into their scorched cloaks and fling something to the ground. A dark haze emerges and envelopes each of them. Bits of stone tile near each of them cracks, shatters into pieces, and is pulled into the haze. In Slakter's other hand, I see a dark orb, like a rotten plumb. He smashes it with his twisted fingers and flings it to the ground, same as the others. The dark fruit strikes the stone walkway in front of us. The fruit vomits a swarm of—oh God—black flies and gnats. The stone under the dark fruit cracks and shatters. Bits of stone swirl and are thrown back. We are being consumed in a buzzing funnel of darkness. That sound—a deafening buzzing sound. Panicking, I look up. Each of the other trolls are enveloped in swarms of black flies. One by one the swarms dissipate leaving craters in the pavement but the trolls have disappeared. Reese is racing to me. I can't hear him over the buzzing. But, I can see his mouth, shouting my name. His outstretched hand almost catches a wisp of my hair before everything goes black.

Chapter 34

Emma Little

I open my eyes and wonder why the card table with assault rifles is hanging from the ceiling. It takes me a moment to realize I'm hanging upside down. My face is bruised and the blood settling in my head is making the pain worse. I don't know how long I've been here. I look around. It's a small room with a garage door on one wall and a small drain in the middle of the floor. I try to bend at the waist. My body hurts all over. I see chains holding my ankles. Where is Reese? Where is Hollis? My breathing picks up. I can't control it. Hyperventilating. I force myself to breathe slowly. Can't pass out now, Emma.

I hear shouting behind me. A door opens and the shouting gets louder until the door closes. A man moves in front of me. He is pale and bald. I think he might be one of the guys I saw waiting for us when we left the airport in Oslo.

"Ah, Hallo," he says. He says something else in a language I don't understand. I'm pretty sure it's Norwegian. I think he's asking questions. He slaps my face when I don't answer. My cheek is hot. Strangely, I'm not scared. Not for me. All I can think about is Hollis and Reese. He shouts at me when

I don't answer again. Just when I think he is about to hit me again, the door behind me opens. I hear another man's voice. The two are arguing about something. The second one, older and stocky with scar running down the back of his neck, he tells the first man to leave. He speaks Norwegian too. I can't understand what he's saying but the body language is universal. While the door is open, I can hear others in the room behind me. I don't know if they are troll or human, but someone is speaking English. My ear is drawn to it and I overhear that some of the trolls didn't make it back.

"Stupid animals, they are. Can't even concentrate long enough to make it through the bloody swarm."

The swarm? The swarm of flies? Is that how they just appeared in the middle of the train station in Oslo?

"Shut your ugly mouth, little man," says another voice that is distinctly troll. "I lost a good jotun out there."

"Aww, don't take it so hard. You still got pieces of his arm …and his foot," the first voice says with a laugh that is cut short by a commotion. The stocky man in the room shouts at them and races out the door closing it behind him. I can still hear the fighting just outside the room. English and Norwegian words shouted back and forth. No one comes back into this room for at least an hour—maybe more. I can't tell. The burning pain clinching my ankles moves through my legs, knotting the muscles in my calves. I glance at the exits: the garage door at the wall across the room and the smaller door next to me. No other windows. I can hear Markham's voice in my head. *Stay calm, darlin'—just keep looking.* The floor drain is a possibility only if I want to risk drowning in a dark metal tube that reeks of garbage and ammonia. Keep looking.

The garage door is raised and a bright light floods the

room from the outside. I blink and my eyes adjust. Outside is just more warehouse with cold concrete, pipes, chains and pulleys. But, even hanging upside down, I can tell there is one very noticeable exception. Across the way from my cell I can see a large troll, like the ones we found in the fishing village. She is covered in an oily fur and dressed in leathers. They have chained her to the wall. A gas-powered generator rumbles providing power to two sets of standing ultraviolet lamps aimed at her. They are simulating sunlight to keep her weak. Monsters.

Two shadows stretch across the floor toward me, one much longer than the other. I see the profile of a man and a troll.

"Whaddid you do? Where's Reese? Wheremyson?" My voice comes out garbled. I notice the troll with the curled shoulders and long tree-trunk shape. He speaks first.

"Shh. Emma. Emma. Emma. I hope your stay with us will be a short one." I recognize the voice of the monster that grabbed me in the square—Slakter. With one arm, he reaches above me and hoists the chain free from whatever held it. He lowers me to the floor slowly. I crumple in a heap and struggle to move at first. His partner, the man with the scar on his neck, is the same one who earlier saved me from being slapped a second time. He kneels at my feet and un-locks the padlock. I rub my ankles and the blood comes back into my legs. The pain comes throbbing back too. The man takes the padlock and lets the brass key retract with a *zip* to a little key fob clipped on his belt and leaves us the way he came, through the garage door. He closes it with a loud clang leaving only me and Slakter in the room—together. I fumble trying to stand. A flare of searing pain hits my ankles as the blood returns. Slakter just watches as if he is amused.

"Take a look out the window, Emma." He points to the garage door with its two small grimy windows. I look back at him and wait. I don't want to turn my back on him. "Go ahead," he says in a sickly but mannered tone.

I move to the garage door with slow steps. I look back at him again just to be sure he hasn't moved. He hasn't so I look. Through the dirty glass, I see the troll, limp and in chains. Her chest moves with rapid shallow breaths. Then I look left and right. There are men, women, and trolls all over the warehouse. The humans look like military types; short haircuts, all business, with faces that all have the same don't-mess-with-me expression. They move hard cases off of trucks and into the open floor. I've seen cases like these before, my mom's boyfriend in Arkansas used them to carry his guns—his really big assault rifles. Another truck backs up and three men hop out of the back. I notice icy slush falling off the tires and leaving wet tire tracks on the concrete. As the men exit the truck, they take what looks like a wooden chest from the bed of the truck. It looks much like a pirate's treasure chest that you see in movies, a square box fastened with metal and rivets at the seams. That chest is certainly not carrying guns.

"You see all of the people out there, Emma?" he asks. "They believe in the work we are doing." He says the word *believe* with a certain relish that makes my skin run cold. "I intend to turn back the clock on humanity… by a thousand years. And they," he says pointing to the men and woman on the other side of the garage door, "they are ready to come with me. But before we can go on this journey, I need something."

"What do you want with my family?" I force my mouth to say the words without shaking.

"Oh, I don't want your family. I don't want you at all. I want the rune stone. The Sleeping Stone. Stein av Minnedag. The Stone of Remembrance… it has had so many stupid names; I cannot keep up." I look at him waiting for an explanation. A story. Something. "Don't tell me. You're going to say you don't know what I'm talking about. Is that right, Emma? I've heard that before."

I don't respond. I don't want to give anything away. If he knows that I truly don't know anything then I'm no use to him. If he thinks I'm lying and I do know something—well, I don't know what he might do.

I hear a thud from behind the garage door followed by shouting. I turn back and look through the little window and see the men who carried the treasure chest now standing over it. The chest is tipped on its side, open, and spilling dozens of the dark fruit—the rotten looking plums they had at the train station. They roll across the concrete; each a fuzzy plum with white veins running across the skin. A white towel is wadded up inside the chest providing padding for this volatile cargo. The soldiers are frozen staring at the fruit rolling loose on the floor, like staring at a grenade. One of the men shouts and points at another. He shrugs and shouts back then he begins carefully collecting each one and placing it back in the chest while the others look on without moving. His hand shakes only slightly as he picks up each and places them gently into the white folds of the towel stuffed in the chest.

"Emma."

I turn at the nearness of his voice at the back of my head. God, I didn't even hear him move. He's kneeling, bringing his eyes level with mine—and no more than six inches away from me.

"Get. Away. From me." I whisper. He looks on me silently and tilts his head, like the wolf looking with dispassionate curiosity at the injured rabbit trapped so far away from its home. I feel the cold garage door against my back.

"I'm not going anywhere, Emma. Not yet." I can smell his breath.

"I don't know what you want. I don't have your stone."

"Are you sure about that?" he asks with a grin. For a moment, I can actually see a silvery gray glimmer deep in the sockets of his skull.

"What? What are you talking about?"

"You're right," he says standing and taking a step back. "No more dancing around it." In one easy step he is at the interior door and gives it an impatient knock. Keys rattle outside and the door swings open with the stocky man with the scar on his neck standing ready. Slakter says one word, "Avtalebok," and the man disappears into the room and reappears with a small leather-bound volume. It's a journal with several loose-leaf pages sticking out of it. Slakter takes it from the man and points it to me.

"Do you know what this is?" I don't answer. It looks familiar. The rough stitching around the binding—the uneven shape—hand crafted. "You should recognize it, Emma. It was in your home. Yes, lying in the black and burned remains of your home. Teddy was kind enough to find it for me." My stomach turns at the mention of Reese's father.

"Although, I do not think he appreciated me taking it. Had to pry it out of his hands." My face is hot and I clinch my teeth, fighting to hold the tears back. He tosses the journal at my feet.

"Pick it up. Look at it. He came back to your house to get

it. Clearly, it was very important to Teddy. Did you and your husband call him Teddy… or just Ted? Theodore seems to be out of fashion these days." I don't answer him. "Pick it up!"

I flinch at the outburst. I slowly reach for the journal and pick it up. I thumb through the pages not knowing what I'm looking for. I have scanned through this little book only a handful of times since Reese and I have been together. It was an heirloom of little value to anyone except family. Most of the pages have lists and charts written in Norwegian. Dates are written next to other numbers that I can only assume are payment amounts for services rendered. Feeling the journal in my hands, I notice it easily falls open to a page toward the back. The binding has been broken where the journal sat open at a page with a sketch of an oval shape with letters inside it. Runic markings aline vertically on the oval. Several notes are scratched out next to the drawing but I cannot read them.

"What am I looking at?" I ask without raising my head from the journal. I can't bring myself to look at him.

"That is the Stone of Remembrance. The prize. You give me that stone, Emma, and I'll go away."

"I… I don't know where it is," I say raising my head. He only stares back at me silently. I avoid his gaze remembering that looking directly into a wild dog's eyes is perceived as a challenge.

"Emma, Emma, Emma." He snatches the journal from my hand, almost jerking my arm out of socket as he does. "Emma, this is a war. And, you want to be on the winning side."

"She knows where it is." I say. Slakter stops mid-speech. "She knows where it is," I say again, pointing to the garage door, to the troll suffering under the lamps and chained against the wall. "Her people are protecting it, like a talisman of good fortune for their village. We just came from her village before we got into Oslo. I saw your handy-work, Slakter. You must be proud of yourself."

He ignores my jab. I shift looking for his eyes inside those dark caverns, looking for any sign that he believes me.

"You didn't find the stone in Alsunndr," he says.

"We weren't looking for it. We were looking for you. You may remember burning my house down and murdering my father-in-law." He tilts his head again and I feel like the injured rabbit all over again.

"Surely, you do not think Muninn sent you all the way here for… revenge?" The look of disbelief on his twisted face transforms to a patronizing grin. "You are truly misguided. And, Muninn has sent you on a fool's errand and placed you in my hands."

"What? What do you mean?"

"Muninn has no interest in your family tragedy. And, Professor Irons is merely a, uh, how do you say? A babysitter to you. I'm sure the professor has abandoned your husband and your son by now and is racing to locate my benefactor and stop him from finding the rune stone."

"She wouldn't do that. My husband… my son… they have no way to get back home."

"That is a shame, isn't it? Unfortunately, adding the professor to this equation means I must speed things up. She's a terrible nuisance." He circles behind me and places his hand on my back. I feel his knotted palm envelope my shoulders. I'm pressed forward toward the garage door.

"It's time I introduced you to Gunhild," he says. "I'm sure she will want to hear your stories about how her village is doing."

Slakter knocks on the garage door and I see the same bald man that unlocked the restraints around my ankles peer through the grimy window. A latch snaps and garage door rises. The bald man stands ready with a rifle over his shoulder. Gunmen warm themselves at a fire burning from a 55-gallon metal drum. They all look over at me and Slakter. He walks me across the main hall of this warehouse and I take in the details as quickly as I can, committing them to memory. Window panes at the far end of the warehouse are painted-over, offering only slivers of light from the dusk outside. Two small pickup trucks sit in their own puddles of loose snow. I look behind me. Against the wall outside the garage door of my cell are several large metallic cases. Sitting on the floor between two tall stacks of those cases is the rustic wooden chest.

A crowd is starting to gather. Men and women, some dressed in tactical gear, line a path between me and the troll like they are getting ready to see a show. The man that slapped me when I woke hours ago is watching me with a grin on his face. I march toward her, trying my best not to let them see me sweat. When I'm still several feet away, I realize that I can feel her breathing. Those shallow quick breaths chill my skin and I slow my approach.

She lies between two rusting pipes as big around as a truck tire and she's propped against the wall with her arms outstretched and raised just above her head. A thick chain wraps around both wrists and that chain pulls both arms toward the pipes on either side of her and then loops back and—God—under her hair, I can see where the chain meets and twists around her neck.

Even if she was not weakened by the floodlights behind me,

the weight of her arms pulls the chain tighter; any movement at all is choking her.

I place a hand on her chest and her eyes open. She flinches against the light. Her belly rises and falls, assisting to push air out of her lungs just so she can breathe in again. I pull away for a moment afraid she might attack out of fear. Shouts go up from the crowd. My face grows hot but I keep my eyes on her. I reach a hand to her face, avoiding the traces of blood matted to her skin and hair, and move the long brown locks covering her face behind her pointed ears. Her eyes don't acknowledge me.

"Gunhild, can you hear me?"

The murmur from the crowd becomes taunting. "She don't speak English. Idiot American." A hand slaps the back of my head throwing me forward into her. I get my footing under me and scurry away from her. Several arms stop me and toss me back and this time I fall fully engulfed in her mass of fur and realize a new fear—she doesn't move at all. She won't wake up. I raise up from my knees and grip her heavy face and pull her head toward me. It's then I see the two small sawn-off horns at her temples.

"Listen to me, Gunhild," I whisper. "I need your help. I need you to wake up. I need you to answer me. I need…" Her eyes do not change. Then I remember the name of her village. "Alsunndr. Alsunndr," I say loud and clear fighting to be heard over the jeers. She twitches and her eyes meet mine. Her breathing slows. "Ranka and Willum. That's your family… right?" The on-lookers shut up when they see the change in her face. I say it again. "Ranka. Willum."

Her face contorts into a grimace and she lets out a wail that pierces. She flails at the chains and a claw rakes across my face and knocks me back. I hit the cold concrete and hands are all over me, dragging me away from her. The Norwegian man that hit me stands over me as I'm drug across the floor. He pulls my hair and spits. I struggle to pull free to get back to her. I lash out, scratching and kicking, but it's no good. Through the angry mass of bodies pulling me across the hall and back to my cell, I look back at Gunhild. She's in pain. She locks eyes with me and, for a moment, she's really there. A large man strikes her across the face with the butt of his rifle…twice. Slakter stands by calmly watching with a look of mild disappointment on his twisted face.

"Let her go," I call out.

I'm tossed back in my cold cell. The man I'd seen earlier, with the scar at the back of his neck, wraps the chain around my ankles and snaps the padlock on. I beg him not to hoist me up. I don't think my ankles can survive it. He waves me off at first and, for a moment, I think he'll grab the chain at the wall and raise me into the air again. I grab his hand and soften my plea. I move his hand to my skin and let him feel the bruise and see the deep red marks wrapped around both ankles. He looks at the bruises. He looks back at me and his eyes show concern, an anxiety that is almost fatherly. He hesitates and nervously scratches at his short beard that's begun to turn white. Then he says something I don't understand and gestures for me to stay put. I understand: don't move, don't cause trouble, and I get to stay firmly on the cold concrete floor. Just before he leaves, he pulls a worn rag from his back pocket, hands it to me, and gestures to my face. He says something and points to my right cheek. I press the white rag to the side of my face, wiping whatever dirt or mess is there. When I pull it away, the white cloth has three red stripes across it. Just then I feel the hot scratches that I'd not felt before. Gundhild must have drawn blood when she lashed out. She didn't mean it.

My jailer, the man with scar and beard, closes the door behind him with a clank as it locks. I look again at the hand holding the white rag he'd given me. Then, I look over at the other hand to see a small key attached to a key fob: the padlock key I swiped from him while he worried over my bruised ankles. I grip the small brass key, steady my breathing, and listen for sounds coming from outside my cell. I listen for the footsteps outside the door. I look across the room watching for any signs of activity through the two small windows on the garage door. Nothing. My hand shakes as I reach for the padlock, insert the key and twist. I commit. I'm getting out of here.

I fling the chain off my ankles and crouch low—listening again. If I'm caught, I won't get a second chance to escape. I listen for movement. I hear voices echoing through the warehouse but none nearby. I race to the garage door. I gently press my face to the metal and look through the window keeping a deep angle so as not to be seen. I look down the large main corridor of the warehouse. I duck and step to the other side of the window and look down the opposite side of the warehouse. In my mind I map the obstacles and hiding places: trucks, large metal cases, a pair of 55-gallon drums. Not much. I look up again. When the crowd dispersed after Gunhild's torment, they must have gone outside or elsewhere in the belly of the warehouse. There's one soldier that I can see, the big guy with the rifle, and he's walking away, shouting orders at someone far off. Not a soul in the main corridor except Gunhild herself…for now. I squat down and reach for the bottom of the garage door. Both hands grip the bottom lip of the door and I only try to raise it. Gently, I tense my arms, rising ever so slightly, I feel the door give and move upward. Just as gently, I let the garage door rest again. I straighten up quickly and glance through the garage window and plan my run. First, raise the garage door. Second, grab the treasure chest and smash it and grab one of the rotten plum things. Third, smash rotten plum into chain and pipe that is holding Gunhild and, hopefully, set her free while sending me back to Reese. My breath clouds the window as I look one more time. Still clear both ways.

I squat down again, place both hands under the garage door and take a deep breath. I lift and feel the door rise when I hear deep voices murmuring close by. Heavy footsteps of two or more men are passing in front of the garage door. I freeze. Holding my breath, I listen. The men walk with strange shuffling steps, boots slap the hard concrete. They cross in front of me just on the other side of the garage door. I hear them talking. The sound of the voices moves further away. They turn the corner and their voices begin to echo in the hall at the other side of my cell. They are just outside the other door. *No. No. No. No. Please, no.*

I race to the center of the room, grab the chain and twist it around my ankles. A rattling at the little door is heard as they fumble to unlock it. Loud voices begin to argue, then there's a loud *click* and the door swings open. I am still bungling the padlock, trying to not actually snap it closed, when they step inside.

Two men carry a third into the room with me. None of them notice the sweat on my face or the padlock in my hand—or that I'm not even dangling from the ceiling. They drop the body unceremoniously in the corner. They pull him upright, sitting against the wall. The body, a man with thinning blond hair and beard, does not make a sound. His wrists and ankles are zip-tied. Blood stains trail from the man's face to his shirt. I try not to stare and avoid drawing attention to myself. I slip the key into my shoe while they are busy with my new cell mate. The two men leave the room mumbling to each other and dusting off their hands.

The garage door rises behind me with a rattling clap. I turn and Slakter steps inside filling the room. He drops the garage door with a bang.

"Efficiency is a virtue. And, I need answers… right now," he says walking in big strides toward me. "We have no need for introductions, Emma," Slakter says gesturing to the body sitting unresponsive against the wall. I turn and look. "We are family here." The body moves, just a little, the head raises and through bruised eyes I see a sign of recognition. Ted.

"Emma." He says my name. Ted. Ted Little is alive! And, we are trapped in a concrete cell with a monster.

Chapter 35

Reese Little

I wake to the snap and pop of a fire. I feel the heat next to me and bolt upright. Professor Irons sits in a simple folding chair in front of a fire place. She leans over and picks up a thin log from a small stack next to the fire place and tosses it in.

"You're awake," she says. "Good. I was worried about you." She stands and approaches me with a cup and saucer. "Drink this."

I feel my body aching but I can't tell if I'm injured or stiff from lying on a rug over a hardwood floor. My head is dizzy and foggy, like waking up from a dream. I reach for the cup she's offered and that's when I see my hand, blood at the cuticles. And, there's an unmistakable smell of burnt hair. Then it comes rushing back all at once. Emma.

"Where am I? What happened to Emma? How long…"

"Calm down, Reese."

"Where is she? We have to find her."

"*Stop.*" The professor's voice is sharp and abrupt. "Listen to me and calm yourself." She thrusts the cup and saucer to me. "Drink this tea. It will bring clarity. Then drink all of this water as fast as you can. You're fighting dehydration." She sets a small jug of water, maybe a half a gallon, on the floor next to me. "You panicked when they took Emma. You became uncontrollable. You were fully berserker and I had to knock you out. Lightning. That's the reason for the blood from your ears and fingers and, most likely, toes as well. Thankfully, as a berserker, you can survive one of my lightning strikes."

"That explains the smell of burnt hair."

"Yes, and the smell too." She turns her chair to face me and sits back down. I gulp the tea. "It was frightening Reese. People saw you. And with mobile phones… I'm not sure if anyone recorded what happened."

"Oh."

"And, you need to talk to your son." She gestures behind me. I turn and see Hollis sitting on a twin bed with no sheets. His knees are pulled to his chest and his eyes are red with tears.

"Buddy," I say reaching for him.

"Daddy, trolls took Momma. And, you… you were scary." He clutches his buffalo but will not come to me. My stomach turns.

The professor explains that I've been unconscious for about an hour. According to the news broadcasting on a cheap TV sitting on top of the micro-fridge, initial speculation is that it was a terrorist attack. A witness recorded part of the attack with their cell phone. It's shaky but I can see the dark form of Slakter holding Emma. The camera is dropped or something and, when it looks back, both of them are concealed in a buzzing cloud of flies and then—gone.

"I haven't been able to reach Gerald by mobile. Hopefully, he'll reach British airspace in the next half hour." She paces across the room and tosses her cell phone on the twin bed. Hollis looks up at me. I give him a small wave. He gives me a small wave back. I finish the last gulp of water and stand.

There's a sink and mirror in the corner. I turn on the water and let it run until it's warm. Then I scrub at the blood at my fingers and my ears.

"Why would they come after us?" I ask. "And, how did they know where we were?"

"Precisely, Reese. Who knew that we would be leaving Norway?"

"The troll king? You think he sold us out?" I finish scrubbing only to realize my hands are shaking. Time is ticking and I have to find her.

"I think it must be considered. But, why come after us if they think we are leaving? It's irrational."

"They're desperate. They didn't want us to leave. Which means they still don't have the stone. And they think we can help them find it. The clock is ticking for Slakter and he has to deliver whatever he promised." I look down and realize I've been wringing my hands. My brain is racing trying to put the clues together—like a puzzle with a hundred pieces and none of them fit. Then, my mind latches on to something. "Do you have the pictures of the ledger," I say, "the ones Gerald sent you?"

"Yes, of course." She rummages through her bag and hands me her cell phone. I scroll through the photos. There's something here; I know it. Then, I find it.

"Here," I say showing her a picture of a page from the ledger. "What's missing?"

"There's a suspicious blank spot where payment should be recorded. Karl didn't get paid for a job?"

"Exactly. The Stone of Remembrance was the only job that he didn't receive payment for. Makes me think my grandfather never delivered it."

"Never delivered it or just didn't find it?"

"I don't know for sure." I look back at the photo on her phone. "What is the Stone of Remembrance anyway?"

"It certainly wasn't a small jewel. It was a rune stone," she says. "Or, I should say, it was two-foot chip of a larger rune stone that was discovered in Nova Scotia." I remember reading something about it at the museum in Oslo. They had an entire wing devoted to runes and runic fortune-telling.

I keep scrolling through the pictures of the ledger. I zoom in on the names and dates. I look back over the locations of where my grandfather went and the names of the objects he obtained. Detail after detail in each picture begins to blur in my mind. The puzzle pieces still don't fit.

"God, I'm a wreck. We have to go find her. Slakter will want to interrogate her." I look at the professor, her eyes are honest and they don't tell me I'm wrong. That sick feeling expands into my chest. I can feel the berserker wanting to rip through my skin and tear this city apart. I go to the window looking for a distraction. Through the curtains, I watch the street three stories below. The place is teeming with police redirecting traffic away from the city center. "Hey, how did you get me all the way up here after you zapped me?" The professor lets out a sigh.

"I attempted to carry you over my shoulder for a block before a good Samaritan took pity on me and Hollis. No one paid too much attention to us considering the number of people fleeing the scene. I'm thankful he stopped by… I'm getting too old to do the heavy lifting, my dear."

"Too bad you don't have a trick to levitate unconscious bodies." I try a bit of levity if only to calm my own nerves.

"Quite right," she says. "Or a shrinking potion to hide you

in my pocket." I chuckle at this but something tickles at my brain. For some reason, I think of the Sons of Ivaldi back in Jotnar Valley.

"We need to go. We need to make a plan… do something." I pace, hands stuffed in my pockets, trying to force a plan of action from sheer will.

"I need to show you something." The professor goes to the bed and reaches under it. She slides a small safe out, just like the ones in hotel rooms, and punches a code into the dial pad. She opens it and pulls out a dark oily—plum is what I'd call it for lack of a better word. Its appearance is—upsetting. Thin white veins run across the flesh. On second glance, it looks less like a fruit and more like a heart, a stained black heart. "They left this behind at the train station. This," the professor says, "is how they travel without being seen."

"That's the thing they all had, and threw on the ground. That thing made the flies and gnats appear."

"Yes. It is a foul piece of magic. True magic. I've only ever read about this. Until today." She is quick to return it to the safe and vigorously wash her hands at the sink. "Jotnar do not conjure that kind of practical magic. Someone supplied those to them." Suddenly, I realize there's a way to find Emma. My pulse races. I stand and cross the room to the professor.

"Professor, can't we use that…"

"I know what you're thinking. Yes, we can use this thing to find Emma. According to ancient texts, the druids in the days of the Picts used these things. They are volatile and deceptively easy to use… and misuse." She turns, drying her hands, and faces me directly. "But, Reese, you have a decision to make. You can use that dark… thing… once and only once. If you think of Emma, it will take you to her. If she's being held captive, then you'll be with her… possibly, with no way out." She peers back at me. Her deep set brown eyes plead that I not do it. I feel options slipping away from my grasp. My brain races, playing out all the scenarios, calculating all the risks. I can't go after Emma alone and the professor can't go alone. Neither of us would last against an army of trolls. We can't go together without putting Hollis in the fight. Damn. *Damn.* I'm helpless. My hands shake.

"Gaaah. So, If I go get her, we'll all be trapped. Or, just sit here… and do nothing." I'm losing it. I can't tell if the room is shaking or I am.

"There are always other options. We have to think, Reese. What else are we not thinking of?"

"There's no time for thinking. He has her. He has Emma and I have to rescue her. He could be torturing her right now."

"Panicking helps no one. Control yourself, Reese." She's subtle but I see her reach for her cane.

"That's just it. I don't have control. I don't. I can't control any of this." I hug my arms, holding myself together. The throbbing in my head is so fast—so deafening. Professor Irons tries to calm me but I can't hear her anymore. I kneel on the floor, doubling over, trying to make myself small. My fingers grip my arms; muscles tighten; have to keep myself from bursting. I feel the cold wood floor against my forehead and press in, hoping to fall through, hoping to be swallowed up. Then a small voice finds its way in.

"One is for Grimnir and his missing eye." Hollis is whispering. "Two are the ravens watching… those gone by." I feel his warm breath against my ear. "Three is for jotnar of mountain, fire, and frost. Four is the berserker furious in blood, bone, life, and loss." His hand is on my arm. My breathing slows.

The throbbing in my head diminishes. I open my eyes. He's lying on the floor next to me. His eyes are wide, scared, but unwilling to look away.

"I don't know what to do." My voice crackles, dry and winded. "I can't do this." I remember the fight with Eklund—*you ain't rekkr, boy*. He was right then. A crippled old man, unarmed, beat me in a fight. There's no way I can beat an army of trolls. And, then it hits me.

"Hollis, get your coat on." I stand, shaky, trying to get my legs under me. "Professor, bring that ugly fruit thing." I reach for my axe and the pair of leather holsters holding Emma's revolvers. The professor steps forward ready to object.

"I know you want to go after her but we need a plan…"

"I don't have a plan." I turn and let her see the clarity in my eyes. "Not really. That's outta my control. I know I can't go after Emma. Not yet." I sling my jacket over my shoulder. "Can you get us transportation to Jotenheimen Park?"

"I can, Reese, but what are you doing?"

"We need an army. And, we're going to get one."

Chapter 36

Ted Little

My breath catches sending a white-hot ache over my chest and a broken rib gets just a little closer to puncturing a lung. I see the woman sitting on the cold concrete floor in front of me through my swollen eyes. I see her. And, my heart sinks.

"Emma," I say with a gasp. I watch the shock register on her face. Tears well up.

"I thought," she says. "We thought you were dead." She nearly leaps off the floor and reaches for me. She's stopped with a jerk just short of reaching me and I see the chain at her ankles. Her hands grab my shoes, the closest thing to her. She squeezes desperately, just to get some assurance that I'm real. I try to lean forward. I raise my hands, zip-tied, shaking, and stained with my own blood. I try to touch her face. Thick red claw marks stretch from her ear to her cheek. She grabs my hand in both of hers and holds it.

"Emma," I say. "Why… why are you here? What happened to Reese? Hollis?"

Slakter strides into the room with a 55-gallon drum tucked under his arm and lets it drop with a loud clang onto the floor.

"Well, enough time spent catching up, yes?" he says. "It's

time to get down to business." Slakter pulls an oily rag from inside the metal drum and lights it. Flames quickly spread over the rag and he drops it back into the barrel.

"I've received many complaints that abandoned warehouses tend to become too cold for some of my human associates." He moves the barrel closer to us and I can see the flicker of flame reflected in the dark glass pits of his eyes. "A little trash and a little charcoal in a metal barrel goes a long way."

"He needs help," Emma says gesturing to me. "Get him to a hospital and I'll take you to Jotnar Valley."

"Emma, stop." I say.

"Yes, Emma, stop. Please," Slakter says turning on her. "You have nothing to offer. And, it is clear from your little show with Gunhild that you are not trustworthy. She knows nothing. You know nothing. But…"

No.

"But, Ted knows. Don't you Ted?"

Don't.

"And, Ted is going to tell us everything, Emma."

Please don't do this.

"Would you like to learn where to find the Stone of Remembrance, Emma?" She doesn't answer. Slakter lowers his twisted frame to her and wraps his hands around her shoulders and raises her to her feet, the chain rattles as she stands. His face and her face are side by side staring at me. For a moment, time freezes. I look back at her hazel and watery eyes. "You know the question, Ted," he says placing a hand against the outside of Emma's face pressing her face against his, cheek to cheek. "Where is the stone?"

"We don't have the stone," Emma says.

"Ted?"

"We don't know where to find it," Emma says flinching and trying to jerk away. "We don't even know what it is."

"Ted, tell her the truth. Please. For her sake." That last part makes me panic. I've been trapped here for almost a week. I've exhausted all my arguments and lies. Slakter knows I have nothing left to tell him… except the truth. "Ah. I notice that made you sit up, yes," Slakter says. "You're paying attention. Good, now out with it."

"Listen to me," Emma says. "I know your mother loved you. I know she tried her best, but she didn't know how to take care of you." What the hell is she doing? Slakter turns and looks at her still holding her between his hands. "I wouldn't know what to do if… if my son was a changeling. I would try to defend him from the taunts of other children. But, your village didn't know. Didn't understand." He's listening to her. "People still don't understand. The world used to think trolls were monsters—you know that. Now, they just think trolls aren't real. You want to prove that trolls are real? Fine. Just don't let them think that you're monsters too. You're not." Slakter is silent as he stares back at Emma. He releases her. For a moment, nobody moves.

"My mother…" he says to Emma. She nods. "Alsunndr, they told you about my mother?" Emma nods again.

"Yes," she says. "The troll king told us…" Slakter lashes out with fury gripping the back of her head and pulling her towards him.

"No," I shout.

"You think you know my mother?" Slakter says spraying spit from his jaws. "Did you know they disfigured her? And left her to rot?" He pulls Emma screaming to the metal drum, her hair twisted in his fist. "She was *burned*. She was marked an outcast and died alone in that same stinking village." He bends Emma over the 55-gallon drum and presses her face toward the yellow flames flickering inside.

"No." I leap toward them with my hands and ankles tied. I land on my belly, crawling and begging for mercy. Emma screams and fights to pull away from the flames. "Stop."

"Where is it, Ted?"

"Let her go." I watch her feet kick out from under her. The chain at her ankles snakes and rattles as she flails against the pain.

"*Where is it?*"

"It's on her hand. The ring on her finger, dammit. The ring on her finger. The stone is on her finger."

He looks at me, then looks at her hand gripping the outside of the barrel. With one fell move, he tosses her away from the barrel, knocking it over and sending coals across the floor. She is a shaking heap on the floor. Her trembling hands reach for her face. He towers over her, snatches her hand up and rips the engagement ring that my son gave to her off of her hand, the same ring that my father handed down to Reese. He raises the ring in the air to catch the cold florescent light. Emma's small whimpers echo against the walls.

"How did he do it? How did Karl make it so small?" Slakter asks with the eager curiosity of a child.

"Have mercy, Slakter. Get her some water, some ice, something."

"The Sons of Ivaldi! That's how! Isn't it?"

"Dammit, help her! Please. Help her."

He turns and marches to the garage door throwing it open. With a triumphant cry he calls his minions to attention. He barks orders in Norwegian and the warehouse lights up with activity. Noise. Chaos. Engines revving. Boots slapping the ground. The garage door slams closed again.

Minutes later, the silence betrays the fact that this warehouse buzzed with the activity of 100 soldiers and a dozen pissed-off trolls. Emma lays quiet and coiled up on the floor.

"Emma. Emma. Talk to me." From her side, I see the rise and fall of staggered breathing. I crawl toward her battling the bonds holding my ankles and wrists together. A sharp ache in my ribs pinches every time I stretch and move toward her. "They are going to Jotnar Valley," I say. "I'm sure that's the next part of their plan." She still doesn't reply. "Can you move? We have to get out of here, we have to find Reese and maybe we can call… or one of Munnin's ravens may have followed us and we…"

"Stop," she says with a forcefulness that is unexpected. I stop.

"Emma," I say wincing against the ache in my ribs. "Can you look at me?" She sits up slowly, facing away from me, and her Auburn hair tumbles against her shoulders and I see the burned edges of hair on the right side of her face.

"I am so tired." She attempts to comb trembling fingers through her hair. She gently pulls out the burned pieces and places them on the concrete next to her. "Ted, you have plans. They have plans. You have secrets. They have secrets. My house has been burned down. My family, my child, has been threatened, hunted. All because your dad stole a dangerous rock from some very dangerous people. And, everyone, including you, seems to know what is going on. *But, I don't know what's going on.*"

"Emma, I'm sorry. I didn't know about the stone. We can find…"

"Shh. You want to talk now… want to get a plan together. Right? Well, it's a little late." She pulls another tuft of hair and lays it in the small pile she's created on the floor and rests her hand on top of it.

"You had years to tell Reese all about this. All about his grandfather, about berserkers, trolls, everything. I'm done waiting for answers. I'm done waiting for someone else to give me a plan." I hear a click. She raises the chain from her ankles and the padlock hangs open. She drops them with a thud on the small pile of burned hair. "So, listen up. Cause this is *my plan*," she says turning around and facing me. I restrain myself when I see the red blistered tissue covering her cheek and temple. "We are getting out of here. You ready?" She stares at me, past the tears welling in her eyes, and I see a defiance warning me that there is only one appropriate answer to give.

"Yes, ma'am."

Chapter 37

Reese Little

We climb and brace against the cold that sinks into our bones. We've trekked up and over a mountain nearly bare of any trees or foliage. The sun has already descended behind the mountains and the temperature dropped below freezing before we ever got out of the vehicle. Professor Irons rented an executive SUV with all-terrain transmission and, two hours later we were driving through the country-side gazing at some of the highest mountains in all Norway. It's amazing what money can buy on short notice.

"This is the spot?" I ask, pointing across the ridge to a range of mountains that are capped with the last slivers of pink twilight.

"It is, more or less. But, Reese, it would be imprudent of me to be anything but realistic in this situation. I don't foresee this meet-and-greet going the way you hope it will."

"You already told me that, Professor." We follow the ridge for another half mile, watching the world on all sides slowly slip into darkness. I've strapped my axe and Emma's guns to me. They are cumbersome as hell for hiking snow covered mountains. I hold Hollis' gloved hand as we cross the rocky ledge. The professor illuminates our way with the head of her cane.

"This would be a fantastic opportunity," she says over the wind, "for me to use that shrinking potion I haven't invented yet."

I wonder if the cold is skewing her sense of humor.

"What? Why?"

"I could shrink to the size of an acorn." She leans forward into the climb. "And, you could carry me up this mountain." I grin but I don't have the breath to waste for a laugh. Then, I think of the Sons of Ivaldi again. I pause the climb.

"So, the Stone of Remembrance. I can't get it out of my head. It's a two-foot rock that broke off of the larger rune stone, right? What if… what if he shrunk it? My grandfather, I mean." Professor Irons turns, leaning on her cane, and pulls her ruby glasses from her face.

"What?"

"What if the stone we're looking for wasn't something that could be carried—not easily, at least? My grandfather could have had the Sons of Ivaldi shrink it for him."

"Well, why the Stone of Remembrance? If he could shrink it, it could be anything. A meteor, a full rune stone, or a geode the size of a bowling ball." Professor Irons shakes her head and turns back to the climb. I know there's something that I'm missing, something close. We walk on for several minutes until we reach a level spot. The professor leans against a boulder to rest. I set Hollis down next to her careful to avoid the snow drift.

"The museum in Oslo, they had this whole bit about the Stone of Remembrance." I rub my temples trying to recall the details of the exhibit. "In the story, supposedly Odin's ravens,

Huginn and Munnin, went rouge, creating this cursed rune stone to put all the gods into a deep sleep."

"Correct. When the smaller piece was removed from the larger stone," she says, "they all went to sleep or …went away, I guess. And they won't wake up until the piece is restored to the larger stone." Professor Irons is very matter-of-fact with the details, careful not to give it too much weight. "I'm aware of that story. Against the accepted body of Norse mythology, it's considered apocryphal. It's more likely a 12th century invention; pagans and those that favored old Norse traditions tried to explain the rise of Christianity and the twilight of their old way of life." She takes a cloth from her coat and wipes her glasses. "And, if it were true, it would implicate Mother Moon and her counterpart in laying down a curse strong enough to effectively decommission the pantheon of Norse gods."

"Whether or not it's true," I say, "don't you see the appeal of a myth like that to someone like Slakter?" I see the recognition in her eyes. She purses her lips. "The troll-king told us Slakter wants strife and bloodshed. He wants the stone to awaken the gods and bring back the old order of things. I think my grandfather and Slakter had the stone. But, when my grandfather realized the danger, he fled Norway without delivering it to Stenholmen. What if he kept it for years in Jotnar Valley? What if he tried to hide it and had the Sons of Ivaldi ply it down to the size of a gem." As I say it, I realize what he did. Oh no. I reach and try to brace myself just before I collapse to my knees on the cold earth.

"Reese? Reese?" The professor approaches me, she lowers the head of her cane, casting a harsh white light over my face. I pull my hands away and look at Hollis. Then I raise my eyes to the professor; "Are you okay?" I struggle to form the words to describe what Grandpa Karl has done.

"Emma's ring. Grandpa Karl gave it to me before he passed. Probably, his way of making sure it didn't get into the wrong hands." The irony of the situation is like a kick in the gut.

"So, Emma had the stone all along?" She raises a hand, covering her mouth. "We can only hope that Slakter hasn't figured it out yet." She paces a moment and pulls her cloak across her. "It can only be reattached to the original rune stone by Huginn and Muninn." I look up into Professor Iron's eyes.

"That means, once Slakter has the stone, his next move is to take his army and go after Mother Moon."

"Jotnar Valley has no idea what's coming."

"That's why we need to call in the big guns." I gesture to the ridge of mountains opposite us that appear to be etched out of iron and dusted in snow. "This is where they are supposed to be, right?"

"Um, so legend would say," she replies. "But, I have to tell you…"

"I know, I know. You don't think this will work. But, Professor," I fight for the words. "I really need to believe in this, because, I don't have another option. This is totally out of my hands."

"Daddy." Hollis looks up at me. His brow is furrowed and his eyes are filled with tears. "Is Momma in trouble?" I can hardly hold back my own tears.

"Yeah. Momma's in trouble." A heaving sigh hits me involuntarily. "But, she's a tough Momma. And, she's full of surprises." The tears come for both of us and I reach down to wipe his eyes. "We need to go get her. But, we need some help. Are you ready?" He nods his head and wipes his face with his sleeve. "Alright." I look over the mountain range again expecting to see something—a change, a sign… anything. "Let's call down some mountain trolls."

Chapter 38

Ted Little

After hammering her padlock through one of the garage windows, Emma pulls a shard of glass and cuts the plastic ties on my wrists and ankles. I lean against the garage door and she races to the back door of the cell and we listen.

"I don't hear anybody," she says after a moment.

"No movement here." I reply. "I don't hear any voices either."

She races back to me. As she gets closer, I catch myself looking at the festering burn on her face. "We go out through this garage door," she says. "It's unlocked. Then, you get the chest sitting just outside the door – looks like a pirate's treasure chest. Crack that thing open and get ready to use the rotten plum things inside to get us out of here."

"Stay close," I say. "We have to be physically in contact with each other if we use those things. I overheard a woman teaching the trolls how to use them."

"Got it. While you do that, I'm going for Gunhild. I'm going to shut off the generator to the lights and get her out of those chains..."

"What? The troll? No. We get the fruit. We stick together. We get out of here."

"If we leave her she dies, Ted."

"Turn the generator off and she'll be able to fight her way out of those chains herself in no time. But we don't have the luxury..."

"My plan," she says through clinched teeth. "We may need some muscle to keep the bad guys away while we try to escape."

"Or, she might just draw their attention and ruin our escape."

For a moment she considers it. Then, tipping her head forward, she says, "My plan."

Lying down with my chest to cold floor, I get both hands under the garage door. Emma grips the bottom of the door as well and we raise it gently only a matter of inches. I scan the hall. Not a soul in sight except the troll trapped under ultraviolet lamps. The hum of the generator powering those lamps seemed to grow louder as each second passed.

"What do you think?" Emma asks.

"Reese and Hollis are waiting for us," I say. "Let's go."

We raise the garage door only slightly to allow us to roll out under it and shut it behind us. Emma glances back and forth across the long stretch of hall both ways as she races to Gunhild. I turn and scan the wall seeing emptied cases of weapons: black metal cases for assault rifles and the occasional case of grenades. All empty. I feel a cold sweat as I realize the fully armed threat that is about to descend on Jotnar Valley.

The silence after Emma switches off the generators is striking. I regret letting her do that before I've found the rotten plums. Sometimes silence is just as loud as fingernails on a chalkboard.

"Come on, wake up," I hear Emma say to Gunhild.

There's no treasure chest. I scan both sides of the hall. More emptied cases of guns. An M-16 rifle is propped all by its lonesome against a small door that looks like it might be a utility closet. The ground is strewn with food wrappers and cans of soda. But, no treasure chest.

"I can't find it."

"What?" She says looking back at me.

"I can't find the treasure chest," I say almost hissing, trying not to raise my voice. "No plums."

"It has to be here. Keep looking."

"I need you looking too. Get over here."

"My key," she says with tears in her eyes. "It won't unlock her chains. It won't work."

"Leave her. Look for the plums. That's our way out." Emma is holding the troll's fur covered face in her hands, raising her head, looking into her eyes.

"Help us… yeah. Come on, Gunhild, help us," Emma says coaxing her back to life. The troll stares back at Emma for a moment and then the fog lifts from her eyes. "Help us?" Emma pleads. Slowly, Gunhild points her long woolly arm in my direction and down at the floor. A drain cover, a heavy steel grate, sits in the middle of the floor. I scurry over and drop to my hands and knees and peer between the wide dark slats. Shimmering in the wet and reeking drain lay three orbs the size of a child's fist.

"We got three plums down here," I blurt out with a smile. I try lifting the cage sitting over the drain with no luck. The slats on the grate are just wide enough to stick a hand in. "See if you can stick your arm through and reach 'em."

Emma races over, nearly falling over Gunhild. She reaches and strains. "We need at least two of them," I say. "One to get us to Reese and Hollis and another to get us all back to Jotnar Valley." She pulls back and looks down the drain once more.

"God, I'm going to be sick," she says and shoves her arm through the cage again. Her eyes close and she inhales through her teeth. "Come on, come on…"

"We need a lever," I say. "Something to lift the steel grate."

"Do you have a lever, Ted?" she says coming up from the drain with a jerk. "Cause I'm fresh out." She's pacing back and forth across the hall. I scan the hall looking for anything strong enough and long enough to act as a lever. Then I hear chains rattling behind me. Emma is standing on her toes reaching over Gunhild and pulling the chain that's wrapped around one of the pipes. She kicks one foot up against the wall to push off and wraps the thick chain around both hands. Leaning back she pulls at the chain with a furious commotion.

"Stop. What are you doing?"

"She can get that grate off the drain," she says throwing her whole body into another tug at the chains. "Get over here and help me, dammit."

"Stop it. Someone will hear," I say looking back down the hall just waiting for trouble to coming walking around the corner and see us. "We need to find a lever, a crow bar, something–

"Gunhild, listen to me." Emma leaves the chains and grabs the woolly troll by the face. "You gotta get us out of here. Do you understand? Do you *hear* me?"

"Shh."

"We need to go right now, Gunhild." The troll's brow is heavy. Her eyes dart back and forth looking up and down the hallway. "You're a momma, right? I'm a momma too. And my baby needs me. And your baby needs you. *Gunhild*, look at me. Ranka needs you. Ranka needs you right now."

With those words, a fire is lit in the belly of the troll. She arches her back with a deep breath and grabs the chain with each hand. She pulls with a fierce strength that rattles the large pipes and effectively tightens the loop around her neck. She winces as her face reddens. With a *Clang* one of the pipes tears away from the wall tossing bits of brick and mortar with it. She snatches the chain looped around the other pipe and rips it from the wall too. She roars, rattling sheet metal panels and window panes.

"Hey," a voice calls out from the distance. Two mercenaries race toward us from the dock side. They both raise rifles in our direction.

"Emma," I call out, "get her to lift the..." A shot rings out and strikes the concrete face of the wall behind my head. I duck and race to the assault rifle propped against the door. The door jerks open and a tall woman wearing a bullet-proof vest steps out with a pistol raised. I grab the rifle. Before she can turn her aim on to me, I slam the stock under her chin, knocking her flat on her back. I take cover in the doorway. I turn the rifle on the mercs and spray bullets hoping they'll retreat. The ground shakes and I stumble against the wall as Gunhild races past me. She charges into the fight with a roar. Just then, a larger troll rounds the corner from behind the mercenaries. He races at Gunhild and the two collide in a snarling fist fight.

I'm shouting for Emma in between bursts of gunfire. She's huddled over the drain, reaching for the dark plums, and totally exposed.

"Get against the wall. Now!"

"Come here," she shouts back. I can see the pair of mercenaries moving towards us, closing the distance, even as they continue to fire.

"We've got to find another way out," I say. "Emma, leave it."

"I need a lever," she says defiantly pointing at my rifle.

An ear-piercing screech is heard. Emma and I see Gunhild flailing at the larger troll. He stands over her and both arms are wrapped around her head. I know what is coming. The report of gunfire goes quiet just as her neck pops. Gunhild's body slumps and falls awkwardly against the concrete floor.

"No," Emma cries out. She stands, losing all sense of where she is. I break from the cover of the doorway, firing rounds as I race to her. I press her to the ground and jam the rifle barrel deep into the grate. I pull back on the rifle but the grate doesn't budge. Emma leans on the stock for leverage. Over the gunfire that is getting closer, I can hear the troll's steps pounding the ground, running toward us. It's only a matter of seconds before...

"Put all your weight on it," Emma shouts.

The grate cracks then lifts. Emma drops to her belly, reaches in. She springs up with a dark plum in her fist already oozing. I turn and see her hurl it. It hits the troll direct in the center of its chest. He stops cold—and then screams. The blood. The gnats. He's eaten away from the core—and Emma stands unflinching. I reach my arm into the drain and snatch another plum. I stand, wrapping my arms around Emma just in time as the gnats envelope her. I look into her face as the world goes dark around us. But, her eyes are fixed on her bloody handiwork.

Chapter 39

Emma Little

The cold bites quick and deep into my muscles. When the swarm of black flies goes quiet, darkness still surrounds me. But, there's wind… and stars. And, then I feel arms around me and I hear my name.

"Emma! Oh my god, Emma!" I know his voice and, with the little strength I have that's not fighting the cold, I reach my arms up to him.

"Mommy!" I feel the weight of a small bundle of elbows and knees crawling into me. I wrap my arms around my son. I smell his hair. Even against the icy wind his smell is unmistakable to me. Something like a blanket wraps around me. Reese kisses me again and again. Then Reese sees him; he sees his father.

"Dad? Dad?"

"Give your old man a hand, will ya?" Ted tries to reach for his son but the pain in his ribs makes him pull back. Reese collapses to his knees and buries his face in his dad's shoulder. They hold each other. Reese removes his jacket and I see his axe and my guns fastened to him. He drapes his jacket over Ted's shoulders.

"I thought you were dead."

"So did I, son. So did I."

Ted lets them know that he'd been trapped for almost a week and all Slakter asked about was the Stone of Remembrance. We tell them how everyone abandoned the warehouse when Slakter got my ring.

Professor Irons applies a bandage to my face. She tells me it's a 2nd degree burn. I don't really know what that means, except that it hurts. I cry and the tears sting my cheek. I want to wipe them away but it can't bring myself to touch my face. The pain of losing my family and the joy of finding them again is in those tears—and I cannot wipe them away.

"She needs a hospital." Professor Irons gestures to me as Reese helps me get to my feet. "And, so does your father." Reese's dad remains seated on the ground. He holds Hollis' mitten hands for a moment just to let him know that grandpa is okay. But, he's not. A few bruises under the collar of his shirt look pretty severe.

"He did that to you." Reese looks at the bandage on my face. He reaches for it and I can't help but flinch. He pulls away and looks over at Ted who hugs his grandson with one arm and hugs his ribs with the other. "He hurt you both." I hear the fury mounting in his voice.

"Reese." I whisper against the wind, hoping to calm him. "Don't think about that now." I reach for him and pull him close to me. He is warm and he is angry. "I need you to decide what we do next. What's the plan?"

"Jotnar Valley. He's headed there now," Ted says, wincing as he reaches for a small dark object tucked in the snow next to him. He holds it up to Reese, doing his best to hide the tremble in his arm. "This ugly little fruit is how they do it.

This is how they got into your neighborhood and got out so fast." The professor walks over, taking it from his hand. As I notice her long skirt and jacket, I realize that I am wrapped in her cloak. She must be freezing but she hides it well.

"We have two of them now." The professor pulls out another of the dark plums from her own satchel. She stares at them, holding them both with a certain respect—and dread. "This gives us options."

"Options or not. We gotta act fast," Ted says just as a round of deep successive coughs double him over. "Jotnar Valley could be under attack any minute." Reese helps his dad stand. Then, he pulls his axe and gives it to him. Ted leans into it like a cane for support. "Hey, that's my axe."

"New plan," Reese announces. "We've gotta warn the valley." He paces, eyes closed, speaking the words as they come. "But, we'll still be sitting ducks when Slakter's army gets there." He turns to me. His eyes gaze into mine intently and he takes my hand. "Come here, Hollis." Hollis rushes to us and wraps both arms around Reese's leg. Reese, raises his eyes at Ted and the professor. "We need to split up."

"What?" Ted lets out a hacking cough. There's a spot of blood at his mouth.

"You two," Reese says, "need to go on to Jotnar Valley and warn them. We're going to stay behind and …see if anyone wants to join our fight."

"I agree." The professor steps forward and hands me one of the dark plums. "You seem to know how to handle one of these, my dear." I cup it in my hands, remembering what I did with the last one I had. The professor moves toward an evergreen shrub several paces away. "I'll be sure that your father receives medical attention when we reach Jotnar Valley."

She raises her cane to the shrub and a purple flame dances from the silver head. I watch as the shrub catches fire and a warm amber light spreads across our little claim atop this mountain.

"Don't start talkin' about me like I can't hear you." Ted points the axe at the professor, attempting to emphasize the point. But, he never takes the other hand away from his ribs. "I'll get medical attention when I want it. But, when we land in Jotnar Valley, you can sure as hell bet I'm gonna get in this fight."

"Reese, do what you need to do." The professor grabs her satchel and throws it over her shoulder. "I hope the Fjell-Trol-let answer your call. Stay by this fire for warmth but it may only last a few minutes against the wind and snow."

"Now, hang on. We aren't just going to leave them here." Ted shifts his weight. He tries to approach us but, even with the axe as support, each step pains him. The lines on his face seem to grow deeper. His eyes give away the realization that the decision has already been made without him. "You'll need this." He takes a step forward and tosses the axe back to Reese.

"Dad, I'll see you again… real soon." With that, the professor tosses the dark plum in her hand against a cold rock. She grabs Ted's hand as the cloud of flies overtake them. We hear his voice, like a distant call across a dark lake.

"I love you, son."

Chapter 40

Ted Little

In my 55 years on this earth, I've been fortunate that I've never had to witness the cruelty and chaos of war. Fate has afforded me the privilege of never knowing what it's like to see my home become a battle ground. Never. Until today.

It's a strange feeling looking around this village, my home for so many years of my childhood. So much is unchanged. But, what catches my attention is the commotion, the frantic families rushing to the caverns, scenes of men kissing their children and wives as they separate and prep for the fight. I see the looks of panic on the faces I pass. A young woman almost collides with me as she admonishes a troll behind her to hurry along.

"Oh! I'm so sorry," she says to me. She turns to the troll —he's wiping tears from his face. "Max, stop dragging your feet," she pleads with the troll.

"Is this your boy?" I ask.

"Yes, yes he... Mister, are you okay? You're bleeding."

I'd forgotten about my wounds. I must look like a nightmare to these folks.

"I'm fine," I say. Just then, a round of deep coughs hit me.

The metallic taste of blood tells me my insides are bleeding.

"Mom, what's going on? Why are we going to the cavern?" Now, I realize the troll is just a boy—and he's frightened.

"Hey there," I say looking up at the boy. "Your name is Max?" He nods his head. "Well, there's not a lot of time for questions, Max. You follow your mom and be brave."

"Okay. I'm scared."

"Tell you the truth, I am too. But, there's a lot a folks 'round here that aren't going to let anything happen to you or your mom. So, get to that cavern and be brave. You hear me?"

"Is it true what they're saying?" the mother asks me. "There's an army of trolls trying to get to Moon?" It was me and Professor Irons that delivered that message the moment the tunnel of flies dropped us in the middle of the valley. We found Mother Moon herself and a troll named Tyra. It was only minutes before the bell was sounded and this whole valley went into siege mode.

"Yeah," I say. "It's true but it ain't gonna happen." Another coughing fit hits me and I taste blood again. "If you'll excuse me, I don't want to be late to the fight."

I leave them and move up the hill toward the gathering preparing for battle. On the way up, I see a squad of trolls escorting Mother Moon down the hill. At the back of the squad is Tyra, her mass of black hair is loosed and she's dressed in full battle leather; she is all business. *Good*, I think to myself, *get Mother Moon to safety—not just for her sake but for everyone's.*

The ache in my chest grows with each breath; I'm almost certain I have a broken rib from my *conversations* with Slakter. As I get closer with each shuffling step, I see the faces of the trolls and men waiting for the fight to come. I count 50 or

60 ready to protect the valley. I wonder if this is all we have to combat Slakter's hundreds and I push down the sinking feeling that weighs heavier inside me. One of the trolls has his three arms wrapped around a female troll and their child. He kisses her. She's weeping. He forcefully tells her to go—not to wait—and she does, taking the child with her. I see him turn back to the group. The anticipation of blood shed can be felt in the air and heard in the nervous shouts and calls from the ridge. The last bits of rust colored sun linger in the sky and frame the profile of trolls and men joined together to protect what is theirs.

Just as I make my way into the crowd, I see Professor Irons. She's working on the handle of her cane; she twists and the cane extends another two feet. A steel spear-head springs from the end. The hat, coat and ruby colored glasses are gone and I see a stern quickness about her that is impressive; this is not her first fight—I'd wager it may not even be her first war.

"Mr. Little, I thought we agreed that you need medical attention."

"We agreed on no such thing, Professor," I say. "I think I'm fine."

She lets the slightest grin slip. "I can see where your son gets it," she says.

"Who's in charge?"

"Scouts have set up a parameter to alert us when and where Slakter's forces show themselves. When they alert us, I'll alert you. Now, I must insist that you get to the cavern and seek…"

"I ain't goin' anywhere, Professor. And from the look of things, we need every available man, woman, and troll." Several faces turn and look. I seem to have gotten their attention. "Now, who is in charge?"

"That'd be me," a rough voice pipes up. The crowd of bodies parts and behind them is a large man with a dirt brown fedora and long-handle axe on his shoulder. The dark blue dusk makes it nearly impossible to see his face but I recognize the voice.

"Markham?"

"Yes, sir. If you come here to fight, you'll need a weapon."

"Markham," I say again. "It's me. It's Teddy Little. How the hell are ya'?"

For a moment he says nothing. Then he steps forward and I see the face of the man that taught me to trap and shoot, the man that taught me to survive three days in the woods with only a pocket knife. The man whose face has hardly aged in 40 years.

"Teddy," he shouts. "Teddy, you're alive! You're here!" He drops his composure for a moment, reaches for me, clapping his big hand against my shoulder. I wince against the stinging pain. "What happened to you?" he asks looking over my bloody bruises.

"Don't worry about that," I say. "Reese and Emma are bringing help. We need to keep the enemy at bay until they arrive."

"We have another problem." Professor Irons steps between us. "Mother Moon confirmed with me that this Stone of Remembrance is very real. And, it's a very real threat now that Slakter has it."

"How the hell did he get that?" Markham's countenance tenses.

"That's a story for later." Professor Irons pulls a set of leather gloves over her hands as she makes the point. "But, Mother Moon insists that if Slakter shows himself tonight, we have to retrieve that stone at all costs. Do you gentlemen understand?"

"I hear you, professor," Markham says. "But, I'll be honest. My priority is to protect everyone in Jotnar Valley. That comes first. The stone comes second."

"Gentlemen, if we don't retrieve that stone tonight, there may not be a valley tomorrow."

I look around and see that we've drawn a crowd and all eyes are on us. They're hanging on our every word. Markham turns and sees their faces. He pulls his fedora from his head and speaks to them.

"They want Mother Moon. You hear me? If they get her, life as we know it is gonna get a lot worse for everyone." The men and trolls draw in closer. "The fight is coming to our front door. Make no mistake, they are willing to die for what they want. So, I say we oblige them." A cheer goes up followed by a few laughs. "We hold them off. Protect your home. Protect your family. Are you ready for a fight?" At this, the crowd roars. Axes and shields wave in the air. Rifles are raised high.

Another coughing fit hits me, nearly knocking me over. Markham steps in a puts an arm around me for support.

"Get this man a rifle," he shouts over the noise of the crowd. "I want you in a perch, Ted. You'll have a sulfur loaded rifle with scope. I need you to pick off their leaders …the ones calling the shots." I pray that Slakter finds his way in my cross-hairs. Even in the dark, I'm certain I'll be able to pick him out easily. Markham leads me to a deer stand hidden in a dense tree line on the ridge. Dag brings a bolt action hunting rifle, I throw the shoulder strap over me and make my way up into the perch.

"Teddy," Markham calls up to me.

"Yeah."

"It's good to see you. I wish it was under different circumstances.

"Me too," I say. "When this is over, we'll have a beer."

"Damn right we will." Markham hustles back to the crowd. He shouts instructions and they disperse; each takes their weapons in hand and race to separate corners of the valley. Each is assigned to watch and call for the first sign of trouble.

A temporary quiet comes on the valley. I check my rifle once. Then, I check it again. I open the case of cartridges, each bullet is an olive-green color, barely visible in the moonlight, indicating a sulfur cast that is the true equalizer for troll-kind. I watch the horizon, hills lit with silver beams, and smell a hint of coming snowfall in the air. I glance through the rifle scope measuring the distances between hills in the dark. I look up and scan the horizon again. I do anything to occupy my mind against worrying about Reese and Emma.

"Help is on the way," I whisper to myself. "Help is on the way."

Chapter 41

Reese Little

"To any jotnar who can hear my voice, this is a call for help. A battle is coming and you are needed." I've shouted and shouted into the wind to the point of howling. But, there has been no response.

"Call out in Norwegian again." Emma is holding Hollis, both are wrapped in the cloak Professor Irons left. They stay near the burning shrub for warmth.

"Babe, I've done that. I've done it again and again." I don't know if it's the cold or just the rasp in my voice that's growing worse but I'm starting to lose hope. Emma calls out too.

"Hey. This is a call to the Fjell-Trollet. We need fighters. We need mountain trolls." She moves a little closer to the fire that's already started dying. The wind has only gotten worse, batting the flames in all directions, and it won't be long before that shrub is only embers. I pace. Maybe, the trolls in this valley can't hear me. Maybe there are no trolls in this valley. Maybe Jotnar Valley is already under attack… and I'm not there. Fighting against the berserker inside, I call out again.

"We need help. Slakter is trying to kill Munnin and start a war." I look at Hollis' eyes, still wide with hope. I press my voice for the last ounce. "He's tried to kill my family. he's tried to kill me and he will not stop until he has war. If you can hear me… we're desperate." My whole body shakes against the cold and doubt that is sinking into my bones. I look back at Hollis.

"Daddy." Emma sets Hollis down. He comes to me and reaches for my hand. "Where are they?" Hand in hand, we both look out across the quiet dark. I feel the tension in his hand lessen, then he let's go altogether.

"They will come after you. They will come after all of us if we don't not stop them now. Get up and fight. Fight, dammit. Fight!"

The last flame dissipates from the shrub. We stand in the cold blue dark once again. Then, Hollis breaks away from me runs toward the valley. He gets only a few feet away when he picks up a small rock, stands, and throws it. It doesn't go far. I can hear the panting and tears through his voice.

"They hurt my momma. They hurt my papa. If you don't wanna help… I'll do it myself." I scoop him up and hold him tight. Emma moves close to us. Her eyes meet mine. It's time to go. I nod and she carefully reaches into her coat pocket and pulls out the dark plum. A sigh escapes her lips.

Just then, a thunderous crack sounds from the mountain opposite us. It echoes and is followed by a rumble. Then we see a portion of the mountain face, shudder and move. Powdered snow and bits of earth spray from fissures shaking loose the rock. A figure emerges, climbing down from the mountain face. It turns and faces us, taking short tottering steps, and raises its arms to the black sky.

"My God. Do you see that?" She grips my arm. I pull her next to me.

"I see it."

"It's… waking up." We watch the troll raise to its full frame, at least 25 or 30 feet, and stretch bulky limbs that are etched in dark stone and smeared with earth. As if, it had been unmoved for so long, its body was becoming the mountain. It turns to face us, fully aware, and stares with big dark curious eyes.

Suddenly, the mountain behind it rumbles—louder this time. Emma falls against me as the ground shakes under us. We watch as two more figures shake off the snow and dirt of the mountain and step down into the valley alongside the first. These are much larger—twice as large or more. Hulking steps scrape the valley floor and send a shudder over the mountain range causing drifts of snow to collapse and slide.

"Look," Hollis shouts. "A family!" The small one moves between the larger two. They're naked except the wet earth and shale covering their skin. They all look at us silently.

"I suddenly feel really small," Emma whispers. Then one of the big ones steps forward. In four thundering steps he is across the valley. I grab Hollis and pull him to me. The mountain troll sniffs the air around us. His eyes shift a moment, looking back and forth across the mountain. *This is it, big guy*, I think to myself. *Just me and my little family.*

I gasp for air, not realizing that I was holding my breath. I let go of Emma and Hollis and decide to step forward. His enormous obsidian eyes focus in on my movement. The lady approaches next to him.

"We need help," I say with the sudden realization that they probably can't understand a word I'm saying. "My friends. My family… is threatened. Some very bad jotnar want a war. And, if they get what they want, no family will be safe. Not my family." I glance over at the small one, tugging at mom's leg. "And, not even your family." They stare at me, brows wrinkled, and I'm not sure if they are confused or empathetic. "Will you fight?" I ask. The father turns and looks back at his mate. Not a word is said between them but a few grunts. She gives a nod to him—the final say. He faces me and sticks out his chest. He places a fist over his heart and, with the other hand, he strikes his shoulder. The Viking salute. A defiant welcome to battle. He does it again and again. *Yeah, boy*, Eklund would say to me. *They're rekkr.*

Chapter 42

Ted Little

A faint buzzing is heard from the hill just south of us, to my right. I hold my breath and listen. The buzzing grows louder. No mistaking it. Markham whistles calling for the defenders of the parameter to gather to him. The buzzing only gets louder.

"Hold," is the only instruction Markham gives. He gestures to the professor and says something to her. She raises what looks like a clunky flashlight to the sky and two flares burst from it, arcing across the black sky, illuminating the valley and hill in front of us. On the opposite hill, we see movement.

Looking through my scope, I see bruisers nearly 15 feet tall and armored next to men that look like militia and mercenaries. The men carry weapons – assault rifles and worse. Though I can't see much through evergreen trees under the cover of night, I can tell that they easily outnumber us and they out muscle us. I look to Markham. He and Professor Irons and the troll with three arms are talking quickly. He glances back up at me and walks over to my perch.

"What do you see?" Markham asks.

With caution, I move into a prone position and take up the rifle. "Were outnumbered 3 to 1 at least. And, they have assault weapons. I see a few AR-15's and a grenade launcher."

"If Slakter's smart," Markham says, "he's not gonna use up bullets until his army can get closer." He chews a cigar as he thinks, then says, "We have to force his army to come to us. To move down and then back up the hill to us."

"How you gonna do that?" I ask. He doesn't answer. I see the small army on the other hill moving into formations. Then I hear the voice of the one who nearly crippled me. The one who attacked my boy and scarred the face of his wife.

"This is Slakter… speaking to the trolls of Jotnar Valley. I am impressed. You are so prepared for our arrival." His rasping voice echoes across the hills. "Since the surprise is spoiled, I'll just come out with it. We want Muninn. She is to answer for her blasphemy."

Markham glances back at me from the front line on the ridge. He wants to know if I can see Slakter. I shake my head. I can't. He's hiding among his army. I wonder if he can feel me searching for him.

"I only want what is right. So give me Muninn and I'll go away." Slakter pauses and waits for a response. Silence. Even the air is still. After a moment, Slakter speaks again. "I offer mercy, for your sake. For your childrens' sake. Just bring her to me and I will withdraw… "

Over Slakter's voice comes another, even louder, and void of diplomacy.

"SKEGGQLD… SKÁLMQLD… SKILDIR RO KLOFNIR." It is Markham. With his axe raised over his head, he shouts it again—the war chant.

"SKEGGQLD, SKÁLMQLD, SKILDIR RO KLOFNIR."

I remember this chant: *an axe-age, a sword-age, shields will be cloven.*

The crowd on the ridge joins the chant as one fierce voice rising to the inevitable fight. A defiant energy overtakes us. Axes clang against shields. An enormous chainsaw roars to life; the troll with three arms holds it high overhead as he shouts. We all shout, taunting the enemy.

"SKEGGQLD, SKÁLMQLD, SKILDIR RO KLOFNIR!"

Suddenly a rocket is fired from the opposing side. A flash streaks across the valley. Then, a glimmering metallic blur leaps in front of the rocket and takes the brunt of the blast head-on. The explosion rocks us but the impact is minimized. Through the smoke, I see an iron giant standing in the center of the impact. For a moment there is confusion. No one is harmed. The metallic monster that took the blast of the rocket stands, gears whirring. The metal face turns to us and the back of the skull pops open revealing the Sons of Ivaldi. A wrinkle-faced elder of their race gives a wave to the onlookers on our ridge and a cheer goes up. Damn if they didn't pull this out at the last minute. That rocket was aimed square at Markham and anyone unlucky enough to be near him.

"Shields," Markham shouts. Every troll raises a metal-plated rectangle the size of a barn door in front of them. The staccato sound of gun fire echoes across the hills.

With a clang, the Ivaldi closes the face of the iron monster. It turns, gears squealing, and makes a bounding run down into the valley between us and them. As it runs down the ridge, tearing through trees as it goes, it raises an arm to the enemy and fires a bolt of blue light as bright as day. The weapon decimates two of Slakter's crew. The iron monster fires again and again. Each hit is a kill shot. I hear Slakter shout the charge and a company of trolls sprint into the valley, heading straight for the mechanized weapon, with clubs and axes raised. Markham calls for our trolls to meet them and they descend the hill shouting for blood. I steady my rifle and breathe. Time to go to work. I scan the hill and count at least 20 trolls descending the hill toward us. No time to line up a clean shot. I fire a shot into the group, immediately reload the bolt with an open hand, and fire again. I fire 10 shots before the two lines of trolls clash at the base of the valley. I look up and see a group of trolls and humans, a second wave, still waiting on the hill to advance on us. I scan the hill trying to find Slakter himself. I don't see him so I turn my weapon to the man firing the grenade launcher. Then I take out the woman using her AR-15 to pin down our trolls. From the number of our trolls lying on their backs bleeding, it's clear the enemy has sulfur bullets too.

The second wave of Slakter's trolls move into the valley all at once. This group outnumbers both sides fighting in the valley. It is messy. The valley shakes. Screams and roars rise out of the chaos that turn my stomach. I aim into the pit and do my best to fire on the enemy. Our iron monster that led the charge is overtaken by a squad of enemy trolls. Boxed in, it continues to blast away at one troll and another and another…until the armor is pierced and then torn apart. I see two of the little guys emerge from the machine even as it is being torn open, no longer able to fight. The two struggle to get free. A swarm of our own pushes the enemy back; Markham leads the fight to guard the Sons of Ivaldi. He is fully berserker and rages against the enemy cutting down brutes left and right that are three times his size. A pair of club wielding trolls assist Markham and form a line to protect the two little guys. The older of the two is barely able to vacate the robot and cannot scramble back up the hill fast enough. The enemy rushes Markham and a cave troll leaps over the line bringing his club down on the old one. A cry is heard from the younger; he is restrained by one of our forest trolls and carried up the hill. Markham turns to see the elder and his face tells me that it is another loss for us. He rocks the cave troll with a swing to the face. It is subdued by a unit of trolls at Markham's side and a killing blow is delivered. The line is broken and enemy trolls are climbing the hill to our ridge. Markham calls the retreat and a horn sounds from the valley. It is echoed by another horn on our ridge. I pop open the case and reload my rifle. I see Professor Irons standing at the edge of the ridge. She fires a ball of purple fire into the valley, vexing the enemy's ascent, but only delaying the inevitable.

"Can't you call down lightning or something?"

She looks back at me. "Afraid not. No conduit. I need an antenna of some kind. Without it, I'd likely burn the whole mountain and everyone on it."

"Where is Dag? We need rifles ready to hold this ridge." She doesn't answer before her eyes widen and she fires a blast from her cane in my direction, mere inches over my head. I spin and see a man in combat gear standing over me. His flesh smokes and he tumbles from the deer stand and hits the ground in a heap. What the hell? I turn looking into the Jotnar Valley behind me and see another man, then a troll, all emerging from swarms of flies.

"They're inside the valley," I shout. I see two more men drop into the valley from the same buzzing cloud and they immediately run for the center of the community. They move frantically, looking for cover. Looking for Mother Moon. Our defense is completely wrecked. We're fighting on two fronts and we've got enemy in the camp. Professor Irons continues to fire down onto the enemy climbing the ridge. Two more men take position just below me and take aim into the valley; we fire several shots trying to slow down the intruders. Markham leaps into the line of fire.

"Forget them," he shouts. "They'll never find Moon. We need to defend the ridge or we lose everything."

I turn and see the surviving contingent of our fighters race up the ridge and collapse. The three-armed troll is applying pressure to a leaking wound at his shoulder. Eight more trolls make it back up to the top. I hear automatic gun fire coming from below the ridge. It's getting louder—and closer. Every man, woman, and troll capable of standing approaches the ridge. Ready to do whatever is necessary. I look over at Markham and Professor Irons. Both appear used up and lacking ideas. "Well?" I say.

"Welcome your destiny," Markham says. "And, let them welcome theirs." He walks forward to the edge of the ridge daring bullets soaring up from mouth of the pit towards us. I follow him, rifle ready. There are just over a dozen of us holding a line at the ridge. Professor Irons grips the spear-tipped cane in her hands. We stand ready.

A thunderous buzzing sounds reverberates the hills. Over the mountain where the enemy once stood, an enormous cloud of flies darken the sky, blocking the moon. Two bodies emerge from the cloud and begin racing down the hill toward us. Even in the blackest night, I recognize my son's face. His wife is with him. Both running to the fight. And, just behind them are two trolls so big as to shake the mountain range itself. Reese brought the Fjell-Trollet, fabled mountain trolls, the biggest of them all.

"Help has arrived!"

Chapter 43

Reese Little

The black swarm clears away and I hear the chaos of battle. Emma runs next to me, down the hill, racing through trees and whipping branches, trying to make it to the fight as fast as we can. The ridge in front of us is crawling with trolls, Slakter's followers and mercenaries. The earth shakes under us and the trees rattle. The giants tearing through the hills happen to be a pair of our new friends: the mountain trolls of Norway.

"Is he clear?" Emma shouts to me. I glance over my shoulder without slowing. The third mountain troll, the little one at nearly three stories tall, carries Hollis gently away from the fight. I see him move north, away from the fighting and behind a cliff for safety.

"Hollis is clear. Time to find Slakter."

We sprint toward a small crowd of humans, soldiers in flak jackets, but no trolls. They are fleeing back up the hill and are too panicked to notice us in the dark. The mountain trolls furiously smash and swat at the enemy trolls scaling the ridge to Jotnar Valley. Even the most blood thirsty troll is no more than a bug in their hands. One of the mountain trolls

is swinging a fallen timber log like a baseball bat. Dirt and
rocks spray from the hill in their wake. In the chaos, there's
no clear distinction between ours and theirs. I only assume
our people are safe in Jotnar Valley. Just then, Emma grabs
me by the wrist and pulls me tumbling to the ground. She
raises a gun over my shoulder and takes aim and I hear a shout.

"Whoa. Whoa. It's Dag… and Astrid."

I look up and see Dag with his hands raised, rifle in one
hand. Astrid is just behind him with rifle leveled back at us.
Emma takes a deep breath and holsters the revolver.

"It's good to see you both," I say standing.

"Not as good as it is to see you," Astrid says. "And, you
brought back-up, no less."

"What are you two doing all the way out here? This looks
like we're behind enemy lines."

"That's because we are," Dag replies. "We're hunting for
Slakter while Markham and the Professor defend the valley."

"Did you volunteer for that assignment?" I ask.

"Hell, no," Astrid says with a smile. "But when you're the
best tracker in the valley, you go where you're needed."

An explosion lights up the ridge. We all look and see one
of the mountain trolls reeling from what had to be a rocket
or grenade. It lets out a roar, raises its foot, and stomps a hole
into the earth crushing Slakter's gunmen.

"We've got to move fast," Dag says. "I just hit Slakter with
a tracer that your professor friend gave us. Slakter was about
100 meters away when I hit him. It didn't slow him down
but we can follow him." Dag turns and points to the south
side of the ridge. I squint looking for it, then I see a thread
of crimson smoke trailing through the air coming from midway up the hill.

"We're going after him," I say moving toward the ridge.

"He's got a squad of trolls and men with him," Dag says reloading his rifle. "I don't think they can buzz outta here and go back to where they came from. They would have done it by now. They'll be desperate."

"Then every shot has to count," Emma replies.

We race to the hill following the red trail of smoke. Explosions and gun fire still echo from the ridge. Keeping my head down, I focus on the forest in front of me; I look up occasionally to find the wisp of crimson in the tree line. We dodge trees and brush but never slow down. I look up just in time to see a ripped evergreen souring over our heads and crash behind us. The mountain trolls are ripping the ridge apart and flinging soldiers bodies through the forest.

A quarter of the way up the ridge our legs ache with fire. We reach a small clearing in the woods and find the red smoke clouding high overhead. Slakter and three other trolls emerge from the opposite side of the clearing with two gunmen with them. Red vapor rises from his curled shoulders. He sees us and freezes. He carries a small leather pouch tied around his neck.

"He has my ring," Emma says. "He's got the stone."

The two gunmen turn to fire and cover their exit through the clearing. Then, a burst of violet light comes through trees and Professor Irons emerges, hovering above the tree line, with another troll, Rolf, following from the ground. She takes up the chase for Slakter.

Slakter turns and runs into the woods, the crimson smoke still following. The two gunmen fire at the professor but are unable to hit her before Dag and Astrid pin them down. One is hit in the arm, the other takes a shot square in the vest—he rolls and pulls himself up and follows Slakter into the woods. Emma and I give chase. One of the trolls turns to meet Rolf; they exchange blows. Emma and I have to run wide to dodge their fight. She pulls both pistols in full sprint and fires at the other two trolls blocking Slakter's exit. She hits one just as he charges at us. The berserker rage hits me, blood thunders in my ears, and I leap with axe raised. I cleave a hole in the monster's collar and send him sprawling on his back, oozing blood. I race into the tree line with Emma, Dag, and Astrid behind me. We follow Slakter's trail of splintered trees.

"Astrid," Dag shouts. "I'm empty."

"I'm on my last." She replies.

The woods open to a river and Slakter has crossed to the opposite bank when I see Professor Irons dive from above. She snatches the pouch and tears it from around Slakter's neck, firing a burst of purple blasts as she rises away. A shot is fired and hits the Professor. She cries out and begins to fall. Everyone is racing into the river to catch Professor Irons, to grab the stone. Dag races to the mercenary that fired the shot, mid-stride he turns his rifle over in his hands and swings the stock like a melee weapon. He cracks the mercenary across the jaw, then again over his head, knocking him lifeless into the river. Astrid fires on Slakter, halting him from getting to the professor. Professor Irons slows her descent but can't stop from crashing into the cold rushing water. She pops up gasping for air, finds her footing and is able to stand against the moving current at her waist. She holds the pouch in a fist against her chest, her cane in the other hand. I see a dark red spot spreading across her stomach. Dag and I race toward the river to help. A roar is heard. A troll leaps over us and crashes into the river almost drowning the professor. It's the troll that went hand-to-hand with Rolf. His face is bleeding. Two more emerge from behind us and race toward the river. I cut one at the knee, he drops and slides against the river bank. Emma opens fire on the next but doesn't stop him before he grabs Professor Irons and raises her high in the air. Two bloodied monsters hold Agatha in their fists ready to crush her. She raises her cane but there is no purple fire. Instead, I feel a stinging heat on my skin. Lightning cracks and the whole forest is a blinding flash of light. A deafening thunder knocks me on my back.

I struggle to raise up and open my eyes. A pervasive burning smell is in the air but I see no fire. Trees are singed and smoking. I turn over and stand. Emma does the same. I hear Dag call out for Astrid, she replies. Then, I see Slakter. He is standing in the river, reaching into the water where Professor Irons once stood. The river bank on both sides is charred. I look, afraid of what I will see. There is no sign of a body, human or troll. There is only a dark burn mark that covers both sides of the river bank. She's gone. The stone is gone.

Slakter plunges his hands into the current over and over, like a child furious at losing a toy. The blood in my head races again and I feel my own fury take over. I race into the river with my axe in hand. He swings at me with a backhand but I duck and cut his leg deep. He turns and faces me swinging, wild and without control.

"You ruined everything," he cries.

He rushes at me against the current and lunges. I time it and throw my axe into his shoulder. He roars and pulls back—the axe still protruding from his shoulder blade—he can't reach it. I leap over him and grab the axe, pulling him backward. I peal the weapon from his back and take another hacking swing as he falls into the water. He flails his arms and knocks me against the bank. I recover just as he lunges out of the water. He's injured and can't chase me. But, I'm not running.

He follows me out of the river bed. I see dark oily blood pouring from his face, leg, and both arms. The blood in my own head pounds even louder. Out of the corner of my eye, I see Markham and a crowd of trolls gather to us. Dag holds them back from the fight. Emma has both guns drawn. I turn and deliver swing after swing, cutting and slashing at Slakter. I do not let up even when he falls to his knees and cannot stand. He swats at me with a mangled arm. My axe is thrown but I turn and pound him with my fists. His jaw cracks. He doubles over and spits blood. Again, he tries to push me away but has no strength left. I step back—and breathe—and look on the pitiful wreck in front of me.

Small steps approach behind me. Emma moves toward us. She has my axe in her hand. I do not take it from her. I feel the pounding in my head slowing. The berserker fury passes. Her eyes meet mine and I step back. She moves firmly in front of Slakter. He sways and raises his head with the little strength he has left.

"You… you all deserve annihilation," he says choking back the oily blood filling his throat. "For turning… against the old gods. For all the… the…"

"For all the terrible evils of mankind?" she asks. She kneels in front of him and wipes her muddied face with the back of her hand. For a moment, his eyes seem to fixate on her scar. "This isn't about gods… or men. This is about family. Somebody hurt your family. So you hurt mine." She raises her chin and breathes deep. "And, I can't let you do that again."

He stares into her eyes and starts to say something; his face is almost apologetic. She takes a step back, raises the axe overhead.

A thundering crack sounds. A giant tree sails over us, cutting through the tree line, splintering branches, and crashes between Emma and Slakter sending them both tumbling. A 40-foot splintered trunk separates Slakter from us all. Shouts are given indicating who is okay and none are injured. I rush to Emma and pull her away. She pushes against me demanding that I finish it.

"No. Stop him," she says. "Don't let him get away." I look back and see him crawling up the bank. He's moving toward a troll collapsed and mangled against a pine tree. Next to the troll is a burlap sack with dark plums spilt from it.

"Stop him," I shout. "Don't let him reach the bag!" I hold Emma as Astrid, Dag, and the rest of the crowd rush toward him but it's too late. Slakter rolls on his belly raising a dark oozing plum and, in one swift motion, he throws it—at Emma. My body reacts before my brain realizes it. I can't move her away fast enough. My reflexes raise an arm to catch it, to stop it. I open my hand. Emma folds herself into me. My body tenses waiting for what will come next. Five fingers wrap around the plum but they are not mine. A thick hand catches the oozing fruit and a cloud of gnats pour from it. Markham holds the dark plum and lets out a fierce wail. Blood rises mixing with the swarm of gnats as his hand is consumed. Trolls rush to him. In the chaos, I pull Emma away from the growing cloud of flies that stretches from Markham's arm to the place where Slakter lay. Dag knocks Markham to the ground and lays across his chest.

"Do it," he cries. "*Now!*" Rolf quickly plants a foot over Markham's shoulder, raises his axe and brings it down just above the elbow, severing the arm in one swing. The gnats swarm over the butchered flesh and then dissipate. Slakter is gone.

"Reese," Dag says, "Your belt. Give me your belt now." I pull my belt and loop it around the bloody end of Markham's right arm. Dag pulls it tight and gets directly in Markham's face.

"Stay with me, Markham. Fight it."

"Is he dying?"

"What? No. He's going berserk. Total berserk. He's losing control." Dag stares into his eyes. Markham is foaming at the mouth and his whole body is shaking. Dag yells to the group. "We gotta hold him down. Pile on, boys."

I'm caught in a collision of enormous bodies trapping Markham against the earth. I see his eyes filling with blood and teeth bared. He tries to flail against us. The breath is squeezed out of me. For a moment, it is all of us versus Markham and I'm afraid we may not win. Then, I hear a rasping voice. A voice that is animal… but distinctly his.

"I'm here," he says. "I'm here. I'm here—I'm here."

We get him to his feet. Incredibly, his bleeding has already slowed. Dag drapes Markham's good arm over his shoulder. They begin the trek back to Jotnar Valley with help of the rest of the pack. Astrid stays with me and Emma and we search, in vain, for the professor. We don't speak about what we are afraid to find. We don't want to find pieces of clothing or bits of flesh. But, what we find leaves a lingering ache, a cruel void that just might be worse. Nothing. We find nothing but charred earth.

We finally climb the ridge and enter our haven again. A

crowd has gathered on the top of the hill. Hollis is there with my father. Emma reaches for our boy and he jumps into her arms.

The crowd gazes across the mountain ridge and we see the family of mountain trolls move between the peaks. Just as the sun throws the first rays of dawn, they each settle into a hill, just like laying down for a nap. The distinction between troll and hill is blurred. And then, they are still. Holding Emma close to me, I turn and face the group of our survivors. I raise my axe high. Silently, each one raises their weapon: axe, rifle, or a closed fist. There is no applause—no victory shout. In each of their faces, I see the cost paid.

Chapter 44

Reese Little

Three days later and all is calm. After all the bodies were buried and we were sure the remainder of Slakter's faction had fled, I came back to the saw mill. Dad is recovering at a nearby hospital and they say he needs his rest. I try not to bother him but once a day.

There's always work to be done. Astrid meets me at the saw mill. A few trolls and humans carry on there, trying to return to life as it was. She trains me on measuring each log as it comes through the line; that's when we hear the applause. The belts switch off and the saw blades stop spinning. The whole crew claps a welcome to Markham. He tips his hat but tries his best to treat it like no big deal—no big deal that he'd protected this valley and everyone in it, including sacrificing his arm for me and Emma.

After the general excitement dies down, Markham asks me to sit down with him, one-on-one. He offers to have me trained on other work besides the saw mill. If I want it. He stares into the cropping of White Ash trees and fumbles for words.

"And, Emma. I know she probably don't like working

laundry in the river," he says, "especially in the winter." He scratches at the sling holding the remainder of his bandaged arm. "We can have her... um. We always need a teacher, you know. Lots of kids in Jotnar Valley. More now than there used to be." He takes a breath and then remembers Emma. "How is she, by the way? Her face, I mean."

"She's healing. Hospital gave us plenty of fresh bandages. But, the doctor said there will always be a scar." He nods but I can see the anger mixed with regret in his eyes just before he looks away. I change the subject. "Markham, my job back home... well..."

"I know. You wanna get back there. You're educated and you got a career. I understand."

"They fired me." His head whips around. "I mean, I essentially disappeared for a month and I never called them back."

"Oh. Oh, I'm sorry 'bout that."

"I'm not." A wide smile fills my face. "I'm not sorry at all. There's plenty of work to be done around here." Markham blinks, staring back at me with mouth open. Then, he erupts with a laugh and slaps his knee.

"Well! Well... you're right about that. Always somthin' to be done around here!"

Later, I take Emma and Hollis with me to find Mother Moon. She's already bundled up for a walk in the cold when we reach her house.

"Mother Moon, I was hoping we could talk while we walk. Are you headed to the lookout on the ridge?"

"I am. Please, join me." I offer my hand to help her down the porch steps. She pulls her shawl tighter around her shoulders. As we walk, I offer my condolences again regarding

Professor Irons… Agatha. I'm struck by how briefly I knew her—yet, how profoundly thankful I am for that short time. We pass the boxcar leading into The Mine and several trolls join us in the trek to the ridge. I can't help but ask Mother Moon a few questions about what Emma and I learned in Norway.

"The stone… must have been a very powerful thing. The professor certainly thought so…"

"Reese, you must have so many questions."

"Just one, really. Where is Huginn?"

"I'm sorry?"

"Slakter had the stone. But, according to legend, you and Huginn are required to make it… work. Is there truth to that myth?"

"To say the Stone of Remembrance is powerful as well as complex would be an understatement, Reese."

"I'd appreciate it if you could sit down with me and Emma and explain that complexity sometime." The glance from her eyes tells me she hears the darkening tone in my voice. I'm not requesting. I'm insisting.

"Certainly." Mother Moon pauses mid-step, reaching a cautious hand to her lips. "Your grandfather accomplished quite the feat," she says. "For years he hid it… right here under my nose." She clinches her jaw.

"So, the question remains. Where is Huginn? And, who wanted the stone?" She glances away scanning the earth, looking through it as if to some other time or some other place. We continue the climb up to the ridge over Jotnar Valley.

Arni and Tyra greet us and the small crowd that has flocked to the over-look. It's a solemn crowd drawn here to commemorate bravery. And sacrifice. Hollis tugs at my arm. I look down only to see him pointing behind us; Dag is leading my father up the hill. Dad is telling some story about pissing off the nurses and leaving before he was discharged. He's bruised and still recovering so I restrain every instinct in my being that wants to wrap both arms around his neck and hug him.

Without a word, the crowd knowingly grows silent. Arni gestures to a square-shaped pit that has been cut into the earth. He tells us this is where the monument to our slain will be erected. Tyra then reads the names of those who died – the names that will be etched into the monument. Among them are Bjorn, Professor Irons, the elder Ivaldi called Dvalinn, Bubba, and two dozen more. When Bubba's name is read, it cuts through me. He didn't leave after all. He stayed. He fought. And, he paid the price.

Dad follows me, Emma, and Hollis as we visit his old house. Not surprisingly, he's rather unemotional about seeing the charred remains of his childhood home. Dag finds us and runs to meet us. Markham follows slowly behind him. Dag's eyes are wide and he approaches with the eagerness of a Golden Retriever.

"So. There's a rumor," he says in a whisper that is actually louder than a person's normal speaking voice, "that you and the family might be staying in the valley, yeah?" Dad overhears and turns. Dag glances at Markham, then back at me, then he looks to my dad.

"Hell, I'm not gonna weigh in on this," Dad says. "Whatever I tell my son to do, he'll just do the opposite!" He laughs and then erupts into a hard cough. For a moment, my dad and Markham face each other without moving. "You look like hell, Markham."

"Well, losing an arm will do that to you. What's your excuse?"

"Ha! I just got old." Both men walk away, swapping stories together.

~

While the sun is still up, Emma and I decide to look through dad's old house. I think I just want to see if I can find mementos of a family history I never knew about.

"So, you're telling me Markham rescued your dad from Grandpa Karl." Emma stands caught in the streaks of sunlight coming through the windows. Dust floats in the still air of the decrepit cabin. For a moment, I admire the sight of her: the streak of hair hanging over one eye, the curve of her breasts under the thin t-shirt, the glisten of sweat at her neck—even the pink scar stretching from her temple, across her cheek, into her jawline. She's got a fortitude now; it was always there, deep down. But, now I see it risen to the surface.

"Yeah. That confrontation started the blaze that took this house." I wipe my pants with the dust and dirt that has collected on my gloves. "I think that's when my dad left Jotnar Valley." A cool wind picks up and whistles over the exposed hole in the roof of the old house. "I guess it's not surprising now, after all we've learned, to find out that my grandpa… had a temper." Emma catches my eye but doesn't say anything. I turn away to find a footlocker stored under the bed.

"You're not like that," she says over my shoulder. "You're not like your grandfather."

"I know." I take a deep breath. "But, I need to be reminded sometimes." I open the foot locker. A loud creak comes from the rusty hinges. Emma gives a slight gasp.

Inside, the footlocker is filled with photos, worn and

browning. I reach deep into the pile of hundreds of photos, some large and some small. I find shoeboxes filled with even more. Some of them are in color with scenes of my dad as a boy playing with other boys his age. Some show groups in black and white, smiling and commemorating the Yuletide.

One photo in particular catches my eye. I pull it from the pile. It's clearly a photocopy of a much older original photo. It shows two boys dressed for a family portrait. The brothers wear vests with a row of buttons on the front and buckles on their shoes.

The older of the two wears a knit drape oddly placed over one side of his face. He appears to have a hump in his shoulder. A deformity. On the back of the photo, scribbled in pen, it says:

Summer 1840—Oscar Lillevik and Karl Lillevik.

About the Author

Aaron Shaver is unashamedly a product of the TV generation.

He found his love for storytelling at a young age through books as well as cartoon shows on Saturday mornings and preachers on Sunday mornings.

Aaron earned his undergrad in theatre and a master's degree in public relations. Which means he's always telling a story. And sometimes, they are true.

He and his wife, who performs and teaches theatre locally, reside in the Nashville area with their wild clan of four children. Their house is a very loud house.

Contact Aaron at
aaron@gentlemanbard.com
or visit him online at
www.aaronshaver.com
www.gentlemanbard.com

A Message from the Author

I relished writing this book! If you enjoyed the story of the Little family and Jotnar Valley, would you consider doing two things?

First, sign up for my newsletter and I'll be sure you're the first to get news on the books that will follow in this series. And, if you sign up for the newsletter, you'll immediately get free short stories from the world of The Berserker Heritage.

For free.

Did I mention it's *free*? But, shh. Don't tell anybody. Just kidding—tell everybody! Visit www.gentlemanbard.com to sign up and get free short stories!

Second (and this is a big request), if you liked this story, would you consider leaving a review wherever you bought this book, or on your favorite social media platform? I want as many readers as possible to discover this story, and your voice can help do that. Leave a review and tell a friend! Word-of-mouth is the best way to introduce this story to other readers.

Lastly, *Thank you*!

Thank you, dear reader, for giving your time to read this book. It means a lot that you trusted me as the author to entertain, and hopefully excite, you with this story. Stories need an audience and I appreciate you being my audience for just a little while. Thank you.

There were also several people who gave their time and voices to the creation of this story. This book was made stronger due to their suggestions, questions, and feedback. Thank you Anna Owen, Nathan Owen, Jennifer Wells, Daren Wells, Kristen Ownby, Kalob Ownby, Jocelyn Ireland, Jeana Hodge, and Ben Hodge.

I also have to say thank you to Mary Lou Statt for constantly pestering reminding me that no excuse was acceptable. Thanks for cracking the whip, Mary Lou.

Thanks for reading **Furious**, the first book in *The Berserker Heritage*. I know, I know, there are still lots of questions that need answers. Like…

Who is the real mastermind behind Slakter's plan?
What happened to Professor Irons? And, where is her family?
What is Mother Moon's history with the Stone of Remembrance?
Who is the man in Karl's memories and why can't he see his face?

And so, just for you, here's a special preview of

Book 2
The Berserker Heritage

Reese Little

I inhale the wet mountain air. Spring is finally here. We're half way through the month of April and Jotnar Valley has only seen four days without rain. Today is one of those days. I climb out of the cab of the diesel big-rig with Hollis bouncing to keep up with me. He stares wide-eyed as Arni and Rolf toss 20-foot Ash timbers onto the flatbed of the truck that I've driven into the logging zone.

"Daddy, look! Look!" Each log tossed soars through the air, landing with minimal bounce.

"I'm looking, buddy. Let's stand way over here—away from the action." I scoot him further up the hill. We get a better view anyway. Morning sun streaks through the tree line. I sneeze.

The crew of trolls leave to return to The Mine for the day. I speak to Arni as he leaves. He wipes his brow and tells me to watch out for Markham and his new toy.

"You'll see," he says with a laugh.

I walk to the clearing and see Markham towering over half a dozen Ivaldi. It's a curious scene with Markham standing in front of a particularly thick Ash tree, his back turned to the dwarves. Without a word, the Ivaldi scamper away and I see the thing on his arm. Attached at the shoulder is a metallic arm forged of stone work and strapped with belts across his chest and back. Markham raises the arm over his head and, with a flicker, a stone axe springs from the inner workings and interlocks at the wrist. He grips the stone axe with his natural hand and swings. He cuts clean through the trunk in only five hits. He lets out a yelp as the tree falls nearly landing on the head of one of the dwarves. He turns to them with a wide-eyed grin. Then he sees me looking on.

"Did you see that? Did you see that?"

After supper, I get to work on fencing the garden I've cut into the plot of earth next to my cabin. I finish dropping the last fence post and setting it when Hollis races out of the house. Emma follows right behind him. She's taking him to a sleep-over with a kid that's his age. They wave as they go and Emma whistles at me, cat-calling with a grin on her face. I flex my arms in response. And, my shoulders immediately regret it.

I grab the shovel and post-hole digger and make my way back to the cabin when I hear a noise. In the tree line, there's a rustle. I turn and look but there's not much to see in the navy twilight. Could be a small animal. Then, I hear it again. This time a twig crunches with the sound of something much bigger than a squirrel or raccoon.

"Call out if you're there." I grip the shovel with both hands. In response, a quiet figure emerges from the tree line. It's a person moving toward me with cautious steps. I assume from the silhouette of hair and the long skirt, it must be a woman.

"Please. I need help." Even in the near silence of the valley, the voice is almost too quiet to be heard. But, the voice is familiar. A pair of deep-set eyes looks at me pleadingly. I take a step back, gripping the shovel handle tighter. Then, I see her brown face and her lips, trembling.

"Reese? It's me," she whispers through staggered breathing. Her skirt is wet below the knees with grass and twigs clinging to the folds. "It's me. I need your help." She reaches a slender hand and grabs mine almost tumbling into me. I catch her as she collapses. Her face looks up at me in the moonlight.

"Professor?" I nearly shout in disbelief.

It is her. But, her face has lost the familiar wrinkles of a middle-aged woman. She is at least 20 years younger than the last time I saw her. But, there is no mistaking the eyes of Professor Irons staring back at me.

"It's not safe." She is not whispering but rather fighting against the loss of her own voice. "I don't know what happened. But, they are coming for me. They are coming for all of us."